Dear Reader:

In the early 1820s, horse racing was a down and dirty sport. James Wyndham, who owns racing stables in both England and America, finds his racing nemesis in red-haired Jessie Warfield, renowned hoyden and champion jockey, who knows as many dirty racing tricks as James does. When either wins a face, the other's nose gets rubbed in the dirt.

Jessie has known James for six years, since she was four-teen years old. She often wants to kick him for the way he treats her, but more importantly, she adores him. She just doesn't know how to show it.

When chance throws Jessie out of a tree, landing her on top of James, she is pronounced Ruined. When she decides to run, she really goes for it, all the way to England, to James's cousins, Marcus and Duchess Wyndham.

James arrives, laden with guilt, to find a Jessie who sounds like the old Jessie but isn't. Jessie has undergone a transfor-mation worthy of Pygmalion.

Will James do the Right Thing and undo Jessie's Ruin? What about Jessie's nightmares that seem to call up some-thing terrible from her childhood?

There's a treasure to be found on the Outer Banks, a mys-tery to be solved, a love story that will plant a smile on your mouth for a long time, and lots of laughter.

Let me know which of the three Legacy novels you like best.

*Catherine Coulter*

**Write me at P.O. Box 17, Mill Valley, CA 94942 or
e-mail me at <u>readmoi@gmail.com</u>**

---

Turn to the back of this book for a preview of *Rosehaven*, Catherine Coulter's stunning novel of romance and power set in medieval England . . .

*In paperback from Jove Books*

## *Titles by Catherine Coulter*

*The Sherbrooke Series*
THE SHERBROOKE BRIDE
THE HELLION BRIDE
THE HEIRESS BRIDE
MAD JACK
THE COURTSHIP
THE SCOTTISH BRIDE
PENDRAGON
THE SHERBROOKE TWINS
LYON'S GATE
WIZARD'S DAUGHTER
THE VALCOURT HEIRESS
THE PRINCE OF RAVENSCAR

*The Legacy Trilogy*
THE WYNDHAM LEGACY
THE NIGHTINGALE LEGACY
THE VALENTINE LEGACY

*The Baron Novels*
THE WILD BARON
THE OFFER
THE DECEPTION

*The Viking Novels*
LORD OF HAWKFELL ISLAND
LORD OF RAVEN'S PEAK
LORD OF FALCON RIDGE
SEASON OF THE SUN

*The Song Novels*
WARRIOR'S SONG
FIRE SONG
EARTH SONG
SECRET SONG
ROSEHAVEN
THE PENWYTH CURSE

*The Magic Trilogy*
MIDSUMMER MAGIC
CALYPSO MAGIC
MOONSPUN MAGIC

*The Star Series*
EVENING STAR
MIDNIGHT STAR
WILD STAR
JADE STAR

*Other Regency
Historical Romances*
THE COUNTESS
THE REBEL BRIDE
THE HEIR
THE DUKE
LORD HARRY

*Devil's Duology*
DEVIL'S EMBRACE
DEVIL'S DAUGHTER

*Contemporary
Romantic Thrillers*
FALSE PRETENSES
IMPULSE
BEYOND EDEN
BORN TO BE WILD

*FBI Suspense Thrillers*
THE COVE
THE MAZE
THE TARGET
THE EDGE
RIPTIDE
HEMLOCK BAY
ELEVENTH HOUR
BLINDSIDE
BLOWOUT
POINT BLANK
DOUBLE TAKE
TAILSPIN
KNOCKOUT
WHIPLASH
SPLIT SECOND

# THE
# VALENTINE LEGACY

# CATHERINE COULTER

JOVE BOOKS, NEW YORK

**THE BERKLEY PUBLISHING GROUP**
**Published by the Penguin Group**
**Penguin Group (USA) Inc.**
**375 Hudson Street, New York, New York 10014, USA**
Penguin Group (Canada), 90 Eglinton Avenue East, Suite 700, Toronto, Ontario M4P 2Y3, Canada
(a division of Pearson Penguin Canada Inc.)
Penguin Books Ltd., 80 Strand, London WC2R 0RL, England
Penguin Group Ireland, 25 St. Stephen's Green, Dublin 2, Ireland (a division of Penguin Books Ltd.)
Penguin Group (Australia), 250 Camberwell Road, Camberwell, Victoria 3124, Australia
(a division of Pearson Australia Group Pty. Ltd.)
Penguin Books India Pvt. Ltd., 11 Community Centre, Panchsheel Park, New Delhi—110 017, India
Penguin Group (NZ), 67 Apollo Drive, Rosedale, Auckland 0632, New Zealand
(a division of Pearson New Zealand Ltd.)
Penguin Books (South Africa) (Pty.) Ltd., 24 Sturdee Avenue, Rosebank, Johannesburg 2196, South Africa

Penguin Books Ltd., Registered Offices: 80 Strand, London WC2R 0RL, England

This is a work of fiction. Names, characters, places, and incidents either are the product of the author's imagination or are used fictitiously, and any resemblance to actual persons, living or dead, business establishments, events, or locales is entirely coincidental. The publisher does not have control over and does not have any responsibility for author or third-party websites or their content.

THE VALENTINE LEGACY

A Jove Book / published by arrangement with the author

PUBLISHING HISTORY
G. P. Putnam's Sons hardcover edition / August 1995
Jove mass-market edition / September 1996
Read for the Heart edition / February 2012

ISBN: 978-0-515-15084-1

JOVE®
Jove Books are published by The Berkley Publishing Group,
a division of Penguin Group (USA) Inc.,
375 Hudson Street, New York, New York 10014.
JOVE® is a registered trademark of Penguin Group (USA) Inc.
The "J" design is a trademark of Penguin Group (USA) Inc.

PRINTED IN THE UNITED STATES OF AMERICA

10 9 8 7 6 5 4 3 2 1

*To Charles Coulter, my father*
*and a very talented gentleman.*
*Thank you for the genes you passed*
*on to me.*
*And the support that never wavered.*
*All my love*

# THE
# VALENTINE LEGACY

NEAR BALTIMORE, MARYLAND
MARCH 1822

*Slaughter County Course:*
*Saturday Races, last race, one-half mile*

HE WAS GOING to lose. He didn't want to lose, dammit, particularly to Jessie Warfield, that obnoxious brat. He could feel Rialto just behind him, hooves pounding firm and steady on the black dirt, head stretched long, muscles hard and bunched. He looked over his left shoulder. Rialto was coming on faster than a man escaping from a woman's bedchamber before her husband came through the door, and the damned five-year-old had more endurance than an energetic man with four demanding wives.

James stretched as far as he could and pressed his face as close as he could to Tinpin's ear. He always talked to his horses before and during a race to gauge their moods. Good-natured Tinpin was always open to James. Tinpin, like most of his racehorses, was a fierce competitor; he had great heart. The horse wanted to win as much as James did. The only time he was distracted from victory was that time when a jockey had slammed his riding crop on his side, sending him into a rage. He'd nearly killed that damned jockey and lost the race in the process.

James felt old Tinpin's labored breathing beneath him. The horse was more a quarter-mile sprinter than a half-miler, so Rialto had the advantage there, in both ability and experience. This was only Tinpin's second half-mile race. James kicked his sides, telling Tinpin over and over that he could do it, that he could keep the lead over that miserable little chestnut, that he could kick Rialto—named after a silly Venetian bridge—in the dirt. He had to make his move now or it would be too late. James promised Tinpin an extra bucket of oats, a dollop of champagne in his water. The horse gave a final burst of speed, but it wasn't enough.

He lost—by only a length. Tinpin's sides were heaving. He was blowing hard, his neck lathered. James walked him around, listening to the groans and cheers of the crowd. He stroked Tinpin's wet neck, telling him he was a brave fighter, that he would have won if James hadn't been riding him. And he probably would have won, dammit, despite James's reputed magic with his horses. Some claimed that James as good as carried some of his horses over the finish line himself. Well, he hadn't carried any horse anywhere this day.

Actually he hadn't even come in second after Rialto. He'd placed third, behind another chestnut thoroughbred from the Warfield Stables, a four-year-old named Pearl Diver who had nosed past Tinpin at the last moment, his tail flicking over James's leg.

Tinpin didn't have much bottom, but then again this hadn't been a four-mile flat race, it had just been a half mile and bottom shouldn't have mattered. What had mattered had been James's extra weight. With a lighter rider on his back, Tinpin would have won. James cursed, slapping his riding crop against his boot.

"Hey, James, you lost me ten dollars, curse you!"

James was leading Tinpin back to his stable lad, his head down. He sloughed off his depression and smiled toward his brother-in-law, Gifford Poppleton, striding toward him like a civilized bull—short, powerful, but not an ounce of fat on him. He liked Giff and had approved of his marriage to his sister, Ursula, the year before. "You can well afford it, Giff," he shouted back.

"I can, but that's not the point." Gifford dropped into a long, lazy stride beside him. "You tried, James, but you're just too damned big to be a jockey. Those other jockeys weigh four stone less than you do. Fifty-something extra pounds make a lot of difference."

"Bloody damn, Giff, you're brilliant," James said, striking a pose. "I wish I'd known. And here I thought only the experts knew that."

"Well, I know a lot of things," Giff said, just grinning at him. "Hell, I wouldn't have wagered on you if Ursula hadn't nagged me into it."

"The brat weighs even less," James said.

"The brat? Oh, Jessie Warfield. That she does. Too bad about poor Redcoat breaking his leg in the second race. Now there's a jockey. You trained him well. What does he weigh? One hundred pounds?"

"Ninety pounds on a sunny day. Do you know how he broke his leg? Another jockey ran him into a tree."

"It hurt me to see it. You know, James, someone needs to make some rules about racing. All this mayhem is ridiculous. I read about a race in Virginia where the favored horse was poisoned the night before the race."

"It might be ridiculous," James said, "and it might be occasionally dangerous, but it's fun, Giff. Leave things be. Just be careful whom you bet with."

"As if you cared. Hey, Oslow, how are you doing?"

Oslow Penny was the head of James's breeding farm. On race days, though, he was the head stable lad who oversaw the handling of all the horses to race at the meet. He was a walking oral history, at least that's what James called him.

The Maryland Jockey Club was beginning to agree. Oslow knew the direct line back, or the tail-male, of every horse that ran from South Carolina to New York. He also knew every current sire and every dam and every get from every racehorse in America and Britain.

Oslow approached them, muttering under his breath, and gently removed Tinpin's reins from James's hand. He was bowlegged, scrawny-looking, and had the most powerful hands James had ever seen. His face was weathered and seamed, his brown eyes as powerful with intelligence as his hands were with strength.

He squinted through the bright afternoon sun up at Gifford's face. "Good afternoon, sir. I'm doing as fine as Lilly Lou did at the Virginia High Ebb races just last week. Better than Mr. James, that's for sure. Aye, and how are you doin', boy? Winded, are you? Well, you did your best, did better than Dour Keg, that knock-kneed creature old Wiggins still persists in racing. Hell, I don't even remember who his sire was, that's how bad he is."

"Did you bet on Mr. James, Oslow?"

"Not I, Mr. Poppleton," Oslow said, stroking a gnarled, veiny hand over Tinpin's neck. "I would have if Redcoat had ridden him, poor lad, but not Mr. James. Mr. James has just growed too big, just like Little Nell, who ate her head off four years ago and couldn't barely shuffle over the finish line at the Dickey races in North Carolina, clean in last place."

Gifford laughed. "You think I could have done better than Mr. James?"

Oslow spat just beyond Tinpin's left shoulder. "Not with that pair of hands you got, Mr. Poppleton. Sorry, sir, but you've got ham hands, not like Mr. James, who has magic running out the ends of his fingers into the horses."

"Thank you, Oslow, for something," James said. "Now, Gifford, let's go see Ursula. I don't suppose you brought our mother with you?'' He patted Tinpin's neck as he moved away.

''No, thank God. She tried to talk Ursula out of coming to this godless place.''

James laughed. He was still grinning when he saw the Warfield brat striding toward him, looking just like a boy, still wearing a riding hat with her violent red hair shoved up under it. Her face was red from the hot sun. A line of freckles marched across her nose.

He didn't want to stop, but he did. It was hard. He'd just as soon ignore her for the rest of his days, but he was a gentleman, dammit.

''Congratulations,'' he said, trying to unclench his teeth. She'd beaten him often since she was a knock-kneed kid of fourteen, but he still hated it. He never got used to it.

Jessie Warfield paid no attention to Gifford Poppleton, president of the Union Bank of Baltimore, as she came toe-to-toe with James and said, ''You tried to shove me into that ditch on the second lap.''

A dark blond eyebrow went up. ''Did I now?''

She came up onto her tiptoes, her nose an inch from his. ''You know you did. Don't even consider lying, James. It was close. If I weren't such a bloody good rider, I would have gone over the edge. But I didn't. I came back and beat you—beat you but good.''

''You certainly did,'' he said easily, wanting to smack her. Some sportsmanship. She was a female. If she were a male, she'd know it wasn't right to rub the loser's nose in his defeat. Although, he thought, when he next beat her, he was going to rub her entire face in the dirt.

''Do you know your lips are chapped? Do you know I can count your freckles from this distance?'' he said. ''One, two, three—goodness, there are so damned many of them it would take me a week.''

She backed up fast. ''Don't try it again, or I'll take my

riding crop to you.'' She licked her chapped lips, shook the crop in his face, nodded to Giff, and strode off.

Gifford said, ''It looked to me like you did nudge Tinpin into her horse, James.''

''Yes, but not hard enough. I just wanted to get her attention. It was nothing compared to what she did to me last year at the June races in Hacklesford.''

''Well, what did she do, this fearsome girl?''

''I was crowding her just a bit, just to teach her a lesson. She knows every dirty maneuver there is. Anyway, she pulled her horse away just enough so she could kick out at me. She got me directly on the leg and sent me sprawling.''

Gifford laughed, thinking that James sure made the Warfield girl bristle something fierce. He asked even as he watched Jessie Warfield striding away from them, her riding crop flicking up and down, up and down, ''Did she win the race?''

''No, she came in last place. She lost her own balance when she kicked me and reeled into another horse. The two of them went off in a tangle. It would have been funny if I hadn't been rolled into a ball on the ground, trying to protect my head from running horses. Just look at her, Giff. She's taller than any woman I know, she looks men straight in the eye, and I wouldn't know she was a female watching her walk.''

Giff wasn't so sure about that, but he could understand James's ire. He said mildly, ''She rides very well.''

''To give the brat her due, she does, dammit.''

''Who's that with Ursula?''

''It's another Warfield daughter. There are three in all. The eldest and the youngest are neither one a thing like the brat. Both of them are beautiful, stylish, and ladies, well, perhaps not entirely, but close enough for descriptive purposes. That's Nelda, the eldest. She's married to Bramen Carlysle, the shipping baron. Come along, you can meet her.

I guess you haven't met her because both daughters were in Philadelphia with an aunt until just two months ago. Hell, you were in Boston until last fall, until the end of the January."

"Bramen Carlysle? Good God, James, Carlysle's older than Fort McHenry. He fought in the Revolution. He was present at Cornwallis's surrender at Yorktown. He's older than dust. How old is this Nelda?"

"Maybe twenty-two."

Gifford just snorted.

Ursula wasn't happy. She sent a look toward her husband that offered substantial marital rewards if he would get rid of Nelda Carlysle.

Gifford, with all the aplomb of a rich banker, which he was, gallantly swept his hat from his head. "Mrs. Carlysle, it's a pleasure, ma'am, to finally meet you."

"And you, Mr. Poppleton. Ah, James. I'm so sorry about that last race. Jessie won but she didn't deserve to, all the ladies around me agreed. She's an abomination. I'm sure Father will speak to her about it. So unladylike of her, so embarrassing for the rest of us."

"I'm sure your father will speak to her, Nelda. He'll probably toast her with his best champagne. Ah, don't be embarrassed, she's damned good. You should be singing her praises." God, he was a perverse bastard.

"Surely not." Nelda sighed, looking down at the toes of her slippers. "She shouldn't be good at such a manly pursuit. A jockey!" She actually shuddered. "I vow I can't go to a ladies' tea without—"

James, who privately thought Jessie should be flogged, said even more perversely, "She's an excellent horsewoman. Surely you can be a bit more tolerant, Nelda. She's just different, that's all."

"Perhaps," Nelda said, lightly touching her gloved fingers to his forearm. "You did well in the race."

"Not as well as two of your father's other racehorses."

"It's just because you're such a big man, James. You haven't come to visit me. Now that I'm an old married lady, I am perhaps freer than I was when I wasn't married."

Ursula cleared her throat. "Well, Nelda, do say hello to Bramen. We must return home ourselves now. My mother is staying with us until Monday."

His mother-in-law. Gifford would have preferred to remain out until midnight. His mother-in-law, Wilhelmina, knew no equal. James, in deference to his own sanity, had moved his mother out of his house at Marathon and into a charming red-brick town house in German Square near the center of Baltimore some two years before. She visited Ursula and Gifford at their home not a mile away in the elegant four-story terrace on St. Paul Street, claiming that her own tiny dwelling depressed her spirits from time to time. However, she complained every minute she was in her daughter's house.

Nelda showed no signs of moving on. She edged closer to James. "Surely dear Wilhelmina can wait for just a bit longer. James, my dear husband tells me you're going to stay in Baltimore forever now."

"I have no plans to return to England anytime this year," James said. "Candlethorpe, my stud farm in Yorkshire, is in good hands. Marathon, on the other hand, needs a lot of work and attention."

"Marathon?"

"I named my stud farm in honor of that ancient Greek who ran his heart out getting to Athens to tell of their victory at Marathon against the Persians. If he'd only had one of my horses, he wouldn't have fallen down dead after he'd given his news."

"Oh," Nelda said. "You should pick another name, James, perhaps something more stately, more easily recognized. Marathon sounds foreign."

"It is foreign," Ursula said. "Perhaps even nasty."

"Oh," Nelda said suddenly, waving, "There're Alice and Allen Belmonde. Over here, Alice!"

James stiffened. He looked at Giff, who winked at him, saying, "Good day, Alice. You're looking lovely. Belmonde," he added, nodding to the man who had married Alice for her money and was now trying to spend as much of it as Alice's father would release, which, thankfully, wasn't all that much a year. He wanted to make money racing, something, James knew, that was just about as tough as marrying a rich girl, which he had managed to do. He'd had one horse race today. The thoroughbred had come in sixth out of a field of ten. He looked up when Allen Belmonde said to him, "I want Sober John to cover one of my mares, Sweet Susie. Your price is stiff, Wyndham, but perhaps it's worth it."

"Up to you," James said easily, then said to Alice, "I like your bonnet. Pink becomes you."

She flushed, something that she managed to do as if on command. It quite amazed him. But he wanted to tell her it wasn't all that effective, at least on him. But he liked Alice, had known her since she was born. So he just smiled when she said, "You're so nice to me, James, and I'm sorry you lost, but I'm glad Jessie won. Isn't she wonderful? I was just telling Nelda how very much I admire Jessie. She does exactly what she wants without being bound down by all the endless rules."

"Rules are to keep ladies protected," Allen Belmonde said as he patted his wife's shoulder. It wasn't all that gentle a pat, James saw when Alice winced. "Ladies shouldn't complain about rules."

"Yes, well, Jessie will do as she pleases," Ursula said. "Come along, James, we really must be leaving now. Nelda, our regards to your husband. Alice, you and Allen enjoy the rest of the day. We will see you in church tomorrow."

James grinned down at Nelda, who'd taken a step closer to him. "I smell like a horse, so you'd best keep your distance. If you see your father, tell him I'll be at his stables tonight with a bottle of his favorite claret, though I'm sure he's already counting on it. He can gloat all he wants."

"You and my father still drink together?"

"Whenever I beat him, he rides to Marathon, bringing me champagne."

"Why then," Alice said, "you should bring the claret to Jessie. She's the one who beat you, not her father."

"It's his stable," James said, wishing the brat were here so he could count her freckles again. That got her mouth shut quickly enough.

"I'll tell my mother," Nelda said. "I don't often see Father anymore. As for Jessie, well, why would I want to see her? She's so very odd, you know. I do disagree with Alice, but she doesn't mind that I do. Ladies need rules. It makes civilization, well, more civilized. We do need you charming gentlemen to protect us, to guide us, to tell us how to go on, to—"

"That's really enough of a list," Ursula said, squeezing her husband's arm in impatience.

James, who thought Jessie the most unnatural of females, said quickly, "She's not at all odd, Nelda. And she's your sister." He turned to Giff. "I'll see both of you tomorrow."

"You'll see Mother, too," Ursula said, her voice as grave as a nun's, her eyes as wicked as a sinner's.

"There is that," James said, gave them all a cocky smile, and strode off through the dwindling crowd.

"Well," Nelda Carlysle said all bright as the afternoon sun overhead, "I'll be off then. Ursula, I do hope to see you again soon now that we're both married ladies. Perhaps I can visit you in town? I've finally convinced Mr. Carlysle that a nice town house on George Street would be ever so convenient. That's quite near to you, isn't it?"

"Quite near," Ursula said, and thought, *I'll move to Fells Point if you come to town, Nelda. You could also be a bit more delicate about your overtures to my poor brother. Oh dear, that would certainly cause a tangle if Nelda managed to get her hooks into James. No, my brother would never poach on a husband's preserves.*

Ursula and Giff watched Nelda lean down to speak to Alice, who was just a little bit of a thing, her hand on her sleeve, then give her a brief nod. She smiled up at Allen Belmonde, nodding pleasantly, though to Ursula's knowledge, Nelda couldn't stand him.

"What are you thinking, Urs?"

"What? Oh, just that Fells Point is a lovely spot."

"Have you been there lately?"

"No, but it doesn't matter, just believe me."

## $\equiv$ 2 $\equiv$

If Lord Derby hadn't won the coin toss in 1780, it's possible that we'd call it the Kentucky Bunbury.

—HISTORICAL OBSERVATION

THERE WAS A full moon. The late-March weather was mild, only a slight night breeze rustling the early spring leaves on the immensely old oak trees that lined the drive to the War-field farm.

James whistled an English ditty the Duchess had written the year before as he cantered astride Sober John, a horse as gray as the exquisite pewter bowl that sat in the middle of his dining-room table, and just as durable. The Duchess, who was actually the Countess of Chase and an English Wyndham, never seemed to run out of ideas, which was understandable, he supposed, what with the idiocy of George IV and all the politicians to provide her with such outrageous fodder. It was a catchy tune. He smiled to think how Marcus Wyndham, the Earl of Chase and the Duchess's husband, would sing her ditties at the top of his lungs in his bathtub, sending maids flurrying off in fits of giggles outside the huge master bedchamber at Chase Park.

James lightly patted Sober John's neck. The stallion was twenty years old now and the mainstay of James's breeding farm. Sober John's get were racing long four-mile stretches from Massachusetts to Kentucky. Sober John was a thoroughbred, a stayer, whose endurance had been renowned on the racecourses. He was now becoming renowned as a stud, thank the good Lord.

The bright moonlight glinted off the white wooden fence that, along with the oaks, lined the drive from the main road to the big house itself. The Warfield Stud and Racing Stable was huge, profitable, and well run. James admired it and prayed Marathon would one day be as successful. He particularly liked all that white fence that went on and on until it disappeared beyond a stand of oak trees into the darkness. He could only imagine what it would cost to keep that damned fence painted white.

When James pulled Sober John up in front of the stables, a young black slave dashed forward to take his reins. "Rub him down good, Jemmy," James said, and tossed the boy a coin.

"Sell me Sober John."

"Forget it, Oliver." He stretched out his hand and shook the older man's. His hair was redder than the brat's, though unlike hers it was threaded with gray and was as grizzled as James's hairbrush. His eyes were a faded blue, unlike the brat's which were a wet-looking green, the color of the damp moss beside a pool of dirty water in the middle of a swamp. "You had four winners in the races today, all of them Friar Tuck's get. That two-year-old filly—Miss Louise—she's going to keep you winning for years, barring accidents. You don't need Sober John."

"If I had Sober John I'd put you right out of business, boy."

"I hope the thought keeps you awake at night."

Oliver sighed deeply. "I'm getting old. Aches and pains keep me up enough at night. Oh hell, if I were your age again, I'd steal Sober John, challenge you to a duel, and put a bullet through your gullet. Now I'm too old to do anything but whine and bark like an old dog.''

''An old dog that likes claret.''

Oliver Warfield grinned, showing a darkened tooth in the front of his mouth that would have to be pulled soon. ''You had three winners—not bad for a young fellow with a dash of skill. You would have had more if your jockey, Redcoat, hadn't broken his leg.''

''He wouldn't have broken it if that lout from the Richmond Rye stable hadn't tried to slash him apart with his riding crop, sending him into a tree.''

''So give your jockeys pistols, James—some owners do, you know. Come inside, my boy. I want my claret. I want to gloat. Jessie told me to do it up right since you tried to do her in today.''

''I don't think it's possible.''

''What?''

''Doing in Jessie. I think she puts glue on the seat of her pants. I'd have to pry off her saddle, too.''

James followed Oliver Warfield into the large office he'd added onto one end of the huge stable. It was lit with four lamps. The air was redolent of the smells of leather, horse, hay, and linseed oil. James breathed in deeply. He loved the smells, had all his life. Oliver waved him to a deep black leather chair. He took the bottle, opened it, and poured both of them a liberal glass.

''To your victory,'' James said, hating those particular words. Oliver knew it, too, the old bastard.

''My victory.'' He clicked his glass to James's, then sat back and drank deep. ''Were there many at the races today? I had to leave early. This damned gout of mine gets nastier by the year.''

''I'm sure Dr. Dancy Hoolahan would tell you the claret doesn't help.''

''Then you should try to win more often.''

"Hell, so it's my fault that you have gout?"

"Well, it's your bloody claret. All I have to do is win and you're here to pour it down my throat."

"The very best bloody claret."

Oliver Warfield grinned, raising his glass again. "Here's to my bloody gout and your damned excellent claret. Now, my boy, were there a goodly number of folk at the races throughout the day?"

"A good number. A lot of ladies, which is a good sign. The Puritans are trying their best to get racing outlawed, but I don't think it'll work here. We're all too big a bunch of sinners."

"You're right about that. Ah, it's fun to gloat. It always makes me feel better. A warm, sunny day never hurts attendance. I wish I could have been there for all of it."

"There were assorted broken bones to liven things up. Look, Oliver, I just nudged Jessie," James said, sitting forward, cupping his wine glass in his hands, "I didn't really try to toss her off. I just wanted to wipe the grin off her face."

"That's not what she says, but she's always ready to look at you cross-eyed, James. I don't know why the girl can't abide you. It's not that she's a little prude, not my Jessie. But she hasn't liked you since she met you—what was it? At least six years ago. She was just a little tyke then."

"She's never been little in her life. When she was fourteen, she was all legs and a big mouth."

"Well, maybe that's true about her mouth," Oliver said. "She beat you soundly, James."

James poured them more claret. "To your victory," he said again, knowing the words would be a litany before the evening was over. The good Lord knew James would need a lot of claret to see him through the evening.

"So many victories over the years," Oliver said as he loosened his cravat. He knew his years gave him the right to wax philosophical every once in a while, particularly with James, who was young and unseasoned. Winning was better than philosophizing any day. Doing both was all a man could desire. "You know, of course, that the Warfield stables have been here since the early seventeen hundreds when it was started by my grandfather. Aye, he'd just stepped off the ship from Bristol, one racehorse to his name, skinny as a rail from puking his guts up the entire voyage, and filled with all the optimism of youth." Oliver Warfield drank deep then sighed. "From father to son and father to son. What a tail-male line."

"I've never heard humans called a 'tail-male line' before."

"Same difference, only I failed. All I could do was breed daughters. Three bloody females. It's enough to make a man weep."

"Maybe this is the start of a tail-female line."

"Not likely. What good are girls? They get married, leave, change their names, and breed—babes, not horses. I'm not complaining. It's what they're supposed to do. Look at my females. Just one husband amongst the three of them, and old Bramen is older than I am, James. Have you seen those skinny legs of his and that huge paunch? He's probably more shriveled than a two-year-old potato. I just shook my head at Nelda and told her she was a fool, but her mother told me to mind my own business, which is horses, and not to interfere. Old Bramen is rich, I'll give him that. What's a father to do, James?"

"Nelda seems happy," James said with no hesitation, lying cleanly. "I saw her today. Don't worry about it. It's done. Enjoy life, Oliver. Enjoy your aches and pains. A son-in-law will turn up. Glenda is pretty, well dowered, and men flock around her. What are you worried about?"

"There's Jessie to consider."

"Why?" James took a drink of claret. The glasses were old and chipped, but they were of good quality; at least they'd once probably graced a grand table. He wondered if Mrs. Warfield had believed them long ago tossed on the trash heap. "She'll outgrow her nonsense. She'll want to be a wife and a mother, just give her a while."

"Poor child. She should have been a boy. Just like me is Jessie, all pride and vinegar and stubbornness. She's even got my red hair. As for those freckles across her nose, well, Mrs. Warfield claims that's my fault for letting Jessie run wild as the colts in the fields since she was just a little mite."

James remained quiet. He and Oliver both knew a lady shouldn't have freckles. Nor should she have chapped lips.

Oliver Warfield beetled his thick red eyebrows. "Jessie doesn't want to marry. She told me so just last week."

James became even more quiet. He looked at the nearly empty bottle of claret and wished he'd brought two bottles.

"She said that all men were pigs and selfish and short-sighted."

"That's quite a lot, even out of Jessie's big mouth."

"Jessie never learned restraint. Except with horses."

"I've never thought I was shortsighted."

"You're young. Of course you're shortsighted. That's why Nelda married old Bramen. She was tired of waiting for you, not that it matters now. Bramen's got more money than either you or I will ever earn in a lifetime. Just mind that you don't become Nelda's lover. Aye, James, I hear things. I know that Nelda would like a lusty young man in her bed and it's you she wants. What am I to do with Jessie? Yes, that's right, give me more claret. You have a good cellar, James. Damn, I think we should have the loser bring two bottles. Just ain't enough tonight. Did I tell you that Mrs. Warfield blames me, claims Jessie is unnatural and I made her that way, letting her ride astride wearing men's breeches will bring her to no good. She says I'm taking away Jessie's womanness. Jessie says womanness is boring and the skirts are too tight. She says she doesn't want to mince around in shoes that make her feet hurt. She doesn't want to have to treat men like they're smart and charming, which they aren't. She says men get married and get fat and belch over their dinner. She says they're clods and can't ride worth a damn. I don't know precisely what she means by all that, but there it is. But she's a damned good rider, is Jessie. Now Glenda, there's a beauty for you, the perfect lady. Don't you agree, James?''

James took another drink of claret. He didn't know Glenda all that well, but from Ursula's glazed expression of social pain, he imagined that Glenda was probably just as spoiled as her lovely sister. At least Jessie wasn't a spoiled brat. She was just a brat, no spoilation about her. As for Glenda, she played the harp and recited poetry that she herself had penned. He'd been spared the poetry but not the harp.

''Glenda would make any man a fine wife. All sweet laughter and giggles.''

James grunted. Glenda was small and round with lovely breasts to which she granted more freedom than other girls of his acquaintance. She lisped occasionally, an affectation that seemed to be making the rounds of Baltimore society. She also had the disconcerting habit of staring directly at a man's crotch. He'd once had to move quickly behind a potted palm when she'd done that to him at a party last year.

He tossed down the rest of his claret. The sweet, heavy wine sat nicely in his belly. ''I'm here to let you gloat, Oliver, not to have you try to marry me off to one of your two remaining offspring.''

''True, but a man has to think of the future. If you married Glenda, you'd combine Warfield Stud and Racing Stables with your own Marathon farm. You could do much worse, James. What's the size of your breeding farm in England?''

"Candlethorpe is small, half the size of Marathon. The Earl of Rothermere who owns—"

"I know all about the Hawksburys, James. One of the finest studs in all of northern England. I hear Philip Hawksbury married a Scottish girl who's magic with horses."

"Yes, Frances is a good sort. Her way with horses is amazing. They oversee my stud along with Sigmund, my head stable lad, when I come to America. Sober John's sire is Ecstasy from the Rothermere stable, who goes directly back to the Godolphin Arabian."

"Sell me Sober John."

"Forget it, Oliver."

"I suppose I could," Oliver said. "But I'll keep after you, maybe send one of my girls to soften you up."

"Just don't send Jessie. She'd just as soon put a knife in my ribs as look at me." James stretched his long legs out in front of him and crossed his ankles. He closed his eyes and crossed his arms over his chest. He said, "You'll not beat me again, Oliver."

"How do you figure that, boy?"

"You'll see, old man, you'll see." He opened his eyes and held out his empty glass.

Oliver Warfield gave a grunt of laughter and poured the last few remaining drops of claret into James's glass.

There was the sound of crashing wood, a scream, and a thud.

Both men were on their feet in an instant, running to the door of the office. They dashed through only to draw up short.

"What the hell?" Oliver Warfield stared down at his daughter, dressed like a boy, her red hair stuffed beneath a woolen cap, lying sprawled on her back, arms and legs flung out, just outside the door, in a trough filled, thankfully, with hay.

"Jessie! What in God's name happened? Are you alive, girl? Is anything broken? Speak to me."

There was a small, unconvincing groan.

James just looked down at her, knew she was quite conscious because he saw her eyelashes twitch, and said, "She's too obnoxious to be hurt. I'll tell you what she was doing, Oliver. The brat was overhead eavesdropping, lying on her belly with her eyes and ears pressed to the cracks between the beams. Isn't that right, Jessie?"

## 3

"SPEAK TO ME, girl!" Oliver lightly tapped his hand against her cheek. She gave another little moan that didn't fool James for an instant. He said in a voice laden with English arrogance he knew would prompt her to attack him, "Yes, do say something, Jessie. Your father and I wish to get back to our claret. Your interruption was untimely. If you don't get up, I'll just have to pour this bucket of water on you. That should make you a bit more alert. I say, Oliver, isn't there a green sheen to that water? Could that be a bit of slime on top?"

Jessie Warfield opened her eyes even though she didn't want to. She resisted the temptation to throw the bucket of water in James Wyndham's face. She would have liked to disappear, but there was nothing for her to do but face the music. "I'm all right, Papa. It was a bad fall, but I was just knocked silly for a little while." She gave her father a pathetic smile.

"You were knocked silly when you were born," James said, extending his hand.

She grasped it and let him pull her out of the hay trough. She brushed herself off for a very long time.

"Were you eavesdropping?" Oliver asked. "As James said?"

She brushed herself harder.

"Come on, Jessie, of course you had your ear plastered

against the ceiling of your father's office. You probably wanted to hear if I would give away any racing secrets.''

"Actually," Jessie said, rising to look James right in the eye, taking the bait he offered with both hands, "you don't have a single racing secret to interest me. I know more about racing than you do, James.''

"Now, Jessie, James admitted that he might be short-sighted, but he is young.''

"What are you talking about, Papa?''

"Don't you remember? You said you didn't want to marry because all men were selfish and pigs and short-sighted.''

"You heard me admit to being shortsighted, Jessie. You heard everything. Refresh my memory. Did we talk about you and your multitude of failings?''

Her eyes fell and he stared down at her. Not far down because she was so damned tall, those legs of hers nearly as long as his. "What the devil do you have on your face?''

Oliver peered closely at his daughter. "Yes, Jessie, what is that stuff all over your cheeks and nose?''

She slammed her hands against her face and took a step backward, hit the back of her knees against the hay trough, and fell into the straw again, arms flailing.

James laughed, crossed his arms over his chest, and said, "I think, Oliver, that your daughter here is trying to lighten her freckles with some sort of concoction known only to females, which makes me wonder how the devil she learned the recipe.''

"Now, James, Jessie's a female. Why, I remember just last month she couldn't ride in a race because—''

Oliver Warfield's voice died a quick, clean death. His daughter struggled out of the hay trough and without another word, fled from the stables, leaving behind her a very embarrassed, silent father and an equally silent James Wyndham.

"Er," Oliver said, "tell me about the Earl and Countess of Chase. Will they ever visit Maryland do you think?"

James looked distracted, which he was. Jessie's unexpected fall through the ceiling had amused him and left him feeling the tiniest bit sorry for her. And even when her father tried to come to her aid, he'd only embarrassed her more. And they'd caught her with that goop on her face. It smelled like cucumbers.

"What, Oliver? Oh, my English cousins. They've got a lot on their plate just now, what with the Duchess birthing her second child, another little boy, just three months ago. They named him Charles James. I'm his godfather. He's dark-haired like his father but he's got his mother's deep blue eyes. Come to think of it, Marcus has deep blue eyes and his mother has dark hair too."

"Duchess. I've always thought that was an odd name."

"Her husband named her that when she was nine years old and he was all of fourteen. She was very contained even then, you see, very collected and calm in any crisis. She still is, except around Marcus. He glories in being offensive and does it particularly well around her. It drives her mad. It occasionally even drives her voice up an octave, though only rarely."

"She writes ditties, didn't you say? Even though she's rich and a countess?"

"Yes, she's quite good."

"That's a man's job."

James looked taken aback. "I suppose so. I never really considered that before. It's just a natural part of her, a talent she has that everyone takes for granted—at least they do now."

"Just the way my Jessie is talented with horses," Oliver said. "A lot of folk just take her talent for granted." He shoved James back into his office. "We've still got a bit more of your claret to drink."

"No, there's just a sip left in my glass," James said sadly. "What earthly good could cucumbers do?"

Sober John covered Sweet Susie two mornings later. Oslow oversaw the lads in their handling of both the stallion and the mare, who'd been in heat now for a good week.

"Aye, it's time," Oslow had said. "I've checked her over and it's time. Sober John's ready."

The breeding shed was large, clean, and attached to the stable. Each of the five lads knew what he was to do. They wrapped Sober John's hooves in soft cotton to protect Sweet Susie. As for her, she was held gently while Oslow guided Sober John to his task. Sober John was excited at her scent and nipped her hard on her rump. For a moment there was chaos, but just for a moment. One of the lads wasn't all that experienced, and Sweet Susie got away from him. Then the lads got Sober John to focus on his duty, which he proceeded to perform with great enthusiasm.

Oslow himself led a trembling Sober John back to his stall, telling him what a grand fellow he was, how he would have an extra share of oats to go with his hay. Keeping weight on the stallions was a problem during mating. Sober John would also have an extra tub of alfalfa.

As for Sweet Susie, James patted her sweating neck as he slowly led her to the paddock to cool down in the shade of three massive oak trees. She was blowing hard and still a bit unsteady on her hooves. He gave her three buckets of fresh water, brushed her down until she blew complacently into his palm. Allen Belmonde had brought her finally, grudgingly paying James the stud fee. Allen had bought a small racing stable just south of Baltimore after he'd married Alice. He'd wanted to marry Ursula at one time, but she hadn't been interested in him. James suspected her dowry wasn't big enough for Allen, anyway. Their mother had been interested, though, in having Allen Belmonde for a son-in-law and that had led to arguments that had led to neighbors giving James impudent grins during the following days.

He hoped that Sweet Susie would foal a winner for Belmonde. It would build Sober John's reputation and that of Marathon. James gave Sweet Susie a carrot, patted her rump, and said, "This is your second time with Sober John. I just know it in my gut that you're in foal. Eleven months, my girl," he said, going to the paddock gate, "then you'll be a mother." Since it would be her first foal, James knew they'd have to watch her closely as her time drew near early the next year.

He walked back toward the house, a big red-brick Georgian surrounded by apple, plum, and cherry trees coming into full bloom in the front and a once-beautiful rose garden on the west side. Thomas, his butler, tended a huge vegetable garden in the back of the house.

James had bought the house three years previously from Boomer Bankes, who'd been caught embezzling from a public water fund. Included in the deal were two dozen slaves whom James had promptly freed. All of them had stayed on with him. He'd spent his money building new cabins for all his married people and had added a large dormitory at the top of the stable for all the stable lads. He provided seed for gardens and good lumber for furniture. After he'd finished, he'd had no money left. The putrid green wallpaper in the drawing room of his home still made him bilious, the floors were ugly and scarred, and the horsehair wadding was poking out of several of the settees and chairs. The kitchen was older than the Ellison flour mills on the Patapsco River, but Old Bess knew how to coax everything to work. The privy had reeked so badly that anyone having to walk near it gagged. He'd had everyone wrap kerchiefs around their faces and they'd dug the old privy under half a dozen feet of earth and built a new one, liming it until no one had to hold his nose within ten feet of it, even if there wasn't an upwind breeze.

Then he'd renamed the farm Marathon, showing off his Latin and Greek education, his cousin Marcus had said, cuffing him, adding that he didn't know the Colonists even knew such things. During the past year James had spent more and more time in Baltimore. Upon occasion he considered selling his stud in Yorkshire, but then he'd just shake his head at himself. He loved Candlethorpe, loved England, and loved his English relatives. No, he wouldn't give up either of his homes.

He came around the east side of the stable, automatically checking off tasks he had already done that morning and thinking about what he had to do throughout the afternoon. He came to a halt at the sound of Oslow's voice, low and deep, a voice that mesmerized anyone who heard it. James's ears immediately perked up.

"Aye, Diomed won a three-year-old sweepstakes in England, at Epsom, way back in 1780. But then he just faded away, didn't win another race, didn't do a bloody thing. They put him to stud, but there he was a failure, too. He lost all fertility. He came over here in 1800, bought on speculation, you know. And you know what happened, Miss Jessie? It was our good old American air and American food and our American mares that worked magic in that old horse. His fertility returned and he covered just about every mare in every state. Aye, if Diomed were a man he'd be a bloody Casanova. Diomed is the forefather of the American racehorse. He stands alone, I say. He'll stand alone forever, you mark my words, Miss Jessie."

"Oh my, Oslow. I remember when he died, I was just a little girl, way back in — When was it?"

"In 1808. A grand old man he was. More folk mourned his passing in old colony land than they did George Washington's."

She laughed—a pure, sweet, long laugh, nearly as long as those skinny legs of hers.

James came around the side of the stable to see Oslow sitting on a barrel, Jessie sitting at his feet, her legs crossed, a straw in her mouth. An old hat was set back on her head and her thick red hair was coming out of its pins, straggling down beside her face. She was dressed as disreputably as any of his stable lads on wash day, her wool pants so old they bagged out at the knees and hugged her ankles. It seemed to him, though, that the freckles over her nose were lighter. Her lips weren't chapped, either.

"So," he said, "what was that stuff you were using, Jessie? I thought I smelled cucumber."

"What stuff?" Oslow asked, nodding to James.

James just shook his head. "So you were telling her about Diomed."

"I wasn't using any stuff. I just like to eat cucumbers. Did you ever see Diomed, James?"

"Once, when I was a little boy. My father took my brother and me to the racecourse and he was there, a grand old man, just as Oslow said, standing there like a king, and all of us went and bowed. It was quite a show. You're telling me that you carry cucumbers around and eat them?"

"Just sometimes." Jessie abruptly got up and dusted herself off. James saw that the wool pants were very tight across her butt. He frowned. Jessie saw that frown and said, defensive as a banker with his hand caught in the till, "I just stopped by for a few minutes to see Oslow. I'm not here spying or anything. Oslow said Sober John covered Sweet Susie."

"Yes. It went well."

"I would like to buy Sober John."

"You don't have enough money, Jessie. You won't ever have enough money."

"When I own my own racing stable I will. I'm going to

be the most famous and richest racehorse owner in America."

Oslow stood up, too. "I wouldn't be at all surprised, Miss Jessie, no, I wouldn't. You be good now, girl. Remind me to tell you about Grimalkin the cat." Oslow walked away, whistling.

"How long have you been conferring with Oslow?"

"I've known Oslow since I was born. He's a friend, and he knows everything about every horse all the way back to the Byerly Turk, the Darley Arabian, and the Godolphin Arabian. Did you know that Sober John goes tail-male all the way back to the Godolphin Arabian?"

"I know. I've never seen you here before. How often do you come to see him?"

She scuffed her boots in the dirt.

"Jessie, I'm not accusing you of spying or putting poison in one of the horse's oats."

"I'd put poison in your oats before I'd ever hurt a horse. All right, I've been coming here since I was a little girl. When Mr. Boomer lived here, he always gave me a glass of claret watered down with lemonade."

"God, that sounds gruesome."

"It was, but he tried to please me. He didn't know anything about children. Poor Mr. Bankes, he didn't make a good criminal. He was too nice."

"He was a sniveling coward, pleading on his knees that no one challenge him to a duel. He preferred jail to facing any of the men he'd cheated."

"He wasn't a sniveling coward to me."

"You didn't have anything to steal. Now, enough of that. I assume you didn't break anything from your fall?"

"No, I was just a bit sore. Papa had the ceiling repaired yesterday. The damned wood was rotted through right where I put my knee."

"I don't suppose that taught you anything?"

He used his obnoxious drawling English accent again, knowing it enraged her. Her jaw twitched, her shoulder actually jerked, but she kept her head down. "Yes," she said, then finally looked up at him. "I learned that I've got to scout out my terrain before I venture into it."

He laughed; he couldn't help it. "Would you like to come to the house for a glass of claret?"

She looked suddenly like a child who'd been offered an unexpected treat. He drew back from that glowing smile. "With lemonade in it, naturally."

Jessie Warfield was back, in spades. She looked away from him, toward the overgrown rose garden. "I must go home, but thank you for your kind offer. The garden is a mess, James. You should have someone fix it."

She didn't wait for him to say anything to that, just turned and strode away, those long legs of hers eating up the graveled drive until she got to Rialto, the damned horse who'd beaten Tinpin. He watched her stroke Rialto's muzzle, check the saddle girth, then swing herself gracefully onto his back. She pulled her hat over her eyes, lightly kicked Rialto in his muscled sides, and rode down the drive. She never looked back. One long tail of red hair had escaped her hat and hung down her back.

He would swear he'd smelled cucumbers. He wondered if she carried them around in her coat pockets; they certainly bagged out enough.

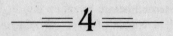

# 4

GLENDA WARFIELD STARED at James Wyndham's crotch. She knew it didn't matter if a man wasn't looking at her, as James wasn't now. He would look at her soon enough, even if he was in the deepest conversation with someone else, as James was now, speaking with Allen Belmonde, that dark-haired, swarthy man whose crotch she'd never stared at because he frightened her with those dark, lightless eyes of his. She couldn't stand his weak, fluttery little wife, Alice, who, strangely enough, seemed to adore Jessie, always praising her independence, nauseating Glenda in the process.

She stared at James. If she just kept staring long enough, he would eventually turn around and she'd see a leap of lust in his eyes and pain as well because he'd quickly realize there was nothing to be done to assuage his lust.

But James didn't turn around for the longest time. He turned around finally when his brother-in-law, Giff Popple-ton, greeted him. He met Glenda's eyes briefly, nodded, but then he listened to something Giff said, and laughed.

Glenda wasn't pleased. She was eighteen, quite pretty, her breasts milky white and full. Men loved to look at her breasts; she'd known that since they'd blossomed two years before. The stable lads were in a constant state of male turmoil whenever she came around, which was often since she had hit sixteen and was more than eager to test her power on anything male.

*Why wasn't James Wyndham interested?* Surely he must realize that if he married her, he'd eventually have the Warfield stables to add to his own holdings.

"It just doesn't make any sense."

"What doesn't, dearest?"

"Oh, Mother, I was just thinking that James Wyndham should be proposing to me rather than ignoring me."

"You're right," Portia Warfield said, frowning at this injustice. "It doesn't make any sense. It is perplexing. Your chemisette is nonexistent, dear. Come with me to the ladies' withdrawing room and I'll arrange it. You don't want to be thought loose by the other ladies."

"Yes, Mama," Glenda said. She dutifully followed her mother from the large Poppleton drawing room.

Portia Warfield said to her daughter as they climbed the wide cherry-wood Poppleton stairs to the second floor, "I just wormed it out of your father—James was married to an Englishwoman. Your father wanted to stop there, but I wouldn't let him. He gave in finally when I offered to let him order whatever he wished for dinner. The woman James married was the daughter of a baron and very young. Evidently she died in childbirth within the first year of their marriage. One supposes that he's still wounded, at least as much as a man is capable of being wounded when his wife dies. Of course he hadn't known her all that long, less than a year. The child died with her. I suppose that would depress a man to have his heir lost, but I understand it's been at least three years since it happened. He should be snapping out of this indifferent stance he's taken with all the lovely girls in Baltimore."

"He has a mistress. He doesn't need any of the lovely girls until he is ready to marry for an heir."

"A mistress?" Mrs. Warfield said, pausing a moment, pursing her lips. "Why haven't I heard anything about that? Do you know who she is, Glenda? Not that you should know anything at all about such improper situations, but anyway, who is she?''

Glenda leaned closer. "Mrs. Maxwell.''

"Connie Maxwell? Goodness, she must be at least thirty-five years old! She's been a widow for years now. Fancy that. Are you certain, dearest?''

"Oh yes. Maggie Harmon told me she heard her papa tell her mama that he saw them together in her garden and they were kissing and laughing and doing other things, too. Her papa told her mama that they disappeared behind a huge rosebush and the laughing stopped.''

"Interesting,'' Mrs. Warfield said. "I'm not saying that Connie's an old hag, but she isn't a fresh innocent like you, dearest. She has kept her figure, I'll have to say that for her. And I suppose she has a pretty enough face, what with all that blond hair of hers and skin so white I've often wanted to shoot her. Ah, well, James is a man, so I'm not at all surprised. But soon he will have to find himself a wife. He must be nearing thirty.''

"James is twenty-seven,'' Glenda said, her voice sounding depressed. "Just three weeks ago he was twenty-six, not very old at all for a man, Mama.''

"That's close enough. Don't frown, dear, it will wrinkle your angel's brow.''

"Maybe when James decides to marry, he'll want to marry another Englishwoman. Maybe he's already met her. His cousin is an earl, you know, and that's nearly royalty. He could marry anyone.''

"Why ever would he want another Englishwoman? The first one didn't even last out the year. Even though his accent hints of an Englishman, he's only half English, doubt-less his worst half, the half that is still wounded, though not so wounded he doesn't see to his man's pleasure. Now, your father tells me that James will be here the rest of the year. That gives you a goodly amount of time, Glenda. But listen, dear, there are other young gentlemen for you to consider.''

"Who, Mother?"

"Emerson McCuddle, for one. A nice young man with a very rich father."

"His breath is bad."

"Let him kiss your cheek and hold your own breath whilst he does it."

"Emerson is a lawyer. He has no interest in horse racing or breeding. What would he do with the stud and stables?"

"There is that. As for James Wyndham, perhaps he will recover himself soon. Perhaps he will tire of Connie Maxwell. Perhaps her years will begin to tell on her, but I wouldn't count on that. You will dance with him this evening. Ah, let's not pull your chemisette up too high, all right, dear?"

Jessie eased back into the shrubbery. She would have sworn that James had looked right at her, but that was impossible. He was inside in all the light. He could only see the black night and that quarter moon just behind the budding apple trees off to her left. She heard the four musicians set at the far end of the drawing room strike up a waltz. Even though she hadn't a clue as to how to dance, she loved the waltz, the sound of it, the feel of it, the way it made her want to sweep around in wide circles and laugh and laugh with pleasure. She eased back up and looked through the window. She saw James bow over Glenda's hand and swing her into the rhythm of the fast German music.

She saw him lean down to listen to something Glenda said. He smiled. Jessie couldn't remember the last time Glenda had said something that had made her smile. She saw her mother moving to stand beside Wilhelmina Wyndham, James's and Ursula's mother. Ursula and her husband were now waltzing, laughing over at James. There was Giff calling something out. More laughter. Soon the whole dancing area was filled. Even Mr. Ornack, as fat as a stuffed clam, was galloping happily about with his thin wife.

She lightly touched her fingertips to her cheeks. The cucumber mixture had hardened nicely. She'd looked very closely this morning. The bridge of freckles over her nose was lighter; she was certain of it. She sniffed. James was right. She did smell like cucumbers. Not a bad smell, but certainly distinctive.

She sighed and watched. She counted off steps, swaying with the music. When it came to a stop, she watched James guide Glenda back to their mother, who was still speaking to Mrs. Wyndham. She turned away from the window when a dark cloud blocked the moonlight. Knowing Baltimore weather, it could begin to rain at any moment. Jessie got to her feet and brushed off her bottom and legs. She heard voices then and recognized James and his brother-in-law, Gifford Poppleton, coming from the open French doors.

"I tell you I saw her with her nose pressed against the window."

"That's ridiculous, Giff. You drank too much of your own punch. Filled it with rum, didn't you? What the hell would the brat be doing here?"

Jessie froze in her boots. Oh God, she had to get out of there. They were coming nearer, coming down the steps that led from the balcony outside the French doors down into the garden. She fell to her hands and knees and began creeping through the low rosebushes that filed all the way to the garden gate, not more than thirty feet away. Just keep down and keep crawling. But she paused when she heard James say, "Does Glenda Warfield stare at your crotch, Giff?"

Giff laughed. "I've heard she stares at every man's crotch. She began doing it about a year ago, Ursula told me. She practiced a goodly bit on me when we arrived from Boston the end of January. It was quite an experience. I understand she's a bit more discreet now. That is, she doesn't stare at every single man, just ones she thinks will marry her. Did you get that succulent look tonight?''

''Yes. It was disconcerting.''

Giff laughed. ''Perhaps Jessie Warfield will learn it from her sister since she was sitting here watching through the window.''

''I think you're mad, Giff. Look, here we are. This is the window, right? No Jessie.''

''She must have heard us talking and run off. Yes, she must have gone through the back garden gate. It gives onto Sharp Street. I'll bet you anything she had a horse tied there.''

''Well, no proving it now. She's gone. I do wonder why the brat was here, if she was here.''

Their voices faded, and Jessie started to breathe again. If James had gone through that back gate, he would have seen Benjie tethered to a scrub bush just beside the gate. She shuddered, only beginning to picture the humiliation had she been discovered. She couldn't do this again.

She ran low to the gate and let herself through.

James stood beside the large French door that gave onto the balcony. ''Good God,'' he said to himself, as he lit a cheroot, ''Giff was right. What was the brat doing here?'' He wondered if she'd been invited. Surely yes. But he couldn't begin to imagine her in anything but disreputable trousers and those large shirts and coats of hers. No, she would have turned down an invitation where being a female was a requirement. He ground out his cheroot, turned on his heel, and made for the stables.

''This road needs some work, don't you agree, Jessie? Lilac here has stumbled nearly a good dozen times.''

She nearly fell off Benjie she was so startled. He must have been riding in the grass on the side of the road.

"James! Oh dear, what do you want? What are you doing here?"

"I saw you and followed you. I hadn't believed Giff when he said he saw your nose pressed against the window, watching all of us. Then I was on the balcony and I saw you slip out the back gate. Why were you there, Jessie?"

"I wasn't."

She didn't say another word. She looked behind his left shoulder, her eyes widened, and her mouth gaped. When he whipped about in the saddle, she was off. But she was riding twelve-year-old Benjie, sweet tempered and slow, so Lilac was galloping next to her in just a few minutes. James leaned over and remarked, "Your hat is just about ready to blow off. Of course your hair is so tangled, it just might hold it on."

She didn't look at him, just clapped her palm down on top of her head.

"Actually it looks like one of Oslow's old hats. Perhaps he gave it to you after it was so old and pitiful he didn't want to wear it anymore?"

She looked over at him then and if her lips could have curled, they would have. She looked madder than James had the morning when Grand Master had bitten his shoulder rather than the mare he was going to mount. "Go to hell. I don't have to talk to you, James. Go away."

Benjie was slowing. Jessie let him. James knew she wouldn't ride the poor old fellow into the road. Soon they were both at a walk, Benjie blowing just a bit. Lilac tossed her head and snorted.

"She sounds just like you," Jessie said, staring straight between Benjie's ears. "Obnoxious and impatient. Did you import her from England?"

"You don't care for my English accent?" he asked, drawling each word into the most supercilious British English he could manage.

"You sound like a pederast."

James's hands jerked on Lilac's reins and she sidestepped. "What did you say?"

"You heard what I said."

"How the devil do you know that word? No lady would say that word, much less know of it."

She turned slowly to look at him, the moon behind her, framing that old hat and the tangles of red hair that hung on either side of her face. "I'm not stupid. I read a lot."

"The question is, what do you read?"

"Everything. In this case, I agree that pederast is very definitely a man's word."

James smote his forehead with his palm. "I don't believe this. It's close to midnight. It's Baltimore and thus it will rain on us any minute and you know about pederasts. Worse, you called me one."

"It's how you sound when you speak with that ridiculous accent. You do it to make yourself sound important, to sound different from all of us Colonists. To make us all feel inferior to you just because your cousin's a bloody English earl. You want everybody to forget you're half a Colonist yourself. You're a fraud, James." She wanted to whip Benjie into a gallop, but she knew she couldn't.

"A fraud, am I? What about you, brat? You with your men's clothes, your hair like a witch's straggling down your back. You look like one of those hooligans who throw rocks at windows over at Fells Point. No, maybe you're not a fraud at all. Maybe your father's wrong. You're only a female because your body makes you aware of it once a month." He ignored her snarl. "So tell me, what were you doing at my sister's party tonight?"

She was as silent as the dark clouds overhead.

"Well? Don't you have an answer? Is it something outrageous?"

She twitched and he continued to push. "I'll just bet I

know why you were there. You were looking at all the men. Perhaps you were trying to find one close to your size so you could go to his house, break in, and steal some of his clothes. The good Lord knows your mother wouldn't let you buy men's clothes. That's it, isn't it, Jessie?''

He'd gotten her. She'd sworn she wouldn't let him get to her, but he had. He always did, when he set out to. She twisted around in her saddle and shrieked at him, ''I wanted to see you, damn you to hell, James Wyndham!''

She was trembling now, knowing she'd just opened herself to utter devastation. She felt raw and exposed. She waited for the blow. And waited some more.

The blow didn't come. Instead, James said, ''This is very strange, brat. Why did you want to see me? Is it because Glenda is after my poor male self and you want to make sure I'm good enough for her? You want to make sure I won't beat her if I marry her? You saw me staring at those breasts of hers that she displays at every opportunity and wanted to make certain I'd manage to restrain myself?''

She could but stare at him. He hadn't ground her into dust with mockery, but he'd hurt her more than even she could begin to imagine at the moment. He was a man; that was it. A man and thus he was as dull witted and as obtuse as her mother's pug, Pretty Boy, whom Jessie called Halfwit whenever her mother wasn't around.

She continued to stare at him and James said, frowning at her, ''Well? It's Glenda, isn't it?''

''Yes,'' she said. ''Yes, that's it. I'm going home, James. You needn't come any farther with me. Good night.''

She clicked Benjie forward. To her relief, James didn't come after her again. She wanted to look back, but she forced herself not to.

James wondered, as he rode Lilac toward Marathon farm, why he'd come after her. His sister would be unhappy with him that he'd left so early. Giff would tease him and poke him in the ribs, all sly and obnoxious, wondering if he'd gone to see someone special. Like Connie Maxwell, who hadn't been in attendance this evening. James could have told him that Connie's son was visiting her from Harvard and thus the two of them would wait until Danny returned to school.

A raindrop landed on his nose. Damnation. He clicked Lilac forward, and she, hating rain more than exerting herself, ran like the rising wind toward her stable.

If Jessie was concerned he would make a good husband for her sister, then people must think he was being particular in his attentions to her. He hadn't been; he knew it. He didn't like Glenda. She made him nervous because her right hand played over him whenever they danced. She annoyed him with her downcast eyes and her talk of seeing beautiful England, in the spring, in the summer, even in the winter, it didn't matter to Glenda. To hear her recite poetry had constituted the most painful twenty-two minutes of his life. He shuddered at the thought of having to sit still while she played the harp.

He urged Lilac to go faster. When he reached the house, he was soaked to the skin, in a bad mood, half afraid that Glenda Warfield was on his heels, and ready to lash out at anyone who crossed him.

He was met by pandemonium.

Oslow and ten stable lads were pacing around, oblivious of the rain, obviously waiting for him. Old Bess was holding a large, black skillet. To protect whom? Thomas was standing in the open doorway, looking stately, his arms crossed over his chest. Even he looked ready for action. Beneath the shelter of the front overhang stood a very angry Allen Belmonde. It seemed someone had stolen Sweet Susie from the paddock while James had been at the Poppleton party. Allen was here because he had ridden directly to Marathon when one of James's stable lads had come to the party to fetch James and found only Allen.

This, James thought, as he was surrounded by shouting stable lads and a furiously cursing Allen Belmonde, was going to be a fine end to his evening.

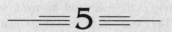

## 5

JESSIE'S HAT, A long-ago gift from her father, kept most of the rain off her face, but the rest of her quickly became wetter than the moss beneath Ezekiel's Waterfall.

She rode with her head down, feeling two parts miserable and one part angry. Damn James anyway.

But damn him for what? What had he done? Nothing, and that's why she was damning him.

When she heard the neighs and hoofbeats of several horses coming toward her, she pulled up Benjie. "It's nearly midnight. Who the devil is out in this wretched rain besides me?"

Then she heard men's voices. They were arguing, cursing the rain, cursing the foul-up with their partners, cursing the mare who was teasing the horse Billy was riding.

Billy was yelling, "The damn bloody mare's still in heat. Damn ye, stay away from me poor old boy! He's too old fer the likes o' ye and yer blood is blue besides, not all mottled and common like my ole boy here."

What damned mare?

"Shut yer trap, Billy," the other man yelled back. "Move yer horse, or we'll be in for it. Jest look, both of them want to mate here, in the road, in all this rain. Damned buggers."

Jessie heard a horse scream, then the man, Billy, scream even louder. She heard a wet thud. His horse must have thrown him to get to the mare.

She clicked Benjie forward, tugging him to the grass-edge of the road. She came around a bend, pulling him quickly to a halt.

There was Sweet Susie, butting against a horse whose rider was sitting in the middle of the road, wet and muddy and cursing. The horse — the common one that was Billy's — was obligingly trying to mount her.

If Jessie hadn't realized that these men had stolen Sweet Susie from James's farm, that they were probably very dangerous, she would have laughed at the sight of Sweet Susie and Billy's horse nipping at each other, their eyes rolling, their manes flying as they reared at each other as the torrential rain poured down.

The other man was trying to pull the horse away from Sweet Susie, trying to keep his balance at the same time, and screaming at Billy to get off his ass and help him. He wasn't having much luck. Billy's horse wanted to mount Sweet Susie, and he looked set upon his course. Sweet Susie looked set upon the same course.

This was her chance, Jessie realized. She wouldn't get another opportunity like this. She shrieked at the top of her lungs, sending Benjie into a furious gallop, steering him right between the two horses, nearly hitting Billy, who was trying desperately to scramble on his hands and knees through the mud out of the way. She saw Billy's horse break away from the other man, jump a ditch, and gallop into the field next to the road. She grabbed Sweet Susie's lead and slammed her heels into Benjie's sides.

He snorted and leaped forward. Sweet Susie, liking Benjie's snort, snorted herself, kicked up her back legs, and ran as fast as she could to catch up to Benjie.

Jessie heard the men shouting behind her to bring back their horse, that she was a thief, and she laughed aloud.

Now all she had to do was make James's farm, Marathon, before they caught up with her. She didn't want to think about what would happen to her if they did catch her. She prayed the man wouldn't leave his partner, Billy. It would take them a while to catch Billy's horse, a good ole boy.

She was only about three miles from Marathon. If she stayed on the road, they'd probably catch her. She waited until Benjie rounded a bend. She guided him off the road into a copse of elm trees, forcing Sweet Susie behind him since it was a very narrow path until they reached Gympsom's Pond, now overflowing its banks from the heavy rainfall. It was tricky, but they made it through. Beyond the pond was a field of hay surrounded by oak trees. Sweet Susie was hungry as well as in heat. Jessie kept telling the mare that Benjie would do whatever she wanted if only she'd keep running with him and not stop to eat. Sweet Susie twitched her tail and ran.

The gunshot startled Jessie so, she nearly fell off Benjie's back. She twisted around and saw just the one man about fifty yards behind her. No Billy.

Before she could flatten herself, there was another shot and this one, to her utter astonishment, hit her. She felt a cold shiver along the side of her head, nothing more, just that blast of cold. If she didn't feel anything, then it couldn't be bad. At least the idiot had shot her and not Sweet Susie. She shouted, "Benjie—run, you devil! Run!" She couldn't fall off. She couldn't pass out, or everything would be lost.

She clung to Benjie's mane and to Sweet Susie's lead. There were no more shots. She supposed the man finally realized he might hit Sweet Susie, and surely that would ruin the plans for the mare.

Rain was running down the side of her face and into her mouth. She licked it away and realized it wasn't rain. It was sweet and sticky and had a strange metallic taste. It was blood, her blood. She felt nauseated and dizzy. In that same moment when she accepted that she'd been shot, really shot, she felt a searing pain through her head. Oh no. She had to be fine—fine enough to make Marathon.

She saw the rich pastures of Marathon just ahead of her, the thick clusters of elm trees spread throughout the fields. She heard the man's cries closing in. She knew then she would make it if only she could hang on. She rode Benjie right up to James's front door, scattering at least a dozen people in front of her. She pulled Benjie to a stop at the sight of James dashing down the deep steps.

"What the devil are you doing here, Jessie?"

"Hello to you, James. I brought you Sweet Susie."

She weaved in the saddle.

"What the devil is wrong with you?" He was next to Benjie then, looking up at her, prying Benjie's reins from her fisted hand to give them to one of the stable lads. "Os-low, you take Sweet Susie and make sure she's all right. Well, brat, what's wrong?"

Thomas brought a lighted lantern. It sent up a ghostly yellow light through the rain.

"Good Lord, what's that on your face, missie?" Thomas said, poking the lantern into Benjie's side. Benjie took exception, quickly sidestepped, threw back his head, and sent Jessie flying off his back.

James caught her. She leaned heavily against him. "Bring the lamp, Thomas."

"Oh my, what's wrong with her purty little face?"

"Why does Jessie Warfield have my Sweet Susie?" Allen Belmonde yelled, running out of the house. "I don't care if she's a girl; I'll see her in jail. She's always giving Alice ideas that don't suit any female, and now look what she's done. She's a common thief. If her damned father thinks he can send his daughter to do his dirty work, then he's—"

"Be quiet, Allen," James said very softly, in a tone of voice he rarely used. It was hard and low and mean and quite calm. Belmonde shut up. James tucked Jessie close.

She was still conscious, but just barely. He added to Allen Belmonde, "I believe she's been shot." He couldn't believe he sounded so calm. God, she'd been shot! "Let's go inside and see how bad it is. No doubt she'll tell us how she came to have Sweet Susie."

He picked her up in his arms. Her old hat fell off her head, and he pulled her against his chest to protect her from the rain as well as he could. He didn't realize until he walked into the parlor that twelve people were pressing at his back.

Old Bess said, "Glory be, Mr. James, jest look at her poor face. All that blood. Poor little baby. What happened?"

Old Bess was right. He stared down at the hair over her temple, matted with rain and blood, at the streaks of blood down her cheek and on her shoulder. "Thomas, please have Dr. Hoolahan fetched immediately. Tell him Jessie's been shot. Now, Bess, get me a blanket. She's soaked clear through."

James just stood there in the middle of his parlor holding Jessie Warfield in his arms. This was not the way he'd expected this particular evening to end. Of course finding Allen Belmonde here screaming about his stolen horse hadn't been in his calculations either. Now everything had changed again. What was Jessie doing with Sweet Susie? He moved to stand in front of the fireplace.

"I can stand, James."

"Shut up. Even though you weigh more than a female should, I can bear it for a few more minutes."

She tried to pull away from him. "Stop it, damn you. Don't move again. I don't want you bleeding on my carpet."

"Mr. James, here's a nice blanket."

It wasn't any good and James knew it. She was wetter than he was. As he wrapped her in the blanket he just knew she'd catch an inflammation of the lung. To his relief he saw that the bleeding was sluggish now, thank the good Lord. "Come along, Bess, we've got to get her out of these wet clothes or she'll get really sick just to spite me. I don't think we should wait for Dr. Hoolahan."

He automatically walked to his bedchamber. Then, realizing what he'd done, he turned and took her to his best guest chamber. "I'll see to her, Mr. James. You go get changed yourself. The good Lord knows you're nearly as sodden as poor Miz Jessie. I'll take good care of her. Don't you worry, Mr. James."

When James knocked on the bedchamber door some seven minutes later, Old Bess told him to come in.

Jessie Warfield had three blankets pulled to her chest and was wearing one of his never-worn nightshirts, buttoned to her throat. He wondered where Old Bess had gotten it. Her hair was spread out over the pillow, and Old Bess was gently daubing a wet cloth to the wound just above her left temple. Thank God the bullet hadn't struck her face. And it was a bullet. He'd known that right away. It had scared the devil out of him. That she'd remained conscious was a good sign. A head wound and unconsciousness could mean death. The thought made him shiver. He was relieved to see that the brat's eyes were bright, not all clouded up with pain and confusion.

Jessie watched him come to the bed. His hair was tousled, his shirt wasn't fastened properly, and he looked worried. About her? No, more likely his concern was for Sweet Susie.

"I'll take over now, Bess. Go downstairs and wait for Dr. Hoolahan."

"Yessir, Mr. James."

Jessie watched her lean down, pick up her iron skillet, and walk from the bedchamber. Jessie said, "This room needs fixing. The wallpaper is so old it's—Ouch!"

"Sorry. You might consider keeping your mouth shut for

a while. Hold still, I want to see how bad this is."

She gritted her teeth and closed her eyes.

"It hurts."

"Yes, I imagine it does. The bullet split through your scalp. That's why you're bleeding like a pig. Damn you, brat, hold still. Don't pull away from me. Don't you dare go to sleep."

It was then he saw the tears seeping from beneath her closed eyes. He didn't like it but didn't know what to do about it. "I'm sorry, Jessie, I won't touch you again. Dr. Hoolahan should be here soon."

He lightly touched the edge of the soft cloth to her cheeks to wipe away the tears. He felt like a clod.

"Just lie still. That's right. Don't move; just lie there and try to relax. And stay awake."

She opened her eyes and stared up at him. "Sweet Susie's still in heat. She wanted Billy's horse to mount her."

"You can explain that later. Rest, Jessie, and—"

"I know. Stay awake. I'm not stupid, James. I won't go to sleep, not with a head wound."

She closed her eyes again, but the pain didn't lessen. Her head seemed to pulse, a dull throbbing that was fast becoming a vicious headache. How could she relax when she wanted to cry and huddle into herself?

"He was stupid to shoot at me when he could have hit Sweet Susie. That's what finally stopped him, the fear of hurting her. She even wanted Benjie. You must keep her apart from the stallions, James."

"I will."

She sighed deeply, gave him a vague smile, and fainted. It scared him to death. She shouldn't have fainted. Not now. God, maybe it wasn't just a superficial scalp wound? What if—"Jessie? Jessie, wake up! I don't like this. Come on, wake up." He shook her shoulders, but her head just lolled on the pillow. He cursed some more. He was still cursing,

ordering her to wake up and stop scaring the devil out of
him when the bedchamber door opened and Dr. Hoolahan
strode in. Actually, the doctor never strode; he minced. He
took short, delicate little steps. He was thirty years old,
barely five feet four inches tall, and had a full head of nearly
white blond hair and slanted blue eyes. That mincing walk
of his made James want to hit him, but now, he was so
relieved to see him, he jumped up from the bed and said,
"Quickly, Dancy, she's been shot, her scalp grazed, but it's
still bleeding sluggishly. She just fainted and I know that's
not good. Oh, Jesus, quickly."

"It's all right, James. Just move aside, that's it. Give me
a bit more room."

Dancy Hoolahan might mince, but his voice was as deep
and soothing as Bishop Morgan's in Washington. He had
light hands and he was clean, necessities for both people
and horses. James watched him lightly probe around the
wound, then lean down and press his cheek to Jessie's chest.
He watched him take her pulse, watched him pry open her
eyes and look at her pupils.

"Ah, she's coming around. Jessie? Come on, my girl,
wake up and stop scaring your host out of his socks."

She groaned and opened her eyes. James saw the pain
deepen her green eyes to nearly black and said, "Can't you
give her some laudanum, Dancy?"

"Not just yet. Head wounds are tricky—you know that.
She can bear the pain, but I doubt she could bear being dead.
Hold on, Jessie. Can you understand me?"

"Yes, naturally. I'm not deaf."

Dr. Hoolahan laughed, a deep, very sweet laugh, which
should have come from a man James's size. "Good girl.
Now, I've got to cut your hair away from the wound. It'll
leave a bald spot but you've got so much hair, it won't
show." He removed a razor from his black leather bag.
"Have Bess get me some very hot water, James. I'll need

a bandage as well, lots of clean white linen.''

It was the longest hour James had ever spent in his life. Jessie was crying, but she didn't make a sound; she just lay there, her eyes tightly closed, her hands in fists at her sides. When Dr. Hoolahan shaved the hair away from the wound, it was James who flinched. Jessie didn't move. Dancy tossed the long strands of wet hair to the floor. She'd been more than lucky. If the man shooting at her had managed just a whisker more to the left, she'd be dead.

All because she'd saved Sweet Susie. He planned to kill her himself for taking such a risk.

When Dancy had finished wrapping the bandage around Jessie's head, she looked so pathetic, James had to smile. He listened to Dancy speak to her, asking her how many fingers he was holding up, asking her when her birthday was, asking her to name all the horses she'd raced in the past week. After each of her answers, he looked up at James for confirmation. James wondered how the devil he was supposed to know if her answers were right. He just nodded.

''Very well,'' Dr. Hoolahan said at last. ''Let's give her some laudanum so she can sleep.''

When she was on the verge of sleep, Jessie said, ''James, there were two men. One was named Billy. Their horses were both chestnuts, at least ten years old. One had a white star on his forehead, and the other one had a blaze that ran all the way from his forehead to his muzzle.''

He didn't ask her to describe the men. He doubted she could. She spoke more about the two horses until her speech began to slur.

''Good enough, Jessie. Go to sleep now. We'll speak in the morning.''

But he didn't leave until she was breathing deeply. He pulled the blankets up to her chin, snuffed out the candles, and quietly closed the bedchamber door.

Allen Belmonde, Dr. Hoolahan, Thomas, Oslow, and Old

Bess were all waiting for him in the parlor. Old Bess looked as though she wanted to hit Allen Belmonde with her iron skillet.

"Did she tell you what happened?" Allen Belmonde said. "Did she admit that she stole Sweet Susie?"

"She stupidly rescued your mare from two thieves. She couldn't describe the men, but she did describe the horses they were riding. They were common, both chestnuts, one swaybacked, the other short backed and muscular. In other words, he had quarter-horse blood."

"She'll remember more," Oslow said, "once her poor head heals."

"Damned girl," Belmonde said. "I can't believe she'd take on two men. It doesn't make any sense."

"You can thank her properly tomorrow," James said, "after I've beaten her."

Thomas cleared his throat. "I've sent word over to the Warfield farm. Oh dear, I believe I hear Mr. Oliver. In a rare snit, he is."

Oliver Warfield stomped into the Wyndham parlor, which looked less shabby in the soft candlelight. He knew enough of what had happened to be terrified. "Where's my little girl? Damn you, James, where is she? Take me to her this instant so I can take a strip off her for being so witless. I can't believe she'd save your damned mare, Allen. Who the hell cares?"

"Your daughter will be all right, Oliver," James said. "If you don't believe me, ask Dr. Hoolahan."

Dancy Hoolahan cleared his throat and took one mincing step toward Oliver Warfield and said in his deep, soothing voice, "She's sleeping now, Oliver. Stop your fretting. A bullet grazed her head, but it just ripped her scalp. No permanent damage done."

"Well, if it isn't Belmonde's fault, then it's yours, James. Damn you, why didn't you guard Sweet Susie more carefully? My little girl could have been killed, and it's because you're incompetent.''

Allen Belmonde added his two cents. "Oliver's right. It's all your fault, Wyndham. I entrust my Sweet Susie to you, and just look at what happens. Damned if you shouldn't go to jail. Maybe you hired those men to steal her yourself."

"You idiot! Don't you dare make threats and ridiculous accusations, Allen Belmonde! James would never steal anything. Well, except a race, of course, and any good jockey would try to do that."

Everyone whipped around to see Jessie Warfield weaving in the parlor doorway. She had a black wool blanket wrapped around her. Her red hair was tangled down her back and around her face, puffing out over the thick white bandage Dr. Hoolahan had wrapped around her head. James's nightshirt, fine white linen, sewn for him by his mama, covered her knees, but just barely.

## 6

"WHAT THE HELL are you doing out of bed?" James was yelling at her even as he nearly ran to catch her, knowing she was bound to collapse at any moment. But she didn't. She leaned against the door.

"I had to, well, see to private things," she said. "Then I opened the bedchamber door and heard all of you yelling." She looked toward Allen Belmonde, who appeared to be nailed to the carpet just beside the sagging pale pink settee. James nearly laughed aloud at her expression. She looked meaner than he did after a night of too much drinking. She started to take a step toward him but quickly changed her mind. She did, however, raise her fist and shake it. "Don't you dare threaten James, Allen. Marathon is the best stud farm in Maryland—except for Papa's and mine. Even if I hadn't chanced to come along, James would have found her. He wouldn't have rested until he had. If you believe otherwise, then you're stupid. I told Alice not to marry you, and yet she did and just look at how unhappy you've made her. And now you're accusing James of stealing your bloody mare."

"Thank you, Jessie," James said, feeling both bewildered and amused. "Now that you've had your say, it's back to bed with you."

"James," Oliver Warfield said, stepping between him and his daughter, "Jessie is an unmarried girl. She can't be here in your house without a chaperon. Damnation, I'll have to stay here as well. Do you have another bedchamber?''

"I'll bet it needs fixing, Papa," Jessie said, sagging now against the door frame. "Mine does, and it's the best one. The wallpaper is green and faded except for the parts that have gotten wet. Those strips are puffing out, ready to peel off the wall."

"Thank you, Jessie," James said again, this time feeling only the urge to smack her.

"This talk of wallpaper is preposterous. I'll have no more of it. I'm taking Sweet Susie away from here right now," Allen Belmonde said. "I won't take any more chances with her safety."

James said easily, "Certainly, Allen. Oslow, get Sweet Susie all rubbed down and ready to go."

"I don't think so," Oslow said. He turned to Allen Belmonde. "Listen to me, sir. Sweet Susie's still in heat. The worst thing would be to try to move her while she's still lunging after every stallion she sees. She could get hurt. Here, we'll protect her."

"The way you did tonight?"

"I'll find out what happened," Oslow said. "I'll guard her myself."

"Do as you please, Allen," James said, "I really don't give a good damn." He took Jessie's arm and pulled her into the front hallway.

"Everyone will hear about this, Wyndham!"

"Let me hit him, James," Jessie said, as she tried to pull free of him. James grinned at her and held her firm. "You could just look at him and scare him to death."

"I look that bad?"

*Oh damn*, he thought, looking at her pale face, at the pain in her green eyes, pain he knew hadn't been there but an instant before. He'd hurt her feelings? No, not Jessie Warfield's feelings. Why, she had no vanity; she wasn't any more female than . . . "No, you look raffish, sort of like a female pirate. Very dashing. What I meant was that mean look you gave him should have frozen his mouth shut. Pity it didn't last."

"I've never liked Allen Belmonde. He doesn't treat Alice well. He doesn't treat his horses well, either. Don't let him take Sweet Susie. You buy her."

"Jessie, she's his mare. Now, you're about to fall over. I'm going to pick you up. All right?"

"I thought you said I was too heavy."

"You are, but I'm very strong and stoic. Be quiet now."

"I'll be up in a moment," Dr. Hoolahan called after them. "I'll give you some more laudanum, Jessie. Now, Oliver, your daughter will be just fine. This is a bachelor's household, but James knows what he's doing. Surely you don't have to worry about such things."

Jessie's head was against James's shoulder. Thick, tangled red hair billowed against his face, tickling his nose. He hadn't realized she had so much hair. "Are you still awake?"

She nodded against his neck.

When he tucked her into bed, he spread her hair over the pillow as Old Bess had done so it would dry. "How do you feel?"

"Like a stall that hasn't been mucked out in a month."

"Pretty bad, then. Thanks, Jessie, for defending me."

"I really do detest Allen. Alice made such a mistake marrying him, and now it's too late. I'll get Allen if he says anything bad about you, James. I promise."

"Thank you," he said again as her eyes closed. Her face was very pale except for the freckles over the bridge of her nose. Dr. Hoolahan appeared in the doorway.

"She's asleep, Dancy. Let's just leave her be." He rose and snuffed out the candle beside the bed. "Tell me what to do for her."

\* \* \*

The following morning, James stood beside Jessie's bed, legs spread, hands on his hips. His voice was low and controlled. "Now you will tell me exactly what happened. You will then tell me why you took such a risk for a stupid horse. You were wrong, Jessie, and you nearly got yourself killed to prove it."

*He is furious*, she thought, watching the pulse leap in his throat. She wondered where he'd dredged up that iron control he was exhibiting. Usually he yelled his head off if he was mad, as he certainly was now. Why hadn't he yelled at her last night? She shook her head. He'd been afraid she'd die; that's why he'd been so calm. But now he knew she'd live, and he was ready to fire his cannons.

"Answer me, damn you. And don't try to tell me that you're in too much pain. Any pain you have, you well deserve and you damned well know it."

"Very well."

"Very well what?"

"I'll answer you. I didn't think at all, really. I saw Sweet Susie, saw my chance when she went after Billy's horse and was nipping at his rump. He'd already thrown Billy, so I just rode Benjie right in between them. Billy's horse jumped a ditch and ran off into the field beside the road. I grabbed Sweet Susie's lead. I'd hoped they'd get Billy's horse, but they didn't. The other man came after me alone. He fired twice before he realized that he might hit Sweet Susie, then stopped. That's all, James. It's not so much of a story."

"You're foolish and brave, and I won't have it, Jessie. Why did you do it?"

"I told you. I just wanted to save Sweet Susie. It never occurred to me the man would have a gun."

"You should have come here and told me. I would have taken some men and gone after them."

She stared at him. The headache, slight until just moments

ago, was pounding through her again. "But what would I have told you, James?"

"I don't know, but you could have taken me back to where you'd seen them."

"Would you have allowed me to lead you back there? It was raining hard. Wouldn't you have been scared I would have gotten ill? After all, I'm so delicate. No, I think you would have made me take myself home and you and your damned men would have ridden around blindly, finding nothing but colds. I saved Sweet Susie. Get used to it, James."

"Jessie, girl, how are you feeling? Bess and I have brought you some breakfast. Dr. Hoolahan told me you'd be starved this morning. Just look at what Bess made for you. Grits and eggs, their yellows all bright, just the way you prefer them, strips of bacon, all crispy and—" Oliver Warfield broke off, staring at his daughter, whose eyes were tightly closed. He glanced at James, who was standing beside her bed, ramrod straight, his arms crossed over his chest, looking as intimidating as hell and madder than the copperhead snake Oliver had ousted off a sun-baked rock the past week.

"What the devil is going on here, James? You're not yelling at my daughter, are you?"

"I haven't yelled a single word. I was just very calmly telling Jessie that she was a bloody fool, Oliver. I still can't believe she just galloped Benjie into the middle of those thieves and played the heroine. It was stupid and ill-advised and—"

"And I succeeded. So just shut up, James."

"That's my girl," Oliver said fondly, stepping into the bedchamber so Bess could come around him with a big silver tray that held enough food for two fat men. "Give him hell, Jessie."

"A little testy, are we?" James said, moving away so

Bess could plump up Jessie's pillows and pull her to a sitting position.

"Now, little honey, it's time for you to eat and ignore these men. What do men know, anyhow? All they do is strut around and give orders and expect a little girl like you to wither away and do nothing. You keep talking, Jessie. You jest snap like a turtle. Mr. James, he ain't used to no snapping, so you do it."

"You order me around all the time, Bess," James said. "Don't give this one any advice. She already does everything she shouldn't do, and more. You call her 'little honey'? That's enough to make a man puke."

"I like 'little honey.' Be quiet, James. You're just mad because I saved Sweet Susie and you didn't. Your wounded vanity is becoming tedious."

"Damn you, Jessie. That has nothing to do with my wounded vanity and you well know it."

"Now that's enough, Mr. James. I don't want the child to come down with a fever."

"No, you want her to eat so much she'll be too fat to get through the door and then she'll be forced to stay here and complain about everything. You see anything else that needs fixing, Jessie? There's not much wrong with this wallpaper, dammit."

Old Bess arranged the tray on Jessie's lap, then beamed down at her. "Now, you just eat all I brung you, Jessie. It'll make your head feel like a plump healthy raisin in no time a' t'all."

"A plump raisin with a bald spot," James said.

"You need fixing, James. I'm sorry, Bess, but I'm not very hungry."

"You would be if Mr. James weren't here twitting you. Out with you, both of you."

James said over his shoulder as he walked through the

door after Oliver Warfield, "Eat, Jessie. I'd rather have you fat than a skinny little brat who presses her nose against windows."

"What's that you say, James?" Oliver Warfield said.

Jessie closed her eyes, her fingers crumbling a slice of bacon. She heard James say, "Actually I was referring to the ceiling of your office in the stables, not windows. I was referring to her ears, not her nose."

"Oh," Oliver said. "That was strange how far afield you got."

When Mrs. Warfield, Glenda, and the carriage arrived to take Jessie home, James had planned to be gone. He had a warning system in place. Gypsom, Oslow's assistant, was supposed to whistle twice, and James would mount Tinpin and ride like the wind. But the plan didn't come off as it should have. James froze on the first step of the stairs as Thomas opened the door to greet Mrs. Warfield and Glenda. What the devil had happened to Gypsom and his plan?

"Mrs. Warfield," he said, pulling himself together. "A pleasure, ma'am. Glenda. I was just bringing Jessie some tea. Where's Oliver?"

"We are your saviors, James," Glenda said, sweeping toward him, her delicious bosom leading the way. "We've come to relieve you of Jessie. Has she been complaining much? She usually does. I'm sure it's been difficult for you."

"No difficulties. Jessie's feeling much better today. Would you like to accompany me or perhaps wait here in the parlor?"

"Oh, we'll come," Glenda said, and walked toward him, her eyes on his crotch. She stood beside him on that bottom step, her breasts brushing his arm. Mrs. Warfield just beamed at the two of them. "Yes," she said, "let's go see dear Jessie."

Dear Jessie was feeling very low. Her head ached viciously. James wouldn't let her read the *Federal Gazette*, telling her it would just make her head hurt more. She was bored. She wanted James here so they could argue—that or she could just look at him. When he suddenly appeared in the doorway, she felt as if the sun had just burst through black clouds. She gave him a big smile. Then she saw Glenda and her mother sweeping past him, bearing down on her, and her smile dissolved into the wainscotting.

"Ah, my dearest Jessie," said Mrs. Warfield, frowning at her daughter.

"Well, sister, don't you look ugly with your hair all frazzled and that silly bandage around your forehead."

James briefly closed his eyes.

"Hello, Mother, Glenda. I'm fine, I just look bad. Where's Papa?"

"Your dear papa didn't have the time to come to get you. You put him out sorely, Jessie, what with that latest exploit of yours. Your poor papa had to sleep in a strange bed just to keep your reputation from being ruined."

But her papa had told her he'd come back to get her himself, and then he'd winked at her, and she knew he would spare her a visit by her mother. But he'd failed. Jessie sighed, looking longingly at the teapot James was carrying and said, "I think Papa liked staying here last night, Mama. He was telling James all sorts of things he needed to do to make the house better."

"That's right, Mrs. Warfield. Your husband isn't shy, and he much enjoyed himself." *And my brandy*, James thought.

Glenda was walking around the small bedchamber, looking at nothing in particular. James couldn't figure out what she was doing. Finally it hit him that she was showing herself off to him—from all angles. Not a bad sight. She turned then and smiled sweetly at him. "Why don't you and I go downstairs, James, and let Mama help Jessie dress?"

"Oh dear," Mrs. Warfield said. "I forgot clothes, Jessie. Oh well, I suppose you'll just have to wear the gown you had on last night."

Jessie thought of her breeches and paled.

James said easily as he set down the tray, "I'm sorry, Mrs. Warfield, but Jessie's gown was ruined from the rain last night. Old Bess tried to save it, but it wasn't possible."

"Your papa never did tell me why you were out riding around in the rain, Jessie. If I've told you once, I've told you countless times, that you must stop acting so strangely. Now what are we to do?"

"If James will lend me this nightshirt and a robe, then I can go home like this."

"My nightshirt is yours, Jessie," James said, giving her a slight bow.

"Shall we go downstairs, James?" Glenda asked, coming to stand very close to him. He could smell her rose perfume. He wanted to sneeze.

"I don't think we have to do that, Glenda," he said. "Here, Mrs. Warfield, let me carry Jessie downstairs. Ah, first, let me fetch a robe for her. Jessie, don't move. I'll be back in a moment."

Glenda watched James leave the bedchamber to get a robe. She turned to Jessie. "James is so handsome. Did he ask you about me?"

"I don't recall that he did," Jessie said.

"Surely he must have. Why, I danced with him at the Poppletons' ball. He was leaning over my hand before I even noticed him. He couldn't take his eyes off me. He told me how gracefully I danced."

Jessie just shook her head.

Glenda twitched her skirt away from a water stain on the wall. "I know you, Jessie. You forced him to pay attention to you, didn't you? You pretended you didn't feel well, and he was obliged to let you stay here. I'll bet you even moaned and carried on so he wouldn't leave you. He held your hand, didn't he? He didn't want to, Jessie. He doesn't even think of you as a female—you know that.''

"That's enough, Glenda," Mrs. Warfield said, looking nervously over her shoulder.

"And now you're forcing him to carry you downstairs. Carry you. That's shameful, Jessie. I'll just bet you ruined that gown of yours on purpose.''

"That's enough, Glenda," Mrs. Warfield said again, seeing that Jessie was alarmingly pale. "Perhaps your sister truly isn't all that well. Leave her be. That's right, go look out the window, dearest. Ah, James, here you are again.''

Without thinking, he walked to the bed and was going to put Jessie into the robe when Mrs. Warfield gasped. "Oh no, James, how improper. No, dear boy, take dear Glenda outside for a moment and I'll see to Jessie. That's right, Glenda, go with James.''

James carried Jessie downstairs. She was stiff in his arms, withdrawn from him; he could feel it. He'd overheard most of what had been said to her, and it made him feel guilty for making her leave. He couldn't imagine that her life at Warfield farm was all that pleasant. No wonder she spent all her time with the horses. She mucked out stalls. She mended bridles. She rode and raced. She beat him regularly. So surely she was well able to handle her mother and her disconcerting sister and if she couldn't, well, she could always escape.

He carried her to the carriage and set her on the seat inside. "There you are, Jessie. I'll be by tomorrow to see how you're getting along. Take care.''

He smiled down at Mrs. Warfield and Glenda. "Ladies, take good care of Jessie. She had a rather rough night of it.''

"I don't see how," Glenda said, and stared at his crotch.

"We'll find out," Mrs. Warfield said, and allowed James to assist her into the carriage.

"Move over, Jessie," she said, as she turned and smiled at James. "Thank you for taking her in."

*As if I were a drowning puppy and he had found me*, Jessie thought.

James stood quietly, watching the carriage wind down the long drive of Marathon. There were weeds coming up through the gravel on the drive. He'd have to send someone out here to pull them up and smooth down the gravel. Everything looked bare, too. He needed to plant more trees, he thought: some oaks and more elms. He wanted Marathon to look lush, to look rich. Jessie was right, curse her. There was so much that needed fixing.

*Poor Jessie*, he thought, then laughed at himself. He'd feel sorry for her . . . until the next time they raced.

# ══ 7 ══

THE SUN WAS shining brightly on that Tuesday morning as James walked down Calvert Street past innumerable publishers and bookstores to Number 27. He'd been coming to Compton Fielding's bookstore since he'd been a small boy. He walked into the shop with its narrow spaces and dark wood and its walls covered from floor to ceiling with books, many in disordered stacks — Mason's astute book on water drainage sitting on top of Richardson's *Pamela* — but Fielding knew where every single tome was. It appeared to be a slow morning. James didn't see anyone else, and that was good because he'd heard from Fielding the previous day that his Corneille plays had arrived from Paris. He was excited. He wanted to talk to Fielding about it.

He rounded a corner and stopped cold. There was Jessie Warfield in deep conversation with Compton. What the devil was she doing here? Surely she didn't read, did she? Surely all she did was horsey things.

He grinned at himself and went a bit closer to listen. If she could eavesdrop, so could he.

"Mr. Fielding, this is the third time you've wanted me to read old diaries. What's this one all about?"

Compton Fielding, a scholarly fixture in Baltimore, a fine violinist who played at civic affairs, a man with wide knowledge of many subjects, gently opened the fragile pages. "See, Jessie, it's well over a hundred years old, from around the turn of the eighteenth century, I'd say. I wish the fellow had dated it, but he neglected to. Old Elisha Bentworth told me I should find old calendars and match days with dates and that would tell me the years, but who has the time? Now, this precious diary covers a span of some three years, most of it spent in the Caribbean. What do you know of those times in the Caribbean, Jessie?"

"Not a blessed thing, Mr. Fielding, but if you want me to, I'll read it. I did enjoy reading the other two, but deciphering some of the words was mighty difficult."

"But worth it?"

"Oh yes, particularly the one set in Charleston in the early Colonial days."

"Ah, Mr. Nestor's memoirs. An odd duck, that Mr. Nestor, but I thought you'd like it. Since you're not all that certain you'll like tales of the Caribbean, why don't you take the diary home and read it over. If you want to keep it, just come back and pay me for it."

Jessie was already thumbing carefully through the diary. "Oh, listen to this, Mr. Fielding. '*We came to Jamaica to find miserable rain and a sour rum that fires the bowels. I had to split my sword in Davie's guts, the little bastard.*' She raised a shining face. "Is this about pirates? Goodness, how bloodthirsty they sound."

"I think the rum merchant's brother might have been a pirate, or known some of those men," Compton Fielding said thoughtfully, taking the diary from her. "You're right. It just might be too bloodthirsty for a young lady."

"I'll take it," Jessie said, and James nearly laughed aloud.

"Well then, if you're sure. You read it through and tell me."

James came around the corner and said, "Good morning, Jessie, Compton. What's all this miserable rain and a sour rum business? What do you have there?"

"You were eavesdropping," she said, then had the grace to look at the toes of her shoes.

"Yes, but I'm still in one piece," James said.

"What she has, James, is a diary from about one hundred years ago. I don't really know what it's about. Jessie will read it through and tell me."

"I didn't know you even read," he said to her.

"Just what do you mean by that, James Wyndham? Do you think I'm ignorant?"

"I've never seen you with a book before. I've never seen you in here before."

"The same is true of you. Now, what are you doing here, James? I would have thought that all you did was ride your acres, break colts, and give orders to all your stable lads."

Since he'd thought the same thing about her, he didn't say what he would have liked to. "I've frequented Compton's bookshop since I was a boy. He introduced me to French novels and plays."

Mr. Fielding was noted for the immense collection of French works he had in his shop, but Jessie, not knowing a single utterance in French, had never really paid much attention. She'd read every novel he had until just recently when he'd begun introducing her to diaries. They were, she had to admit, rather interesting, but thin on plot. There were no handsome gentlemen to sweep a girl off her feet. Oh yes, she adored lots of plot.

"You are a horse breeder and racer, James. You couldn't possibly speak French."

"Well, I do. In fact, I've spent a good deal of time in France." He eyed her up and down. "You're wearing a gown. Where the devil did you get it? It's too short and quite an ugly color of yellow, and it bags in the bosom. Ah, I know. It must be one of Nelda's or Glenda's castaways. Would you like to borrow a pair of my socks to stuff down the front?"

Compton Fielding cleared his throat. "James, would you like to come see the collection of Corneille's plays I just received? You particularly wanted to read *Le Cid*. The collection also has *Cinna* and *La Mort de Pompée*. I myself prefer *Le Cid*. The others are a bit tedious in that pompous classical sort of way."

James gave Jessie a final look of acute dislike and followed Compton Fielding to his small desk at the rear of the store. The air was so heavy with the smell of wood, books, and rag dust that James wondered how Fielding could breathe after a couple of hours in the bowels of the shop.

When he held the Corneille plays in his hands, he gently opened the pages to *Le Cid*. He began reading the first scene between Elvire and Chimene.

"You can really understand that?" Jessie had wandered up and was standing at his elbow, staring down at the page. "It looks like gibberish."

"Yes, of course. Why would I want to buy it if I couldn't even read it?"

"Perhaps just to put me in my place. Me and all the other ragtag Colonists. That's it, isn't it, James? You think we're all ignorant buffoons."

"I've never thought you the least bit ignorant, Jessie, and how could I, given what you're buying? Here you are reading a diary—something of historical interest. I'm impressed."

"Before I got her on the diaries, she read every gothic tale I could find her."

"I'm not surprised," James said, and laughed. She looked as if she wanted to peel a layer of skin off him, but she kept her mouth shut, which surprised him.

Feeling a touch guilty, James thought he'd try to make it up to her. "Come on, Jessie, I'll buy you an ice cream over on Baltimore Street. Would you like that?"

She glowed with pleasure. "Perhaps I'd like it, just a little bit."

James paid Compton Fielding for the Corneille and escorted Jessie and her diary down Calvert Street. He was stunned to see she even had a parasol, a flowered confection that she held like a club. Her red hair was pulled too tightly back from her face and tied with a black velvet ribbon at her neck.

"We're going to Balboney's?"

"That's right. Mr. Balboney's son, Gray, wants to learn stud management. I'm thinking of taking him on."

"Oh dear."

" 'Oh dear' what?"

"There's your mistress, James, Mrs. Maxwell. She's waving at you."

Sure enough, Connie Maxwell was just across the street standing in front of Hezekiah Niles's newspaper office, waving frantically at him. He waved back, motioning her to wait for him. He turned back to Jessie. "For God's sake, you're not supposed to know anything about mistresses."

"Perhaps not, but Glenda knows all about her. I heard her discussing Mrs. Maxwell with Mama. Glenda's afraid you'll marry Mrs. Maxwell and not her, but Mama said that wouldn't happen. Mrs. Maxwell is too old for you and you'll want sons, and she is too old for that as well. She said you'd want a young virgin, a lady who is malleable and submissive and sweet, someone who would bring you money, someone just like Glenda. She did allow, though, that Mrs. Maxwell was very fine-looking, which she is. She's lovely. She doesn't look at all old."

James stared at her, fascinated by what was coming so guilelessly out of that mouth of hers. "Jessie, I have no intention of marrying your sister."

"You don't?"

There it was: that hopeful look, as wistful as that of a child being offered a Christmas cookie.

"No. Were you eavesdropping again?"

"Oh, no. Well, maybe. Sometimes they talk in front of me. It's as if I'm not there."

"But this time they didn't? You eavesdropped?"

"Yes. At least I didn't fall through the door or make any noise."

"Jessie, do you know what a mistress is?"

"She's someone you mount whenever you want to."

"Horses mount. Humans have sex. Do you know what sex is all about?"

"I suppose it's a lot like the stallions and the mares, regardless of what you say. All very loud and messy and painful."

"Painful?"

"The mares are always screaming and thrashing around, and the stallions bite their necks and rumps. But they keep doing it, so I suppose it must please them. Sweet Susie was eager for any stallion available, even poor old Benjie. When we were racing away from those men, I told Benjie to promise Sweet Susie that he'd give her anything she wanted just as long as she ran as fast as she could. She did run fast, James."

"Jessie, I can't believe this conversation. Now, I want you to go to Balboney's. I'll join you in just a few minutes, all right?"

"All right. Oh, James, I like Mrs. Maxwell. She's ever so pretty and she laughs a lot. She's always been very nice to me. She always bets on me, too."

"I know, she told me. You're right. She is very nice. Wait for me, Jessie."

She watched him make his way through the drays, the horses, the carriages, and the beer wagon to get to the other side of the street. She watched him greet Mrs. Maxwell and saw the lady smile up at him, her gloved hand on his forearm. He leaned down to hear what she was saying. Mrs. Maxwell was very small, barely coming to James's shoulder. Jessie turned away, twisting the handle of her parasol with such violence that it split apart. "Well, damn," she said, and walked to Balboney's Ice Cream Emporium on Baltimore Street.

Jessie was eating a vanilla ice cream out of a small blue bowl when James strode into the shop not five minutes later. He sat opposite her, ordered himself an ice cream, and said, "Connie says hello. She also said my taste is improving. I told her she needed spectacles. She said I should ask you nicely to give me some pointers on racing."

"I could give you lots of pointers, James, but I doubt you'd listen. You'd box my ears even if I managed to make gentle suggestions, wouldn't you? Besides, you don't really need all that many pointers. The fact is, you're just too big to ride in races. I'm sorry for you, it's too bad, but you're just going to have to face up to it. Besides, you wouldn't be able to swagger around the way you do if you were a real jockey who weighed one hundred pounds. How's Redcoat? Will he be able to ride at the Axminster Races Saturday?"

"No, it's me again. Redcoat's leg won't be healed properly for another couple of months, at least. I've been training Peter, but the lad's not ready yet. You'd eat him alive. The male jockeys would toss him off his horse's back and into a ditch without even breaking stride. No, he needs more time so I can make him mean. You've got me as an opponent on Saturday, Jessie. Are you going to ride Rialto?"

"No, he has a sore hock. I don't know what happened, but I suspect his stable lad wasn't all that careful with him. No, since it's quarter-horse racing, I'll be on Jigg and Bonny Black. They can run faster than the wind for that quarter mile. How about you?"

"Tinpin. He'll beat you this time, Jessie. You haven't got a chance. I've been speaking to him privately all week, offering him bribes, telling him that you're just a twit female and that if he lets you beat him again, he'll have to retire in ignominy. He's ready. He'll be out for blood."

"Just you stay away from me, James. No pushing me into a tree or a ditch. Do ride Console, too. He's got more heart than any horse I've ever seen."

He shouldn't be surprised. He said slowly, "You're right. Console is a bit too long in the back, but he does have heart. I'm always afraid that if I race him for longer than a quarter mile, his heart will burst because he'll push himself so hard."

"You wouldn't push him. That's why you're an excellent horseman. Not as good as my father or I, but you're good nonetheless. Now, I've been thinking about this, James. I've decided that Connie Maxwell isn't really your mistress."

"You're quite right. She's a friend and I like her and she likes me and we enjoy each other. A man pays a woman to be a mistress. Connie is independent. She can order me out of her life whenever she tires of me. Now, Jessie, you're unmarried, a virgin, and this sort of talk isn't right. It wouldn't fluster Glenda, but with you, no, it's just not right. Eat your ice cream."

"I am. It's delicious. I'd like another one."

"Just don't ask me to carry you around anymore."

"You think I'm fat?"

"For God's sake, Jessie, you're as skinny as that table leg. I'm just jesting with you."

"Nelda and her husband, Bramen, came to dinner last night. He's fat, James, and he eats like Friar Tuck, who's in stud now and can eat like a pig if he wants to. I don't think Nelda likes him very much."

"Friar Tuck or her husband?"

Jessie took another bite of her ice cream. "Nelda doesn't

like horses at all, so I guess it's both. Glenda told her about how she was going to marry you by the end of the summer. She said she'd be a beautiful September bride. She said you would be ready by then. Mama agreed with her. She said that you would be over your grieving, if in fact you were still grieving, which she doubted because you were a man and men evidently don't grieve. Grieving about what, James?''

He said in a voice as remote as that faraway desert in Africa, ''I was married. My wife died in childbirth. That was three years ago. I told you I wasn't going to marry your sister. Why don't you weave that into your dinner conversation this evening? I don't wish to be rude to her, Jessie, but I have no intention of marrying her.''

''Do you like me?''

''No, not particularly. You're a pest. At least you're a good horsewoman. Don't get that punctured look. All right, I like you sometimes. I see you're finished. Do you want another ice cream?''

''No. If I could gain weight in my bosom, I'd eat another one, but I can't. Glenda is always showing off her bosom. She's very pretty.''

''Who cares?''

On the following Tuesday, Jessie was a mite depressed as she went into Compton Fielding's bookstore because James, just as he'd promised, had beaten her at the races the previous Saturday, cajoling Tinpin over the finish line a good two lengths ahead of her and Jigg. She'd had to hear her father grumble, then take a bottle of champagne over to Marathon to toast James until the both of them were as drunk as stoats.

She'd prayed James would have a vicious headache, but he'd been at church Sunday morning, with his mother, Ursula, and Giff, to hear Winsey Yellot exhort everyone present to exercise more moderation in their daily lives. She'd given James a nasty grin.

She waited inside Mr. Fielding's bookstore until he finished with a customer, then walked toward him, the diary in her hand.

"What did you think of it, Jessie?"

"It was fascinating. He made me think I was there, his descriptions were so vivid. Not all of them to be sure, but enough to hold my interest."

"You're frowning. Why?"

"Oh, I was just remembering how a couple of times I thought for certain that reading the diary was somehow familiar. That's silly, of course. I'd like to buy it, Mr. Fielding. Perhaps you have another one for me? Well, if you don't have any more novels, that is."

He did have another diary, and she paid for this one on the spot. It was written by an English sailor who'd tracked and hanged pirates in the early years of the eighteenth century. He followed her from the shop and onto the road, saying, "Give this one some time, Jessie. He isn't a very clever fellow and he tends to repeat himself, but perhaps you'll find him amusing."

"I hope—" Her voice disappeared in her throat. She heard and saw the oncoming wagon at the same time. The man was driving it right at her at a furious pace, the horses snorting and blowing, pounding the packed earth. There was no time for anything. The man must be mad. He must be drunk. She managed to jerk herself back onto the sidewalk, panting hard, frozen with the worst fear she'd ever felt in her life. Then the wagon was coming right at her, the man yelling at the horses, whipping them up, swinging them toward her.

Compton Fielding grabbed her at the last instant and literally threw her against the door of his bookstore. She hit her head against the door frame and knocked herself out.

"My God, Jessie. Wake up!"

She did in just a few seconds and stared up at Compton Fielding, who looked as pale as the sheets that hung on the rope lines behind Warfield house every Tuesday.

"My head hurts. That man was mad. He tried to kill me."

"No," Compton Fielding said slowly. "No, I think he was drunk. It was a stupid accident. Don't worry about it, Jessie."

"Then why did he drive on?"

"I don't know, but I'll ask around."

"Maybe he was after you, Mr. Fielding."

"That's a possibility, I suppose," Fielding said, and grinned. "Perhaps he wanted me to give him violin lessons and I turned him down."

She did laugh, a little.

Jessie told her family that evening at the dinner table. Her mother said when she'd finished, "No one in his right mind would want to kill you, Jessie. It was obviously some sort of strange accident. That or Compton Fielding was right. Someone wanted to knacker him."

Glenda took a bite of blancmange, licked her lips only to purse them, and said, "Mother's right. Who would have enough interest in you to want to kill you? It's really quite absurd. So is your story."

Her father, who hadn't spoken up to this point, said slowly, "Everything happened just as you said, Jessie? All right, I'll speak to Compton about it. Forget it now, my dear. Eat your stewed pork. That's a good girl."

Her father never mentioned it again. By the next racing day, when she swore she'd beat James to hell and back, she'd forgotten about it—a good thing, because a jockey from Virginia tried to butt her off her horse with the handle of his riding crop. It was a wild racing day, many jockeys were injured, and neither she nor James did very well.

# 8

The ideal thoroughbred is born to run, bred
to win, and will literally race to death.

WHEN JAMES SAW her coming out of a small dress shop,
he wondered what in blazes Jessie Warfield would be doing
there. He waved at her. When he caught up to her, he asked
her to Balboney's for some more ice cream. He didn't know
why he did it, but he did. Perhaps it was because they'd
both lost at the last races.

Yet again, Jessie's delight was alarmingly obvious. They
discussed the race and found themselves in the rare situation
of commiserating with each other. By the time James ordered her another bowl of ice cream, he still hadn't delivered
a single snide comment.

At that moment, Mr. Parvis, a longtime newspaper man
from the *Federal Gazette*, burst into the emporium shouting,
"Allen Belmonde was just found shot through his mouth!"

"Oh my," Jessie exclaimed. She called out, "He's dead,
then, Mr. Parvis?"

"Oh, Jessie, it's you. Yep, he's deader than a mackerel
caught in the Patapsco and lying out on the dock for a week.

The back of his head was blown off. His poor little wife found him in one of the tack rooms.''

"Good God," James said blankly. "I can't image Allen shooting himself."

"Oh, he didn't," Mr. Parvis said, rubbing his hands together. "Someone killed him dead." *Oh dear*, Jessie thought, her sweet, helpless Alice—frail and weak-spirited, but still Jessie had always liked her, probably because Alice had never had a negative word about her racing horses and wearing men's breeches. It was Alice who'd told her about the cucumber mixture for lightening the freckles. She pictured Allen Belmonde with the back of his head blown off and nearly gagged into the melting ice cream in her Balboney blue bowl.

Oslow Penny said, "Jessie, you're depressed about poor Alice Belmonde. You'll see the lady tomorrow, and you can flutter around her all you please. But no more sighs and tearful expressions now. That's right. You just chew on that piece of straw, pull your hat over your face to protect that pretty white skin of yours, and listen to the story of Grimalkin the cat."

"I'm listening, Oslow." Jessie pulled the disreputable old leather hat over her eyes, sank back against a hay bale, drew her knees up, and chewed on a fat straw.

"You remember that all thoroughbreds are descended from three and only three stallions."

"Yes, the Byerley Turk, the Darley Arabian, and the—"

"The Godolphin Arabian. That's right, Jessie. Now be quiet. The Godolphin Arabian was foaled way back in 1724. Now, the Godolphin Arabian's companion wasn't a stable lad or his owner or even a donkey. It was Grimalkin the cat. That damned brindle cat rode on his back, sitting up, all proud and smug, neck stretched out, surveying the world as if he were a bloody proper prince. The cat ate beside him, clawed through his mane to keep the tangles out, and slept draped around his neck. No one could figure out why that horse and that damned cat were so inseparable, but they were. It came in time that Grimalkin the cat died.

"The horse went wild. He wouldn't eat for days. He wouldn't let anyone near him. He looked to be pining away. Then he appeared to be normal again, but he wasn't. He wouldn't let another cat near him. He tried to kill any cat he even saw. He'd go wild if he even saw a cat in the distance. It's said that when he died, they buried him beneath the stable gateway next to Grimalkin the cat."

Jessie shoved her head back. "That's too good a story, Oslow. I think you made it up."

"No, he didn't, actually."

"James, goodness, whatever are you doing here?"

"Peter told me the two of you were swapping outrageous tales."

"She's all upset about poor Alice Belmonde. I don't know why since the girl's now quit of a scoundrel of a husband. I wanted to cheer her up. I've succeeded."

"Good. Now, don't disarrange yourself, Jessie. That's a new hat, isn't it?"

"I found it in a trunk in the attic. It just needed to be cleaned and reshaped a bit. I like it."

"It does have character. It does keep the sun off your nose. However, I think I smell moth powder. How old is the thing, Jessie?"

"I think it was my grandfather's."

He looked at that hat a moment longer, shook his head, and said, "Gordon Dickens, the magistrate, is here. He wants to talk about Allen Belmonde. It seems Gordon heard that there was quite a commotion here just a few days before Allen was shot and that Belmonde was so mad he wanted to take Sweet Susie away that night. Jessie, why are you rubbing your throat? Why have you turned whiter than my stable cat's belly?''

"I did threaten him, James. In front of witnesses. You nearly had to drag me off him. Do you think I'll be hanged?''

"No. Did I really drag you off him? Odd that I don't remember it happening exactly that way. Now, come along, the both of you. Dancy Hoolahan is here—the whole cast of characters, I guess you could say.''

Gordon Dickens had hated tea since his stepmother made him drink it until he'd peed in his pants. An excellent punishment for a smart-mouthed little boy, she'd told him with a good deal of satisfaction when he'd finally lost control. He even hated to see anyone else drinking the foul stuff because it made him want to relieve himself. He could barely contain himself, watching Jessie Warfield drink that dreaded tea, but he knew he had to. He was here to do his duty. He had to be alert. He not only had to listen to everyone's words but also carefully study their expressions. His father had always told him that you could see guilt on a man's or woman's face if you knew what to look for. He wasn't quite sure what that meant, but he always looked carefully. He couldn't think about his luscious bride, even now lying in their bed, all warm and naked and tousled. He swallowed and forced himself back to his duty. He looked from that tea-drinking female, Jessie Warfield, to Dancy Hoolahan to James Wyndham. He cleared his throat.

"Would you like a muffin, Gordon?''

"No, James, thank you. I'd like to hear what happened after Jessie Warfield brought the mare back here. Yes, Thomas, you come in here as well. You were one of the parties present that night.''

"It wasn't really a party, Mr. Dickens,'' Thomas said, all austere because he knew this was proper business. "Poor

Miss Jessie was all bloody and Mr. James was holding her up. No, it weren't no party.''

"That's not what I meant. Tell me what happened.''

When all the facts had been wrung out of all of them, Gordon Dickens stroked his whiskers, stared at Jessie, and said, ''I understand that you and James Wyndham are rivals. I always wager on James, but you beat him at least half the time, which surely isn't the thing to do. I've seen you try to shove your horse into him. I've seen you kick out at him. I've seen him try to ride you into a ditch. You're enemies. Why would you defend him and threaten Allen Belmonde? Why would you even bother saving that mare? It wasn't your mare.''

"I like Sweet Susie. She's a fine mare. I don't suppose you've found the two men who stole her? Or whoever hired those men to steal her?''

He'd been too busy getting married and learning the awesome joys of the marriage bed to pursue the matter, but Gordon Dickens didn't say that. He thought about how he'd spent the early-morning hours and blushed. He shook a bit. Who cared about a damned horse when Helen was lying there waiting for him, smiling at him, her arms out? ''Not yet,'' he said, and his voice was as chilly as a Baltimore spring rain. How dare the damned girl question him? ''You haven't answered my questions, Miss Warfield.''

"It didn't matter that Sweet Susie belonged to Allen Belmonde, who wasn't a very nice man. I would have tried to save Sweet Susie if she'd belonged to Mortimer Hackey, a truly despicable man. Anyway, Allen Belmonde was annoying everyone, shouting accusations at James—totally unfounded accusations—and I wanted to hit him.''

"Perhaps you shot him instead.''

James, who was leaning his shoulders against the mantel of the fireplace, jerked forward to tower over Gordon Dickens. He pulled him up by his collar out of his chair and shook him. "That is the most ridiculous thing that's emerged from your mouth. Just look at her—she's perfectly white with fear. Mind your tongue, or else I'll mind it for you."

"See here, James, I'm just doing my job. She did threaten him, she plays at being a man, just perhaps she also uses a gun like a man, and—"

Wanting only to distract James, who he could see was itching to send his fist into Gordon's jaw, Dr. Hoolahan said quickly, "I don't suppose you know that Allen Belmonde had once wanted to marry Ursula Wyndham, James's sister?"

James whipped around, staring at him as if he'd grown an extra ear. "Well, he didn't marry Ursula, so I had no reason to shoot him. How the devil do you know about that, Dancy?"

"Mr. Belmonde's wife became ill shortly after they were married. She was also depressed, pale, and on the verge of tears the whole time. She told me that he began avoiding her almost immediately after their marriage, that he'd even called her Ursula several times during moments of, er, affection."

James turned to stare at Dancy Hoolahan. He released Gordon Dickens, absently brushed his coat front, and gently shoved him back down into his chair. "I told Alice not to marry him," James said. "He married Alice Stoddert out of spite after Ursula married Giff, hoping to make her jealous I suppose, only it didn't. He wouldn't believe she didn't want him, that she preferred Giff Poppleton. And Alice didn't believe me either." He looked Gordon Dickens straight in the face. "You will contrive to keep all this behind your teeth, Gordon. All of it, do you understand? And you as well, Dancy, and yes, I well understand why you dug it up and spit it out when you did. Well, I'm under control now and I won't throttle Gordon, at least in the next five minutes. Remember—all of you—that none of this has anything to do with Belmonde's murder.''

Gordon Dickens fiddled with his cravat. "I must do my duty. However, I agree with you, James, that none of this seems to have any bearing on Belmonde's unfortunate death."

Jessie said, "Who do you think killed Mr. Belmonde, James?"

"I haven't the foggiest idea. As you said, Jessie, he wasn't a particularly nice man. Listen, Gordon, Allen Belmonde had two business partners. There was probably a good deal of strife among the three of them. Have you looked into that?"

"Oh, yes. They all hated one another. They accused one another of villainy, of embezzlement, of cheating." Gordon Dickens rose, looking gloomy. "This is a proper mess. I was hoping that one of you would be guilty. It would have made things so much simpler."

"Why, thank you, Gordon," Dancy Hoolahan said.

"There's the horse racing," Oslow said. "Mr. Belmonde made bets at the racetracks, big ones, I heard, and he didn't always pay up when he lost. There're also rumors that he was responsible for poisoning Rainbow—a four-year-old thoroughbred whose sire was Bellerton and whose dam was the Medley mare—at last year's Baltimore Plate. The horse he backed won, so he also won, a lot of money. All unproved of course."

"Everything is unproved," Gordon Dickens said, and sighed. "The world is unproved." He sighed again as he rose. He straightened his waistcoat. It was loose. He'd lost weight. It felt good. He knew it was from all the unaccustomed activity he was getting at night and in the early mornings. "Damn Belmonde's eyes," he said, looking at everyone with gloomy irritation. "Why couldn't he have just ridden off that cliff over at Miller's Jump? That way I could have called it an accident, and that would have been the end of it.''

Mrs. Wilhelmina Wyndham had a firm hold on her son's arm. ''Whoever is visiting poor Alice? You will get rid of who it is, James. We are here now and thus the only ones who should be offering sympathy to the poor girl. Some folks have the manners of rodents.''

James had ridden to the Belmonde town house on St. Paul Street, to offer Alice whatever support he could. And here was his mother, just emerging from the landau he'd bought for her three years before. ''Ah, my dearest boy,'' she'd said, allowed him to assist her to the ground, and took hold of his arm.

''Did you tell Alice you were coming to visit her?''

''Certainly not, but that doesn't matter. Go see to it, James.''

He just smiled down at his mother, knowing nothing short of a hurricane could ever dissuade her from anything. Maybe not even a hurricane.

Her visitors were Glenda and Jessie Warfield.

A thin woman with stooped shoulders ushered them to the large Belmonde parlor. Glenda was prettily arranged on the settee wearing a pale yellow muslin gown. Jessie was standing beside Alice, with her hand on the widow's bowed shoulder. She was wearing another of her sister's castaways, a pale gray wool that made her look like a young nun trying on the mother superior's habit. Like the other gown, this one was too short and too big in the bosom. James heard her say, ''Alice, Mrs. Partridge has told me that you've scarcely eaten at all. Come now, here are some fresh scones. Shall I spread some butter and strawberry jam on one for you?''

Alice gave her a helpless look that made James want to enfold her in his arms and pat her. He expected that most people reacted to Alice like that. But evidently not Jessie. She floored him, saying "Now this is quite enough, Alice. You're going to eat the scone or I'll stuff it down your throat."

That brought a smile to Alice's pale lips. Her frail shoulders even lifted a bit. She looked up when Mrs. Partridge cleared her throat.

"Oh, Mrs. Wyndham! James. Do come in." Alice leaped to her feet, and Jessie knew why. Everyone leaped to their feet when Mrs. Wilhelmina Wyndham came within striking distance. The lady scared her to death. In the past, she'd easily managed to avoid her, but not today. There was no escape from her today.

Wilhelmina looked at Alice, who had two hectic red spots on her pale cheeks, and said, "You have grieved for three days, Alice. Allen Belmonde deserves no more than three days of having you wilt around not eating. It is the shock of finding him that has prostrated you, not your loss. Now, I would like a cup of tea and one of those fresh scones Jessie was talking about."

"Yes, ma'am," Alice said, and scurried out of the parlor.

Jessie said, "I didn't know Alice could move that fast. Well done, ma'am."

Wilhelmina looked at Jessie briefly, lifted her chins, then turned to Glenda, who was now sitting on the edge of the settee, at attention, ready for inspection. "You're looking well, Glenda, but that gown of yours is cut too low. There is too much bosom on display. Here." Wilhelmina handed her a white lawn handkerchief. Glenda took it and stared at it helplessly. "Arrange it over your bosom, dear," Wilhelmina said.

"Now, Jessie, I had to settle myself before I spoke to you. You are as you always are, so no surprise there. At least you don't smell like a horse today. I have no more handkerchiefs, or else I'd give you one to help fill out the chest of that gown. I shall speak to your mother. She needs to have gowns made for you.''

James, who should have been used to his mother after all these years of watching her in action, nonetheless fairly choked on his words. ''Mama, I think you should sit down. Ah, here's Mrs. Partridge with your tea and a scone. That's right, take two. Now, Alice, stop hovering. I want to speak to you. Come with me to Allen's study.''

Allen Belmonde's study was a dark room with heavy leather furniture, a dull brown Axminster carpet, and books lining the walls that James knew the dead man had never opened. James gently pressed Alice Belmonde into a chair, lowered himself on his haunches in front of her, and took her white hands between his. ''My mother's a bully, Alice, but she's right. Allen was a rotter. You have a large estate to deal with. There are people depending on you.''

''I'm a woman, James. I don't know anything. Allen never told me anything, either. He always said I was to be here whenever he wanted me. He said that was my only role, that and having children. Now he's gone. I feel, well, I feel sort of frozen. There's no one to tell me what to do.''

''Did you love him, Alice?''

''I wanted to, James. You know that. I believed I could make him forget Ursula, but he never did. He was always saying that Ursula would never say such stupid things the way I did. He said she would never whine and complain and cry as I did. No, I didn't love him anymore. I suppose that now I'll go to Hell.''

''No, I rather think you've been liberated from Hell. You'll get through this, Alice.''

''His partners have already been here telling me the business is worthless, that they're sorry, but there's no money for me. I really don't care because my father will take care of me. He doled out my dowry on a yearly basis to Allen, and believe me, Allen hated it. My father's already told me that he will continue my yearly allowance, that I don't have to remarry if I don't want to.''

''I'm pleased, Alice. Now, don't worry about his damned partners. Allen's lawyer, Daniel Raymond, will see to those villains. You might not care about the money, but there's got to be justice. Now, there's the farm, Alice. I think it would be good for you to learn about the management of a stud farm.''

''That's what Jessie said. She said she'd teach me.''

That gave him pause. What the devil was Jessie up to? ''I didn't realize you and Jessie were such good friends.''

''Oh yes, for years now. Nelda and Glenda, too. I was always very protected by my papa and mama. And there was Jessie, so free, doing exactly as she pleased, not minding if her mother yelled at her or ordered her to stay in her bedchamber for a week if she got sunburned or tore her dress or got kicked by a horse. Jessie was always brave. I was always a coward. But she says that doesn't have to be true. She says there's no man now to tell me what to do. I can do and be whatever it is I choose. She believes I can unfreeze myself. She says money will help me unfreeze even more quickly.''

Jessie had said all that? Could he possibly be wrong? James had always thought that Alice Stoddert Belmonde was one of those ladies who absolutely had to have a husband to take care of her, or a brother, whose role he, James, had taken. He would have staked a good amount of money on his belief. He could just stare at her now. Was there a firmness he'd never heard before in that insubstantial voice?

He said, ''Jessie's not all that free, Alice. She's still a female. She's still a daughter living at home. Her mother still tells her what to do.''

Tears shone in Alice's eyes. ''You don't think she can help me, James?''

''I didn't say that. I'm just saying that all isn't necessarily what it looks to be. Now, Raymond and I are meeting with Allen's erstwhile partners. He will come by later with papers to sign. You just see to eating more and unfreezing yourself, just as Jessie said.''

''There's Mortimer Hackey,'' Alice said with a delicate shudder.

Hackey owned a small racing stud to the west of Baltimore. He was petty, dishonest, and gave racing a worse name than it deserved. ''What does that scoundrel have to do with anything?''

''He wants to buy the stud. I think he wants to take Allen's place, too. He's been here at least five times a day since Allen was killed. He holds my hand overlong, James, and once he even kissed my cheek. I wanted to vomit. He's horrible.''

''Tell Mrs. Partridge not to let him in again. I'll speak to him, Alice.''

When they returned to the parlor, James heard his mother bellowing loudly enough for the watch at the far corner of St. Paul Street to hear. ''There is nothing more deplorable than a girl who lacks respect for her elders. You, Jessica Warfield, will not speak to me like that again. You will not disagree with what I know is perfectly true.''

''But ma'am, Nelda married her husband because she wanted to. You're wrong about Mama making her marry Bramen. As for Papa, he said it turned his innards to have his own daughter married to a man older than he was. No, ma'am, it was Nelda's idea.''

Wilhelmina Wyndham snorted, an inelegant sound, but effective. ''You're nothing but a girl, Jessica. You don't know anything at all. I know your mother. She connives. She schemes. She's quite good at it, actually. I taught her quite a lot. She wanted buckets of money for Nelda and she latched onto Bramen. Nelda had no say in the matter. Now, don't disagree with me or else I'll have to speak to your mama about you. Indeed, I would tell her how to deal with you.''

Jessie jumped to her feet. ''Glenda, we must be on our way. I'm going to say good-bye to Alice.''

''I'm not going anywhere, Jessie. Don't be rude to Mrs. Wyndham. If everything works out as it should, then she will have every right to be involved in our lives.''

''What is that supposed to mean?'' Wilhelmina Wyndham said, turning an awful stare on Glenda. ''I know you, Glenda Warfield. You want my son. Well, my dear, if you are willing to be guided by me, perhaps it might be done. I have reminded him that his ill-advised English marriage wouldn't have ended so tragically if only he'd listened to me. Indeed, it never would have happened.''

James said very quietly from the doorway, ''Mother, it's time we took our leave. Alice is tired and wishes to rest. That is, she wishes to eat two scones and then she wishes to rest. Come along, Mother.''

''I shall, dear James.'' She swept to her feet, patted the curls around her still-handsome face, and offered her hand to her son, who wanted to throttle her. Jessie looked pushed to the limit and madder than a wild dog. Glenda was humming softly to herself, pleating the material of her gown with soft, white fingers.

James said, ''Jessie, would you like me to escort you home?''

Glenda immediately rose, the handkerchief Mrs. Wyndham had given her falling out of her bosom. ''That won't be necessary, James. Jessie and I must be on our way. Good day to you, Alice.''

As they were all leaving the Belmonde house, Nelda's carriage drew up. The sisters only nodded to one another.

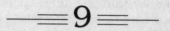

# 9

JESSIE PRAYED HARD that it wouldn't rain, but she didn't think God was listening. It was Baltimore, after all, and most folks believed that God, in His more whimsical moments, allowed the heavens to open up on them ten minutes after the sun had been blazing in the sky.

It was chilly, the air heavy, the night blacker than a sinner's secrets. Jessie huddled in her man's coat and leaned through the rosebushes so she could see into the large Blanchard ballroom. She saw James almost immediately. He was taller than most men. When he laughed, he threw back his head, showing his tanned throat. She wondered what made him laugh. She certainly had never done so, at least not like that—laughter so free and irresistible.

She'd been invited to this ball, but she'd declined, as she always did, but this time only after her mother had looked at her, up and down and up and down, and once again, up and down, and given her that thin-lipped smile of hers that had nothing to do with humor. It wasn't that her mother didn't want her to have a frivolous evening. It was just that she knew Jessie would make a fool of herself, a fool of her family, and most importantly, a fool of her mother, were Jessie to appear dressed like Glenda, trying to be a lady.

No, it wouldn't work. Her mother was right. But still. Jessie sighed and pressed closer to the window. She knew tonight was the night. She'd overheard Glenda planning this evening with their mother.

She knew she couldn't let them betray James. He deserved a lot of things, but he didn't deserve to have Glenda at his side for the remainder of his sentient days on this earth. If he'd wanted Glenda, that would have been another matter, but he'd said clearly that he wouldn't ever marry her. No, she wouldn't allow her mother and Glenda to serve him such a turn.

Ah, there Glenda was, on a course set straight for James. How odd of her; she was staring at his waist, not his face.

Jessie saw James turn finally and give Glenda a smile and a nod before turning back to speak to Daniel Raymond, the lawyer who was helping poor Alice Belmonde pull her life together.

But Glenda wasn't to be put off. Jessie recognized all the signs. Her chin was up, her bosom thrust forward, and there she was again, staring directly at James's waist. She stretched out a soft, white hand and laid it on James's black sleeve. He frowned, turning to look at her.

In but a moment, he'd said something to Daniel Raymond and escorted Glenda to the dance floor. It was a waltz. This was it.

Jessie backed out of the rosebushes and quickly ran to the lovely old elm tree that stood in the middle of the Blanchard garden. She shinnied up it, then grabbed a long, thick branch and pulled herself astride it. She couldn't have her legs dangling down; they might see her. She stretched out on her belly along the length of the branch.

She waited.

And waited some more.

The waltz should have ended an eon ago. Glenda had had enough time to feel faint at least a dozen times. But Jessie was afraid to move. What if they were already in the garden but not close enough for her to hear them? What if they came beneath the tree and looked up? She'd be caught. She would have failed.

Her left foot went to sleep. She raised her left leg and shook it. It didn't help much. She felt herself slipping and hugged the branch. It scraped her cheek.

She heard voices, grasped the branch tightly, and tensed. Oh goodness, they were nearly right beneath the tree. But Glenda wasn't there. It was two men, and one of them was James.

They were arguing.

"Listen, Wyndham, I'm going to buy her out and you have no say in it." Jessie recognized Mortimer Hackey's deep, rough voice. She knew him as a man of vicious temper who'd managed to come by money in a mysterious way. He had a jockey who always used his riding crop on any other jockeys who came near him at the races.

"Why I came out here with you I don't know," James said. "I have nothing more to say to you, Hackey. She's going to learn to run the stud farm herself, so forget it."

"You son of a bitch, you won't interfere! Why, I might even marry the little piece, who knows? Allen told me she was worthless in bed, but I don't care. I'll have the stud farm."

"I'll say this just one more time, Hackey. Leave Alice alone. If I hear about your bothering her again, I'll beat you to a bloody pulp."

"Threaten me, will you, you prissy little boy with all your damned English airs!"

The rage in his voice scared the devil out of Jessie. She'd heard him speak like that once to one of his jockeys who'd just lost a race right before he'd sliced open his face with a whip. She managed to pull the pistol from the pocket of her man's coat. She shinnied backward on the branch, then swung astride it so she could more clearly see the men below her. What she saw scared her nearly witless.

Mortimer Hackey had drawn a gun on James and was waving it at him. "No one knows you came out here, Wyndham. I looked. I made sure no one was paying any attention. I know all about you and Alice Belmonde. I heard you bedded her while poor old Allen was sleeping with every whore in Baltimore. But you'll give her up. You'll not interfere. I won't beat you, Wyndham, I'll blow your puny brains out."

"Slept with Alice? You stupid bastard!"

Hackey jerked his pistol up, aiming it at James's heart. In that instant, James leaped on him, his hands grabbing Hackey's arm and wrenching it upright. There was a sharp report. A cascade of leaves fell down to the ground. The two men were grappling, struggling wildly, punching to little effect, each trying to gain the upper hand. Jessie watched James, the larger and younger of the two men, slam his fist into Hackey's belly. Hackey howled and jerked backward, freeing himself for an instant. He raised the pistol, panting now, hard, as he said, "You miserable whelp, you—"

"James! Where are you?" It was Glenda.

James didn't move. Hackey's attention wavered a bit. James yelled, "Stay away, Glenda!"

Hackey brought the pistol back and laughed. "You little bastard, I—"

Jessie aimed her pistol and fired it. She heard a yelp of surprise followed by a groan. The gun recoiled, spinning her backward. She grabbed madly at the branch and only succeeded in scraping her fingers. She cried out as she plummeted to the ground.

James only had time to look upward in the direction of the unexpected shot before Jessie came hurtling down, knocking him flat on his back. She landed on top of him, her arms and legs sprawled out.

Mortimer Hackey stood over them, his pistol loose in his hand. "Dear God, Jessie Warfield! You tried to kill me, you miserable little girl. You shot me in my damned foot. Why, what you need is—''

James was nearly unconscious, but he held on. He saw Hackey standing over them. He was terrified that Hackey would shoot Jessie. He prepared to roll over on top of Jessie. Then he heard Glenda call out again, ''James!''

Then he heard Mrs. Warfield, loudly scolding, saying, ''Now, my dearest, you mustn't come out here with dear James. Why, do you know what everyone is already saying? You know what this will mean, don't you? Wait a moment, Glenda. Something isn't quite right here. Where is dear James?''

They were just feet away. Jessie was shaking her head to clear it. James was breathing beneath her, but he was lying very still. She was afraid she'd knocked him out. She managed to gasp, ''Mr. Hackey, you'd best get out of here. You can't kill both of us. There are other people coming. I didn't mean to shoot you in the foot. Actually I was aiming for your arm.''

Mortimer Hackey cursed fluently, kicked James's leg, kicked Jessie in the ribs, and took himself off through the rear of the garden.

Jessie reared up a bit and began to pat James's face. ''Come on, James, wake up. I'm sorry I landed on you. Please, wake up. Don't be hurt, please.''

James blinked and opened his eyes. Jessie was lying on top of him, her breasts pressed against his chest, her thighs against his, spread wide. Her face was so close to his he felt her breath warm on his mouth. If it hadn't been so dark, he could have counted the freckles across her nose.

''You killed me,'' he said. ''Are you all right?''

''Just a bit shaken, I think. Give me a minute and I'll get off you.''

''Take your time,'' he said, and brought his arms around

to gently push her over a bit. His right leg hurt, and a lot of her weight was on it.

"You feel female, Jessie."

"Well, I am a female. Oh dear, I see what you mean, that is, goodness—"

"No, don't go all maidenly on me. Catch your breath, then just slide off."

"I heard Glenda and my mother."

James didn't have time to shove Jessie an inch either way, much less shove her off him and out of the garden.

"Oh, my God!" Mrs. Warfield bellowed. "Glenda, it's your sister with James, not you. Dear heavens, she's lying on him. How could this have happened?"

Another bellowing voice rained down on them. "James, my dear boy, what are you doing with Jessie on top of you, kissing you, stroking you?"

James couldn't believe it. It was his mother. He heard other voices behind them. At least half a dozen. He closed his eyes. He couldn't believe this.

Glenda yelled, "Jessie Warfield, you're a wretched bitch. You get off James. He's mine. You'll not have him. I can't believe you're letting him have you right here in the garden. You're not even dressed in a gown."

"Well," Portia Warfield said, hands on her hips, "it seems that this is a muddle of major proportions. But don't worry, Glenda dear, it will work out."

"Oh God," James said.


Jessie was sore and bruised, but not, she thought, as sore and bruised as James was. She held a cup of tea between her hands, sipping slowly, trying to warm herself. James wasn't drinking tea. He was drinking brandy. He was staring off at nothing in particular.

They were seated in Mrs. Wyndham's parlor, a very nice parlor, Jessie thought, but it jarred her, what with all the shades of peach. Pale peach brocade on the settees, dark peach silk on the chairs. Peach everywhere. Mrs. Wyndham's town house was next to the Blanchards' and thus the obvious place for everyone to gather. She wanted to die. She looked at James again. He was staring at the mantelpiece as if he wanted to eat it or perhaps just chew on it and spit it out at someone—probably at her.

Her father, her mother, and Glenda were there, now blessedly silent for the moment.

Mrs. Wyndham was seated on the settee across from Jessie. She looked to be deep in thought.

Glenda ran gracefully across the room to fall on her knees beside James's chair. "Shouldn't you have Dr. Hoolahan examine you, James?"

"No," James said, not looking at her. "He's doubtless fixing Hackey's foot. That's where you shot him, isn't it, Jessie?"

"I think so. He was sort of dancing around on his left leg. He kicked you with his left foot."

"He kicked you, too. In the ribs?"

"Yes, but I'm just a bit sore, nothing more."

"Oliver, are you ready to listen now?"

Oliver Warfield rubbed his jaw. "I don't know, James. I saw Jessie sprawled out on top of you. I saw her kissing you."

"She didn't kiss me."

"She was sliding her fingers all over your face. Everyone saw that. Oh, all right. Say what you have to say."

"I was having an argument with Mortimer Hackey. He was threatening to go after Alice Belmonde. He wants her and he wants the stud farm. He wants me to keep my nose out of it. Our argument became rather heated. I hadn't intended to go out into the garden with him, but I did. There was no reason to cause a scene in the middle of the Blanchards' ballroom. It would have gotten back to Alice, and she would have been hurt by it. So I went into the garden with him. When he drew a gun on me, I jumped him. The gun went off wildly and we fought. He got the upper hand after I smashed him in the belly. He broke free and he still had the gun. It was then that there was another shot, followed by Jessie hurtling out of the elm tree to fall on top of me. There was nothing more to it than that.''

Oliver Warfield sighed.

Mrs. Warfield said, ''I don't understand why you were there, Jessie. You weren't going to the Blanchards' party. Why did you have a gun? Why were you up in that tree?''

Everyone was looking at her, James as well. She stared at her scraped fingers. She wished she could become a peach shade and fade into Mrs. Wyndham's parlor rug. She looked over at James, and in that instant he knew he didn't want to know the truth of why she'd been up there in that damned elm tree with a gun, not in front of this group. He said quickly, ''I was wondering why there were suddenly so many people in the garden. I heard Glenda calling me. I heard you, Mrs. Warfield, asking Glenda where I was.''

''Ah, well, that was nothing, really,'' Mrs. Warfield said, and called out, ''I should like some more tea, Wilhelmina.''

''So that's it,'' Wilhelmina Wyndham said slowly, staring at her girlhood friend whom she'd always bullied. ''You had told me to come into the garden and bring my friends because you had a wonderful surprise for all of us, me especially. My God, you wanted all of us out there as witnesses. I told Glenda that you schemed and connived well, Portia, but this time it didn't work. You wanted all of us to see Glenda and James together. It was all a plot, and you didn't tell me a bit of it.''

''No!''

''Yes, Portia. Just look at Glenda. Her face is all red, and there might as well be a sign on her forehead reading GUILTY. But Hackey and Jessie here botched everything.

Now Jessie is ruined, my son looks like a seducer of virgins, and will thus become far more romantic in every silly female's eyes. I do wish you'd stop trying to deny that you and Glenda plotted between the two of you to trap him into marrying Glenda. If only you'd discussed it with me, I could have helped you foresee all the possible difficulties. But you didn't, and look what's come of it."

Jessie had had enough. She managed to get to her feet without moaning from all her bruises. "This is ridiculous. I'm not ruined. I'm the very last virgin James would attempt to seduce. All of you know it was just a silly mix-up. I'm going home. Father, will you come with me?"

"Your face is scraped," James said, rising slowly himself. "Be sure to wash it well."

"I will. Don't worry about Hackey, James. Tomorrow at the track he'll be racing that knobby-kneed three-year-old of his and I'll make sure his jockey winds up in the dirt."

"Jessie, mind your own business. Now, is everyone quite through with all of this?"

"I want to know what Jessie was doing there," Mrs. Warfield said, standing now, staring down at her daughter. "Why were you there, Jessie? The truth now."

James was on his feet in the next instant. "I'm through with all this. I don't give a good damn why Jessie was hiding up in that elm tree, but I'm glad she was. I fancy she saved my hide because Mortimer was going to shoot me. Now, I'm leaving. Ladies, Oliver, good night."

"I don't know, James," his mother said, "maybe you'd best wait a bit."

"I'm leaving, Father," Jessie said, and walked with a limp to the front door, ignoring her mother's loud voice behind her.

James was there beside her. "Come along, Jessie, I'll see you home. It's the least I can do in payment for your shooting Mortimer in the foot."

They rode side by side, down Sharp Street, crossing over to Waterloo Road, then to Calvert Street. It began to rain— heavy, cold sheets of rain. The sky was blacker than a bucket of coal. They both were wearing hats, but it did little good. The rain was coming down sideways, slapping at their coats and their unprotected necks. A sudden gust of wind sent Jessie's old hat into a ditch and out of sight. She slapped her hands to her head too late. "Oh dear," she said. "It was the only one I could find in the trunks."

He handed her his gentleman's top hat.

She just shook her head, and he slapped it back down on his head. They rode side by side shivering, each cursing the rain silently, each wondering what the other was thinking until James said, "Jessie, why were you in the elm tree?"

"To save you."

"Well, you did save me. But why were you there in the first place?"

"To save you."

He sighed and got a mouthful of rain. "Ah, I guessed as much. You knew what Glenda and your mother had planned, then?"

"Yes, and I did eavesdrop—lucky for you, James. So don't rip a strip off me."

"Oh, I won't. If you hadn't saved me from Mortimer and possible extinction, then you would have what, Jessie? Shot Glenda when she swooned against me or grabbed the buttons on my breeches and pulled them open?"

"I was going to shoot the ground near both of you. Glenda hates guns and jumps ten feet into the air whenever one goes off close to her. She would have run as fast as she could back into the ballroom."

"Why did you want to save me from Glenda?"

She turned to look at him then. Her hair was plastered against her face, falling in sodden strings down her back and over her shoulders. Her lips were blue from the cold. She had to look as wretched as he felt.

"I had to," she said finally, then kicked her booted heels into Benjie's sides. He obligingly scuttled forward, eager for dry hay and a dry stall.

James called after her, "I'm cold and wet. I hurt. I know you feel the same way. I'll make you a deal, Jessie. Tomorrow, after the race, you and I will make some sense out of all this."

"No."

"What did you say to me?"

"There's no sense to be found anywhere, James. Just forget all of it. I don't want to be forced to save you again, so take care with all those vicious jockeys tomorrow."

She bolted away from him, soon turning off onto the beautiful wide drive of Warfield Stables and Stud Farm, the words all fashioned over the top of the wide gate in iron letters at the beginning of the drive.

He didn't slow Dimple, the sweet old mare from his boyhood. She liked a steady pace. She didn't like the rain any more than he did, but she was old enough to know that if her legs kept moving she'd be home soon enough.

If he'd only known what was going to happen in the next two days, he would have been sorely tempted to ride north and never look back.

# $\equiv$ 10 $\equiv$

**If he were a horse, nobody would buy him.**
                                    —WALTER BAGEHOT

IT WASN'T RAINING, thank the good Lord. But the track was pitted with mud puddles. As a result, few ladies were present for the races today. Only the hardier men were there, betting with less abandon than usual, but still, there was excitement in the air. Everyone liked a quarter-horse race. It was fast and hard.

James would ride Console in the third race. Console was eager, snorting and throwing his head around. Oslow patted his muscular gray neck and said, "You just wait a minute, old boy, and Mr. James will be here to give you a fine ride."

"That's right," James said, and quickly checked the girth, tightening it automatically as Console breathed out. "Now, let's you and I take a nice walk and talk about things."

James led Console away from the crowds, talking to him all the time. "We won't try to run Jessie off into a ditch today. Maybe next week, but not today. But that jockey of Mortimer Hackey's is another matter. See that withered beggar old Mortimer has entered?" Console turned his head around and snorted.

"Exactly," James said. "I want to make him very sorry."
Console snorted again.

*     *     *

It was a dangerous flat stretch because of all the wretched mud and fallen branches and uncovered rocks. James pressed himself close to Console's neck and talked to him. Then he listened. Console was ready. He was bored. He wanted to fly.

Console passed Jessie, riding the black three-year-old Jigg, in a matter of moments. He didn't acknowledge her at all. There were twelve horses on the flat. Since this was the third race, it was rapidly becoming an obstacle course, with clumps of mud flying, slamming against the horses and their riders.

Console would have danced with enjoyment if James had let him. He was running his heart out, not caring if he barely missed a jagged rock in the middle of the track, ready to kill any other horse or jockey who tried to push him out.

James saw Mortimer Hackey's horse just to his left and whispered to Console, "There he is. Let's get him."

Console veered to the left, smashed his big head into the other horse's neck, sending the horse stumbling away and his jockey flying into a shallow pond of mud, and raced over the finish line with all the joy of a vicar who's just baptized every sinner in his flock.

Console won two hundred dollars. He tossed his head, not even breathing hard, ready to go again, but James handed his reins to Oslow. "Give him an extra bucket of oats. He smashed Mortimer Hackey's horse out of the race."

"I saw him do it. Well done, my fine lad." Oslow patted the big gray's neck, and Console neighed loudly.

There were six more quarter-mile races that day until just after three o'clock, when it started raining again—heavy sheets of rain that sent all the spectators scattering.

James also won first place in the fifth race and second in the sixth. Bonny Black, ridden by Jessie, won the sixth race.

Tinpin, grumpy and indifferent, managed to pull in third. James was surprised he had done that well.

Oslow and three of the stable lads were covering the horses with blankets and leading them off for the long trek back to Marathon when Mortimer Hackey stomped into view. James grinned at him. "How's your foot, Hackey?"

"You bloody bastard, you sent your horse right into my horse! My jockey has been knocked crazy in the head, thanks to you. Hoolahan says it'll be three weeks before he's fit to ride again."

James yawned. "You did try to shoot me, Hackey. Did you think I'd turn the other cheek? Besides, that jockey is always too ready to use his riding crop. He deserved a lesson."

"You take one step closer, and I'll shoot you again, Mr. Hackey."

James shut his mouth on another yawn. "Jessie, for God's sake, Mortimer isn't up to no-good, at least not today. He's just a mite miffed because his jockey took a tumble in the third race."

Mortimer snorted, waved his fist at the two of them, and walked off in a snit. He barely avoided careening into a deep mud puddle.

"I saw it. Well done."

"Thank you. Console enjoyed himself. He can be a mean bugger when he wants to. How are you feeling, Jessie?"

"Me? Oh, I'm fine. You?"

"I'll live. Wyndhams are too ornery to croak."

Jessie just nodded and walked away, with rain running over her in waves. She was bareheaded. He wanted to ask her how her family was treating her, but he didn't. She seemed just fine. She'd been right when she'd told her father that it was all ridiculous.

It stopped raining as suddenly as it had begun. Of all the perverse things: the sun was brighter than a fireball in the sky. But there was no more racing as more entries had already headed home.

James was whistling as he came to Luther Swann's famous wagon covered with its white canvas and painted with blue stripes. He went around the corner of the wagon and stopped dead in his tracks. Jessie was pressed smack against the side of the wagon. Luther, as mean as a snake whenever he touched a bottle of whiskey, which was too often, was all over her, kissing her, his hands fondling her breasts, pressing his groin against her.

James roared as he strode forward: "Get off her, you damned, sorry bastard!"

Why the hell wasn't Jessie fighting him? Why was she just standing there, letting him do whatever he wanted to do?

"Eh? Oh, James, I was just enjoying myself a bit of fluff here. Yep, I always wondered what Jessie Warfield would feel like. Lordie, she's got breasts, nice 'uns."

"Get off her, Luther. Now!"

"You want her, do you? Well, that's the word. You took her last night in the Blanchards' garden and everyone saw you take her and you didn't care, just cast her off, you did, and her pa let you. So why can't I have her, too?"

James grabbed Luther by the scruff of the neck and literally jerked him off her, hurling him to the muddy ground with a thud and a yelp.

He whirled around to see Jessie still pressed against the wagon, pale and silent. "Jessie, for God's sake, why'd you let him touch you like that?"

It was then that he saw the trickle of blood staining her throat. He touched the small gash. "He held you still with a knife?"

She was even whiter, if that was possible, not moving, not even pretending to pay attention to him. She just stood there, staring at Luther, who was now shaking himself as he rose slowly to his feet. She saw him put the knife away in the pocket of his wet coat.

James turned on his heel, grabbed Luther Swann by his coat lapels, jerked him forward, and sent his fist into his face. He kept hitting him until he fell, then he just hauled him up again, and hit him until he felt hands pulling him away, heard men's voices telling him to stop it, to control himself.

He finally realized that Luther was unconscious at his feet. He shook his head.

"What's going on here, James?" Oliver Warfield shook him again. "Why the hell did you beat Luther up?"

"What the devil do you mean? You're her damned father, for God's sake. He was forcing himself on her, Oliver. He made her stand still for it with a knife to her throat. Ask her yourself."

"I can't ask her, James. She's gone."

Luther was sitting up now, shaking his head. "I was just taking what she offered, James," he said, and whimpered when James took a step forward.

"Stop it, James! Look at your hands. Your knuckles are bleeding."

"It's true, Mr. Warfield," Luther said, seeing possible help from Jessie's own father. "Your daughter acts just like a man, and she wears those tight trousers. All of you know she's just asking for it. Well, she gave it to Wyndham last night. It was my turn, that's all. You, Sam, you told me you wanted her, too. Don't you remember? We flipped a coin to see who would get her first."

"My God," Oliver Warfield said. He jumped on Luther, pounding him in the belly with his fists. James managed to pull him off. "My God," Oliver said again. He shook his head and walked away.

James strode after him. "Oliver, wait. Dammit, we've got to do something."

Oliver stopped. He turned and looked at James, silent for a very long time. Then he shrugged. "You walked away from her last night. What do you expect me to do today? You want me to beat up a dozen men? Is that what you plan to do?"

"I don't know," James said slowly. He felt more helpless than he had when he'd been dragged by a huge black stallion for fifty yards. "I just thought it was all nonsense, just as Jessie did. I couldn't imagine anyone believing that Jessie and I would be making love in the Blanchards' garden."

"Folks love scandal. If it isn't real, they'll tug on it and jerk on it and mold it about until it's real enough to hurt a person really bad. You had a good day, James. You beat Jessie in all three races. If you don't mind, I'd just as soon not come to Marathon tonight with that God-awful champagne you like so much."

He turned and walked away.

James just stared after him. He felt swamped with guilt and anger. None of it was his fault. Damn Glenda and her wretched mother. And curses upon Jessie's head as well. If she hadn't interfered, well . . . actually, if she hadn't been up in that elm tree with a gun, he would have been dead and none the wiser today for it.

Glenda came into Jessie's room without knocking. At first she didn't see her sister. She rarely visited this particular bedchamber. Indeed, she hadn't been inside for some three or four years, since she was young and tended to idolize her older sister until she'd learned that Jessie was peculiar. Since Glenda was a lady born and bred, she couldn't afford to pay any attention at all to this strange female who just happened to share her parents with her. The room wasn't all that large; indeed, it was a bit smaller than Glenda's bedchamber. But what it had that Glenda's didn't have was a nearly full wall of windows that faced west. Precious Baltimore sunlight streamed into the room, so bright it hurt the eyes to look directly into it. There were no draperies. None at all, which of course wasn't the right thing. Glenda wondered if her mother knew that Jessie had removed them. Other than that ghastly bright sunlight, there was only a bed, a large armoire, and a small writing desk. There was no vanity table. There was, Glenda remembered, a long skinny mirror on the inside of the armoire.

"What do you want, Glenda?"

"Ah, Jessie, there you are. I didn't see you sitting there in that window seat. The sun's so bright. I just wanted to speak to you for a moment."

"Yes?" Jessie didn't move. She was tired, was sore from her adventure of the previous night, and bruised and battered from the five races she'd ridden in today. The knife cut on her throat throbbed gently. She'd bandaged it herself and loosely wrapped a colorful scarf around the bandage.

"Mother asked me to come tell you that you shouldn't come to church with us tomorrow. Not after what happened today. Mother doesn't think it wise for you to show yourself for a while. She said that if the men were trying to get at you, the ladies would shred you."

"Shred me?"

"Yes. Mother says that ladies swoop down on their own sex with more abandon and joy than an army of men. She said they'd make hash out of you and shred you."

"Mother didn't send you, Glenda. Doubtless she doesn't want me with you tomorrow, but I'm sure she'll come to tell me herself. Now, what do you want?"

"I want you to go to Aunt Dorothy in New York City. If you ask Papa, he'll send you as soon as possible."

Aunt Dorothy, her father's younger sister, was as gracious as a mad dog, more pious than a reformer, the widow of a minister of too ample means. She'd terrified all three Warfield sisters since they'd been born. Jessie had overheard her father telling her mother once that he never doubted his brother-in-law's money came from stealing half the money in the tithing plate every single Sunday.

"I would rather die than go to Aunt Dorothy. You know what she's like, Glenda."

"Yes, but what else can you do? If you go out of the house, men will think they can take you at their whim. They believe you're a slut, that James has already had you. The ladies will shred you. I heard Papa say he couldn't allow you to race anymore. You're ruined, Jessie. It's that simple. You must leave."

"If I leave, then you and mother will somehow try to trap James again into marriage."

"It's none of your affair. Oh yes, I realized last night that you were there because you'd eavesdropped on us. You were there to keep me from having James. I deserve James and I'll have him."

"He doesn't deserve you, Glenda."

"If he is really honorable and generous, then perhaps one day he'll come to deserve me. He will work to deserve me. But he must know that the Warfields would bring him great consequence. Marriage to me would bring him Warfield Stables."

"What about me? Aren't I entitled to some of Warfield Stables?"

Glenda smiled, wandered over to the small chair in front of the writing table, and sat down. "Surely Father will do something for you. You have been a prize jockey for some time now. Yes, he'll see that you're taken care of." When Jessie didn't say anything, Glenda said, "I will provide you with enough money to get to New York City. It's all that I've saved, but I'll willingly give it to you. It's three hundred dollars."

"That's quite a sum." Jessie herself had saved nearly a thousand dollars beginning with the small coins tossed to her when she'd been little more than a toddler.

"Yes, but I think you deserve it. I shan't regret giving it to you if that's what you're worried about. No, take the money, Jessie. I'm sure everything will work out well for you. I even have two gowns you can travel in to New York. I've even written to Aunt Dorothy telling her that you're coming. Naturally, I pretended the letter was from Mama. You see it's for the best, don't you, Jessie?"

"Three hundred dollars?"

"Yes, and two gowns."

"Two of your *best* gowns or two gowns from three years ago?"

"Well, oh all right. I'll give you one of my best gowns and three older ones."

"I would also like that velvet-lined lemon-colored cloak of yours."

"That's robbery!"

"Take it or leave it, Glenda."

"You swear to leave?"

Jessie looked out over the rose garden, a triumph of her mother's ability to find the best gardener in the area. Soon the air would be filled with the scent of roses. But she wouldn't be here to smell those incredible white blooms the gardener had managed to succor into vivid life the previous year. But what did the damned roses matter to her now?

"I swear," she said.

James went to church. He always went to church. It pleased his mother to have him accompany her. Besides, he was very fond of Winsey Yellot, the minister. Winsey believed the French were the Unredeemed. He proved every one of his points with quotes from Voltaire, who was endlessly witty in addition to being an atheist. James usually lost their arguments because he laughed so hard at Winsey's execrable French pronunciation when he quoted Voltaire.

This morning it was overcast. Nothing new in that, he thought as he assisted his mother from her carriage. He found himself looking for the Warfields. He saw them in their usual seats in the fifth row. ''Not too close, mind you,'' Oliver had said to him, ''to prevent a nice snooze, but far enough away so Winsey doesn't harangue me personally.''

Jessie wasn't in her usual place. He frowned even as he looked at the people in the other pews. He wanted to dismiss it, but he couldn't. She wasn't here because her mother knew she'd be shunned if she'd come. They'd left her behind. He felt rage building. Everyone had smiled at him, spoken to him, asked him about his health, his horses, and Marathon. Jessie would bear the brunt of all of it.

He couldn't wait for Winsey to finish his exhortations, this Sunday, his subject being slavery. Baltimore had just voted that no future state of the Union could allow slavery. James had heartily agreed.

He didn't know what he was going to do about Jessie, but he had to do something. When the service was finally over, he looked up to see Glenda staring at his crotch.

He didn't find out until Sunday night that Jessie was gone, to New York City, Glenda had told everyone, to their Aunt Dorothy. James, who'd heard Jessie whisper tales about Aunt Dorothy since she was fourteen, felt like the biggest bastard on earth.

# = 11 =

*Chase Park, home of the Wyndhams*

"MY LORD."

Marcus Wyndham, 8th Earl of Chase, looked up at his butler, Sampson, who'd managed to glide across thirty feet of oak floor without his hearing a single footfall.

"You did it again, damn your eyes. However do you manage it, Sampson?"

"I beg your pardon, my lord?"

"Never mind. Someday my ears will attune themselves to you. At least I've learned to lock the door whenever the Duchess and I are involved in, well . . . never mind that. What do you want?"

"There is a strange young person here, my lord. Not a young person who is strange, just a young person I've never seen before. She asks to see you. She walked right up to the front doors and knocked. She looks somewhat like my dear Maggie playing the role of a disreputable waif, demanding to see the lord of the manor."

"She wants work, you think? Send her to Mrs. Emory."

"Well, you see, my lord, there's something about her,

other than the obvious fact that she's from the Colonies.''

''What? The deuce, you say, Sampson. The Colonies?''
The earl rose, rubbing his hands together. ''She must know
James. She must be here because of James. You're certain
it's not Aunt Wilhelmina, aren't you, Sampson? She asked
for me, you say?''

''No, my lord. It isn't That Woman. As for the young
person, well, actually, she wants the Duchess. I doctored the
truth just a bit since the Duchess is feeling a bit on the
poorly side.''

''She's off the poorly side as of luncheon. Tell you what,
Sampson, get the Duchess and the both of us will see this
young person from the Colonies who has the look of Maggie. Does she have a name?''

''Jessica Warfield, my lord.''

Ten minutes later, Sampson, the Chase butler since his
twenty-fifth year, led a very pale, very determined young
person into the Green Cube Room, a chamber that had intimidated a baron only last month with its magnificent
painted ceiling set between beams covered with lavish ge-
ometric designs and opulent gilt furnishings. The Turkey
carpets on the floor were at least a hundred years old, yet
their reds and blues and yellows shone in the afternoon sunlight coming through the front windows. There were paintings on the walls that had to be older than the Colonies.

Jessie was intimidated. Even more, she was terrified. She
was the greatest fool to be born on this planet. She dutifully
walked behind a very handsome man who was obviously
the butler, but who hadn't turned his nose up at her. Indeed,
he'd been stiffly kind. She remembered James speaking of
handsome Sampson, who'd married Maggie, the Duchess's
red-haired maid, who'd been an out-of-work actress before
she'd come into the Duchess's employ. She hoped this was
Sampson, for James had always grinned whenever he spoke
of him, telling her how he was the only one who could

control Maggie, and he had to grow more clever by the year to succeed.

"My lord. My lady. This is the young person from the Colonies. Miss Jessica Warfield."

So this was Marcus and the Duchess, she thought as she forced her feet to move forward. Marcus was dark and tall and so handsome even she wanted to swoon, something she'd never before considered doing in the company of any man. So dark he was yet he had the deep blue eyes of an angel. Except angels smiled, didn't they? He wasn't smiling. On the other hand, neither was he frowning. She looked at the woman standing beside him. The Duchess. She wrote the clever ditties that James occasionally hummed or sang at the top of his lungs. She'd supported herself long before she'd become the Countess of Chase. Surely she was too beautiful to be so resourceful. Surely God wasn't being fair to dish out so much to one single individual. Like her husband, the Duchess had black hair and blue eyes and the whitest skin Jessie had ever seen. Unlike the earl, the Duchess smiled at her, a full, easy smile that made Jessie even more nervous.

"Oh dear," she said, looking again from the earl to the countess, "this is certainly a flagrant intrusion. I know it is and I'm so sorry for it. But you see, James has told me so much about both of you—and all about Badger and Spears and Sampson and Maggie—that—"

The earl broke in easily, "James Wyndham? My cousin?"

"Yes, I race against James and many times beat him. Oh dear, I didn't mean to say that. Now you'll never believe I'm a lady."

The Duchess stepped forward, her hand held out. "I thought your name sounded familiar, Miss Warfield. James has spoken of your family over the years. Welcome to our home. Since you're a friend of James's, you're welcome here. Now, come and sit down. Sampson, bring some tea and seed cakes. Let me take that pelisse.''

Jessie willingly gave it up. It was an ugly mustard color, but she'd believed she had to have something to make her unquestionably female. The one Glenda had promised to give her hadn't materialized, damn Glenda. She hadn't gotten any gowns either, damn Glenda again. The Duchess folded the pelisse neatly, as if it were very valuable, and laid it over the back of a chair that had probably had kings sit in it. The current king, George IV, was very fat. She hoped he didn't visit and sit in that chair. It would collapse, surely. She didn't want to sit in it either. It would realize she was a peasant and disintegrate in shock.

''Now,'' the Duchess said as she sat gracefully in a narrow, terribly French-looking chair across from Jessie, who'd gingerly sat herself on the edge of a blue brocade settee, ''how is James?''

''Don't forget Aunt Wilhelmina, Duchess.''

The Duchess sighed. ''One hesitates even to speak her name, but all right, I'll include her in the question. And dear Ursula. How are all of the American Wyndhams?''

''As of six weeks ago, they were fine, ma'am.''

This was interesting, the Duchess was thinking. She resumed her charming smile. ''Miss Warfield, tell us how we may help you.''

''Well, you see, ma'am, I'm here not to race because I know that in England all females must be extra proper and that ladies can't wear trousers and can't be jockeys and can't ride in races and—''

The earl raised his hand. ''How old are you, Miss Warfield?''

That took her aback a bit but she managed to say, ''I am twenty, sir. James is twenty-seven and—''

''Did you travel from Baltimore to England all by yourself?''

Jessie knew the English were very particular about things like this and thus lied swiftly and cleanly. "I had a maid to accompany me, but she got vilely ill on board ship and then there was this ghastly storm, so violent, and everyone got very sick, me included, and poor Drusilla went on deck, vomited over the railing, and fell overboard she was heaving so hard. So I had no choice but to come here from Plymouth on a mail coach."

The Duchess looked to her husband. He looked on the point of bursting into laughter. She looked quickly at the very serious, very frightened face, and said, "These things happen. It is tragic that poor Drusilla had to meet her maker in such an unfortunate manner, but you managed very creditably to get here all by yourself."

"Well, there was one horrible thing that happened. It was near the town called Hayfield and there were three men with masks on their faces and they wanted to steal everything. I'd hidden my money beneath my gown—oh dear, anyway, I gave them my five dollars and they just looked at it. The leader spit on it and tossed it back to me and said he didn't want any of that odd stuff from the Orient. At least that's what I think he said. He was very difficult to understand."

Jessie came to a halt all by herself this time. She was appalled at what she'd freely admitted. Surely they believed her a vulgar, brainless twit. She said, "Forgive me. I'm talking so very much and usually I don't. I'm just so very scared."

The past two months, held at bay until now, collapsed in on her. She dropped her face in her hands and sobbed. They weren't delicate sobs, but hoarse, deep ones.

Suddenly, she stopped, raised her face, and swiped her hands over her eyes. "Forgive me again. I'm never afraid. I don't know what's happened to me."

"Ah, here's Sampson. You need some tea."

''James always says that tea is the solution to every problem in England.''

''Why, I suppose that it is,'' the Duchess said. She poured a cup and handed it to Jessie. ''Now, drink it down and see if you don't feel just a bit better for it.''

Jessie took a big drink and wheezed for breath. ''It's stronger than the whiskey Old Gussie makes in his own still. This is tea? Just innocent tea?''

The earl rose to pat her on the back. She was thin, he thought. It must have taken her a long six weeks to get here. Alone on a ship. Then a good five days on the mail coach from Plymouth to Darlington. Just to contemplate it curled his toes. He gave her one of Badger's famous lemon seed cakes. Jessie didn't mean to, but she ate it in two bites, then felt like a coarse savage doing that in front of these magnificent people.

''Have another,'' the Duchess said, smiling at her.

She gave this one three bites, but it was difficult.

''When was the last time you ate, Miss Warfield?'' Marcus Wyndham asked easily.

''Well, yesterday, really. You see, all my American dollars were stuffed in my, er, chemise, except at night of course. Someone slipped into my bedchamber and stole all of it. I have a dollar left that I hid in the toe of my left boot.''

''Well, I'm relieved you didn't get robbed until you were close to us.'' The earl rose and stood over her, looking down at the vivid, curling red hair that was poking out riotously on all sides of the very ugly straw bonnet. Yes, she had hair the color of Maggie's, perhaps even a more vivid, richer red. ''How long have you known James?''

''Since I was fourteen. He doesn't know I'm alive. That is, he knows I'm alive, it's just that he doesn't care. It's very depressing. Oh goodness, I've done it again. Truly, sir, I don't talk like this all the time.''

"Please don't shut down on our account," the earl said. "Now, you must be tired. You are our guest, Miss Warfield. I daresay we'll get all this straightened out after you've had a good rest. I'll have Cook send you up a nice late luncheon."

Jessie couldn't allow this. She bounded to her feet, tripped on the hem of her gown, and went crashing toward the beautiful silver tea service that had surely served multitudes of earls and dukes and princes. She felt the earl's hand clasp her upper arm and pull her upright.

He smiled down at her as he released her. "Are you all right, Miss Warfield?"

"Yes, sir, but I can't be your guest. James doesn't know I'm here. No one does. I ran away because everything was impossible at home. It will remain impossible, so I can't go home. I want to work for you. I know I can't be a jockey for you since ladies can't do that in England, but I love children and James has told me that her ladyship just had another little boy and James is his godfather. I would like to be a nursery maid. I think the baby is probably too young for a nanny, probably even too young for me to take him riding and teach him all about thoroughbreds, particularly the founding sires, and my favorite is the Byerley Turk, who was captured at Buda in 1688."

"He's just a bit too young for the Byerley Turk," the earl agreed. "But he's a smart lad, and I daresay he'll want to be up to snuff by his first birthday. Well, Duchess, what do you say? Shall we set Jessica—"

"Excuse me, sir, but my name's Jessie. I know that sounds perhaps too provincial, perhaps too Colonial, but it's my name. It can't be helped."

"It's charming," the earl said easily, quite charmed by this unexpected female. "'Jessie' it is. What do you say, Duchess?"

The Duchess rose and walked gracefully to Jessie, who

scrambled to her feet. She took her right hand between her own and said with a smile, "Charles is a handful, just like his father. I imagine he will adore you, particularly your splendid hair. You will take care that he doesn't bald you. Welcome to Chase Park, Jessie."

"I don't have splendid hair. You're just being kind because that's what James said you were."

"Of course you have lovely hair. Say 'thank you,' Jessie."

"Thank you, ma'am."

Soon Jessie was trailing after Sampson, who was casually telling her that he'd always fancied visiting the Colonies. He'd never before seen an Indian and said he'd like to borrow some of their war paint for his wife. It would amuse her, he said.

In the Green Cube Room, the Duchess was saying to her husband, "Marcus, this is interesting. What do you think happened between her and James that sent her scurrying here all by herself? What she's done is foolish beyond belief."

"I'll wager you she wore trousers until she got close to us, then changed into that god-awful gown. Don't worry. We'll find out everything soon enough. Now I wonder what Maggie will say when she meets a woman younger than she is with hair that just could be redder?"

Maggie, Sampson's wife of six years, was magnificent. Jessie just stared at her as she clutched the threadbare dressing gown more closely about her. At least she was clean and had lain down on that incredible bed with its pale gold brocade overhang and four tall posters, each beautifully carved, and closed her eyes. The mattress was goose feather if Jessie wasn't mistaken, and she'd thought she'd collapsed onto heavenly clouds, but still she hadn't slept. She'd been too scared and too relieved, both at the same time. The gown

Maggie wore when she came to Jessie's bedchamber, which was next to the nursery, was finer than the one the Duchess had worn when Jessie had first been shown in to that awesome Green Cube Room. Ah, but her hair, it was glorious.

"Redder than a sinner's passions," Maggie said comfortably when Jessie just stared at her and blurted it out. She patted that beautiful hair and grinned. "You've not a bad head of hair yourself, Miss Jessie. It's not as pure a shade of red as mine, but it's acceptable nonetheless. Now you have all these dancing curls that won't obey even my fingers, so we'll—" She paused and struck a thoughtful pose.

"Oh, please call me Jessie. I'm not a Miss. You're right, my hair won't do what anyone tells it to. I'm going to be Charles's nanny of sorts."

"Yes, my Sampson told me you were going to teach Charles all about racehorses and thoroughbreds and the Byerley King—"

"Well, it's actually the Byerley Turk. He's a horse, you know, not a man."

"That's a pity. Men provide so much more sport than horses, but I suppose opinions do vary on that score. I daresay you'll do just fine no matter what kind of a Turk it is. Now, let me see what I can do with this very nice head of hair. You'll be having dinner with the Duchess and his lordship this evening. You scrubbed your hair really well, didn't you, in your bath?"

"Oh yes, it was dreadfully dirty," Jessie said as she sat down and stared at the nearly dry wild tangle of red curls in the mirror.

"Don't you worry now, Jessie. The Duchess told me you needed me, and I can well see that you do. She wants me to bring you up to the mark. It's a good thing I'm so talented—Did I tell you I was an actress before I saved Mr. Badger's life in Plymouth? Oh, you haven't met Mr. Badger or Mr. Spears yet. You will."

"James has told me ever so much about everyone. He said you were incredibly beautiful."

What James had actually said was that Maggie froze his tongue in his mouth ever since she'd patted him on his butt when he'd been twenty years old.

"Yes, well, James is a nice man. He grew up well. We're all very proud of him. Those deep green eyes of his appeal to the senses. Have you ever noticed those long eyelashes of his? And that nearly blond hair that's sort of curly? He's a handsome man, our James, and he grew to be so big, nearly as big as the earl, his cousin. Now, you just relax and close your eyes. I shall proceed to work my magic."

"James does have beautiful green eyes," Jessie said. Her eyes were closed, so she didn't see Maggie's smile at those wistful words. To Jessie's surprise, Maggie didn't immediately begin brushing out her hair. No, she rubbed a very sweet-smelling cream onto her face. "Isn't that nice? The Duchess told me you'd been on board a ship for a good six weeks. That ocean air isn't good on a lady's face. This will make you soft again. We'll use it every day. You will use it on the rest of yourself as well, after every bath. You have nice skin for a Colonist, Jessie. Now, let's see what we'll do with your hair."

Jessie felt like a fool. She didn't want to leave her bedchamber, which was more lovely than even her mother's at home. Maggie had told her it was called the Autumn Room because of all the lovely golden shades in the draperies and the counterpane. This was the room they gave to Charles's nanny?

She didn't want to walk down that long, wide corridor with its niches holding naked Greek statues or the endless stretch of walls filled with paintings of Wyndham ancestors.

She didn't want to trip on the hem of this incredible gown

that the Duchess had sent for her to wear and land on her nose beneath one of those paintings.

When there was a knock on her bedchamber door, she was nearing a state of panic that had her shaking and cursing herself for shaking.

She opened the door to see a tall older gentleman who was dressed more elegantly than any gentleman she'd ever seen in her life. He had thick black hair threaded with interesting silver and dark eyes that surveyed her calmly.

The personage smiled down at her. "I'm here to escort you downstairs, Miss Warfield. The Duchess thought perhaps you'd be more comfortable on my arm rather than marching past all those Wyndham portraits that give her bile, she's always saying."

"Thank you, sir." She gingerly placed her hand through his arm. "My name's Jessie."

"You Colonists are so informal, but it's charming. Chin up. That's better. I fancy Mr. James is very worried about you."

"Oh no, he doesn't care, he—"

"Yes?"

"I'm sorry. You couldn't possibly care that James doesn't even know I'm alive. I suppose it is possible he's a bit worried since he was a part of my downfall."

"Interesting things, downfalls. Was yours an interesting downfall or just a simple, everyday sort?"

She burst into laughter. She laughed and laughed, trembling with it, and the Grand Personage beside her merely smiled benignly until finally she subsided.

"Do you know I don't think I've laughed for nearly two months now? Goodness, that felt quite good."

"I daresay you'll laugh even more when you ride tomorrow."

"Ride? As I did at home? Oh no, sir, surely the earl and countess couldn't be that lax with their servants, and that's what I am. In America I'd be an employee, but here, surely, I'm just a servant of no account at all.''

"You're dining with the earl and countess.''

"That's different. They just want to know all about James. They miss him.''

"Yes, he's an interesting man. He's been through a lot, but he's survived, and gotten all the stronger for it.''

"Yes, I know about his wife and child dying.''

"That was one thing, yes. Ah, now mind your steps, these stairs can be treacherous to females, males too if they've imbibed too much.''

Jessie said nothing more until the Grand Personage had guided her down to the last magnificent oak step and her feet were solidly on the black-and-white Italian marble entrance hall that was larger than the entire downstairs of her father's house.

She felt very provincial. Her laughter was long gone. She looked around her and felt the same terror she'd felt when she'd walked through those cathedral-like double doors with their huge brass lion-head knockers.

"I never imagined a house like this, sir.''

"You'll become used to it. The Duchess hated it as a child, thought it was cold and overwhelming, but now she's proud as the devil of it. Let's take you to see the earl and the Duchess. They're in the small gold room this evening. Mr. Sampson believed you would feel more comfortable there on your first night here.''

"James told me that the earl named her the Duchess when she was nine years old.''

"Yes, he did.''

"Are you visiting here, sir? Are you also an earl? Or perhaps a duke?''

"Not to my knowledge. Now, I want you to keep your head high, keep those shoulders squared, and smile. Act as if you were the queen of America come here deigning to visit. Will you try to do that?''

Jessie gulped. "I'll try. Aren't you coming with me?"

"Not this evening. I'll see you tomorrow."

"Thank you, sir."

"You're most welcome."

# ===12===

JESSIE JUST COULDN'T take it all in. Here she was sitting in a priceless chair that must be hundreds of years old, holding a silver fork that weighed as much as her arm, picking at fresh garden peas that rolled around on a plate that had more gold on it than every wedding ring in Baltimore melted together.

She realized this wasn't a state banquet hall, but rather just a cozy little dining room no larger than her mother's huge parlor. The walls were painted a light yellow. Windows lined the front, and the light silk draperies were drawn back to show the front lawn with its well-scythed grass that melted into an oak forest. She heard a strange sound that so startled her, she dropped her fork.

"It's all right," the Duchess said. "That was Fred."

"Fred?"

"The peacock. He's currently infatuated with Clorinda, but she's having nothing to do with him. She's a fickle little brown peahen. He is constantly fanning his magnificent tail, but alas, no luck. He's complaining about it to us. Just ignore him."

"All right." Ignore an infatuated peacock? Well, she supposed that since this was England she would have to adapt to any number of strange things.

"Do you like what Maggie did to your hair?" the earl asked.

Her hand went self-consciously to the thick braids wound around and interwoven to form a circle atop her head. "And now some little streamers as I call them," Maggie had said, "to soften the effect around your sweet face. Like that. Just pull them loose and let them curl where they will."

"I don't feel like me at all," Jessie said.

"From a male perspective, you look lovely," the earl said as he forked down a bite of boiled leg of lamb in white sauce and closed his eyes in bliss. He grinned. "Forgive me, but Badger is the chef tonight. He wanted to prepare a special dinner just for you."

Jessie dutifully took a bite of the veal cutlet garnished with young carrots and rice. It was delicious. She took another bite then another. "James told me how Badger could cook the socks off the king's own chef at Carlton House."

"Try the ragout of duck and the green peas," the Duchess said. "Yes, James always claims he's died and gone to glutton's heaven when Badger cooks for him."

"Ah," Jessie said, and closed her eyes just as the earl had. "How do both of you remain so thin?"

If Jessie wasn't mistaken, the earl was grinning at the Duchess like a man who'd just stolen a kiss from the preacher's wife.

His wife frowned at him and said, "Badger doesn't cook for us like this all the time."

"That's right," the earl agreed very quickly. "Now, what do you really think of Maggie and her talents?"

"Maggie said I looked splendid." There was such disbelief, such utter bewilderment in her voice, that both the earl and the Duchess laughed.

"You do," the earl said. "Try the trout à la Genevese. You also look splendid in the Duchess's gown. It has always made her look sallow, what with that dull black hair of hers and that washed-out complexion. Yes, that emerald green is becoming on you. I'm just surprised it wasn't in Maggie's armoire."

"Maggie decided to allow Jessie to try it," the Duchess said. "She did say, though, that if Jessie didn't do it justice then she'd remove it while Jessie slept and wear it herself since it was a rather acceptable gown and deserved to be shown off. Did Maggie believe it became you, Jessie?"

"She just looked me up and down and hummed."

"An excellent sign," the earl said. "You mentioned that you were a jockey."

"Yes, I'll admit it since I've already spit it out. I know you probably have some very proficient jockeys here who are of the right sex."

"Becoming a nanny is very different from being a jockey," the Duchess said. "Are you certain you wish to deal with Charles?"

"He drools a lot, Jessie," the earl said. "Except with Spears. He never drools on Spears. It isn't fair. He looks at me, grins, gets this evil look in his eye, and waters from the mouth the moment he's in my arms. He's teething right now as well as drooling. He likes to bite my chin."

"He bites anything that doesn't move quickly enough."

"I look forward to meeting him. I'm sorry, but the fact of the matter is I've never been around babies all that much, but you see, I love the new foals. I play with them and brush them and speak to them and—"

"Well, that's a relief. It's very nearly the same thing, isn't it, Duchess?"

"Almost exactly," the Duchess said. "I must also warn you, Jessie. Charles's brother, Anthony, just turned six years old. He'll be jealous that Charles has you. Thus you'll have the two of them hanging onto your skirts."

Jessie's eyes lit up. "Anthony rides?"

"Like a little centaur," the Duchess said fondly. "Perhaps you can be his horse nanny."

"Yes," the earl said. "You could teach him all about the fact that most horses are Barbs imported via France from northern Africa."

"Oh yes," Jessie said, forgetting her delicious dinner, forgetting the exquisite Aubusson carpet upon which her cheaply shod feet rested, forgetting that she was a Colonial in the presence of near-royalty. "That would be wonderful. You don't mind?"

"Not at all," the earl said. "Ah, here's Badger, come to be praised. Badger, this is Jessie Warfield, come to us from the Colonies. She's a friend of James's."

He was ugly and big, with huge fists, a full head of white hair, and a big smile. He was dressed like a gentleman who'd just chanced upon a huge white apron and tied it around his middle.

"You're Badger?"

"Aye, that I am. You liked the Julienne soup?"

"Oh yes."

"And the boiled leg of lamb and white sauce?"

"She did her duty by every dish, Badger. Now, what have you there?"

"Nesselrode pudding, my lord."

He served the pudding as three footmen deftly and silently removed the plates and set down new ones, these with just as much gold as the others.

When he finished, he nodded to Sampson, motioned to the footmen, and said, "I'll speak to you tomorrow, Miss Jessie. You rest well tonight. Master Anthony will be so excited to meet you, he's liable to roar into your bedchamber and jump up and down on you. It's because you're an American, of course. He'll look closely to make certain you don't have an extra finger or an extra ear. Good night, my lord, Duchess."

He was gone. As were the footmen. Sampson said,

"Good night. Mind what Mr. Badger said, Miss Jessie. That Master Anthony is a wild monkey."

"I'll mind," Jessie said, and watched Sampson leave the small informal dining room that had, she was certain, an echo.

"Now, my dear," the earl said, sitting back in his chair, "before we adjourn to the drawing room for some of Badger's incredible coffee, tell us what happened between you and James to send you flying to a foreign country."

She looked from one to the other and blurted out, "I didn't want to go to Aunt Dorothy in New York. She's my father's younger sister and she's petty and mean and pious and expects you to be grateful when she tells you what a bad person you are."

"I shouldn't consider going to her either," the Duchess said. "She sounds as bad as James's mother."

"James's mother is a terror. She makes me want to disappear under the floor. She once said to my face that I was a tart and should be whipped. Then she tried to cover it by saying that I hadn't heard her aright, that she'd said I was smart and that my skirt was ripped. It wasn't, I looked." Jessie sighed, then said, "There was no place else. I'm sorry I just knocked on your door and disrupted your lives."

"Lives occasionally need disrupting," the earl said. "We get so bloody complacent. Disrupt all you like, Jessie. What happened between you and James?"

"I was found by everyone lying on top of him in Blanchards' garden, but I really wasn't kissing him, truly, I just wanted to make sure he was conscious so I was patting his face and perhaps I was breathing too close to his mouth, I'm not really certain now but James does have a lovely mouth, not that it matters now, for you see, I was ruined. James wasn't because he's a man. What could I do? James doesn't want me. Nobody did except one man who isn't a gentleman who attacked me at the racetrack and tried to take liberties. But James saved me. I would have saved myself, mind you, but this one man had a knife to my throat. James was very angry, not that it changed anything. I'm truly sorry.''

"I see," the Duchess said. "Perhaps you could tell us what you were doing on top of James?"

Jessie took a deep breath, then recounted the sorry string of events.

"And you were ruined," the earl said.

"Yes. It isn't fair that the man isn't ruined as well."

"Well," the earl said, "the man is supposed to marry the woman if he's caught with her lying on top of him. Isn't that right, Duchess?"

"In the usual course of events, yes."

"He would have, but I know that James doesn't even like me. I would never do that to him."

"I see," the Duchess said, looking into Jessie's eyes. Beautiful green eyes, a lighter green than James's, and filled with a pain that was much too much for such a vulnerable creature as Jessie Warfield. She'd been delighted when Jessie had walked into the drawing room all proud and scared at the same time and ready to show off her new plumage and try not to puke at the same time. She'd told her she looked lovely, an observation Jessie took as a rank fabrication. But the Duchess wasn't deterred. She would continue to build her confidence. Perhaps that was all she needed, confidence and a bit of training. The Duchess wanted to see her on horseback.

Maggie had done a fine job with her. She wasn't a classic beauty, but there was intelligence in those green eyes of hers, and a mouth that curved up naturally with humor. She had lovely white teeth and a jaw more stubborn than James's. She was tall and slender, and she carried herself well. She had lovely white skin, and the Duchess found the sprinkling of freckles across her nose charming. What was wrong with

James? Surely he wasn't still brooding over Alicia, now dead three years?

Jessie cocked open an eye to find herself staring into two deep blue eyes that were only an inch from her face.

She shrieked.

"Shush," a very young male voice said. "Spears will come and put me under his arm and carry me away if you don't be quiet. I didn't mean to scare you."

It was a child, and he was speaking with that ludicrous starchy accent everyone else in this strange country spoke. "All right," she said. "I'll be quiet. I can't imagine what startled me so much. I mean, you're not precisely touching your nose to mine. I can't stand people who yell."

"I can't either."

"You're rather heavy. Do you think you could move a bit to the side?"

"Oh certainly. I say, is that better?"

Jessie could breathe again. She thought now that turning blue from want of air was what had awakened her in the first place.

"Much. Now—"

"You talk very funny, like Uncle James when he first arrives home before he learns how to speak properly again. Papa says it's because he comes from a savage land and we have to civilize him over and over. I'm always there to help Uncle James learn English again."

"You're Anthony."

"Yes. I'm named after Anthony Welles, the Earl of Clare, a very good friend of my grandpapa's. I never met either one of them, but the Earl of Clare was supposed to be a dashing gentleman who lived in Italy half the year and here in England the other half."

Jessie was fully awake now, utterly charmed by this out-pouring of confidences from a little boy who would surely grow up to be at least as handsome as his papa. "Your mama told me you ride like a centaur."

"Mama truly said that? A centaur? You're certain you didn't misunderstand her because you're an American?"

"I promise I have it right. Now, Anthony, I'm Jessie. I'm going to be Charles's nurse and your horse nanny. I ride like a centaur, too, you know, and I also race."

"Really? Mama said Aunt Frances was the only lady she knew who rode sometimes in races."

"You're introducing me to a lot of names I've never heard before. Give me a while to get my bearings, Anthony, then add a new name a day, all right?"

"I should have known you'd be tormenting poor Jessie."

"Papa!" Anthony rolled off the bed, his nightshirt flying around his ankles, and dashed to the door where his father stood, dressed in riding clothes and lovely black boots that shone as clear as mirrors. The earl lifted his son high in his arms, then lowered him to give him a hug and kiss. "Your mama thought you might have slipped through Spears's net. You're slippery, my boy." He looked at Jessie, who was struggling to pull the blanket to her chin. "We've considered locking him in the dungeon at night, but he's got the knack of quivering his chin, and the servants fall for it every time. They'd never let him stay in the dungeon for more than five minutes. What are we to do? But I found him, right where his mama knew he'd be. Now, Anthony, you didn't awaken poor Jessie, did you?"

"Oh no," Jessie said quickly. "I woke up all by myself and there Anthony was, standing in the doorway, as quiet as a mouse, just waiting for me to do something."

Anthony gave her an approving look and said, "She talks funny, just like Uncle James. Can we take her riding with us, Papa? She claims she's good. I told her about Aunt Frances, but she said she's got too many names on her plate now and I had to slow down."

"An excellent idea. Go to Spears now and let him get you dressed. After breakfast, we'll all go riding."

Anthony squeezed his papa's neck once more and scrambled down to his feet. "I'll see you at breakfast, Jessie," he yelled as he ducked behind his father and out the door.

"He's the very image of you, my lord," Jessie said. "He'll slay women in droves when he grows up."

"I'll try not to let it bother me that you're in a lady's bedchamber, my lord." It was the Duchess, and she was wearing a lovely dark blue riding outfit with a jaunty blue velvet riding hat that had an ostrich feather curving around her cheek. Jessie had never seen anyone so beautiful in her life. Actually, seeing the two of them side by side, she realized they looked remarkably alike. They were cousins, after all. Beautiful cousins.

"Good morning, Jessie. How did you sleep?"

"Like a dead rock," Jessie said, and yawned, unable to help herself.

"I'll take my husband from your bedchamber so you can bathe and dress. Here's Ned with your bathtub and some water. We'll see you downstairs."

"What about Charles?"

"Unlike his brother," the earl said, "Charles still doesn't quite grasp that you're here for him and thus at this moment, he's quite uncaring, being burped by his other nurse after the Duchess here let him eat for nearly an hour."

Maggie came into her bedchamber twenty minutes later, just as Jessie had finished braiding her own hair, she hoped just as Maggie had done it the previous evening. Maggie was carrying over her arm a riding habit of dark green velvet.

Maggie looked at her for a few moments, then said, "Sit down a moment, Jessie. I think you've half the knack of it."

Jessie sat.

"Now, my pet, you don't want to look outrageously beautiful the way I do all the time. I owe it to the house and to my husband to be a pearl during the day and a diamond during the evening and during the night—well, that's something you don't need to know just yet. But you, Jessie, you're not like me. You don't want to be unbraiding braids all the time. You want to be comfortable. Let's save all the plaited braids for the evening. How about just a single one for the morning? Now, here's how you make it straight. Yes, that's it. Now we'll just loop it up like this and pin it. Nothing to it. The last thing you do is loosen it all up." Maggie looked at the tightly pulled-back hair, took the handle of the comb, and eased the hair looser on the top and sides of Jessie's head. Then she pulled loose "streamers" to curl haphazardly about her face. The one that fell over her ear itched, but Jessie decided she could become used to it. She just stared at herself. It was amazing.

"See, that's all you need to do. Tomorrow, you will try it while I watch."

"Thank you, Maggie. I can't quite believe what a difference it makes. Oh, you're going to cream my face again."

"Yes, and this time I will leave the cream for you. Use it in the morning and just before you go to bed at night. Now, if you were married, you'd have to use it before your husband visited your bed. My Sampson says that if Badger would only add some vanilla to the cream that he'd like to lick . . . well, never mind that. Just wait until we get you into this riding outfit. The color should make your eyes a richer green."

"I can't keep accepting clothes from the Duchess."

"Oh, this one doesn't belong to the Duchess. It's mine. She wanted to lend you one that would have made you look bilious, yards of apricot velvet and dull as dirt. No, this one will suit you perfectly. I don't ride, but dear Sampson likes to see me prepared for every occasion. Every once in a while, to please him, I sit atop one of the earl's horses and pose. It does please Sampson no end. I am his Delilah, you know.''

When Jessie stepped out of her bedchamber twenty minutes later, Maggie's riding outfit on her back and a pair of the Duchess's boots on her feet, there was that tall, handsome gentleman waiting for her again. He smiled at her.

''Very fetching,'' he said, and proffered her his arm.

''Do you really think so, sir?''

''Another week of hearing the truth of things and you'll have the self-confidence of his lordship. No, perhaps that isn't all that healthy a thing. I will think about it. Now, let me escort you to breakfast.''

Jessie walked happily beside him. She was certain he must be some famous personage and he'd simply found it amusing to befriend her. He left her at the breakfast-room door.

''You will not eat with us, sir?''

''Not this morning. I've already consumed my morning victuals. You enjoy yourself riding, Jessie. Don't let Master Anthony ride off Monmouth's cliff, which is at the south end of Fenlow Moor.''

''I won't.''

He smiled down at her, turned on his stately heel, and left her. She hadn't time to open the door. A footman dressed in stunning gold and dark blue eased forward as smooth as a snake and opened the door for her.

So this was what was called dining *en famille*, she thought, forcing herself to stand still while the same footman pulled out her chair for her.

Anthony was in high spirits, waving a strip of bacon around on his fork as he made a point about his pony.

''My God.''

Jessie brought her head up fast at the earl's stunned voice.

"My God," he said again. "Isn't she utterly delicious, Duchess?"

"It's that red hair, Jessie. My husband lusts after red hair."

"What is lust, Mama?"

"It's a new feed for the horses," the earl said, and laughed. "Your mama thinks it's about the best feed we've ever had. I think she wanted to eat it herself."

The Duchess threw a piece of toast at her husband. She hadn't yet buttered it. "Jessie isn't yet married, my lord. Mind your tongue, or it won't go well for you."

The earl said to Jessie, his voice pensive, "Did you know that last month she threw a plate at me? It had eggs on it. Luckily she hasn't become all that good a shot since we've been married, so only my coat was ruined. Spears wasn't even put out by it. He just smiled and said her aim was getting better."

"What did you do, my lord, to deserve having a plate of eggs heaved at you?"

"Call me Marcus. What did I do? Naught of anything. So naught I can't even remember."

"I will remind you later, my dear," the Duchess said, eyeing her small son, who was staring at his papa.

Jessie wondered if the plate had broken. She certainly hoped not. It was probably worth more money than her father's stud. She looked back and forth between the Duchess and Marcus. The Duchess was scolding Anthony about stuffing porridge down his little gullet like a savage. As for his papa, Marcus was forking down his porridge like a big savage.

She was lucky. More than lucky, not that it wasn't about time that her luck turned. She would try to be a good horse nanny to Anthony and a good nurse to Charles.

She missed James damnably, curse him.

# ═══ 13 ═══

THAT FRIDAY EVENING, when Jessie had been in residence for a week and a half, the countess and earl gave a dinner party. She was invited. She was their guest, not Charles's nurse or Anthony's horse nanny.

She agreed because of the excitement in the Duchess's beautiful eyes. When the earl gave her a gown of the softest yellow silk, all low-cut over her breasts, the sleeves long and fitting closely at her wrists, she wanted to cry. She'd never before seen such a lovely gown in her life. She doubted if anyone in Baltimore even knew such a gown was possible. Maggie arranged her hair with only three inter-woven braids atop her head. The rest of her hair she brought through the circle and arranged the curls in a fall that came nearly to the middle of her back. Her streamers fell down her neck and beside her face. She just sat there and stared at herself in the mirror.

"Now, just a bit of lip cream."

"Oh goodness, my mother would have apoplexy."

"Yes, isn't it wonderful that you're here and she isn't?"

"Maggie, is it possible? Are the freckles all gone?"

"No, there's this adorable little line—little soldiers, I think of them—marching right over the bridge of your nose. They're charming. I should imagine that all the young ladies here tonight will see them and go home and paint some on their own noses. Now, this gown. Your breasts look mighty fine. I'd brought some handkerchiefs to stuff in there just in case, but you don't need them. Mr. Spears said we didn't want to flaunt your cleavage but that you should have one. Yes, he would approve. No freckles on those pretty shoulders. Nearly as white as mine except my skin's creamier because it's the way I am, but yours isn't all that bad, Jessie. You're ready.''

"I don't dance, Maggie."

"You what?"

"I don't dance."

"Oh goodness. How much time do we have?"

"Not enough."

Maggie was looking thoughtful. "I have an idea," she said. "You go on downstairs, Jessie, and don't worry. You want to have a nice time."

He was waiting outside her room, as he'd been so many times since her arrival at Chase Park. He looked magnificent in his evening garb, his cravat as white as his teeth. He looked her over thoroughly. She found herself holding her breath for his opinion. He said finally, stroking long fingers over his jaw, "Maggie did a fine job. You're ready to meet all our illustrious neighbors. I want you to stretch out your charming drawl. I want you to emphasize it. You're to show them you're different and that you're very likely better than they are. Can you do it, Jessie?"

She looked at this gentleman who surely had to be a duke at least and said, "You truly believe I can, sir?"

"I truly do. Give me your hand and let's get you downstairs."

This time she didn't ask him if he were dining with them. She simply smiled up at him at the bottom of the great staircase and said, "Thank you, sir."

"Now," the earl said as he drew her into his arms, "we're going to waltz. We have time for one lesson before the guests arrive. Maggie tells me you're smart and will learn quickly.''

Sampson was playing the pianoforte. He marked the first beat of the three heavily as he played. Jessie was terrified and delighted. It was true that the earl practically held her off her own feet most of the time, but before the end of the waltz she nearly had the knack.

''You've got to relax and trust your partner,'' he said. Then he frowned. ''Well, trust is perhaps too strong a word. Many of the men are clods and would land on your feet. Others are lechers and would try to make love to you. I'll tell you whom to dance with, all right?''

Jessie agreed to that. Dinner was in the state dining room. There were twelve couples, twelve footmen, and more food than Jessie had ever seen in her life. She sat between the Earl of Rothermere—the gentleman who oversaw James's stud when he was in America—and a Mr. Bagley, the local curate, whose abiding interest was in the Norman cathedral in Darlington. After the boiled salmon in lobster sauce, roast quarter of lamb and spinach appeared, the Earl of Rothermere, Philip Hawksbury, said to her, ''Just taste this boiled salmon. Badger cooked this evening, praise the Lord. I prayed he would. I've offered him anything he wants to come to Rothermere, but he refuses, damn Marcus and the Duchess. I tell Badger my wife and I are so thin our ribs knock together, but he just smiles and offers me a taste of his new creation. The last time it was an oyster patty of sorts. I thought my belly was going to expire on the spot from happiness.''

She laughed even as she felt like a fraud. She watched the Duchess and tried to copy her. But the Duchess was so graceful, so utterly serene and calm, even the movement of her fork from plate to mouth was done exquisitely and naturally, without conscious thought. There was simply no way she could be like the Duchess.

She was utterly relieved when the Duchess rose and took the ladies into the Green Cube Room. Jessie met all the ladies, who didn't know what to make of her. However, since the Duchess introduced her as a friend from the Colonies, they were reserved but polite. Jessie stretched out her Colonial drawl as much as she dared. She couldn't tell if the ladies were gratified or not hearing it. In but moments, the gentlemen came into the huge room and the orchestra tuned their instruments.

She sat beside the curate's wife during the first waltz, her foot tapping heavily on the first beat. The second waltz, she danced with Marcus, and he only had to lift her off her feet three times to prevent disaster. Then he handed her over to the Earl of Rothermere.

"Take good care of her, Hawk. This is the third waltz in her entire life."

"A pullet then," the Earl of Rothermere said, and gave her a dazzling smile. He was more energetic than Marcus, whirling her around until she was laughing aloud and gasping for breath. When it was over she said, "The earl told me he would be careful not to give me to clods or to lechers. He said nothing about volcanoes, my lord."

"He never does," Philip Hawksbury said. "You're doing well, Jessie. Very well."

She went upstairs some time later with an ice cream for Anthony. He was sitting at the top of the stairs, ready to hide in one of the niches whenever a lady came up the stairs to go to the withdrawing chamber. When he saw Jessie, he said, "You look different, Jessie. Your face is very red."

"That's because your papa is dancing my feet off. Now, here's an ice cream for you from Badger. He said he knew you'd already eaten at least four others and this was to be the last."

"How odd that Badger wouldn't count right," Anthony said, looking puzzled. "It's five actually, but they were small. I do wonder how Badger miscounted—he never has before.''

When she returned from her bedchamber, he was licking his fingers. ''It's a wonderful party,'' she said. ''Everyone is being very nice to me.''

''They have to be or else my mama and papa would nail them behind the wainscoting.''

She had to smile at that. ''I must go back now. Isn't it time for you to go to bed?''

''Not yet. Spears said I could have an extra thirty minutes tonight. He said I was to watch the gentlemen in particular. He said I was to make a list in my head of all the things they did or said that I didn't think were right. I am to tell him in the morning.''

''Do you think your papa will do anything that will go on that list of yours?''

''I asked Spears that, and he said that my papa was unique and exempt from any list.''

She kissed him goodnight and started down the huge staircase. She heard the knocker on the front door and watched Sampson, resplendent in magnificent evening garb, open the great doors. There stood James, his black cloak billowing out behind him in the stiff evening wind, his head bare.

''Ah, at last you've arrived, Master James,'' Sampson said.

''Is that damned twit here, Sampson?''

''Which damned twit, Master James?''

''Don't you rub my nose in it, Sampson. She's here, isn't she?''

''Naturally she is here. Where else would she be?''

He looked up then and saw her. He looked away from her, back to Sampson. ''The Duchess and Marcus are having a party?''

''Yes, but your arrival won't inconvenience anyone.

You're expected. Mr. Badger doubtless has dinner for you. He's had dinners prepared for you for the past three days. We all discussed it and decided that you'd realize within a week that she'd come here.''

"Tell me she's all right, Sampson."

She said then, "James."

He looked up at her, shook his head, and looked away. "Where the devil is she?"

"James!"

This time he took several steps forward and looked up at her again. "Jessie?"

"Yes."

"You're not Jessie. You look nothing like Jessie, but you have her voice. What did you do to Jessie?"

She walked slowly down the stairs because she had no choice. She didn't want to trip on her skirts and break her neck. But she wanted to run. She wanted to leap on him and hold him hard against her and not let him loose, even to let him eat Badger's dinner.

She reached the bottom step. He'd walked toward her and had stopped three feet away. He was staring up at her.

"Hello, James. I'm very surprised to see you."

He stared at her silently for another very long minute. "My God, I don't believe this. Just look at you. What did you do to yourself? Oh, I know. Maggie got hold of you."

"Yes," she said, her chin up, feeling like a queen, feeling like a female that James Wyndham could admire, perhaps even lust after as he did Connie Maxwell. "Everyone got hold of me." She knew her breasts were round and white and there was ample cleavage. Her hair was exquisitely arranged and the fall of curls from within the circle of braids surely looked romantic cascading down her back. A streamer waved down each side of her face, nearly touching her shoulders. She was wearing lip cream. She only had a single file of freckles marching across her nose. She had looked at herself when she'd gone to her bedchamber. She knew she looked as lovely as any lady in the Green Cube Room waltzing around. Even her hands were soft from all Maggie's cream.

"You look ridiculous."

Her mouth dropped open. "What did you say?"

Sampson said smoothly, "James sometimes falls into his dear mother's speech habit, Jessie. I believe he really said that you looked *ravissant*, in the manner of the French."

"That wasn't even close, Sampson," James said over his shoulder. "My mother could take you out in the first round. Stay out of this. Now, my girl, just what the devil do you think you're doing? You look like a painted hussy with that red cream smeared all over your mouth. Your breasts are about to pop out of your gown, breasts I didn't even know you had, or maybe you puffed them out with handkerchiefs? You've lost your freckles—Why is that? Have you locked yourself in a dark room for the past two months and sacrificed an acre of cucumbers? Just look at that bloody gown. You can't even walk for fear you'll trip over that damned flounce or your equally damned feet. Your hair looks like you're ready to go on the stage in some Medieval play. I bet you can't even move your head without fear of it all spilling out of its pins. Dear Lord, you've got pins in your hair, you! What is the meaning of all this?"

She felt crushed, her illusion of beauty in shambles at her feet, feet that did hurt just a bit because the Duchess's slippers were on the small side. She said, "I can move my head without my hair falling apart."

He waved his hand through his hair, strode up to her, and clasped her upper arms in his hands. He lifted her off her feet and set her down again on the marble floor. "All that is nonsense. Forget I said anything. I lost my head for a moment. You're here and you're safe. I prayed Marcus would take you in. You're so damned pathetic, I doubted he'd boot you out.''

"I'm not pathetic, at least I'm not anymore, but you don't like me either way, do you? Damn you, James, I'm beautiful, Marcus said so. Sampson said so. Maggie said so."

"They did, huh? Well, they haven't known you since you were fourteen years old. They haven't seen you plunge out of a tree like a shot duck. They haven't watched you munching on a piece of straw, an old felt hat pulled down over your eyes and singing a ditty the Duchess wrote. Nor have they smelled you with cucumber all over your face."

"What does that have to do with anything? What does that have to do with my being beautiful now? Look at me, James. Damn you, look at me."

"I'm looking. I'd be afraid to touch you for fear you'd fall into shimmery little female pieces. Now, what did Spears say about all this?"

"I haven't yet met Spears."

"That's odd. Usually Spears heads up this cast of meddlers. Where the devil is he, Sampson?"

"He is here, Master James. Not immediately here, you understand, such as he isn't at present standing here beside me, but he's in residence, just as he should be, just as he wishes to be."

James waved his hand through the air again. Then he jerked his fingers through his hair, standing it on end. "I keep getting off the track here, and the good Lord knows I've rehearsed everything I was going to say to you over and over again the past seven weeks. Now I can't keep everything straight, and it's all your fault for being so damned different. I was expecting you to be you, not this female I couldn't have imagined even existing. Are you even wearing stockings?"

Without hesitation, Jessie lifted the beautiful yellow silk skirts and petticoat to show him pale yellow silk stockings.

His eyes crossed. "Pull your dress back down. A simple yes would have sufficed. You don't know how to behave. You're as much a lady as the Duchess is a gin-soaked sinner in Soho. Now, why the hell did you run away, Jessie? Yes, that was the first question I'd planned to ask you. Thank God I finally remembered it. Why, Jessie?"

"It's a stupid question. You know very well I ran away because I was ruined. Everyone knew that. Glenda paid me three hundred dollars to leave. She also promised to give me some gowns and a cloak, but she didn't. She thought I was going to Aunt Dorothy in New York, but I didn't."

"Yes, that is what Glenda tearfully announced to all. She said you knew you'd disgraced yourself and thus had left, not wanting to bring more shame upon your family. I never thought you'd go to Aunt Dorothy. That old besom is more a terror than my dear mother. You're an idiot, Jessie, but I've never believed you were stupid. I immediately went to the docks and found out what ships had sailed for England. The *Flying Buttress* had sailed the morning you'd disappeared. One of the dockhands remembered you, seen you race a number of times. He told me you were all garbed in your trousers, trying to look like a man, but not fooling anyone. Damn you, Jessie, you didn't even bother to leave me a note. You didn't even leave your father a note. You just packed your damned breeches and left. I told Oliver I was coming over to England to get you. He told me he wanted you back. I don't know why he would, but he does."

"Papa might want me back, but Glenda is right. No one else does."

"That's nonsense and not true. By the time we get back to Baltimore, no one will even remember that you were lying on top of me, your hands all over my face, your mouth not an inch above mine."

"Actually, Master James," Sampson said, moving just a bit closer to Jessie, "Mr. Spears, Mr. Badger, Maggie, and

I have discussed this thoroughly and it is our opinion that Jessie won't ever be accepted again back in the Colonies. At least not in her current condition.''

"I would agree with that. Just look at her. This current condition of hers would bring her countless propositions. Men would lose all sense just looking at her.''

That, if Jessie wasn't mistaken, in no way resembled an insult. "What sort of propositions?''

"Be quiet, Jessie. Sampson, go away. At least back up three steps. I'm not going to strangle her—not yet, anyway. Thank you. Now, Jessie, this was the most foolish thing you've ever done. Wait, I remember in one race you wanted to beat me so badly you refused to take the longer way around. You tried to jump your horse over a tree that had been uprooted the night before in a storm, but your horse didn't make it and you went flying into a ditch filled with water.''

"Yes, I was riding Abel. I remember you laughed until your belly must have ached. I remember you stopped your horse, didn't even finish the race, and just stood at the edge of that damned ditch and looked at me and laughed and laughed.''

He remembered too being so scared he'd nearly lost his breakfast until he'd seen her floundering in at least three feet of water, looking like a drowned sheepdog, her red hair all plastered over her face, with nothing broken. Only then had the laughter bubbled out of him. Only then. He grunted.

"But it's done, James. I'm here and now you're here and I want to know why you're here.''

"I don't care what your father says, what anyone else says. I'm not responsible for ruining you, Jessie.''

"Of course you aren't. I told everyone that, including my father.''

"That doesn't matter to him. He's made me feel guiltier than hell. I had no choice but to follow you here and fetch

you back home. I had to leave Marathon, I had to leave
Alice, who I hope will keep herself away from Mortimer
Hackey, I had to leave Connie. All for you, Jessie, you
damned female, who just happened to shoot Mortimer
Hackey in the foot and fall on top of me.''

''I saved your life, James. I also saved you from Glenda.''

''That's true, but it doesn't matter. What matters is that I
hadn't planned to come to England before the end of the
year, and now I'm here. Just to fetch you back home.''

''I'm not going home. Nothing's changed, James, nothing
at all. I can't go back.''

''We all agreed, Master James,'' Sampson said. ''She
can't go back in her current condition. As I said before, all
of us have discussed this thoroughly and agree on this.''

''That's right, James. Nobody wants me back except that
man who tried to take liberties with my person.''

He banged his fist against the wall and yelled at her,
''You will do as I bloody well tell you!''

''Cease your ranting. You have no authority over me.''

''Think of me as taking your father's place. He wants you
home. I am his emissary.''

''Ha. Forget it, James. I will do as I please, and what I
please to do is remain here. I'm employed now. I have a
job and important responsibilities. Don't you dare sneer at
me, James Wyndham.''

''Is that so? And just what do you do?''

''I'm Charles's nurse and Anthony's horse nanny.''

''Oh my God, it's worse than I thought. Listen, Jessie,
Charles has a nurse. He probably has three nurses. He probably has three nannies waiting in the wings. Anthony has
his father and mother and Lambkin and every other stable
lad to teach him all about horses. Marcus and the Duchess
are letting you do this because they feel sorry for you. It's
beyond absurd, and it won't continue.''

Sampson cleared his throat. "Master James," he said quietly.

James slowly turned to see the Duchess and Marcus standing in the entrance hall, staring at him.

"Welcome home, James," Marcus said, and strode to him. He hugged him, then pushed him back. "You look like bloody hell. Haven't you slept at all? You're as thin as a stick. Worried about Jessie all these weeks, huh? Well, she's safe and sound. And beautiful. Just look at her."

"Thank you, Marcus, for all your observations. Hello, Duchess. I'm sorry to interrupt your party, but I came directly here, thinking the brat would be here and here she is, only she doesn't look like herself. Why did you let her paint herself like a hussy and dress like a London courtesan? She couldn't even keep her skirts down. She had to show me her stockings, which are far too enticing for her to wear."

"James, dear," the Duchess said in that perfectly modulated voice of hers, "we're delighted you're here. We've all been expecting you, but I do counsel you to moderate your tongue. Jessie looks exquisite. She looks more lovely than any other lady here. We do not feel sorry for her. She's right. Her jobs are very important to the boys and thus to us."

"Ha."

"Damn you, James. What's wrong with you?"

"Jessie, you keep out of this. Oh, the hell with it. You're all right. I'm going home to Candlethorpe."

"Not until you've had your dinner, Master James. It's a two-hour ride to Candlethorpe. You'll remain here tonight. Mrs. Emory is already preparing the Blue Gusset bedchamber for you. Come into the kitchen. Badger is waiting for you. Duchess, my lord, Jessie, go back to the party. I will deal with Master James."

\*    \*    \*

Jessie danced until three o'clock in the morning.

"I fancy I'm very good now," she said, smiling up at Marcus as he whirled her around in the last waltz.

"Yes, you are." He yawned. "You're also too young for me, Jessie. You've frazzled me. Even the Duchess is sitting over there looking like a beautiful wilted rose. I think we'll wait until tomorrow before we begin your lessons in the various country dances. Sampson likes to play country dances on the pianoforte."

Jessie climbed into bed thirty minutes later, after having pulled all the pins out of her hair. It felt good to have her hair loose. The pins had stuck into her scalp. She'd taken off her slippers just after midnight, toeing them beneath a chair. She'd ruined her beautiful stockings, but it had been worth it. With her two pounds a week, she could afford to repay the Duchess. She dreamed of James. This time it wasn't that terrifying dream about that horrible-smelling dead man who opened his mouth and accused her of stealing his treasure, a dream she'd had four times in the last several months. No, in this dream, James wasn't angry with her. Actually, he was far from angry. He was pressing her hard against him, kissing her, and his mouth was wet, very wet, and hot.

She awoke to find Anthony's small spaniel, Damper, sitting on her, his nose pressed against hers, licking her chin and her mouth.

She shoved him off, laughing and wiping her mouth with the back of her hand. "You miserable loving little lout! Did Anthony slip you into my bedchamber?"

"No, I did."

# ═══ **14** ═══

JAMES LOOKED SPLENDID, all windblown from riding, his buff leather breeches fitting him as tightly as Maggie's York tan leather gloves. His hair was lighter than it had been when she'd left Baltimore, all streaked with different shades of blond, and longer than it should be and really quite lovely, as were his green eyes, a green much more green than hers, deeper and darker and more pure.

"What the devil are you staring at?"

It didn't occur to her to lie to him. "You. You look very nice. I like all the different shades of blond in your hair."

She belatedly pulled the covers over her chest and pushed herself up in bed.

That gave him pause, but not much. "You still don't look the way I'm used to seeing you. Your hair is wild around your face, all tumbled about like you've had a lover in your bed, instead of pulled back so tightly your eyes look slitted." He stepped farther into the bedchamber, nudging Damper out the door with the toe of his black boot. "I've been riding with Marcus. You wore him out, he said, dancing his shoes off until he begged for mercy. He said you learned quickly, that you dance nearly as well as the Duchess. I didn't believe him, of course. It's time you got out of bed. It's nearly ten in the morning. I'm going to Candlethorpe. Would you like to come with me?"

"You're asking me to come to your English home?" she

said slowly, so excited it was difficult to keep her voice steady, but she wanted to be certain she'd heard him correctly. She didn't want him to know she was ready to throw off the covers and dance if he'd indeed asked her to his home.

"Yes, come with me. I don't trust you here without me. You just might tear off again to escape me."

"Oh." She didn't leap out of bed.

"How long will it take you to dress?"

"An hour."

"An hour? The old Jessie could be out of bed and in her trousers in ten minutes."

"You prefer the old Jessie?"

"Yes. No. I don't care. Just hurry."

"A moment, James. I'm an employed person now. I must ask the Duchess if I could have a day to myself."

"Actually, the Duchess suggested you accompany me to Candlethorpe. She said you'd been spending too much time with the children and she feared for your sanity. Hurry up."

He strode from her bedchamber, leaving her sitting up in her bed, wishing he'd left out all he'd said. A simple nod would have sufficed. She sighed as she pulled the bell cord.

It was closer to an hour and a half before Jessie came out of her bedchamber to see that elegant tall personage waiting for her, a smile on his face.

"Good morning," he said as he offered her his arm. "I understand you were a great success at the party last night. The earl and the Duchess said you sparkled and laughed."

She sighed. "That was last night. Have you seen James this morning, sir?"

"Oh yes. I was with him at breakfast early this morning. He was still full from stuffing himself with Mr. Badger's delicious late dinner, thus he was just fiddling with his porridge and sipping black coffee. He demanded to know what was going on here."

"What did you tell him, sir?"

"I told him that you were now a part of this household, that you were a young lady of excellent parts."

"He laughed, didn't he? Or cursed? That's more like James. He curses very fluently, every bit as well as the earl when Clancy bit him on Wednesday."

"As I recall, he just grunted."

"Then the Duchess told him to take me to Candle-thorpe," she said, looking briefly at a portrait of a long-ago Countess of Chase, who wore a massive white wig on her head decorated with three birds of undetermined species and a full-size nest.

"Spears, what the devil are you doing with Jessie?"

"I'm her lady's gentleman."

Jessie whirled around to face him. "You're Spears? *The Spears?*"

"I have that personal honor," Spears said, and gave her a slight bow.

"You promise you're not an earl or a duke?"

James shouted up to them, "Spears, did you tell her to take over an hour to make herself look like a trollop? Just look at her. That riding habit belongs to the Duchess—I recognize it. It looks ridiculous on Jessie. She's American, a hoyden. She doesn't wear such stylish—"

"I believe, James," Spears said in his very firm voice, even as he continued to guide Jessie down the wide stair-case, "that at the end of your verbal trail you will step off a cliff that will drop you directly into your grave."

James chewed on his lower lip. He cursed, then said with a sigh, "Perhaps you're right. What is this, Jessie? You didn't know this was Spears?"

"No. I thought he was a visiting earl or duke who felt sorry for me and helped me get around here." She lowered her voice and giggled. "We've got to cease meeting like this, James—at the foot of the staircase."

"Now you're sounding like a twit schoolgirl. That was a titter, and it came from you. You need to get home quickly, Jessie, before you become someone entirely different."

"I would say, James," Spears said as he released Jessie's arm at the bottom of the staircase and patted her gloved hand, "that Jessie is a woman who adapts well to her surroundings. Now, she must have her breakfast."

"But James wants to leave, Spears, and—"

"Your breakfast, Jessie."

"Yes, Spears."

Candlethorpe was a snug property, much smaller than Marathon, yet it looked as impressive and solid as the rolling surrounding hills. It looked as if it belonged exactly where it was, almost as if the stone and wood had long before blended into the landscape, becoming one with it. The house was at least two hundred years old, square, three stories high, red brick, not overly large, ah, but the stable was freshly painted, long and low, and very modern with fenced paddocks on each side of it. There were oak and elm trees all over, many of them so ancient-looking Jessie thought they'd probably been there in the Roman times.

"James, were the Romans here in Yorkshire?"

"Yes they were. There's quite a pretty village called Aldborough that was really a Roman city. Not much has been done to it, but there are two quite excellent mosaic pavements. Perhaps in the future they will find more. Why do you ask?"

"The trees. They look so old, they were probably here with the Roman centurions. It's very romantic, don't you think?"

James heard a horse whinny loudly and grinned. "That's Bellini, the most beautiful Arab I've ever seen in my life. Marcus gave him to me last year. He's already sired two fillies and three stallions. Come see him, Jessie."

Bellini was as black as a coal bin and surely as intelligent as James, Jessie told him as she patted the magnificent stallion's black nose. "He's a sweetheart."

"All the mares think so. Last winter, just before I came back to Baltimore, a mare from the Rothermere stud jumped poor Bellini. She kicked one of my stable lads badly when he tried to pull her off."

"You're making that up."

"No, no. Come meet everyone."

She met his head stable lad, Sigmund, who had come to James from Croft's stud just twenty miles away, a stud famous for its Byerley Turk blood.

"Stop drooling, Jessie," James said as he watched her pat every single horse, feed each one a carrot she'd snatched up from the bucket outside the stable, and tell them how very lucky they were.

"It's hard," she said, turning to smile at him. James froze. He didn't make a single move, utter a single noise. There was a shaft of sunlight coming over her shoulder from the open stable door, framing her hair, making the redness of it glisten like a sunset on the west coast of Ireland where James had visited a racing friend. She was smiling at him, and that hair of hers, in a simple braid, somehow looked different. He realized that it was looser, that there were myriad lazy curls framing her face. He turned away. He didn't like this at all.

"This is Caliper, an old fellow who's seen more changes than any other stallion in Yorkshire."

Caliper got two carrots and more pats from Jessie than he deserved.

"Come to the house now."

It was obvious to Jessie that the Duchess had overseen turning the inside of Candlethorpe into a livable dwelling. She wished she could tell James that she, Jessie, could do wonders with Marathon, if only . . . well, enough of that.

She shook her head and ran her hand over the top of a chair that was covered with lovely dark blue brocade. Very new dark blue brocade. There were two Aubusson carpets on the floor of the drawing room and several groupings of settees and chairs. There were several landscapes on the walls, but unlike Chase Park, there were no family portraits. The walls were freshly painted, a pale yellow, making the drawing room light and airy.

She met Mrs. Catsdoor and her son, Harlow, who took care of Candlethorpe when James was gone.

She met Mr. Goodbody, the gardener, and his undergardener, Carlos, who'd washed ashore off Scarsborough some five years before. He was from Spain, he told everyone in his broken English. He never gave any details.

"The gardens are beautiful," Jessie said as she stepped out the wide French doors that gave onto the east lawn, not even a fraction of the size of Chase Park, but quite lovely in high summer, hydrangeas, roses, hyacinths, daisies, all blooming madly. "The Duchess insisted," James said.

"You sound almost embarrassed. Isn't it manly to admire beauty?"

"The Duchess adores flowers. I let her have her way," James said, ignoring her question. He turned to face her. "Which do you prefer—Candlethorpe or Marathon?"

"I'd like to own both. Each is special in its own way. You won't sell either one of them, will you, James?"

"Not unless I go bankrupt. Would you like some lemonade?"

"What I'd really like is to ride Bellini."

He grinned down at her. "Perhaps on your next visit. He's a devil, though he acts charming enough when he wants to. Are you wearing stockings with that sinful riding outfit, Jessie?"

She didn't hesitate, just pulled up her riding skirt to show him pristine white stockings that disappeared into her black riding boots.

"The Duchess must be going bankrupt clothing you." He was frowning—why, she didn't understand. She thought it was a jest, nothing more, yet James had lost his sense of humor.

"No she's not. I'm paid two pounds a week. I plan to shop tomorrow and pay her back."

"Two pounds a week? What riches. She pays you the money to pay her back. Come now, you know you can't remain at Chase Park until you're old and doddering."

She walked away from him to touch the petals of a deep red rose. "I know," she said, not looking at him. She leaned down and inhaled deeply.

"What are you going to do?"

She turned now and stared up at the man she'd loved since she was fourteen years old. It had been hero-worship then, yes, she knew that now. James had been a god to her, perfect in all ways, a splendid being who occasionally smiled upon her, yelled at her, recognized that she needed a kind word sometimes and gave it freely. But then she'd grown up and seen that he was a man, not a god, but oddly enough her feelings for him had just grown stronger, more abiding. They had changed into something very deep, as deep as the Ft. Point reservoir.

But it didn't matter. James still looked at her as if she were fourteen years old, or a trollop in her new finery. No, it didn't matter.

"I think I will work for the Duchess and the earl for several years. I will save all my money. Then I will come home and buy my own stud. I will race horses and I will win."

He didn't laugh. She was surprised that he didn't. She was also thankful. She didn't think she could have borne it had he laughed. Nor did he sound remotely condescending as he said, "That will require a lot of money, Jessie. Two pounds a week is about forty dollars a month. In two years, if you saved every pence, you'd still have less than a thousand dollars."

"I know that. It will be enough. My father will surely sell me several stallions and mares at a cheap price. All I need is a start. I can grow and succeed just as you have."

He looked away from her then toward the rich-leafed maple trees that climbed up a rolling hill. "I had more help than you know, Jessie. I married a girl with a large dowry. I had a great deal more than a thousand dollars to start up the stud here. In fact, Alicia's father gave us Candlethorpe as a wedding present. So you see, Marathon had the chance to succeed just because I had ample funds to begin the stud here, and ample funds to lose money that first two years."

"How much money, James?"

"Alicia's dowry was nearly twenty thousand pounds."

Jessie did a fast calculation. "Goodness, James, that's much more than a hundred thousand dollars, that's almost—"

"Yes, I know. I'm a rich man because I just happened to fall in love with a girl whose father was a baronet and very rich. She was his only child. He loved her very much. He urges me to visit him. He thinks of me as his son, though the good Lord knows I don't deserve it. He doesn't blame me for Alicia's death, though I know his loss is great."

"Why should he blame you for her death?"

"I planted my seed in her womb. She died in childbirth, the babe with her. We hadn't even been married a year."

"I see."

"No, you don't, not really. You're young, Jessie, you've never considered a man as other than a competitor to beat at the races. You can't possibly know what it's like to, well, that's not important. So you see, money would be difficult."

"Why do you blame yourself for her death?"

"The doctor was a fool. He dithered. Her labor was difficult and long. I was banished from the bedchamber and told it was women's business. Foolishly I left only to return to hear her screams. When I got into the bedchamber, she was nearly dead. He'd let her die because he was too ignorant to know what to do. Since then I've done a lot of reading on childbirth, I've spoken to physicians in London. I know now that she could perhaps have been saved. If I had only taken the whole business more seriously, Alicia could still be alive today, our child as well."

Tears fell down her cheeks. She made no sound. James saw her shoulders shake and turned her to face him. "Tears, Jessie? I don't think I've ever seen you cry before. It happened over three years ago. I shouldn't have told you about it. Now, dry your tears. Jessie, please."

But she didn't. She lowered her face into her hands and cried harder. James cursed quietly, then pulled her against him. "Shush, Jessie. It was a long time ago. The pain's not close anymore. It's in the past where it belongs, all vague and blurry, not sharp and prodding anymore. Hush, you'll make yourself sick."

She raised her face and stared up at him. Slowly, she raised her arms and closed them around his neck. "James," she said only.

He didn't know why he did it, but he did. He lowered his head and kissed her mouth. Her closed mouth. Her very soft closed mouth that had just a light smear of the lip cream. He felt a shot of lust so strong, he trembled with it. Lust? With Jessie Warfield? It was ridiculous. He ran his tongue over her bottom lip, saying against her mouth, "Open your mouth just a little bit, Jessie. Yes, that's right."

The lust was incredible. It was piercing and powerful, and he simply lost his wits. He cupped her bottom in his hands and lifted her to press her against him. She froze like a rabbit in the sights of a fox.

He felt like a near-rapist. He immediately released her and gently pushed her back.

"I'm sorry. Forgive me."

She was staring at the buttons on his riding jacket. "You startled me. No one's ever done that to me before. Perhaps you shouldn't have let me down so quickly. Perhaps you should have let me grow accustomed to having your hands around my bottom. Perhaps—"

"Be quiet, Jessie. Damnation, I'm sorry. Despite your new plumage, you're still Jessie Warfield, and it wasn't good of me to attack you like that."

"It was a very nice attack. Perhaps you could kiss me again?"

"No," he said, then pulled her against him and kissed her, not a very gentle kiss, but one that was hot and wet and—She giggled into his mouth. He drew back and smiled down at her. "I made you laugh?"

"I dreamed about you last night. I dreamed you were kissing me, that it was hot and very wet and that you were pulling me tightly against your chest. When I woke up, it was Damper sitting on me and licking my nose."

He dropped his hands to his sides. "You conjure me up in your dreams when a damned dog licks your nose. That puts me in my place."

"Oh no. I can't imagine you sitting on my chest." She stared up at his mouth and swallowed. "Again, please, James?"

"No," he said more violently than he'd meant to. "It's time for luncheon. Come along. Mrs. Catsdoor will have prepared something for us."

# === 15 ===

HE FELT AS if he were standing in front of a tribunal. All they needed were those rolled white wigs on their heads and long, thin noses. He wondered if Maggie could ever be convinced to cover her glorious hair with one of those things. Probably, if she cared enough. He wasn't actually standing in a docket. He was seated on a gilt chair given to him by the Duchess, in his own drawing room, drinking Mrs. Catsdoor's tea. The tribunal were all staring at him over their teacups. A silver tray lovingly loaded by Mrs. Catsdoor with small delicately trimmed cucumber sandwiches and slivers of lemon cake hadn't been touched. He knew she'd prepared them to impress Badger, whom she held in awe. He wondered if Badger knew that Mrs. Catsdoor admired him excessively, and that admiration had nothing to do with his cooking. They continued to stare at him. He felt like a criminal.

"All right, out with it," James said. "Why are you here? What have I done now?"

Spears lay down his cup of tea and cleared his throat. "James, we came to Candlethorpe today because we've discussed the situation thoroughly and have come to a decision."

"Did you tell Marcus and the Duchess your decision first?"

"No, we're telling you first," Badger said.

"What situation?"

Maggie smoothed her brilliant emerald green satin skirts as she said, "You've grown up into a fine man, James. That's what I told Jessie and I mean it. We're all very proud of you. However, it's time for you to get a good hold on yourself and do the *Right Thing*."

"The *Right Thing*?"

"Yes, James," Sampson said, the judge of the tribunal. "We also agree that you know our decision first. It concerns you, not his lordship or the Duchess. It does concern them, but not as directly as it does you."

"Just what is this *Right Thing*, if I may inquire?" James rose to stroll over to the fireplace. It gave him an illusory sense of freedom to be able to walk even across his own drawing room. The grate was empty, swept clean. He leaned negligently against the mantelpiece, his arms crossed over his chest, which was difficult since he was still holding his teacup. "Come, Spears, spit it out."

"Very well, James," Spears said, and rose, all austere as a judge ready to deliver his verdict. He took three measured steps, then turned to face all of them. He cleared his throat. Garrick acting on Drury Lane couldn't have done it better. He said, "We believe you should marry Jessie."

James stared at him. He'd known all along what they meant by that *Right Thing* business, but he just hadn't wanted to accept it. Now it was all said, all out in the open. He'd not wanted to confront it like this, well, perhaps he already had in the deepest recesses of his brain, but he'd dismissed it. Surely he had. He didn't ever want to consider such a thing, at least not when he was fully conscious. He stared some more. He fidgeted. Finally, he spoke. "This is none of your collective business. Jessie has nothing to do with any of you. She has nothing to do with me. She's whined to you that I ruined her? I didn't ruin her. I had nothing to do with anything. When I didn't ruin her, when

I told her father I hadn't ruined her, he still kept after me. It was Jessie who refused to let it continue. So she's changed her tune now, has she? Now she wants not only my hide, she also wants my name?"

Maggie studied her thumbnail, then turned the wedding ring slowly, ever so slowly around her finger. "That is quite the stupidest thing I've ever heard you say, James. Jessie is innocent; she's extremely vulnerable; she's in a foreign country; she still doesn't know what's good for her, though our hints have become a mite more specific over the past three days. She'll go to her grave protecting you, or trying to. She hasn't changed any tune. I don't think she even wants to marry you."

"You see? I was right. She has no interest in me at all."

Badger cleared his throat. "As Miss Maggie was about to point out, the only reason Jessie won't hear of marrying you is because she believes you don't even like her. I believe, Miss Maggie, that you made that telling point last evening over my dessert of stewed pears and sponge cake."

"Damn all of you meddlers! You want the truth? Very well. I rarely like her. I can count on my left hand the number of times I've liked her more than rarely."

Spears cleared his throat. He waited until all the murmuring had died down. He waited until all eyes were on him. Then he said, "We questioned Jessie closely. She was shut down as tightly as a clam protecting its innards. All she would allow was that she found Candlethorpe splendid. We all found that observation very telling."

"What the hell does that mean? *Telling?* That tells me she's got eyes in her head and a modicum of sense. Candlethorpe is an excellent property. Why shouldn't she acknowledge that?"

Sampson and his wife, Maggie, exchanged glances. Badger was studying those delicate slivers of lemon cake. He ate one, chewed for a very long time, his eyes half closed, then nodded to himself. Spears looked more austere than ever.

"This is gaining us nothing," Badger said, the lemon cake forgotten, his voice now colder than James had ever heard it. "Listen, Mr. Spears, let us just lay the cards on the table. James, you must marry Jessie Warfield. You will do it immediately. There is no other choice. She will never be able to return to the Colonies with her head up unless you do. Regardless of your part in it, she's the one who is blamed. If you're a gentleman, you will put things to right and you will do it very soon."

"James," Maggie said, fingering the exquisite emerald earrings that dangled from her white ears, "Jessie has loved you since she was a girl. She will make you a splendid wife."

"She hasn't liked me any more than I've liked her, Maggie. You're quite wrong."

Sampson cleared his throat. "Are we in error to assume you are no more mourning your late wife?"

"Yes," Badger said. "If you're still mourning her then we've a problem."

"No, I'm not still mourning Alicia. She's been dead for over three years. I have learned to live without her. All of you know it was difficult for me for a very long time, but no longer. My life is full to brimming. I don't want another wife. I don't want an American girl who's a hoyden, who many times beats me in races and who's changed her stripes completely and now dresses like a damned trollop since she crossed the hallowed threshold of Chase Park."

"She's beautiful," Maggie said, as indignant as Clorinda when Fred the peacock managed to sneak up on her and get in a free peck. "She just needed a bit of adjusting, that's all. Certainly she doesn't look like a trollop. That's very unfair of you, James."

"She doesn't look like herself. At least I knew what to

expect when she looked like herself, but no longer. She shouldn't have been adjusted, she didn't need it, I didn't need it. Just the other day I was noticing that even with her hair in a braid, it's not all slicked back as tight as stretched material the way it used to be. You've taught her to have those silly little female curls dangling down on either side of her face. She couldn't strut around in her breeches and race with those silly little curls.''

"I call them streamers," Maggie said.

Spears said, "We've gotten far afield here. You will marry her, James. It's imperative. Do you want her to remain an employee of his lordship and the Duchess for the rest of her life? It would be a blight on your good name. It isn't fair that his lordship and the Duchess be responsible for her until she becomes an old woman and passes on. She deserves much more. She has wit and spice and good sound common sense. Marry her.''

"Aye, do it.''

"Hear, hear.''

"How about next week? The Duchess and I can manage it. Ah, I know just the wedding gown for her. I've pictured it in my mind. You will be immensely pleased, James.''

"I'm sure it's a treat, love," Sampson said, and kissed his wife's soft white hand.

Badger ate one of the dainty cucumber sandwiches. This time he frowned ever so slightly.

James threw his teacup at the wall.

Jessie walked into the nursery, Charles in her arms, tickling him and telling him he would break female hearts when he gained but another year to his ticket, telling him that little females would find his gnawing on anything that didn't move fast enough quite charming. She nearly ran into James, who was standing just inside the doorway, staring at her with acute dislike.

"James! What are you doing here?"

"Where have you been?"

"Charles wanted to see his mama's roses. They're beautiful, particularly the red ones, just like velvet—"

"Shut up, Jessie. You know very well why I'm here, damn you."

Charles looked at James then back at Jessie. His chin trembled. "Don't raise your voice," she said, bouncing Charles up and down in her arms. "There, little love, it's all right. Your cousin James is just a bit like a volcano. He blows up, then cools. The cooling part is all right, but the other—"

"Shut up, Jessie," he said, this time in a near whisper. He held out his arms to Charles. That insensitive little tot gurgled in delight and went right to him.

"It isn't fair. Have you ever burped him? Has he ever wet on your shirt?"

"Once he did," James said, rocking Charles. "Wet on me, that is. My little godson recognizes I'm a man. He knows men should be in charge of their lives, should make their own decisions. He knows that I can't, thus he feels sorry for me and he's comforting me in the only way he knows how. He's pulling my hair and drooling on my neck."

"What do you mean you're not in charge of your life? You've got Candlethorpe and Marathon both. What more do you want or need? You probably even have a Connie Maxwell over here in England. It's true, isn't it, James? What's her name? Stop shaking your head—I'll never believe you. My mother always said that men are driven to seek out all sorts of females because their natures are unsteady. What are you talking about, James?"

"That gown you're wearing should make you look more like the old Jessie, but it doesn't."

"That's because it fits me. It isn't too short nor is it baggy in the bosom."

"I like the color on you. I wouldn't have thought you'd look decent in gray, but you do. You look modest, at least from the neck down. As for those streamers all around your face—"

"You've been speaking to Maggie."

"Yes, she corrected me. She said they aren't curls, they're streamers."

"What about them?"

It was at that instant he knew she was afraid he was going to insult her streamers, call them ridiculous. He wanted to. He wanted to tell her she was a blight, that he didn't want to marry her, that he just wished he'd never met her. Because if he hadn't seen her striding beside a quarter horse some six years before at the Weymouth racecourse, then lost to her in the third bloody race, she would never have been in that blasted tree to fall on him and ruin herself. She would never have run off to England.

Instead, he said, "The streamers are charming. But when you race, the wind will blow them into your eyes. You will have to be careful."

"You really like them, James?"

Her voice was so wistful that James gave Charles an unexpected squeeze, with the result that Charles gave a big burp. James rubbed his back. Charles obligingly burped again.

"The Duchess just fed him," Jessie said. "You do that well."

"I like children. Would you like to walk with me in the Duchess's rose garden?"

They left Charles sucking his thumb as he fell asleep in his crib.

The afternoon was cloudy, the summer air heavy.

"A rain will clear everything up soon," James said for

want of anything better. Jessie was walking beside him, her head down, staring at the toes of her slippers.

"Rain is usually a good thing," he said, frowning at her profile.

She looked up at him then. "What do you want, James?"

"Didn't Spears, Badger, Maggie, and Sampson tell you?"

"No, they just caught me one day in the kitchen and asked me all sorts of questions until my eyes crossed."

"It's their collective specialty. They're quite good. Damn their eyes, they're usually right. Even when you want to shoot them, you end up brooding, sitting alone in the dark, unable to sleep, because you know they're right."

"They spoke to you?"

He decided she didn't need to know they'd all trooped over to Candlethorpe, leaving Chase Park defenseless, and trapped him in his drawing room. It would hurt her to know that they'd come after his skin, wanting to nail him to the altar. Dammit, it would hurt her, he had no doubt that it would, and for some reason, he didn't want to hurt her.

"They're always speaking to me," he said, sounding irritated. "They've tried to improve my character for the past seven years."

"Have they succeeded?"

He frowned at that. "You know, I'm not certain, but perhaps they have in some ways."

"The Duchess's roses are exquisite."

"Yes, everything she touches turns exquisite except for Marcus. She says that's just fine because she likes him offensive. She says it keeps her mental works well oiled when he's being himself."

"Why are they so nice to me, James?"

He looked up to see the rain clouds nearing. He said, cutting to the chase, "Because they're fond of me and they're fond of you and they believe we will wed." There, he'd said the word. He plunged ahead. "Would you like to marry me, Jessie?"

There, it was done, only the result wasn't quite what he'd expected. She jerked as though he'd just kicked her. Then she blinked as if awakening from a dream. She turned on her heel and walked away—well, she walked for about three feet, and then she picked up the skirts of her modest gray gown and broke into an Old Jessie run, flying across the ground, faster than most boys, her petticoats white and flounced, flapping about her ankles, which were encased in lovely white stockings. Even lovelier white slippers were on her feet. He was used to seeing those feet only in boots, sturdy, ugly boots.

"Jessie! Dammit, wait!" He was off after her. He got a slap in the face by a low-hanging elm-tree branch. He cursed the tree and her and kept running. He caught up with her near the small lake. She was leaning against a tree, her arms around it, hugging it, her face pressed against the bark.

"Jessie," he said once he had caught his breath. "Why the devil did you run away from me? You're going to scratch your face if you keep shoving yourself against that bark."

She didn't move, just seemed to press herself more tightly against that damned tree.

"Don't you want to marry me, Jessie? Is that it?"

Her silence continued. He felt his irritation blossoming like one of the Duchess's roses after it had been well manured. "Why, damn you? I've known you since you were fourteen years old and looked like a knobby-kneed boy except you didn't, not with all that flyaway red hair that never stayed hidden beneath those disreputable old hats of yours. I know you so well that I always know when you're lying. You're no good at it. I know you don't have any breasts, at least I thought I knew, but after seeing you in that trollop ball gown with your breasts falling over the top, I'll have to think about that some more. You can scrub down a horse and a stable nearly as fast as Oslow. You know horses, nearly as well as I do. You ride, nearly as well as I do. You race—again, sometimes nearly as well as I do.''

''I've beaten you regularly, James, over the past six years.''

''Ah, so that got you a mite testy, huh? Now that you've turned around and given me the courtesy of facing me, well then, will you marry me?''

''You want to marry me because you know when I'm lying?''

''There are other reasons. I've already listed them. We would deal well together. We share the same aims—we want to race and own studs, which I already do, and with marriage you would be part of it, too.''

''These are damnable reasons, James.'' This said, she turned her face back against the tree. ''Go away. I have nothing more to say to you. You didn't ruin me. I'm not your responsibility. I told you what I planned to do with my future. I will own my own stud and racing stable. I will succeed.''

''You have about as much chance of success as Charles does in growing a complete set of teeth in the next week. Don't be an ass about this, Jessie.''

''I see it clearly now,'' she said slowly, turning to look up at him again. ''Spears and company came to see you. They told you that you had to marry me. That's it, isn't it?''

''No.''

''This was all your own idea?''

''Yes.'' Distraction, he thought, that was what he needed, and thank the good Lord he had it. He didn't think he was a much better liar than Jessie. ''I've got a letter from your father for you.''

Thunder cracked overhead. It was midafternoon and the sky was a muddy gray, darkening by the minute.

That brought her around. "A letter from Papa?"

"Yes, he gave it to me to give to you. Do you want to read it?"

"Have you read it?"

"Naturally not. It's addressed to you."

She frowned as she opened the envelope and pulled out a single sheet of folded paper. She read:

*My dearest Jessie:*

*I hope James has found you and you're safe and well. I am more worried about you than I can say. You must marry James and come home as soon as possible. If dear James hasn't yet come to reason, you must propose to him. He's a gentleman. He'll accept you. Come home, Jessie—*

*Your loving father,*
*Oliver Warfield*

Without a word, she handed the letter to James. She didn't look at him while he read it. She couldn't bear to see the disgust on his face. She looked up to see that the sky was now nearly black. They would never make it back to the house before the heavens opened up and made a good effort to drown them. She pushed off the tree and began walking back toward Chase Park.

James fell in beside her. He was looking thoughtful, not particularly angry. "Would you have proposed to me, Jessie?" he asked at last, "if I hadn't proposed to you?"

"No."

He shook his head, took her hand, and said, "Let's hurry. Your streamers won't weather this storm well."

Jessie picked up her skirts again and ran beside James, laughing even as the first raindrop fell on her nose. They came around the corner of the great mansion to see Fred closing in on Clorinda, her tail feathers pressed against the stone.

"Fred, you lecher," Jessie shouted. "Let her go."

James was laughing as Fred turned on them and squawked as loudly as the next clap of thunder. James grabbed Jessie's arm and pulled her along with him. "He might attack us for our interference with his ladylove. Come along, we're nearly to a door."

They were just a bit damp when they rushed through the long glass doors in the massive Chase Park library.

"The letter," Jessie said. "Where is it?"

"I tucked it in my pocket to keep it dry." They both turned to the long glass doors when there was another loud clap of thunder. A streak of lightning sliced through the sky. The rain was coming down in earnest now.

"That was close," Jessie said, patting a curl that curved around her cheek. "I think my streamers survived."

"Yes, they did." He wrapped one streamer around his finger. It was softer than it should be, even damp. When he released it, it fell lazily over her ear down to her neck. "But you must take care. You don't want to risk Maggie's displeasure, though she normally doesn't have to show any."

"Do you really think I look like a trollop when I'm wearing clothes that fit me?"

James wiped his hand across his forehead. Sweat and rain, he thought. Jessie could always run fast. "Jessie," he said finally, "have you ever seen a trollop?"

She gave that profound thought. He guided her to the fireplace, where a fire blazed cheerfully. "Warm yourself," he said, rubbing his hands together.

She shook out her skirts, saying, "I don't think I've ever seen a trollop. Do they truly look like I do when I look nice?"

"No, they look tawdry and garish, things like that. They look obvious, their clothing an advertisement to men."

She swallowed, not looking at him, just shaking those skirts of hers more than they needed to be shaken.

"No, you don't look like a trollop," he said with a deep sigh. "Are you going to propose to me, Jessie, if I tell you that my proposal was a sham?"

"No. I would never do that to you."

"Why not?"

She sat down on the floor and stretched her hands toward the fire. "It's no great mystery, James. You don't love me. I want to marry someone who loves me for what I am— both the new Jessie and the old Jessie. My father loves me but that's different, isn't it? I'm an excellent employee and he doesn't have to pay me anything, just feed me and give me a place to sleep." She eased back a couple of feet from the fire and settled her skirts around her legs.

"I think you're being harsh."

"Perhaps. But it doesn't change anything. I simply have to realize what I can have and what I can't have."

"Do you want to have children?"

"Yes, but that's something I probably won't have. A husband is necessary first."

He turned on her then, and she realized he was quite angry. It surprised her. "Damn you, why do you think so little of yourself? Look at you, you're lovely in a modest sort of way." He stalled.

"I know," she said.

"Stop sounding like a whipped hound. Stop trying to sound so reasonable, so self-effacing. Why don't you want to sacrifice me to cancel out your ruination? I'm here. I've asked you to sacrifice me."

He came down beside her, grabbed her arms, toppled her backward, and came down over her.

# —≡ 16 ≡—

JESSIE WAS A good fighter. She brought her legs up and struck him in the back, then slammed her fists into his shoulders and chest. He flattened himself over her, grabbed that braid of hers to hold her still, leaned down, and kissed her.

She jerked her head to the side and he missed the first time. He got her chin, then the tip of her nose, then finally her mouth.

"Stop it, James. You're pulling my hair out."

That got his tongue into her mouth, but for only an instant. He barely escaped with his tongue still intact. She was really mad, he thought, if she were willing to bite off his tongue. He reared up on his elbows, not trying to force her anymore. He leaned up just a bit and stared down at her.

"Your hair smells like lavender and rain."

"Go to the devil, James. That's drivel. I don't know what you're thinking, but this is—"

He leaned down quickly and kissed her again. He managed to push her legs apart and came down to lie between them. He closed his eyes at the feel of her. He could feel the heat even through her gown and her petticoats. He pressed down and she gasped.

"Will you rape me in the damned library, you idiot?"

James shook his head. He looked bemused. "I'm ruining you but good. It's better when the man's on top and trying to stick his tongue in the woman's mouth and pressing himself against her belly. Yes, this is the right way to ruin a woman. I never much considered it before, but you feel good, Jessie. Don't you like me against you? Can you feel me?'' He knew she could. He was harder than the leg of that gilt chair just a foot away from him.

"Yes, and it's strange. You're just like a stallion, aren't you?''

"More or less, but not really, which is something for which you should be profoundly grateful. Now, Jessie, will you marry me?''

"No, nothing's changed. All you feel now is a bit of lust. My mother has told all her daughters about men and their lust. She says that a gentleman's lust is usually the only thing a female can exploit to get her way. She says that all men feel lust with great regularity. Even after they're wedded, she says, their lust doesn't stay at home where it should.''

"Your mother should be shot.''

"It isn't true?''

"No, well, perhaps a bit of it. Why the devil do you think Glenda is always leaving her breasts very nearly naked? No, don't struggle anymore. I'm trying to keep some of my weight off you. If you try to hurt me more, I'll flatten you. Do you want to know what else Glenda does? She stares at a man's crotch. My crotch has been stared at more times by your sister than any other crotch in Baltimore, so don't go on and on about how men are the predators, always on the lookout for new females.''

"Is my mama wrong?''

"Sometimes.'' He pressed himself hard against her simply because he couldn't seem to help himself. "Where is the damned bell cord?''

She punched him in the jaw, not all that hard, but hard enough to get his attention. He reared back, managed to grab her arms, and pinned them to her sides. "It does no good to ruin you in this obvious sort of way if there isn't someone to catch us at it. Damn, where is that bell cord?''

"I fancy, James, that you are no longer in need of one. I am here. Mr. Badger is here. Mr. Sampson and Maggie are here as well. We are pleased."

Jessie looked up to see them closing in a circle around her, all smiling and nodding with satisfaction.

"You may get off her now, James," Badger said. "The deed has been done."

"I don't think she's properly ruined yet," James said. "Could one of you fetch the Duchess or his lordship?"

"I will bring both of them," Sampson said. "Remain as you are, James. I will return shortly and it will be done."

"I can't believe all of you are just standing around letting James lie on top of me. He's kissed me and even tried to stick his tongue in my mouth. Why aren't you doing anything?"

"We are doing something," Badger said, a sweet smile on that ugly face of his. "And I've prepared some delicious crimped cod and oyster sauce for our celebration dinner."

"I tasted it," Maggie said, tapping one lovely violet slipper against the Aubusson carpet. "Mr. Badger, you have outdone yourself again."

"James, damn you, let me up!"

"Jessie, your language isn't what your soon-to-be husband would appreciate," Maggie said, twitching her lovely violet satin gown away from James's boot. "My Glenroyale — that's Mr. Sampson's first name — says that an occasional explicative, uttered in moments of extreme excitement, is acceptable, but this isn't one of those times."

"No, it isn't, Maggie," Spears said. "Ah, I do believe I hear them all coming. Perhaps you'd best improve upon your current tableau, James."

James grinned down at Jessie, then kissed her closed mouth. He was still kissing her with mounting enthusiasm when the Duchess and Marcus strode through the door on Sampson's heels.

"Well," the Duchess said, coming to make up part of the circle surrounding the pair on the carpet. "James, dear, I'm not all that certain that Jessie is still breathing."

"Let your mouth up a bit, James," Marcus said, coming down on his haunches. "I remember I had to teach the Duchess how to kiss properly. It took a while, but she's fairly proficient at it now. Before, though, she turned quite blue in the face, just as blue as Jessie's face is now."

James raised himself up on his elbows, still looking down at her. "Well, Jessie, are you now sufficiently ruined?"

"I'll kill you, James. This is horribly embarrassing."

"She was breathing, Marcus," James said, and lowered his head again. She tried to get away from him, but he finally found her mouth and stayed there.

"It does appear she's breathing through her nose," Badger said. "We all told James that Jessie's a good sort," he added to the Duchess. "We assured him that she'd make him a fine wife."

Jessie turned blue, not from want of air, but from rage. She began to struggle, catching James by surprise, truth be told. He was so busy enjoying the taste of her that he'd momentarily forgotten what he was doing. She managed to get one arm free and box his left ear. He yowled and fell off of her.

She immediately bounced to her feet, staring down at him, shaking her fist, her foot raised to strike him, but she thought better of it at the last minute and yelled, "You wretched liar! You told me that they hadn't talked to you about marrying me. They nailed you, didn't they? Played on your guilt, made me sound like a sorry, pathetic female who would probably wander off and dive from a cliff. Damn you, James, you told me it was all your idea."

"Oh dear," Badger said. "I'm very sorry, James. An unwary tongue isn't what this situation required. I do hope my poor crimped cod and oyster sauce isn't in jeopardy now."

"The road to true love shouldn't be strewn with rose petals," Maggie said. "Just look at his lordship and the Duchess."

"I would have preferred just one or two rose petals, Maggie," the Duchess said, to which her husband replied, "That doesn't sound like such a bad idea, Duchess. I can see you walking across the bedchamber to me, your white feet all bare, as well as the rest of you, the soles being caressed by some of Maggie's petals. What do you think?"

"I think, my lord," Spears said, "that your levity is singularly misplaced at this particular moment in time. James has a problem now because of Mr. Badger's unfortunate lapse. Jessie isn't happy with him."

James came up on his hands and knees, shaking his head. "Maggie, that was the most god-awful metaphor I've ever heard in my life. True love and rose petals? As for you, Marcus, your digressing to the bedchamber is just like you. I suppose next you'd nibble the rose petals that stuck to the Duchess's feet. As for you, Jessie, you've made my ear ring." He shook his head and gently rubbed his ear with his hand. "What do you say about that?"

Jessie was slowly backing away from all of them. "I'm leaving. This is bedlam. James doesn't want to marry me. Why won't all of you just accept that? Obviously you've made him feel so guilty that he forced himself to propose to me. When I said no and saved him from himself, he forced himself to fall on me and hold me down. He even forced himself to kiss me until I didn't fight him anymore."

"Damn you, Jessie, how do you think I got as hard as that fireplace iron if I wasn't interested?"

"I'm sorry about your crimped cod, Badger." She ran to the glass doors, pushed one of them open, and dashed into the storm.

"Oh damn," James said. "I've got to catch her again. She's fast, even in her skirt and petticoats. Badger, get some hot tea ready. She's only wearing those ladylike little slippers. Her feet are probably already wet."

"Wet clothes," his lordship said as he watched his American cousin run out into the storm, "and the subsequent removal of them tend to lead most usually to interesting afternoon diversions."

"We'll see, my lord," Spears said. "Mr. Badger, let's get some blankets and that hot tea. I hope neither of them becomes ill through all this excess of emotion."

"Jessie will ruin her streamers," Maggie said, and touched her fingers to the soft curls that lovingly hovered over her white ears.

He cornered her in the Chase Park stables, trying to get a saddle on Clancy's broad back. It wasn't that the saddle was too heavy. Clancy was seventeen hands high, and she simply couldn't heave the saddle up onto his back. She dropped the saddle, stomped her foot, and cursed. As for Clancy, that brute of a stallion who had been known to throw the earl a good dozen times in fits of pique, was neighing softly, nudging Jessie's shoulder with his nose—all in all, behaving like a besotted swain or an obsequious pet. James imagined that the bloody horse would have collapsed onto his knees so she could hug him better if he'd had the brains to realize it.

"You aren't going anywhere, Jessie. Why did you pick Clancy? He's a brute, he could kill you if he had a mind to do so, and you can't even get a saddle on his back. Just look what you've done to him—you've broken his spirit. Why, he'd lick your face if he thought about it. Give him one final pat and let's go back to the house."

"No."

"Jessie, you will do as I tell you. I'm tired of chasing you. I'd forgotten you're like a mountain goat. I'm tired. So just stop all these dramatics and come back with me to the house.''

''House, ha! It's a bloody mansion. It has more rooms than an entire block of houses in Baltimore.''

He stared at her a moment, bemused.

''Clancy isn't a brute. He's a sweetheart.''

''That's what the Duchess says about Marcus. Oh God, you haven't tried to ride Clancy, have you?''

''Naturally. We've had great rides. He's shown me the countryside.''

''You're telling me Marcus allowed this?''

''He doesn't know. Lambkin allowed that it was better not to awaken his lordship's choler.''

''Jessie, you're soaked. I'm soaked. You're not going anywhere. Come along with me now.''

''Will you try to pin me to the floor again?''

''No, not the floor. The next time I pin you it will be to a bed.''

She picked up the saddle and threw it at him, only to have it fall several feet short.

He leaned back against the stall, careful not to irritate Clancy, who was rolling his eyes at the sight of that flying saddle, and said, ''Just look at what you've become. You put on a gown and you lose all your strength. Your streamers are plastered to your head. The bodice of your gown is plastered to your breasts. That looks interesting. Perhaps I can flatten you against this stall.''

He took a step toward her, looking wet and wicked. She ducked beneath Clancy and came up on the other side.

''Are you out of your damned mind? Clancy could hurt you, Jessie. Come along, now, at least let's get out of this stall.''

She'd already decided that. Clancy liked her, she knew that, but she also knew he found humans occasionally irritating. His tail was beginning to twitch. She patted his neck, kissed his nose, and slipped out of the stall, James on her heels.

He caught her arm before she could break into a run.

"Enough," he said. He pulled her against him. She was trembling—undoubtedly from the wet and cold. He ran his large hands down her back. Her back didn't feel like a lanky girl's. It was disconcerting. Her breasts didn't belong to a lanky girl, either.

He breathed in the scent of her, nibbled on her ear, the wet streamer sticking to his mouth, and said, "Marry me, Jessie. Let's just get it done."

She was crying. That's why she was trembling. He pushed her back against his arm and raised her chin with his fingers. "Why?"

She made no sound. The tears just welled out of her eyes and fell over her cheeks to her chin. "You cry well, Jessie, but tell me why you're crying? Are you giving up? Do you have to think of this as losing to me? Actually, we're both winning, if you'd but give your brain a chance to think all this through."

She leaned her forehead against his shoulder. He knew when she'd stopped crying. She stood very still. Then she said quietly against the wet batiste of his shirt, "James, you're the only man who's ever kissed me."

He grinned as he kissed the top of her wet head. "I'll kiss you until we both cock up our toes if you'll let me."

She stepped back and looked up at him. "I'll let you. But first I want you to agree to something."

He was still. He didn't think he was going to like this and he was right, even as he said, "Agree to what?"

"You're like a dog with a bone in his mouth and you won't stop until you've gnawed it—or me—to death. You're now looking at this situation as if it's a race to be won. You've got to beat me, to make me yield. It doesn't matter any longer if you truly believe that what you're doing is right. It's beyond that. I should have said yes immediately. Then you probably would have paled, stammered that you'd made a ghastly mistake, and scuttled off. But I didn't. I turned you down, and you couldn't bear that.''

"What's your damned point, Jessie? What do you want me to agree to?''

She drew a deep breath, pulled one of her streamers off her cheek, and said, "I look at marriage as forever, James. I know that men do, too, but they are incapable of remaining faithful to one woman, namely their wives. Since you don't love me, you will tire of me quickly, then you'll want to go back to Connie Maxwell or to any number of other women. I'm willing to accept this as long as you agree to allow me the same courtesy. When I tire of you, I can take lovers. I don't want any lies between us.''

"That's a lot of things you've said, Jessie. Let me take the most basic thing first. You can't take lovers. Unlike a man, you can get pregnant. I won't claim another man's child.''

"Oh, I hadn't thought of that. Isn't there a way not to conceive a child?''

"Yes, there are several ways.''

"Well?''

"You wouldn't understand even if I told you.''

"So you're saying the women you'd have sex with would know how to prevent conceiving your child.''

"Yes, but there are always accidents.''

"Then surely a prospective lover would exercise equal care. One assumes that a man who's unfaithful to his wife wouldn't want his mistresses to give birth to his bastards.''

"You will take no lovers, Jessie.''

"If you won't, then I won't.''

James plowed his fingers through his wet hair. "Damnation, I don't believe this. Clancy just nudged my shoulder. He thinks I'm bloody crazy to stand here listening to this nonsense flowing from your ignorant mouth. No, just shut up, Jessie. Let me tell you about Connie Maxwell. She wouldn't be my lover if I were married. Does that surprise you?''

''I suppose it does. If I were she, I believe I wouldn't be able to turn you away.''

He sucked in his breath as if he'd been punched in the belly. ''Be quiet. I can't take much more of this. Now we're both soaked. I don't wish to have either of us contract an inflammation of the lung. Let's go back to the house now.''

She fell in beside him, silent now, looking straight ahead. The rain was still falling, more lightly now, becoming a fine drizzle. A fog rose, as if shoved up from the bowels of the earth, shrouding everything in a soft, gray veil. They heard Fred chortle what he must have thought was a fine mating call. It sounded like a buzzard in its death throes.

Jessie laughed.

James looked at her, but she didn't explain. He took her hand. They continued walking to the house, hand in hand.

Neither of them succumbed to a cold. When they went into the kitchen, the tribunal was waiting for them, armed for any disaster.

''Here you are,'' Badger said. ''We hoped you'd come into the kitchen. Now, we have dressing gowns for both of you. Jessie, you go first into the pantry and take off those wet things. Then you, James. Then you'll have hot tea and some delicious apples à la Portugaise, a recipe I just received in the post from a Frog chef who lives in Rouen.''

''Then we'll discuss your wedding,'' Spears said. ''His lordship will speak with Mr. Bagley, our curate. Oh dear, we must post bans, and that will take three weeks. None of us wishes to wait that long.''

''James, with his lordship's assistance, a special license can be procured,'' Badger said.

"I've already spoken to the Duchess about your wedding dress, Jessie," Maggie said.

Sampson poked his head into the kitchen. "I've alerted his lordship and the Duchess that you're both here."

The earl peered over Sampson's shoulder. "Well? Are we to fetch Mr. Bagley?"

"Yes," James said.

"Yes," Jessie said.

"Perhaps," Marcus said to James, "you'd care to tell me how you won the day? Did you do something romantic and dashing? Did you perhaps pin her in the wet grass and teach her how to breathe? Or did you protect her from the rain and caress her until she was panting for you?"

"My dear husband," the Duchess said, slipping around him and Sampson, "I believe Jessie is a bit flushed—no wonder, since you never seem to curb your thoughts before they become words."

"She loves it," the earl said. "Just look at her. Her eyes are nearly crossed. She's staring at James. We'd best get them married as quickly as possible before she flings him to the kitchen floor and has her way with him."

"A special license," James said. "Just tell me what to do, Marcus, and I'll see to it."

Spears said, "While you and Jessie are changing into dry dressing gowns we will discuss what is to be done. Then we will tell you."

James threw a towel at Spears, who looked eloquently pained.

The earl laughed. "I'm hungry, Badger. Do you have any of those currant dumplings left over from luncheon?"

# $=17=$

A thoroughbred and a husband: both must have uncommon endurance, boundless nerve and heart.

—COMMON WISDOM

"I WILL," JAMES said, and looked expectantly down at Jessie, who was remarkably pale even with the rich emerald green wedding gown that made her shoulders look more creamy than he would have believed possible. Emerald green. An excellent color on her. It made her hair seem even brighter. He realized that during the past five days things like this had been sticking in his mind.

He'd bought her a pair of white slippers to replace the ones ruined during her escapes from him in the rain. He remembered her reaction when he'd handed her the new slippers wrapped in silver paper. She'd looked down at the lovely white shoes and become completely still. "They'll fit you, Jessie," the Duchess had said. "Maggie and I traced out your own shoes for Mr. Dobbs, the cobbler." Still, Jessie had just looked down at those white slippers. Then she'd looked up at him, and he would have sworn that she was afraid of something, which was surely unlike Jessie. Afraid of what? "Thank you, James," she'd said, then she'd turned around and walked off.

The Duchess said with a sigh, "She's off to see Charles

again. He doesn't make her feel frightened or unsure, you know,'' to which James had said nothing himself, turned around, and walked off himself.

He looked down at her now while the Bishop of York, that exalted personage who'd agreed to conduct the ceremony as a favor to the powerful Earl of Chase, exhorted her to obey her husband. James would have preferred Mr. Bagley, but Marcus had decided they needed to have the ceremony presided over by one of the highest in the land. Two whimsical streamers curled lazily down over Jessie's ears. White, delicate ears. He'd never imagined that Jessie Warfield could have white, delicate ears.

So much had changed since that day and yet so little. She'd become a Jessie even the new Jessie didn't resemble. She was restrained, that was it; she didn't say a word unless directly spoken to, and surely that wasn't either the old or the new Jessie. Perhaps she was trying to be like the Duchess. She wasn't succeeding, if that was her aim. She avoided James after he gave her the new slippers, spending most of her time with Charles and Anthony. James wasn't troubled. So busy was he with his horses at Candlethorpe, he was frankly relieved Jessie didn't look hurt or reproachful when he finally did come to Chase Park on those days when the Duchess sent him invitations to dine. He couldn't imagine himself playing the smitten suitor, not with a girl he'd wanted to beat into the ground in every race where they'd been competitors. He figured Jessie couldn't imagine him that way either. She couldn't possibly expect him to ride all the way to Chase Park every day to coo poetry in her ear. James had played the romantic only once before — in wooing Alicia — and he had no intention of playing the role again. He'd been another man back then, so head over heels in love that he'd scarcely been able to construct a coherent sentence in her presence. And he'd wanted her. He'd hurt with want. It was all he could think about when he was near her. It was all he could think about when he wasn't near her. He'd embarrassed himself many times, become as hard as a stone by merely touching her hand. All he could think about was having her naked beneath him, moaning for him because, surely, she'd want him as much as he wanted her.

James forced himself to listen a moment to the bishop's mellifluous voice, soaring richly now, as he praised this union, brought about by his illustrious lordship, the Earl of Chase. James wondered if Jessie realized the bishop was saying in so many words that they were a couple of savages, kindly brought to order by a peer of the realm. Marcus must be spitting at such nonsense, that or waiting until it was all over so he could laugh his head off. James stopped listening before he punched the bishop in his long, thin nose. He hoped the Duchess had a good hold on Marcus; he was probably quite tempted himself.

Actually, now that he thought about it, neither could he imagine Jessie playing the wistful maiden, sitting beneath the Duchess's rose arbor waiting for him to come recite some nauseating poetry to her, any more than he could imagine himself reciting it. He was startled when suddenly Jessie said, "I will," in a voice as thin as the lovely stockings he'd glimpsed when she raised her skirt to allow him to tie the ribbon more securely around her left ankle.

He'd never before in his life considered what seeing a lady's stockings could do to a man. He'd become instantly harder than the heels on his boots.

The Bishop of York blessed the young couple, then said to the Earl of Chase, not to the groom, "It is done, my lord. They may wish to embrace as many young married persons do upon completion of the ceremony. God believes a modest tendering of affection following dedication to Him bodes well for a union and enhances the pleasure of those witnessing the event."

James gently placed his index finger beneath Jessie's chin

and pushed up. He leaned down and lightly touched his mouth to hers. Her lips were as cold as the carrot soup Badger had forgotten to heat for dinner the previous night. No one had remarked upon the cold soup. Badger had insisted upon preparing all the wedding dishes and had thus been distracted for the past four days.

"It's going to be all right, Jessie," he said, and lightly touched his mouth to hers again. "Trust me. It will be all right. Come, kiss me. Let's enhance everyone's pleasure."

She said nothing, merely stared up at him, wondering how this could have come to pass. She was married to James, something she'd dreamed of since she'd met him six years before when she'd seen him at the Weymouth racecourse striding confidently beside a quarter horse, speaking to Oslow, speaking to the horse, telling both of them that no one could possibly beat them. She remembered he'd beaten her in the second race, just as he'd said he would to his horse and to Oslow.

The sky had been clear that day, but she'd been struck by lightning. One big strike and it was all over for her. She fancied that lightning strike would stay with her for as long as she lived.

She kissed him. Not enthusiastically as she would have liked, but there were many people here and it was a bit embarrassing, even if that bishop said they could do it. She kissed him just once more for good measure. He smiled down at her and patted her cheek. "Well done. Let's speak to our guests."

Mr. Bagley and his wife were present. A very nice man, Jessie thought, having met him and his wife at the Duchess's first dinner party for her. The poor man shouldn't torture those poor strands of long blond hair, brushing them from one side of his head to the other, pomading them to his scalp. Jessie liked him, but to no avail. The Duchess had said since they needed a special license and no delays, Marcus had spoken to the bishop, more's the pity. Marcus's and the Duchess's doctor, George Raven, and his young bride from York were there as well. Since George Raven, Marcus had said, had saved their respective hides more times than he cared to count, he didn't mind at all having him close since one never knew what could happen, even at a wedding. And besides, Marcus no longer minded Dr. Raven coming to tend the Duchess now that the good doctor was married and wouldn't lust after the Duchess the way he had in the past, or tried to.

The Bishop of York would have been gravely disappointed had he but realized that no one else at the wedding wondered how the devil Master Charles's nurse and Anthony's horse nanny could be marrying the American male Wyndham. Being a discreet bishop, however, he'd mentioned this distressing fact only once to the earl, who'd carefully begun pulling at the magnificently tied cravat that had taken a good ten minutes to get just right, just so he wouldn't pound the man into the Aubusson carpet.

Frances Hawksbury, the Countess of Rothermere, congratulated James, then turned to Jessie. "Now that you've got him in harness, my dear," she said, lightly patting her shoulder, "give him his head when he's kicking at the traces, then rein him in gently but firmly."

"James," Marcus said, coming up to them, "I see you're being likened to a horse."

"It does seem to fit nicely," Jessie said, smiling at the Countess of Rothermere.

"And I'll nip her neck to keep her obedient," James said, "perhaps nudge her rump a bit to move her in the directions I choose."

The Duchess laughed. "You're both abominable. It's over, finally, the bishop is already at the champagne bottle, and Badger has prepared a wedding breakfast that will have everyone begging to move in."

"They will all move in or they will all try to kidnap Badger from us."

"I do wonder how you remain so thin," Jessie said.

"It's those damned traces," Marcus said. "I kick and I kick to try to get to her, but she just smiles and tells me to keep moving, that occasional restraint is good for my manly parts."

After a half dozen toasts with the very dry champagne from the earl's cellars, James looked at his bride and whistled. "You're tipsy, Jessie. Come to think of it, you never drink spirits, do you?"

She hiccupped and asked for another glass.

"Oh dear," the Duchess said. "Do you still want to go to Candlethorpe for the night, James?"

"Yes. I want to go home."

"Come along, Jessie," the Duchess said in that serene voice no one ever resisted, and led her upstairs. Since they were riding to Candlethorpe, the Duchess and Maggie helped her change into a magnificent riding outfit that the Duchess had had made for her. It was a soft burnished gold with darker gold braiding on the shoulders. It was pinched in tightly at the waist, with three layers of thick braiding at the hem. It made her skin glow and her hair look like a fierce sunset.

When Jessie was dressed and Maggie had lovingly placed the last streamer to frame her face, the Duchess set the riding hat on her head and stood back. The dyed ostrich feather curled around her cheek.

"You're beautiful."

"Will James say I look like a trollop?" The effects of her two glasses of champagne had long fled.

"If he does, he's an idiot. If he's an idiot," Maggie added, "then you just bite him. Men love little love bites or little *correction bites* as I call them. Dear Sampson purrs like his lordship's bloody cat when I nip his shoulder, and then he—"

The Duchess cleared her throat. "Maggie, would you please see if James is ready to leave?"

Maggie, no fool, winked at Jessie, then took herself off, saying over her shoulder, "You look a treat, Jessie. You surely do. I want you to look at every man when you come downstairs. You'll see that all of them will be undergoing bouts of lust when they lay eyes on you."

"It's true," the Duchess said once Maggie was out of the bedchamber, the door closed. "Now, Jessie, do you wish to ask me anything?"

"Ask you anything? Oh, you mean about sex?"

"Well, yes. Just think of me as your older sister."

"I think I know everything, Duchess. I was raised with horses, after all. James will come up over my back and stick himself inside me. That's all there is to it."

The Duchess gave her an engaging smile. "Well, perhaps you're in store for a bit of a surprise. But you can trust James to do everything properly."

"Yes." Jessie turned away and walked to the wide bank of windows. She stared onto the west lawn. She wondered where Fred and Clorinda were today, on her wedding day. She said quietly, "He was married before. He knows all about wives."

"Jessie? Does that bother you?"

She waved her hand, as if to ward off unpleasant thoughts, turning away from the windows to face the Duchess again. "No, that would be foolish. I only just thought of it now. He's had a wife and thus knows all about everything. Was she beautiful, Duchess?"

"Alicia? Well, yes, she was, actually. She was very small, with hair as blond as those paintings you see of angels and the bluest eyes you could imagine. But enough about Alicia.

The poor girl died years ago. A tragedy, really, but she's nothing to do with you, Jessie.''

"Did she help James with Candlethorpe?"

"If you mean did she help him train horses and muck out stalls, no, she wouldn't have considered such a thing."

"She just sat in the drawing room and served tea? She didn't race or ride?"

The Duchess smiled at the acrimony in Jessie's voice. "Forget her. Now, let's go see if your new husband is ready to leave."

The Bishop of York eyed Jessie as if she were an exotic bird from another world in her glorious gold riding outfit. She wondered if after all the champagne he'd consumed he even recognized her as the bride. "I suppose," he said, his voice even more resonant, "that a gold riding ensemble is very American. Did her ladyship approve of this unexpected spectacle?"

"I did," the Duchess said, and quickly took Jessie's hand and pulled her away.

Jessie said her good-byes to all the guests, then turned and looked at the Duchess. "You've been very kind to me. I don't deserve it, but you were kind nonetheless. May I come to see Charles and Anthony?"

"You may visit anytime you wish," the earl said, coming up to take Jessie in his arms. He hugged her, then said, "Those damned martinets are all waiting to wish you and James well."

"Yes, come along, Jessie," James said, and took her gloved hand. He led her from the great massive doors of Chase Park, down the well-worn stone steps to where the four martinets stood, huge smiles plastered on their faces.

Badger handed James a huge covered basket. "I've packed you some lamb cutlets and cucumbers, a bit of apple pudding, and one of James's favorites, boiled knuckle of veal. You'll get thirsty on your ride, so there's also some of the earl's champagne. It's very cold, so drink it soon."

"Here's a packet of cream for you, Jessie," Maggie said. "Don't forget now, you can't wear it on your face to bed anymore. It would make your husband laugh or cry, depending on his whim at the time."

"I would like to present you with a pair of earrings, Jessie," Sampson said. "My Maggie assures me that they'll look exquisite in your little white ears."

"Goodness, Sampson, they're sapphires."

"Yes, my Maggie tried them on to ensure that they would be becoming to you. Yes, hold them up and let's judge this. What do you think, Mr. Badger?"

"I don't think," Badger said slowly, studying them carefully, "that they flatter the gold. They are too bold a color and fight with that particular shade. Yes, just as I would never serve sweet potatoes with blueberries, you should never wear the sapphires with this gold."

"I think the colors complement each other well enough," Spears said, gently edging Badger aside to eye them himself. "But I agree, Mr. Badger, that sweet potatoes wouldn't at all enhance themselves served alongside blueberries."

"Well," Maggie said, "I can't keep them since dear Sampson already gave them to you. What do you think, James?"

"I like her ears naked," James said.

Badger looked like a cook whose cake had just collapsed in the middle.

Spears looked like a disapproving judge.

Sampson looked at his wife's ears and grinned shamelessly.

Maggie just patted Jessie's hand and told her to do as she wished with them. "You trust James to select the outfits that will complement them best."

Spears still looked stern, his face set in austere lines, and Jessie realized he was looking at James. He was all garbed in black.

"Thank you, Spears," she said.

"You will take good care of James," he said, and she nearly laughed at that thought. "Yes, I will try to."

"You will see that he stays on his course."

"What course, Spears?" James said, hefting the basket of food from his left hand to his right. "These damned cutlets weigh as much as the new saddle I bought for Jessie."

"What new saddle?"

"Forget it. It's a surprise. Do you swear you'll act surprised when I finally present it to you?"

"Yes, I promise. What course, Spears?"

He broke into a smile. "You'll know the course when it appears, Jessie. If you need us, just send a message. We'll be there as quickly as can be. Do you promise?"

"I promise," she said, stood on her tiptoes, and kissed his cheek. "You smell good, Spears. Are you using some of Maggie's cream?"

Badger roared with laughter. Maggie giggled. Sampson guffawed. Spears did nothing at all. The new bride and groom laughed and waved as they rode side by side down the beautiful tree-lined drive of Chase Park, James on Bertram, a gray Barb with a white nose out of Croft's stud and Jessie on Esmerelda, a Byerley Turk bay mare from the Rothermere stud.

The afternoon was warm, the sun bright overhead, the sky studded with white clouds. Jessie said after fifteen minutes, "James, can we open that champagne now?"

He eyed her. She'd not said a single word since they'd left Chase Park. She'd ridden Esmerelda with single-minded intensity; he recognized that from watching her race, but why the intensity now? Her cheeks were flushed from the ride, her hair flying in long loose streamers from beneath that very provocative riding hat perched on her head with that feather curving around her face to stroke her chin.

He pointed to the left off the road beyond a white fence

to a small copse of maple trees. "Just behind those trees is a small meadow."

They took the fence in an easy jump. Jessie fell in behind him through the copse of trees on a narrow trail that suddenly ended in a small, circular meadow filled with wildly blooming pink and red hollyhocks, purple gayfeathers, white baby's breath, and yellow wood violets. James searched around until he found a moss-covered rock flat enough and large enough for the two of them, bowed to Jessie, and with a flourish, said, "I don't want to smash the flowers. Moss is a different matter."

They spread a cloth between them and arranged Badger's offering. James popped the champagne cork, pulled two glasses from Badger's basket, and poured. He laughed when he poured too quickly and sipped as fast as he could before too much champagne was lost.

"Here, Jessie."

He poured himself a glass, then clicked it against hers. "Why did you want champagne?"

"I thought if I drank the whole bottle, then you could just get it all over with."

"Get what all over with?"

"Don't be stupid." She downed the entire glass and held it out for more.

"Oh, you want to fall into a stupor. Then while you're stuporous I'll do degenerate things to you and then the deed will be done and you won't have to worry about it anymore?"

"That's right, though I would have phrased it a bit more circumspectly."

"I'm a man. I'm rarely circumspect. Now why are you worried about having sex with me? You've known me forever. You already know all my bad habits—well, most of them. You don't know as yet if I snore or not."

She wouldn't look at him. She studied the clump of foxgloves just beyond her left boot. She drank another glass of champagne. He obligingly poured her another half glass when she thrust the empty glass toward him, her eyes still on those foxgloves.

"As foxgloves go, they're not bad," James said as he watched her down that half glass, then thrust her glass at him again.

"No," Jessie said, thinking the foxgloves looked lovely the way they were fading in and out of her vision.

He supposed dithering wasn't bad, at least for the moment. It was difficult enough for him, he knew that. He'd acknowledged the problems before he'd offered to marry her. He'd always regarded her as a brat, a younger sister who irritated him and provoked him until he wanted to smack her bottom. And now she was his wife, and it was equally obvious to him that she was as skittish as Sober John was during a Baltimore storm. Did she think of him as an older brother? One with whom she was in competition?

At the moment, he simply couldn't imagine how he was going to approach making love to her. Making love to Jessie—the brat. It boggled the mind. Except that he had been looking at things a bit differently during the past week.

He drew a deep breath and prayed. "Jessie, I've known you for a very long time. I admit I still know the old Jessie more than the new Jessie. But, never have I known you to be a coward. What's wrong?"

"You've never known me married before, either. That's what's wrong. You and I, James, we're married only because—" She paused and shrugged. "There's no reason to repeat the dreadful sequence of events again. They're as painful to you as they are to me. Do you really want to mount me, James?"

# ═══ 18 ═══

"MOUNT YOU?" HIS eyes nearly crossed picturing her naked, bending over, looking over her shoulder at him as he
neared her, as he touched her. He shook his head. He'd been
too long without companionship of a sexual sort. If any
female spoke to him of mounting her, he would have seen
the same sequence of explicit images in his brain.

"Maybe," he said at last after he'd drunk a bit more of
his own champagne, "but not for a while." Jessie was right.
The champagne had been a good idea. It was probably the
only way to get through this.

"I'm not Alicia. I'm sorry but I had to ask the Duchess
about her. She said she was beautiful, all small and blond
and blue-eyed. You loved her. I'm none of those things, and
you don't love me. I can't imagine what will become of
us."

"We will survive, I daresay," he said, eyeing her glass
until she emptied it and he could pour her more champagne.
The damned bottle was empty, and he didn't even feel the
least bit tipsy. He prayed she did. He said, "Badger should
have realized that a bride and groom have a greater need
for spirits than ordinary folk. He should have packed another
bottle."

Jessie picked around in Badger's basket. "He did," she
said, lifting another cloth-wrapped bottle.

James offered a prayer of thanks toward Chase Park's vast

kitchen. "An excellent man is Badger. Well, why not? Let's get drunk then here in this lovely meadow. It's warm. When you're too intoxicated to know what I'm about, I'll pull up your riding skirt, unfasten my breeches, and take your virginity. Then it will be over, and we can go along to Candlethorpe and get a good night's sleep. Tomorrow it will all be forgotten, and we can muck out stalls side by side. Perhaps we'll be so at ease with each other that we'll whistle together, perhaps even sing some of the Duchess's ditties. What do you say to that, Jessie?"

She didn't say anything. He'd hoped for a smile; just a hint of a smile would have relieved him, but she didn't dredge one up. She was trying to remove the cork on the other bottle of champagne. She couldn't get it out. She put it in her mouth and gnawed on it.

James leaned back, the sun on his face, the scent of the flowers in his nostrils, and laughed. She was the old Jessie, the brat, chewing on a straw, licking the remains of a candied almond from her fingers, gnawing on a champagne cork, it was all the same thing. When he heard the cork pop, he simply lifted his glass and thrust it toward her.

Jessie began to laugh after her fourth glass of champagne, thank the munificent Lord. She waved her hand to ward off a bee and James said, "Careful, Jessie, you nearly knocked over our remaining precious bottle."

She shoved the bottle down between her legs. "There, now it's safe."

He looked at that bottle and knew he had to act before he was too drunk to do more than belch. "Do you think you're feeling silly enough now to lie back and let me kiss you?"

She stared down at him. She looked worried, eager, and more afraid than a sinner in a roomful of preachers. "Yes," she said, "let's kiss."

"Put the bottle over there. Yes, that's right. Now, just relax, Jessie."

"Just one more small glass, James," she said, poured it, drank it down in one gulp, and then gave him the silly smile of a girl who, sober, would have been terrified out of her mind. She lay on her back, stretched out, and arranged her hands over her chest as if she were dead. He felt he should pick a foxglove and put it between her fingers.

He leaned over her and kissed her closed mouth, smiling even as he said, "Open up, just a little bit. Pretend I'm a small but succulent piece of something good to eat, say a bit of Badger's garnished tongue."

She opened her mouth beneath his, and James felt as though he'd been struck in the gut. She tasted of champagne—he'd expected that—but she also just tasted sweet and strangely exotic, and he wanted more. She didn't taste like a brat. He was careful to keep his hands on her arms, careful not to stick his tongue in her mouth, careful to control himself. He feared he'd kiss her yet again and really get things started when suddenly she'd turn into the fourteen-year-old again—a girl, not a woman.

He stopped a moment and pulled back. Her eyes were open, as was her mouth. She was staring up at him.

"What is it?"

To his surprise and amusement, she flushed. She actually turned red and looked away from him.

"What's the matter? Come now, I'm your husband and you've known me since you were barely able to ride a horse."

"The champagne is wonderful, but I have a problem."

"Yes?"

"Don't be obtuse, James. I have to relieve myself."

He tried not to laugh; he couldn't help himself. "Undone by a bottle of champagne. Well, I'll wait for you here, Jessie. There are some lovely bushes just over behind that stand of maples.''

She struggled to her feet, smoothed down her skirts, and turned to walk with exaggerated care toward that stand of maple trees. She never looked once at him.

He lay back against that sun-heated rock and began humming one of the Duchess's ditties. He hummed another ditty, and then a third. He drank another glass of champagne. Then he frowned.

He rose, cupped his hand around his mouth, and called out, ''Jessie? Are you all right?''

There was no answer, only the soft rustle of the summer leaves in the light afternoon breeze.

''Jessie!'' He was on his feet, worried now, surprised that he wasn't all that steady. He dumped the rest of the champagne on a bed of nestergroot, hoped they wouldn't croak, and went to the trees.

He found her on the ground, on her side, her face pillowed on her hands. She was in a sodden stupor.

''Well, hell,'' James said. Now he'd have to do it all over again. He wondered if she'd be ill when she came out of her stupor. He was willing to bet Badger hadn't thought this would be the outcome of his generous gift.

Jessie wanted to die. She didn't want to say good-bye to anybody. She just wanted to breathe her last, slowly, gently, and then waft away. She opened her eyes just once, but the intense bright light made her head pound so violently and her belly twist in gigantic knots that she knew the end must be very near.

''It's a hangover, Jessie. Here, Mrs. Catsdoor made you a special brew that should help a bit. I'll just lift you, there, that's it. Now drink it all down.''

''James? You're here with me?''

''Yes. Drink.'' He got it all down her but it was a chore

because it only seemed to make Jessie sicker. The concoction kept dribbling down her chin, and she kept choking. It was a foul brew; he knew that because he'd had a glass of it himself. But it would help in the long run.

"Poor Jessie," he said, and laid a cool, damp cloth on her forehead. "No, keep your eyes and your mouth shut. You're at Candlethorpe, in your bedchamber. I managed to get both of us on top of Bertram though he didn't want to volunteer for the duty, the selfish sod, and complained most of the way home, slapping that long tail of his against my leg. I held you, all boneless, your head falling over my arm, and held the reins to Esmerelda in my left hand. That mare found the entire ride to Candlethorpe something of an adventure. She was also eyeing Bertram with a good deal of filly interest."

Jessie wet her lips with a dry tongue but was wise enough to keep her eyes closed. She had to know. Because she felt ready for death, because she knew a person couldn't bear this agony for very long, she was able to ask, "Did you mount me, James? Is it all over now? Was it all right? I didn't make a spectacle of myself, did I? You will remember me fondly, won't you, once I die?"

He was so surprised he just stared down at her, quickly pulling the cloth down a bit farther to cover her eyes. He knew he couldn't lie to her any better than she could to him if she were looking at him. What to do?

"Oh dear, was it that bad? You can tell me the truth. Was it horrible for you? Do you want me to leave? I don't think I can because I'm sure the end is near, so that will be just as well, won't it?"

"Well, I wouldn't say it was horrible—no, not at all. And yes, I'll always remember you fondly, Jessie."

"That's a lie. You've cursed at me more than you have at your horses."

"Perhaps, but death softens and blurs memories. I'll wager after you've been gone only six months or so, I'll have only fond memories of you.''

"How did you manage to mount me with all my clothes on?"

"Well, I wouldn't call it difficult. You were very pliable, very cooperative. Don't you remember how you wanted me to get it all over with so things could get back to normal between us?"

"The last thing I remember is thinking the hollyhocks were the brightest pinks and reds I'd ever seen. I don't remember anything else. And now it's too late. I'll die a virgin in spirit if not in flesh.''

"You are a very nice virgin."

"What do you mean 'are'?"

"Well, actually, I was thinking spiritually.''

"Was my fleshly virgin part acceptable, James?"

"Well, you must remember that you were extraordinarily pliable, Jessie. It required a lot of skill and concentration on my part just to accomplish everything and get us back to Candlethorpe.''

He watched as she lifted her left hand and touched her fingers to her nightgown. "You took off my clothes? You undressed me and put me in my nightgown?"

"Well, someone had to make you more comfortable. We are married, Jessie.''

"Oh dear, I don't like this at all, James. I can't even remember your taking off my clothes there in the meadow, much less remember your doing it again here. Did you even pull off my boots and stockings? However did you get me to stay up on my hands and knees so you could mount me? I would have thought I'd collapse.''

"Well, one doesn't always have to pull off all of one's clothing. Boots can stay on sometimes. It's occasionally seductive, as are stockings held up with garters. Another thing,

Jessie, men don't always mount women. Men and women aren't horses all the time."

"I suppose I should thank you for getting it done so adeptly that I don't remember a thing about it."

"If you will remember, Jessie, I did tell you to trust me."

If he wasn't mistaken she suddenly turned a vile shade of green. He wasn't stupid and he was fast. He got the basin to her just in time. She shuddered and heaved and retched while he held her, careful to keep her braid from falling in her face. When finally the spasms were over, he said, "Poor Jessie, I'm sorry. Here, rinse out your mouth. You'll be better now, you'll see."

She lay back against the pillows, moaning, her hands clutching at her stomach.

"Let me die now, James, please. Go away. I want to breathe my last by myself. Please say good-bye to Esmerelda for me. You will take good care of her, won't you?"

"Yes, I swear I will."

"Good-bye, James. I'm sorry you have to be a widower again, but it's for the best." She sighed deeply, saying in a whisper, "For you to become fond of me in six months isn't bad."

"It might not even take six months." He laid the cloth over her eyes again, gently folded her arms over her chest, and said, "The six years went quickly, Jessie." She moaned as he rose. He waited until her breathing evened into sleep.

Mrs. Catsdoor was waiting for him in the corridor. "How is she, Master James?"

"She wanted to die alone."

"Aye, it's like the darkness before the dawn. That was my granny's special brew. She always said that my grandda was a man who couldn't hold more than a small dram of demon rum but that she knew he couldn't help himself and thus if she wanted to have a husband for longer than a year, she had to invent something to ease him."

"Did your grandda last longer than a year?"

Mrs. Catsdoor looked philosophical. "Yes, indeed, Master James. He's all of seventy-two now, no teeth at all in his head, and drinks like a thirsty goat. We buried my granny twenty years ago. We found gallons of her brew in the cellar. He finished the final one some five years ago."

"There's something passing strange if that's the moral to that tale, Mrs. Catsdoor."

She sighed. "I've always thought so, Master James. Your new bride isn't used to spirits, is she?"

"No, I believe, though, that the bottle and a half of champagne she consumed today will keep her free of intoxication for a good ten years."

"That's what my grandda used to chant like a monk when he felt particularly revolting. His vow never lasted out the day."

James decided he wanted to meet grandda. "We'll let her sleep through the night, Mrs. Catsdoor. If she does wake up, though, could you make something she could eat and keep in her belly if she's hungry?"

James didn't particularly want to eat either, but he liked Mrs. Catsdoor's porridge with the honey she mixed in it. He finished the bowl just before he took off his clothes and climbed into bed next to his sodden wife.

He leaned over her for a moment, lowering his ear to her chest. Her heart was slow and steady. "You're not dead yet, Jessie."

# ═══ 19 ═══

*I'M ALIVE*, JESSIE thought, reasonably pleased, and then unutterably relieved once she realized she wasn't still so vilely ill that she wanted to die. She raised a tentative finger, then her whole arm. She was wearing her own nightgown, one James had put on her the day before.

Was it still the day before? Bright sunlight shimmered through the light muslin draperies. She remembered Mrs. Catsdoor's brew and how she'd believed it unjust to die with that vile taste in her mouth. But she didn't die, and James had known she wouldn't die. She'd made an ass of herself and he'd let her do it. It was morning. She realized that now.

And James had done everything a husband was supposed to do, and she had no memory of it, so that was all right as well. She heard a snort, jumped, then turned to see her groom lying on his back, one arm flung over his head, the other hand on his belly, which was barely covered with a sheet. He gave two more short snorts then fell silent.

Everything that was deep within her responded to the sight of him lying there beside her. He was her husband. He had thick gold hair on his chest, all crispy-looking and a tuft of soft gold hair beneath his upflung arm. He was hard and lean, lightly tanned from working in the sun without his shirt, and she wanted more than anything to shove that sheet down just a little bit more. She wanted to see just how much like a stallion he really was so she could try to remember what he'd done to her.

She moved her legs. Nothing hurt. Recalling how she'd seen mares teetering around after mating, she began to wonder. She didn't think she was going to teeter at all. James must have been very careful with her. She eased out of bed before she could resist the temptation to pull that sheet down no longer and walked across the bedchamber. When she did, she didn't teeter at all.

She whistled to herself as she stripped off her nightgown, then bathed in the basin of cool water on the dressing table. Every few minutes, she looked back at the bed. James hadn't moved a bit. Well, perhaps that sheet was just a bit lower. She took a step toward the bed, then stopped, and settled for craning her neck a bit. The sheet *was* lower. She saw the narrow line of golden hair that disappeared too soon for her taste beneath that dratted sheet. He had a flat belly, but she'd already known that, still seeing it in the flesh pleased her. His flesh was whiter here, and she found that fascinating though she couldn't begin to explain why.

She dressed quickly, still whistling, took one last look at James, and regretfully left the bedchamber.

"Mrs. Catsdoor?"

"Good heavens! Mrs. James. Now, don't you look like a lovely little summer posy, all bright and eager and ready to blossom for the sun."

Jessie thought of those foxgloves and smiled. "Your brew was excellent. Thank you very much. I thought I loved champagne, and I surely did, but it did me in. I'm sorry I wasn't quite attentive enough when I arrived here yesterday. Goodness, I'm starved."

"Of course you are," Mrs. Catsdoor said, grinning as she remembered Master James carrying in his bride in his arms, and she looked dead. Dead drunk was more like it. "Come eat some porridge. Master James tells me it's the best por-

ridge in all of England and the Colonies. It's my honey, you
know. I have a special breed of bees, and no one else knows
of their hives. Just three of them and all the honey's for me.
Just sit down here, Mrs. James, and I'll fix you up right and
tight.''

James awoke with a start. He'd dreamed he was kissing a
woman who was moaning into his mouth, whispering how
magnificent he was, how much he pleased her, how she
enjoyed him touching her and coming inside her and he was
so big and so—James shook his head. A typical man's
dream. Nothing but a damned dream.

Something wasn't quite right. He was in his bed, but he
wasn't sleeping on the left side. He was on the right side.
He never slept on the right side; it made him have strange
dreams, although this most recent one wasn't bad at all.
Then he remembered he'd placed Jessie there sleeping like
a drunken stoat, convinced she was going to die, and he'd
slept beside her. The pillow was still pressed down, the
sheets rumpled.

She was gone.

"At least she didn't die," he said to the empty bedchamber, climbed out of bed, and shrugged into his dressing
gown. An hour later, he found her grooming Esmerelda,
chatting to Sigmund as if she'd known him all her life. She
wasn't wearing breeches as the old Jessie would have, but
the pale blue gown was of sturdy cotton, plain and func-
tional. So this was the new Jessie in her working mode.

She'd braided her hair atop her head with those streamers
curling lazily down over her ears. He wondered if she'd
brought her old leather hat to England.

"Good morning," he said.

"Good morning to you, Master James," Sigmund said as
he continued to pick at Bertram's left front hoof. "Got a
pebble here. Ah, there, got it. Nasty thing. Ye got it from

yer long ride yesterday, didn't ye? Good old boy, all right now.''

''Good morning, Jessie. You seem to be no worse from your excesses.''

Jessie had wondered about this moment of truth. James had told her that once it was done, then they could return to normal. So be it. She grinned at him. ''Doesn't Esmerelda look grand? She's ready for a ride, James. Would you care to join me? We could try whistling a duet.''

''No, Bertram, ye just stay away from Esmerelda,'' Sigmund said.

''She was teasing him mercilessly yesterday,'' James said.

''She ain't interested today, that's fer sure,'' Sigmund said. ''Come outta heat, she has, with a vengeance. She's already bit poor old Bertram, jest for being a mite friendly to her.''

''Females,'' said James, shaking his head. ''Jessie, I can't ride with you. I'm expecting a Mr. DeWitt this morning with a mare for Minotaur to cover.''

She just shook her head, saddled Esmerelda, and was gone. He looked after her.

''Don't ye worry, Master James. Mrs. James knows wot she's about. I took her all around and introduced her all over again. She spoke to each one of 'em, gave 'em sugar and a sweet pat. I swear they all remembered her and gathered around her like little kiddies. I ain't niver afore seen a female what know'd so much about horses, an' she's easy wit 'em, never makes 'em nervous. None of the horses screwed their heads about the way they do when they don't trust somebody.''

''You should see her race.''

Sigmund guffawed, shaking his head. ''That's a kicker. Race, ye say? That feminine little bit of red hair and white skin can race? You're jesting me, Master James. She grooms a horse well, never complained once, no she didn't, but race? That little sweet lady?''

''So little you know,'' James said, slapped Sigmund on his skinny back, and took himself off to see to Minotaur.

''We've got six stallions and three mares,'' James said as he handed Jessie a dish of compote of gooseberries, one of Mrs. Catsdoor's specialties. Badger, in a moment of weakness when the four martinets had come to force James to the altar, had presented the recipe to her and she'd now made it three days in a row. ''Minotaur covered the DeWitt mare, a smart little Byerley Turk out of Tomikins from Croft's stable.''

''I was reading the *General Stud Book*. Goodness, James, things are so very organized here.''

''It's really nothing more than a genealogy of horses but needed, that's certain. I've been talking with many men in racing back in Baltimore. None of them believes it's all that important. For the most part, they're content to just pass things along, word of mouth.''

''Have Oslow write down what he knows.''

''Good idea. Do you like the compote of gooseberries?''

''It's fine. Badger, though, he made it once and everyone tasted it and swooned.''

James just grinned. ''I'm glad you didn't die, Jessie. You've been a good friend and an irritation for too long to croak just yet.''

''You knew I wouldn't. You let me make a fool of myself.''

''Yes, forgive me, but you were so completely convinced it was the end. I swear to you, I didn't laugh once.''

''You slept with me, James.''

''Well, yes. It's my bed.''

''The earl's cat, Esmee, slept with me once. I rolled over

on her by accident. She yowled, hissed in my face, and left me, never to return.''

''She likes to sleep on Marcus's chest and knead his hair. He wakes up yelling.''

She pushed some garden peas around her plate, then went back to her compote. ''What will we do now?''

He raised an eyebrow. ''You can help Sigmund and me with the horses this afternoon.''

''Of course I'll do that, but it isn't what I meant. I mean, what will we do about, well, the other?''

''What other?''

''James, I won't allow you to make sport of me again. You know very well what I'm talking about. I have no memory of having been mounted. When I woke up this morning, I wasn't at all sore. I didn't teeter on my legs the way I've seen some mares do who have been mounted. I didn't look at all different when I stared into the mirror.''

''Oh, that.'' He studied his thumbnail. He had a thick callus on the pad. Finally he looked over at her. At the moment she looked very much like the new Jessie, and he felt a surge of nice heavy lust. However, when she'd returned from her ride this morning, she'd looked just like the old Jessie, her hair in wild tangles around her face, her riding hat tied to the saddle by its ribbons, sitting astride Esmerelda, not in a decorous sidesaddle, laughing and talking all at once, telling him everything she'd seen, telling him every clever thing Esmerelda had done, and he'd thought blankly as he'd tried to listen to that mishmash of sounds coming from her mouth that it would be impossible to make love to the girl he'd considered a little sister for more years than he cared to count. But now she was as silent as the Duchess. She looked elegant. She'd never in his memory looked elegant until she'd come to England. He wanted to take that gown off her.

''It's all right, James,'' she said very quietly. ''I understand, truly I do. You're too kind to tell me that you would just as soon I kept away from you." She very carefully folded her napkin and pressed it into the tablecloth beside her plate. She rose. "I am going over the household and the accounts with Mrs. Catsdoor. Please tell Sigmund that I will come and help with the horses later."

She was nearly to the door when he said from right behind her, "Don't leave, Jessie."

She felt his hands on her shoulders, the warmth of him, the strength of him. She opened her mouth only to close it again when she realized that something had changed. He was no longer simply resting his hands on her shoulders. His fingers were lightly digging into her flesh, kneading her, making her feel very nice indeed.

"Turn around."

She did, wondering what he would do now.

"Look at me."

She looked at him, all the curiosity she felt written plainly on her face. Her lips parted a bit. He leaned down and kissed her—a full, deep kiss since this was the new Jessie standing in front of him and he had no memories of her at all as a sister or a brat or an irritating constant in his life. Actually, he thought as he licked her bottom lip, she was his wife. And that had to be the strangest thing of all. And she believed he'd already consummated their marriage. While she'd been in a drunken stupor. He nearly laughed aloud, but he didn't.

She raised her hands to flatten them on his chest. She felt his heart pounding deep and fast beneath her palms. She felt the pressure of his lips, fascinating, that mouth of his, and she tasted the gooseberry compote they'd shared. She'd never imagined anything like this. She'd dreamed about it, wondered what it would be like if James pressed his mouth against hers, but to feel his tongue, to feel all of him pressing against her, it undid her completely.

She stood on her tiptoes, grabbed him, and pulled him hard against her. He laughed in her mouth. "Easy, easy, we've all the time in the world."

"No, we don't."

"Perhaps you're right." He stuck out his hand and pulled the breakfast-room door shut behind her. He managed to turn the key in the lock. He wrapped his arms around her back and pivoted until he could see the table.

A lovely white linen cloth. All the dishes he could shove aside. He lifted her, never releasing her, never stopping his kissing, and carried her to the table. He eased her up onto her back, her legs hanging over the side, her feet to rest on the seat of her chair. He gently pushed her back, quickly shoving a plate of red mullet out of the way.

She was staring up at him, looking bemused and interested, that curiosity still lively in her eyes. "James, what are we going to do?"

"We're going to be people, not horses."

Now she looked a bit alarmed. "I'm lying on the table, James. There's a bowl of Julienne soup beside my right elbow."

He moved the soup bowl and the too-close plate of rolls. "That's better. Now let me move this chair. Just let your legs hang down for the moment. Yes, that's it."

He moved between her legs, bent down, and kissed her some more. Immediately she brought her arms around his neck to pull him closer. "Let's bring you down just a bit," he said between wet, sharp kisses, grasped her hips in his hands, and brought her halfway off the table.

"Goodness, this is passing strange, James. I feel like—"

She didn't finish. He pressed himself against her, and she flopped her hands to the table beside her as if he'd just shot and killed her.

"It's just me, Jessie. No, don't try to wriggle away from me. Just get used to the feel of me. Stay still." He pressed in more closely. He closed his eyes, his fingers digging into her hips, raising her slightly. He could feel the heat of her. His fingers trembled and twitched. He wanted to touch her, to stroke her.

"Did you do that yesterday?"

"No, I didn't do this yesterday. We were lunching on a rock, not a table. I don't even remember yesterday." He moaned when she arched a bit. "Wrap your legs around my waist, Jessie. No, don't look at me as if I've lost my wits. Just trust me. That's right, lock your ankles behind my back. Ah, that's good." Now he leaned over her and began kissing her again. Her wonderful gown buttoned up the front, the heavens be praised. He kept kissing her as he pulled each of those rotten little buttons out of its loop. Damnation, there had to be two hundred of them. He ran out of patience and ripped the last few free. He came up a bit over her and opened her gown. Maggie had struck again, he thought, both shocked and inordinately aroused by the sight of a peach satin chemise bordered with the most wicked little snippets of lace imaginable, none of the lace covering much of anything, just framing those breasts of hers that were the new Jessie's breasts, not the old Jessie's.

His hand hovered. Her breasts were rising and falling, looking as delicious and white as the frosting of the wedding cake Badger had baked and decorated until the wee hours of the morning the night before their wedding. Lightly he touched his fingers to her left breast. He closed his eyes and let his fingers trace over her flesh, warm flesh, warm Jessie flesh. Surely she hadn't always looked like this, all white and full and round, arching up, staring at him as if he were a god from some ancient and exciting myth come to earth to claim her. Suddenly, with no invitation at all, he saw her as she'd been on a long-ago night when he'd come over with a bottle of port to her father's tack room to toast his racing victory of that day. She'd been sitting cross-legged in a rickety chair next to her father's desk, dressed in the most disreputable old shirt and breeches he'd ever seen, wearing no shoes, just thick black socks that he was certain had holes. Her hair was plastered down to her head and yanked back in a severe braid. Then she'd said in that snide, bratty voice, "Papa said I could stay a moment to greet the loser. I beat you but good today, James. You lost all your concentration in that second race, nearly fell off your poor horse's back when that jockey tried to kick you. I laughed and laughed and won, naturally." Then she'd stood, still grinning at him. "I'll keep beating you, James. It's your fate."

And she'd sauntered out of the tack room like an arrogant boy, her father laughing his damned head off at what she'd said, and James just standing there wanting to tie her up in strong rope and throw her into the Patapsco River.

His fingers stopped caressing that white flesh.

# ≡ 20 ≡

"JAMES? WHAT'S WRONG? Are my legs squeezing you too tightly? Am I hurting you?"

"Oh no."

She tightened her ankles.

"That's a bit much, Jessie. Yes, a bit much, nearly too much actually but don't loosen up any."

He felt her heels pushing against his back, forcing him more closely against her. He brushed his fingertips over that wicked satin lace. It felt nearly as soft as her flesh.

"You've never touched me there before. It's interesting. Do you like the chemise?"

"It's not much like you," he said. He was staring down at his brown, callused fingers that were again lightly stroking her breasts.

"Maybe it's like me now that I'm different."

"Or maybe it's Maggie trying to mold you into her shape."

"She has a shape that would be very nice to be molded into. The chemise was her wedding present to me."

"She did well. Now, Jessie, just be quiet. Don't you know what I'm doing here? How can you just chat about nothing at all when I'm touching your breasts?"

She turned her face away from him and was on eye level with a small dish of calf brains. Looking at those brains, all soft and cooked in butter, she said, "I'm scared."

"So you're scared, and I'm thinking that if I make love to you it will be incest. What a combination we are. Damnation."

"What do you mean, 'incest'?"

"Six years, Jessie—for six years you've been like a little sister to me. You've annoyed me endlessly. I've felt protective of you countless times. Remember how I'd come up to you and ruffle your hair or pull on your braid? Then, of course, I'd want to thrash you, but that was denied me, more's the pity. Even when you sprawled all over me in the Blanchards' garden, I didn't think of you as a female. You were just Jessie, the brat in breeches who was always in the way."

"I'm not your bloody sister, James. You didn't even think of this incest business at all yesterday, did you?"

"No, I didn't, but today's different."

He leaned over her, kissed her hard, and said into her mouth, "Yesterday you were tipsy, you were giggling, you had those cute little streamers hanging down."

"So I have to get intoxicated for you to think of me as your wife and not as your sister?"

"No, it's not that. Damnation, Jessie, if you want the truth, yesterday I didn't do a damned thing to you. Do you think a man wants to be intimate with an unconscious female? You even snored a couple of times when I was hauling you to the horses. Do you think that's conducive to amorous feelings?"

"*You didn't do anything?*" She shoved at his chest, and he pulled back, standing between her legs, her ankles still locked behind his waist, her breasts still covered. Suddenly, he ripped open her chemise and pulled it wide. She gasped, trying to cover her breasts, but he grabbed her hands and pulled them over her head. He leaned down, kissed her, then brought her hands down and held them at her sides.

"I never realized you looked so nice, Jessie, or is this

something you've added since you got to England?''

Not just nice breasts, he thought, unable to look away from them. Lovely breasts. Whiter than a cow's fresh milk, her nipples all soft-looking, a warm pink, and he wanted to touch her and kiss her, but he held himself still.

''I just rub Maggie's cream all over me every time I bathe, nothing more.''

''A magic cream. Fascinating. You don't have any freckles on your shoulders or breasts.''

''No, just the line across my nose.''

''Your skin is very white.'' He sounded in pain but Jessie was dogged, teetering on the edge of fury. ''You really didn't do anything to me yesterday?''

''Not a thing.''

''You didn't take my clothes off when we got here?''

''No, Mrs. Catsdoor took care of you.''

''So this is the first time you're seeing me at all unclothed?''

''Yes.''

He released one of her hands because he had to touch her breast. The instant she was free, she made a fist and hit him in the jaw, so hard his head flew back. He grabbed her hand again, cursing.

She tried to rear up, but he was heavy against her. She fell back against the tablecloth, panting, shrieking, ''You bastard! You lied to me. You made me think that it was all over and done with so I wouldn't have to worry about it anymore. And now here I am, still both a physical and spiritual virgin with you standing between my legs, my ankles locked behind you, and you've ripped my beautiful chemise that Maggie gave me and you're staring at my bosom. All for the first time, not the second time so I wouldn't have to be all that embarrassed. I hate you, James. Damn you, let me go.''

''No,'' he said, and he leaned down and kissed her left

breast. "You're not my damned little obnoxious sister, not with breasts like these you aren't." He shoved himself against her and she tried to struggle away from him. She unlocked her ankles and her legs fell down over the end of the table. She was sliding off, pressed so hard against him now that he thought he'd die if he didn't come into her this very instant. Not an instant from now, but this instant.

It was more than a man could take. He kissed her other breast because he couldn't help himself, then he reared back, pulled up her gown and petticoats, stared at those long legs of hers, now covered with soft white cotton stockings, tied mid-thigh with garters of peach satin. The garters matched her chemise? He trembled. He stared down at her.

It took him a moment to realize she wasn't struggling anymore. She was just lying there staring up at him, watching him look down at her.

"You're not wearing drawers," he said. She was wearing only her peach satin chemise that came merely to the top of her thighs. He was shocked. Even Connie wore light muslin pantalettes that tied with pretty ribbons just below her knees. Lots of pretty lace trimming, of course, but they were still drawers and covered everything. He'd always enjoyed kissing up her legs, pulling those ribbons loose with his teeth, then slowly pulling them off her.

"No," she said, her voice as thin as the layer of sweat on James's forehead. "Maggie told me not to wear any pantalettes for thirty days after we were married. She said it would drive you mad knowing I was naked beneath my riding skirt or my gowns."

"Why just thirty days?"

"She said after thirty days I was to do it only randomly, that you would never know when you looked at me if I was wearing anything beneath my chemise or not. She said that would drive you mad as well for at least six months."

"And after six months?"

"Then I was to leave them off only as a reward. She said a man started showing his true colors after six months and needed to be handled with more guile. I told her I knew all your true colors already. I told her I'd seen you punch a stable lad who'd drunk a bottle of gin and slept next to one of your horses, that I'd heard you yelling your head off crying foul when someone better than you beat you in a race. I even told her I'd heard you belch, but that was just one time and you didn't know I was there."

"Good God," he said, aware that he was but a pair of breeches away from coming into her, that her breasts were quite naked, and she was talking his ear off. He had to regain some semblance of control here. If he didn't, he'd do something stupid.

"Jessie, be quiet now. We'll speak more about Maggie's underwear strategy a bit later. Right now, while you're not looking at all like the old Jessie, I'd just as soon come inside you and get it over with. Would you like that?"

"You're looking at me."

"Yes. Your woman's hair is as red as the hair on your head. It's incredible, really, with all that white flesh of your belly. There's so much of you that's balm for a man's lust, I don't know where to look first. Now, will you bash me again if I let your hands go so I can kiss your breasts?"

"No, but perhaps later I will when I've had time to think about it some more."

He released her hands, leaned down, and took her nipple into his mouth. He was flooded instantly with lust and warmth. He blew on her nipple, then said, "Do you like that?"

She didn't say anything, but she grabbed his face between her hands and pulled him down to her again. He didn't leave her breasts for a very long time. And even when he eased his fingers up her thigh, he still kissed her breasts. She was shaking. Surely that was a good sign. When his fingers touched her flesh, she heaved upward so violently she nearly knocked him off her.

"Goodness, should you be doing that, James? No one's ever touched me there before. Only me, and that's when I bathe."

"Yes, I should touch you here every day, perhaps four times a day. At least I should be doing this to the new Jessie. Promise me something." He lightly stroked his fingers over her, even as he looked at her glazed eyes.

"What?"

"You've got to stay the new Jessie, at least when we're making love."

She closed her eyes, arched her back, and moaned. The old Jessie had never done that.

He eased a finger inside her and felt her ankles lock behind his back again. "Yes," he said, stroking her now, feeling the wonderful heat of her, the loosening of her flesh, that delicious arching of her back. When he touched her belly, then delved into those red curls to find her, she nearly bucked him off her again.

"That's it," he said, coming over her to kiss her. Her breath was hot, she was panting, and he didn't wait any longer. He freed himself from his breeches and came slowly into her.

"James! That's your stallion part."

"Hold still, Jessie. Just hold still and I'll come in really slowly. That's it, just relax. That doesn't hurt, does it?"

She was staring at him, watching the pained, utterly absorbed expression in his beautiful eyes. She tightened her ankles and it brought him farther into her.

Suddenly she gasped. "Oh dear, stop, James. This isn't good anymore."

"It's your maidenhead, Jessie." He was panting, his voice sounding like a creaking door that needed oil. His hands were shaking and he was inside her, but not far enough, not nearly far enough. "Trust me, Jessie. Every woman has one. I don't mean she has one trust, she has a maidenhead." He was staring down at himself pushing into her. He knew he wouldn't stop, he couldn't, not without dying. And if he did stop and he didn't die, then he'd kill himself anyway.

He smiled down at her, not moving, until he felt her ease and smile up at him. Then he shoved hard.

She yelled at the top of her lungs. He prayed Mrs. Catsdoor wouldn't start pounding on the door. He prayed she wouldn't scream anymore. She was small, he'd hurt her, but it was over, finally, it was over, and he didn't feel as though he'd violated his damned sister. No, she was his wife and he was touching her womb.

"I'm not moving. Don't shove at me and please don't move. I'm a man, and things of the flesh are different for me. All right, Jessie?"

He leaned down and kissed her mouth, her throat, then her breast. He nuzzled her breast with his chin, rubbed his cheek over her. "Is that better? Is the pain lessening?"

"A little bit. The Duchess didn't tell me about any of this. Is this the normal way of things?"

The Duchess told her something about sex? She moved in that moment, and he knew it was all over for him. He heaved over her, feeling the release wash through him, making him shudder like a man with a violent fever.

"Oh, Jessie," he said, and fell over her. Her arms were around his back, holding him tightly against her. Her hair was against his cheek. He felt the heat of her drawing at him, and he shuddered with the pleasure of it. He didn't move until he could finally breathe again. She squeezed him, then thumped him on the back with her fists.

"Is that all, James? Oh dear, you'd best be careful. Your right hand is nearly in the calf brains."

Calf brains? He was inside Jessie Warfield, the eavesdropping twit who'd fallen through her father's tack-room ceiling. He managed to pull himself up. He looked down at himself, a part of her, that white flesh of hers and that sinful red hair. He looked up her body, pausing at her breasts before he managed to get up to her face. She was staring at him, looking confused.

"What's the matter?"

"That's all there is to it?" she said, then unlocked her ankles. Her legs were sore, the muscles pulling.

He smiled and lightly touched his fingers to her woman's flesh, soft and swelled and wet with his seed.

"No, but it's all for you right now. Before I leave you, Jessie, what did the Duchess tell you?"

"She told me to think of her as my older sister and ask her anything about sex. I told her I knew everything. All about mounting, that is. She just said that wasn't all there was to it, that I knew enough for now and that you'd take care of things. She didn't tell me it would hurt. She didn't tell me you'd be so free with my womanly self."

"It doesn't hurt so much now, does it?"

She thought about that. "Not so much now."

"Just lie still and let me clean you up a bit." As he fastened his breeches again it hit him hard what he'd just done. He'd taken his wife's virginity on the dining-room table. He closed his eyes a moment. No wooing, no extended time to ease her and to make her really ready for him. But she'd nearly bucked him off her, twice. Surely she'd been ready. He shook his head, poured a glass of water onto a napkin, and pressed it against her. He didn't think the napkin was as soft and white as her flesh.

As he washed her, he looked up to see that her eyes were tightly closed, her face turned away from him.

"Poor Jessie," he said. "I'm sorry for being such a clod."

"I wonder," she said, not opening her eyes, "if stallions ever apologize to mares."

"Yes, they do."

Her eyes flew open. "You're lying. You have no idea. Oh dear, James, could you help me up, please." It seemed she realized her breasts were free and she quickly began buttoning her gown only to realize that the bottom part of her was naked as well, and she slapped down her petticoats and skirt.

"Let me help you."

He began the endless task of fastening those damned buttons. "I don't like this gown," he said after he'd managed two of them. "Let me just fasten some of the buttons. Promise me you'll change your clothes and then toss this miserable garment in the kitchen midden."

Jessie met James's dead wife's father that same afternoon when she was swimming naked in the small pond only fifty yards from the east of the house. It was bordered by water lilies and willow trees and tall water grass.

"Who the devil are you?"

Jessie swallowed a mouthful of water at the sound of the man's voice, whipped around, hoping the water covered her to her neck, and said, "I'm Jessie. Who are you?"

"You're James's new bride?"

"Yes. And you, sir?"

"Lyndon Frothingill, Baron Hughes. I'm Alicia's father. James is my son-in-law."

"Oh," she managed. Her feet were sinking in the mud, and she wanted out of the pond. "Do you think you could leave, sir? I'd like to come out now."

He stilled. "You're an American. Just listen to the way you talk. Like an illiterate nobody. And just look at you. No young English lady would even consider swimming in a pond, much less naked. My beautiful Alicia couldn't even swim. You look like a trollop with all that red hair. You're pregnant, aren't you? That's why James married you? He had to because he's a gentleman.''

Jessie wondered if that one time just after lunch in the dining room could have gotten her pregnant. He took that thoughtful look as a proof of her sin. He took a step closer to the edge of the pond and actually shook his fist at her, nearly yelling, ''You damned little bitch, you trapped him before I could act. I wanted to give him time to forget Alicia. He loved her more than life, James did. I feared for him after she died. I've given him well over three years to recover. I was bringing him Alicia's dear cousin, my own brother's child—Laura. She should have been the one to wed him, not you, you damned Colonial trollop.''

''Sir, I'm getting cold. Could you please leave now?''

Baron Hughes stood on the grassy bank, his hands on his meager hips, staring at her, a sly look in his eyes. ''Why don't you just come out now? I'll see what James has gotten in his second wife.''

Jessie saw a very angry, very bitter man, who looked older than his years. Surely he couldn't be older than her own father, but he seemed to be, deep lines scoring both sides of his mouth. His eyes, though, looked vicious, his mouth thin and mean. She wondered what he'd been like before his daughter's death.

''I'm sorry about your daughter, sir. I know James did love her very much. I didn't trap him, sir, at least not in the way you believe. I'm not a trollop. I'm a horse racer.''

For a moment, the vicious look left his eyes, leaving blank amazement, then returned quickly. ''You're not even a good liar, are you?''

''James says I'm not. Please, sir, I'd like to come out now. Won't you leave?''

''No. Since you're pregnant, perhaps you won't be on this

earth much longer, though strumpets like you tend to flourish while sweet angels like my Alicia are taken. I'll just
pray you'll die in childbirth just like my poor Alicia.''

"If I do, will you wait another three years before you trot
out your niece?''

"I won't have to. James will have forgotten you in
months. I daresay he'll want to remarry before the grass
grows over your grave.''

"This isn't very pleasant, sir. Please leave now. I'm being
nice because I realize you're still upset by your daughter's
tragic death. But it wasn't my fault, sir. James is now my
husband. You must accustom yourself to it. If you don't
leave me alone now, I'll be forced to do something you
perhaps won't appreciate.''

"What would that be, you damned chit?''

"Well—''

"Actually, sir, I think my wife would like the privacy.''

"James!'' The baron whirled around to see his former
son-in-law standing beneath the waving branches of a willow tree.

"She didn't lie to you. She's not a trollop. She's a horse
racer. Come along, sir. You need a brandy. Jessie,'' James
added, giving her a nod, "dry yourself well. I don't want
you to take a chill.''

The baron gave her a malicious look, shrugged, and followed James.

When she was tying the ribbons on her slippers, Jessie
wasn't too certain she wanted to see the dead Alicia's papa
again.

She went to the stables and spent the next hour grooming
Selina, one of the Arabian mares James raced in York.

She was on her knees oiling Selina's hooves, as filthy as
any stable lad, when she saw a shadow. She looked up the
length of James's body. He was wearing black boots, tight
dark brown buckskins, and a white shirt, open at the neck.

He looked healthy, tanned, as savory as Mrs. Catsdoor's nesselrode pudding. She realized she was staring at him, her mouth open, and snapped it closed.

"Is that your last hoof?"

"My last what? Oh, yes, it is." She patted Selina's leg. "She's a beauty, James. How old is she?"

"Seven. She was sired by Janus. She's foaled two stallions, both racers. Now, it's late and you're in dire need of a bath. You look like the old Jessie. I don't want that anymore. It makes me feel depraved." He paused a moment, then came down to his haunches beside her. He wrapped his finger around a loose curl. "Even your streamer is sweating."

"The old Jessie didn't have any streamers."

"No."

"You must strive to remember that, James. The old Jessie didn't have a peach satin chemise either."

"I'm sorry I ripped it."

"Mrs. Catsdoor said she'd mend it for me. She fancied I wasn't too handy with a needle, seeing as how I was from the Colonies and lived with horses all my life. I told her I fancied you weren't too good with a needle either, for the same reason. She *tskd-tsked* and patted my hand and said I needed guidance and she would provide it."

"She's right, but you're young enough to learn."

"Is he gone?"

"Yes, the baron's gone. He's an angry man, Jessie. I'm sorry he behaved as he did to you. On the other hand, what the devil were you doing swimming naked in the pond?"

It was a silly question, so she didn't answer it. Instead, she finished polishing Selina's hoof. As she rose, she ran her hands over Selina's legs, her shoulders, and her withers and combed her mane with her fingers. "You're beautiful now, my girl, more beautiful than I am, and I can't run as fast as you can. Here's a carrot for you. That's right, don't bite my fingers. Just nibble. That's it.''

Jessie brushed off her skirt, knew she looked a mess, but she did have her streamers, soaked with sweat though they were. Nor was she wearing any pantalettes. She gave James a sideways glance.

"What does that look mean?"

"I'm not wearing any underwear," she said, laughed, picked up her skirts, and ran, looking over her shoulder to see him standing as still as a fence post, staring after her.

# ═══ 21 ═══

"JAMES?"

*"Hmmm?"*

"Do many women die in childbirth?"

He stopped nuzzling her neck and leaned back in the chair, closing his eyes. "Yes, too many. But you won't, Jessie, I swear it to you. I told you that after Alicia's death, I read every book I could find on childbearing. I spoke at length with George Raven. Had he but been here when her time came, I doubt she would have died. Don't worry."

"Maybe I won't get pregnant. Maybe I can't since I've ridden horses all my life."

"Where did you get that errant bit of nonsense? No, don't tell me. It was your mother, right?"

"Yes. She said I had probably ruined my female parts."

"You still had a maidenhead."

"I did, didn't I?" she said, sounding as pleased as Fred who'd probably cornered Clorinda again and stolen another peck. "Well, that's a relief. Maybe everything else is in order as well. I hope so. I certainly like foals and Charles and Anthony."

The thought of rending that small barrier made him tremble with lust. He could practically feel himself again as he'd shoved through it, so frantic with urgency that he'd nearly spilled his seed at that moment. He pulled her closer to his chest and began nuzzling her neck again. She was sitting on his lap in a large winged chair in the bedchamber. It was *their* bedchamber, he'd told her when they'd come up after dinner. She wasn't to sleep alone in the adjoining room. He didn't like that at all.

Jessie, who knew nothing about the proprieties of sleeping arrangements between husbands and wives, solemnly nodded. "I'd rather sleep with you. I've never slept with anyone before. It's an adventure." She wrinkled her forehead. "You know, James, I don't think Papa and Mama sleep in the same bed."

"You're chattering again, Jessie."

"Sorry. I'm nervous, James. I'm in my nightgown, and you don't expect me to be wearing any pantalettes. You're in your dressing gown, and I know you don't have anything on beneath it. This is unnerving."

He smiled as he kissed her hair again. He hugged her close to him as he said, "You're right—this is unnerving. I never thought I'd want to do anything with you other than beat you on the racecourse. And now that I've untied that very pretty bow, I can slip my hand inside and touch your breast. Ah, you're as soft as Selina's belly, after you brushed her. You know, Jessie, I didn't get to see all of you on the dining-room table today, just those important strategic parts. Let's get that nightgown open."

He untied three more bows and pushed the soft muslin apart. It parted all the way to her feet. He looked, nothing more, just looked, for a very long time. He lightly laid his hand on her hip, turned her toward him, and began kissing her. He was surprised and inordinately pleased when he felt her hands untying the sash of his dressing gown. "Yes," he said into her warm mouth, "I want to feel your breasts against me. My God, Jessie, that's incredible."

It was, she thought, trembling now, those strange urgent feelings pulsing low in her belly, even when it was her breasts hard against his chest. She moved a bit, and they both moaned.

He laughed. He had to because, after all, he was the one with the experience here; he was the one who shouldn't just fall apart and slaver all over her, baying like a hound at the moon, just because her she was brushing the hair on his chest.

"I like your legs," he said, watching his brown hands stroke her white flesh, feeling the sleek muscles, admiring the long length of her legs.

"Thank you. May I see your legs, James?"

"Actually, you can. I can't take too much more of this, Jessie." He lifted her in his arms and carried her to the bed. He set her on her feet, stripped off her nightgown, and pressed her down until she fell onto her back. She stared up at him, embarrassed—he knew that because her cheeks were becoming nearly as red as the hair on her head. He slipped out of his dressing gown, planning to let her look her fill at him, but he couldn't manage it. He came over her, lying with his full length on top of her, her legs spread beneath him.

"No more maidenhead, Jessie—just pleasure for you." He came up on his knees, lifted her hips in his large hands, and brought her to his mouth.

He felt her freeze in shock. He paused a moment to look at her face. She looked utterly bewildered.

He watched her wet her lips with her tongue. "I don't know about this, James."

"Well, I do. Just be quiet and enjoy yourself."

"I can't. It's too embarrassing."

He wondered if he would fail with her and nearly laughed at himself for his impatience. This was the first time for her and he hadn't done much to soften the shock of it, just came between her legs and lifted her in his hands. He'd just wanted to take her with his mouth and he had. He would have to slow down. He eased away from her and came down beside her. He kissed her once, again, and yet another time.

He stroked her, learning her, hoping to ease her after his frontal attack. It did ease her. When her hands were on his back, stroking his shoulders, kneading his chest, he wondered how he could be such a reasonable, rational man one moment and a ravening beast the very next.

He knew she was ready for him, and he couldn't wait to stroke her more. He just couldn't. He came into her quickly, pushing hard, and felt her flesh accommodating him, but it was still tight, so incredibly tight that he lost his head.

The release was even more powerful than the one on the dining-room table. He'd thought a release like that had to be only once in a marriage, when the man took his bride's virginity—a heady act, that. But it wasn't true. His heart was pounding so loudly he doubted he could hear anything. He felt her hands, those palms as callused as his own, stroking up and down his back.

He'd given her no pleasure. Again.

He didn't want to apologize again, at least while his brain was still at low ebb. He had to regain his wits and talk to her, explain that he wasn't usually such a selfish sod, that sometimes a man just lost control and veered off the proper path and that's what had happened with her, though he couldn't begin to explain it since he'd known her since she was fourteen and had never once even considered what she'd look like without her clothes. Yes, he'd promise her that he'd take care of her the next time. Not, he realized vaguely, as fatigue tugged at him, that she could begin to understand what he would even talk about. What did she know about pleasure?

Not a blessed thing. He cursed softly even as he fell off her onto his back, jerking the covers over him as he fell.

Jessie lay there for a very long time, staring up at the

ceiling that was painted the same soft white as the walls. The molding around the ceiling was nicely done, she thought, with carvings of fruit and vines and such. She'd been married now for two days. James was lying like a felled log beside her, snoring, occasionally twitching, sprawled out on most of the bed. He had nice feet, both of those appendages showing below the covers. She rose slowly, feeling the tightness of her thigh muscles, and walked to the basin to wash herself.

She wandered to the windows, pulled back the lovely pale gold draperies, and looked out. There wasn't much of a moon to lighten things up. The grounds looked shadowy and vaguely menacing. She walked back to the bed and stood there a moment, staring down at her husband. She wondered where she was supposed to sleep. In the few minutes she'd been gone, he'd sprawled over all the bed, his arms and legs flung out. She found herself smiling. He'd enjoyed what he'd done to her. She was quite certain of that. She was happy that he had. She lightly touched her fingers to his chin, to his nose, to his earlobe. He was the only man she'd ever really seen, the only man who'd come to be part of her. She would give him whatever he wanted.

"Jessie, what are you doing out of bed?"

He startled her so badly, she jumped a good foot. "Oh dear, you're awake, James? Yes, I can see you are. I'm not beside you because there isn't any beside you to be beside."

"You're right. I've got all the bloody bed. Come here, Jessie. I want to kiss you."

Then he'd want to do those other things to her as well. So be it. She loved him.

It was as dark as the bottom of a witch's cauldron. James realized soon enough that Jessie was easier with him in the dark, less embarrassed. *Good*, he thought. This time he would make a thorough job of it. This time she would have pleasure. When he kissed her belly, she was trembling, her heels dug into the mattress, her fingers tangled in his hair. He raised his head a moment. "Jessie, I'm going to kiss you and caress you now and I want you to just relax."

"All right," she said, and jumped when she felt his tongue slide in and out of her navel. When he parted her with his fingers, she raised her hips, felt his hot breath on her, and arched wildly. He was talking to her while he kissed her, whispering sex words. She didn't understand everything he was saying, but his words excited her, particularly the way he said them. When he eased his finger into her, she went wild. The feeling was awesome, unexpected, and she never wanted it to end. She heard herself crying out. She couldn't seem to stop. On and on it went. She didn't know she was panting, clutching his hair, digging her short nails into his shoulders, but James did.

James gave her all the pleasure he could. When he felt the passion begin to lessen, he eased his rhythm, soothing her, easing her. It was wonderful. She was his now, all of her.

He grinned up at her in the dark. "What do you think, Jessie, about this sex business?"

She groaned. "I'm dying. I don't have any bones. I'll never walk again. I'll never even move again."

"Good, that's what a man likes to hear from his wife." Then he came over her and slid into her, and she was slick and wet and her arms were around him, holding him tightly, and her hips were moving to draw him deeper, and it was over for him in moments.

"I'm a good husband," he said before he was asleep, his head beside hers on the pillow.

"Well," Jessie said into the darkness. "That is something I never expected." She kissed his ear, his chin. She squirmed out from beneath him, settling against him. This was good, she thought, very good indeed. Together, they drifted off to sleep.

James had believed that a cannon bombardment couldn't have awakened him, but he was wrong. Jessie's scream penetrated his brain. In an instant, his heart was pounding, he was alert. Jessie cried out again. This time wide awake, it wasn't quite a scream, but a cry of pain and fear. He shook his head and leaned over her. She was dreaming. He started to shake her, then stopped when she opened her eyes and yelled, ''No! Get away from me! No, Mr. Tom, don't touch me like that. No, no, stop!'' She screamed again, a thin cry actually, and jerked upright.

''Jessie, wake up, you're having a nightmare.'' He shook her, but she didn't awaken. She moaned again, whimpered, trying still to struggle away from him. ''Wake up, come on, it's just a bad dream.''

''James?''

''Yes, stop shaking, you just had a nightmare. It's over now.''

''Yes, it's over,'' she said, and fell back against her pillow. He doubted she'd really come awake; he'd just roused her enough to break off the dream. He unplaited her braid and tugged his fingers through the deep ripples it left in her hair. She didn't stir. Her hair was so thick and curly. He smoothed it out over the white pillow.

Yes, she had lovely hair for a girl he'd known for too long to possibly consider her as a wife, as a mate, as a woman he desperately wanted to come into again. Yet he knew he would have to wait. But sometime around lunchtime he'd make her scream with pleasure again.

As he drifted off a second time, James wondered: *Who the hell was Mr. Tom? What had he done to her?*

''Jessie, wake up.''

She moaned and pulled away from that hand on her

shoulder, pulled away from that insistent voice.

"Come on, wake up. It's very late, later than you've ever slept in your life. Wake up."

She pulled the covers over her head.

He pulled them off her. She felt the bed give when he sat down beside her. "Jessie," he said, and kissed her cheek, her ear, smoothing her wildly curling hair from her face.

She opened her eyes and looked up at him. He was so beautiful, so precious to her that she didn't think she could bear it. But of course she could. She remembered the pleasure he'd given her in the dark of the night. It was daylight now and it was difficult to look at him, knowing that he knew what he'd done to her.

James was grinning down at her, feeling a good deal of male satisfaction. Triumphant even. He felt wonderful, well rested and filled with delicious sated feelings. He leaned over and smoothed his fingertip over her eyebrow. "I'm going to do that to you again today sometime. What do you think? Nothing to say? That's all right, Jessie. Embarrassing you is a treat, something I never managed to do until I was running my tongue down your white belly and then—"

"James."

He leaned down and kissed her. "Good morning," he said, and kissed the end of her nose, her left ear, her chin. "Whatever are you doing still asleep? I exhausted you, is that it? You're supposed to feel all energetic, Jessie, not swooning in bed until half the day is gone."

She smiled at him, the new Jessie gaining a hold. "After you've taught me everything about this marriage business, then I'll be able to tease you as well."

"There's lots to learn, Jessie. It will take me more time than you can imagine to teach you every nuance, every slight movement that brings a different kind of pleasure."

Her eyes nearly crossed. "Oh," she said.

"I lied to you. Half the day isn't gone. I just wanted to

have breakfast with you so we could discuss what we'll do today. It's only seven o'clock. I've already bathed and dressed. Harlow is bringing up hot water for you. Would you like Mrs. Catsdoor to help you?''

She didn't want anyone to help her, unless it was James. She couldn't quite bring herself to ask him to rub her back with the bathing cloth. He turned in the doorway. ''Oh, Jessie, who is Mr. Tom?''

She stared at him. She repeated so softly he barely heard her. ''Mr. Tom?''

''Yes, who is he?''

Jessie seemed suddenly remote. Her eyes took on a far-away cast that made James feel her thoughts, whatever they might be, were miles away. ''I don't know,'' Jessie said slowly, her voice distant. ''I remember a long time ago that I had dreams about him but then they stopped. This is odd, James. I haven't dreamed about Mr. Tom for years. Why would I dream about him last night?''

He had no answer to that. He'd known her for six years. He'd never heard her or her family say anything about a Mr. Tom.

The day stretched out endlessly, one slow minute at a time. James could hardly believe that it wasn't noon, the time he'd set to take her to bed again.

The sun was hot overhead. Jessie wiped away the sweat on her brow. Every few minutes she looked at her husband, and when he looked back at her, she knew exactly what he was thinking. She also knew she didn't have a stitch of undergarments on underneath her clothes. She scrubbed the horse harder until he tried to dance away from her.

She heard James laugh. She shook her fist at him. They worked the horses all morning, companionably because they'd been companions for so very long. At ease around horses, they knew how to behave, what had to be done. And they were at ease with each other. After all, they'd been companions long before they'd been lovers. Jessie began to hum.

It didn't occur to her to believe James loved her just because he enjoyed lovemaking with her. No, what was important was that they were friends. She would build on that. There was a race in York, and James intended to ride Bertram in two heats.

Jessie rode Selina just before lunch, putting her through her paces. She was surprised at the horse's smooth speed, her flawless endurance. She suspected there was some blood other than Arab in her. No pure-blooded Arab could have as much stamina as Selina did.

When Jessie returned to the stables, she saw that James wouldn't be riding anything on Saturday. He was sitting on the ground, cursing the air blue, holding his ankle with one hand and waving his fist at Clothilde, one of the bay mares, with the other.

George Raven arrived two hours later at Candlethorpe, fetched by Mrs. Catsdoor's son, Harlow.

"Hello, Jessie. What happened to James? Harlow couldn't seem to put two words together for me."

"It's his ankle. I don't think it's broken, but I didn't want to take the chance I was wrong. You are the doctor, after all."

He gave her an angel's grin, for surely George Raven, shorter than Jessie and very slim, was the most beautiful man she'd ever seen in her life. No wonder Marcus had always complained about his attending the Duchess.

"A horse kicked him?"

"Yes, Clothilde. I do think she was laughing at him while he was sitting on the ground, cursing her. She did have this unholy look in her eyes."

"Let's see how he's doing."

James had refused to go to his bedchamber. He was reclining on a beautiful blue brocade settee in the drawing room, the kicked foot propped up on several cushions. He was miserable, furious, and in a foul mood. It was past noon and here he was with his ankle hurting like the very devil. Jessie had all her clothes on, and he was nowhere near getting her into bed. Well, hell.

"I should have known Jessie would fall apart and send for you. Why didn't you tell me you'd been such a fool, Jessie? Ah, no answer, huh? You knew I'd box your ears, curse you."

"He sounds practically well already. Now, James, leave poor Jessie alone. You've only been married three days. She did the right thing. Now let's see how hard Clothilde kicked you."

"Bloody mare. I had to give her a physic. Sigmund was holding her and I was doing the offensive deed and she jerked loose from Sigmund and turned on me."

"Clothilde was pretty angry?"

"She didn't even pause to question what she was doing. No, she just kicked out that hoof and got me good. Sigmund just sent me word that she's just fine now. Seems the release of her bile took care of her other problem. Ow! Go easy, you damned torturer."

"Sorry. Jessie's right. The ankle's not broken, thank the good Lord, but James, you're going to be a gentleman of leisure for the next two days. Stay off that foot. Stay seated as much as possible, and keep the ankle up high. Now, here's some ointment for Jessie to rub into the ankle. It won't do much for the pain or swelling, but it will make you feel a bit better."

"I'm racing on Saturday."

"Not this Saturday you're not. No, don't complain or whine to me about it. Keep the weight off the ankle and relax. Jessie, will you keep him chair-bound?"

"Certainly, though he is capable of cursing the ceiling down on our heads."

George Raven raised a very blond eyebrow. Jessie could just picture Marcus looking at him and telling him to go bugger himself. That word, the Duchess had told her once, had led to a great deal of consternation in the house when she'd wondered aloud what it meant. "You should have seen the look on Badger's face," she'd said, laughing. "I thought he would throw the tureen of turtle soup he was making at my head."

Dr. Raven said, "You curse in front of your bride of three days?"

James snorted. "You should have heard her curse when she was only fourteen years old."

"He's right," Jessie said. "I listened to him one day, admired his verbal ability vastly, and searched out every foul word spoken by every stable lad in Baltimore. My father wasn't such a bad source either."

"What about your mother?"

"Don't sound so snide, James, just because you feel rotten. Ah, Mrs. Catsdoor, you're just in time."

George Raven poured three drops of laudanum into a glass of lemonade and handed it to James. "Drink it and don't complain. It won't put you to sleep, but it will reduce the pain in your ankle to a dull ache."

James drank the whole glass, wiped his hand over his mouth, and said, "I'm waiting. It still hurts."

Jessie chose to ignore him. "As to my mother," she said to George Raven, "she taught me other things."

"Like what?"

Dr. Raven looked from one to the other. They were scrapping like two children. Of course James wasn't feeling all that ready for action at the moment, but he supposed he expected to see Jessie, the new bride, wringing her hands, hovering over James, giving him ineffectual but loving pats—all in all, behaving like a besotted newlywed. But no, these two were behaving like two people who'd known each other for a very long time, two people who weren't particularly in love with each other. He wondered what the truth of the matter was. Neither the earl nor the Duchess had breathed a word of anything interesting to him or to his own new wife, Rowenna. He smiled as he straightened up. Rowenna would have been consoling him continuously had he been hurt.

"Go away, George."

"All right, James. Jessie, just make sure he doesn't move around. Keep him chair-bound and bed-bound—well, that's not quite what I mean. No waltzes. No riding. I'll see you on Saturday. Not at the racecourse in York. I'll see you here."

"Do come for luncheon, Dr. Raven. Perhaps you'd like to bring Rowenna as well?"

When Jessie returned to the drawing room some minutes later, James looked her up and down and frowned. "I will say this just one time, Jessie. You will not dress like a boy and ride Bertram on Saturday."

She grinned at him like a pickpocket who had just snaggled St. Peter. "I daresay I could win some guineas for us, James. Candlethorpe is very nice inside, but we do need money for Marathon. It looks like an old barn inside. How much could I win at York?"

"Not enough, so you might as well forget it."

"Perhaps enough just to buy new wallpaper for the parlor."

"Jessie—"

"You look very interesting, James, like a languid poet—perhaps Shelley, though he's dark, isn't he?—with your foot propped up, that lock of hair hanging over your forehead, all slouched down in that chair."

"Promise me. I don't want Sigmund running in here in

hysterics because you and your breeches are gone and Bertram's gone as well.''

"I daresay I'd take Sigmund with me. I wouldn't know where to go, you see."

"Do you want me to tie you to that chair? I will, Jessie, if you don't give me your sacred promise this very instant. Say it, Jessie. Say 'I swear I won't go to York on Saturday.' ''

She gave him a shameless grin, an old-Jessie shameless grin. He wanted to come inside her so badly he hurt worse than his blasted ankle. He'd never before realized that the new Jessie was the old Jessie beneath her clothes.

# ═ 22 ═

HIS TWISTED ANKLE provided respite. Jessie knew he wanted to have sex with her—goodness, before lunchtime, he'd said with a wicked laugh—but she also knew that the way it would have to be accomplished would be a method that would doubtless shock her to her toes. She eyed James and decided he wouldn't have the guts to ask her to do it, which was a pity, but in the long run, better for the welfare of his ankle.

Because James knew her so well, he just sighed deeply, squeezed her hand, and sighed again. Jessie grinned at him. "My ankle will heal soon enough," he said.

"It had better."

"That's my Jessie." But he'd wanted to cement what he'd gained. If enough time passed, perhaps he'd see that look of bewildered embarrassment on her face again. He didn't want her to retreat, to freeze up on him. Well, damnation. Sigmund and Harlow had helped him upstairs. It had been Harlow's request to be his gentleman's gentleman, and he'd not done a bad job of getting his clothes off him and putting him to bed.

Jessie hadn't volunteered, and James wasn't about to ask her. He didn't even know if it had occurred to her. Lovemaking after proper preparations was one thing, undressing a man with an ankle swelled to the size of a Darlington melon was quite another.

His ankle was throbbing, his belly wasn't too happy from Mrs. Catsdoor's attempt to reproduce Badger's green-pea soup, and he was bored, conversation between him and Jessie having dwindled during the long evening into inquiries about his ankle followed by his own curt replies. She'd tried, he'd give her that, but his ankle still hurt like the devil and he made a terrible patient.

Once he was in bed, the covers pulled up to his chest, and Harlow removed from his bedchamber, he called out, "You can come in now, Jessie. I'm all shrouded in blankets and sheets, everything repellent covered, except for my damned foot."

She came through the adjoining door. He knew she'd just been waiting in there for him to call her. She was wearing a very plain dressing gown, probably one that belonged to the old Jessie. Did she fear he'd attack her if she wore one of her new-Jessie dressing gowns? Probably.

He eyed her anew for any interest. "Are you going to sleep in here with me?"

"I'm concerned that I might roll over on you or kick your ankle."

"I'm not worried. I want you here."

She started to shake her head, and he said quickly, "I might need you during the night."

She nodded slowly then. He closed his eyes as she eased another pillow beneath his foot, her fingers lightly touching his big toe as she said, "Is that better?"

"Better than what?"

She sighed. "George told me you'd be difficult. When Papa got kicked in the leg some years ago, I was the only one who would spend any time with him. Mother told him he could drown in his own bile for all she cared."

"I don't want to do that. Why are you wearing that hideous dressing gown?"

"I don't want to torture you, James. One of the confections Maggie gave me, well, you just might break your ankle trying to get to me. I don't want that on my conscience.''

He swallowed hard. ''Shall I tell you a story?''

''No. I'm very tired. I want to go to sleep. Oh, I nearly forgot. Dr. Raven said you were to have another glass of lemonade with laudanum.''

He decided he wanted it. He didn't want to lie awake, his ankle hurting like the devil, listening to Jessie breathe next to him, within arm's distance, within touching distance. No, better to retreat into oblivion.

He slept through the night. Jessie, a light sleeper, kept waking up, listening to him. He didn't wake up in pain.

The next day his ankle was very much improved. ''Perhaps,'' he said at breakfast between bites of toast and eggs, ''I'll be able to ride Bertram tomorrow.''

''Not in your wildest fantasies. No. I won't allow that, James.''

''I wouldn't even have to leave until later tonight. Some years ago, Frances, the Countess of Rothermere, worked with an architect in York and invented a carrier for horses. That way the racehorse arrives all rested at the course, not exhausted from having walked the whole way.''

''That's ingenious,'' Jessie said, dropping her fork and sitting forward. ''What does it look like?''

''A covered smallish wagon that's pulled in turn by two horses. You just secure the horse's reins to the bar to keep him still, and off you go. The rear upper half of the wagon is open, so there's plenty of fresh air.''

''Goodness, how I'd like to see that. A woman, Frances Hawksbury, had the idea?''

''Yes. Contrary to popular belief, her husband wasn't at all dismayed that she, his wife, came up with the idea and not he. He tells everyone he knows about it. I've seen several of them around now.''

"I wish I were smarter, then maybe I'd have thought of that."

"You're smart enough. Be quiet. I thought I'd build a couple so I could race horses at courses farther away, say in North Carolina or Washington City."

"Oh, James, that would be wonderful. I remember we raced the local ponies on the Outer Banks, near Ocracoke. It's odd, you know, but we haven't gone to the house on Ocracoke since I was a young girl. I suppose Papa just grew tired of listening to Mother carp about all the insects that were always biting her. They bit Glenda as well, but not Nelda or me. Isn't that strange?"

"I've heard it said that bugs only bite succulent flesh."

"I daresay that the Duchess would have thrown her peas at Marcus if he'd said that to her."

He liked the way those streamers of hers curled lazily down to nearly touch the collar of her pale yellow gown. The new Jessie was in full bloom this morning.

"Are you wearing your underwear underneath that gown since I'm incapable of doing anything?"

Her fork hit her plate. She looked down at the small yellow pile of eggs. She said, "No."

His eyes nearly crossed. The throbbing in his ankle was nothing compared to the sudden surge of lust in his groin.

"You're torturing a sick man."

She tilted her head to one side, the streamer falling loose beside her cheek, and grinned at him, a teasing grin, one that Glenda wouldn't hesitate to copy if she'd had the pleasure to see it.

"I've been thinking about what would please you today. I've decided I'm going to take you for a ride in the landau. We're going to have luncheon with the Duchess and Marcus. What do you say?"

He thought about his ankle being jostled around for two

hours to Chase Park and two more hours back to Candlethorpe, and nodded.

"Good," she said, tossed down her napkin, and rose.

An hour later James was very comfortably ensconced in
the landau, his foot propped up on pillows, all secured with
ropes tied to the sides of the landau. No jostling.

"Frances's horse wagon gave me the idea. You know,
tying the reins to keep the horse steady?"

He just shook his head and relaxed while Jessie click-
clicked Phantom, his magnificent gray Barb, who was snorting happily, and broke into a trot.

But they didn't go to Chase Park that morning. They were
only thirty minutes from Candlethorpe when two riders
came into view. It was the Duchess and Marcus coming to
see the felled master of Candlethorpe.

Amid the laughter, the questions about James's ankle, the
shaking heads at the quirks of coincidence, and Jessie's in-
ventive way of tying James in place, Phantom suddenly
reared up, shook his great head, and tried to jerk the reins
from Jessie's hands.

James jerked the reins from her gloved hands, stood up,
barely, and began to execute a very strange series of movements, bringing Phantom first sharply to the left, then pulling him inexorably to the right. He did this three times.
Finally, Phantom heaved a great sigh and stood docilely in
the middle of the road, his head facing the hedgerows.

"What was that all about? What happened?"

Marcus reached over and patted Phantom's neck. "Good
fellow," he said, then added to Jessie, "James was a robber.
He bought Phantom for fewer guineas than the Duchess
spends on a pair of gloves."

"Yes," the Duchess continued. "He all but stole him
from this squire who was going to put him down because
he nearly trampled his nephew, a repellent little boy who

would probably have been better off for the trampling.''

James laughed. ''Poor old Phantom has this habit of seeing double. When Marcus and the Duchess stopped their horses right in front of us, Phantom saw four horses and four riders and decided it was time to leave. I tried many maneuvers, and finally hit upon the solution. I keep his head turned slightly to either the left or to the right. That way he can't see the horses and double their number.''

''It works,'' Marcus said. ''Now, since the Duchess and I have come all this way, let's go to Candlethorpe and we'll spend the day amusing you.''

''You knew about James's ankle?'' Jessie asked, eyeing James carefully as he turned Phantom around. Marcus and the Duchess didn't ride in front, but rather they stayed on each side of the landau.

''George Raven came to Chase Park yesterday. Anthony had decided that Marcus's cat, Esmee, would make a fine napping companion for Charles and put her next to his little brother. Esmee, who'd just eaten an entire trout for her luncheon, snuggled next to my sleeping son. Charles woke up, yelled his head off when he saw Esmee's face only an inch from his, and his nurse, Molly, fell, hit her head, and knocked herself unconscious trying to get to him to see what the matter was. She's fine now, just a ferocious headache. Marcus was forced to discipline Anthony.''

''What did you do, Marcus?'' James asked.

The earl gave his wife a sideways look, then mumbled, ''I smacked his bottom, made him apologize to Molly, then sent him to his bedchamber and told Spears he wasn't allowed to eat or play for at least fourteen hours.''

''We then left so Spears could change Anthony's punishment to suit his own opinion,'' the Duchess said. ''It was well done of you, my dear. I suspect even Spears was impressed with your firmness.''

''I'm glad I'm not there to see what Anthony's doing,''

the earl said. "About you, James, what happened?"

"James was giving Clothilde a physic. She didn't like it."

"No man or animal would," Marcus said. "Serves you right, James."

The Duchess carefully lifted off her riding hat, a lovely affair with a band of bright red around the black base, and hit her husband's arm with it. "You think a woman would enjoy such a thing?"

"I was speaking for all mankind, and that includes women."

After the ensuing verbal debris eventually cleared, James realized he hadn't felt his ankle at all.

The Duchess and Marcus didn't leave Candlethorpe that evening. After dinner, they left Mrs. Catsdoor rendered nearly speechless at their praise for her boiled knuckle of veal and her *vol-au-vent* of plums. The evening was spent singing some of the Duchess's ditties and playing whist.

That night when James was lying on his back in their bed, his foot propped up on its complement of three pillows, Jessie getting ready to snuff out the candles, he screwed himself to the sticking point and said, "Jessie, would you like to try something a bit different?"

"What?"

"Perhaps you'd like to kiss me a bit?"

"I don't know, James," she said, frowning down at him with great interest. "It might not be wise. You tend to lose control of your hands when you kiss me."

He sounded desperate. "I know, but I was hoping that perhaps you'd like to follow my instructions and we could do more than just kissing. You could, well, basically, you could sit on top of me and—"

"Sit on top of you? Why on earth would I want to sit on top of you, James?"

''Not just sitting. That wouldn't accomplish anything, unless you were reading a book, and I don't want you to do that. No, you would actually take me in your hands and—'' She was looking at him as if he'd told her he was going to strap her down on the rack and start stretching. He stalled. He lost his nerve.

She wished she knew what to do. He wanted her on top of him? She'd never seen a mare atop a stallion. It was a fascinating thought, but not with that swelled ankle of his. No, it had to wait, curse the fates. She began whistling, snuffed out the candles, and climbed in beside him. She wished the bed were larger. She could feel the heat of him, feel each movement he made. When his hand touched her side, she squeaked.

''Hold my hand, Jessie,'' he said, and she did.

She fell asleep rubbing the callus on his thumb.

James lay awake longer than he wished. Somehow he'd imagined Jessie would be more willing to try new approaches to lovemaking. The good Lord knew she'd always been brash, more confident than a female should be, eager for new experiences, always twitting him, mocking him, beating him at the damned racecourse, and protecting him from Glenda.

But she hadn't been at all eager to sit on him. She wasn't stupid. Surely she could imagine what she'd have to do. A shy Jessie was something he hadn't thought would plague him.

His ankle throbbed. The laudanum pulled on him, finally easing him into sleep, for which he was profoundly grateful.

Toward noon the following day, Badger arrived in a wagon loaded with enough food to feed the village of Tutleigh just to the south of Candlethorpe.

Instead of having her nose out of joint, Mrs. Catsdoor looked as if God himself had deigned to visit her. She exclaimed in delight, her hands pressed to her ample bosom, at all the dishes he'd prepared and brought to them. "Oh, Mr. Badger, if it isn't an incredible ragout of ducks! Look at the onion sauce you've prepared to accompany it. Just smell that wonderful fresh basil. Ah, and black-currant pudding, one of Master James's favorites. You're so good, sir, a genius, a master, a—"

"Please, Mrs. Catsdoor," the earl said, "Badger already runs the kitchen at Chase Park. I'd just as soon he didn't proclaim himself master of the entire house."

Badger allowed he had no real interest in running the entire house, although he just might have a few suggestions that Mr. Crittaker, the earl's secretary, might look into. As for Mrs. Catsdoor's praise, Badger took it in stride. When James hobbled into the entrance hall, he said, "I've brought something very special for you, James. A poultice that will shrink that ankle back to normal size within an hour. Dr. Raven is excellent at his bone mending and belly remedies, and relieving the ladies of their little plaguing ailments, but he knows nothing of brews to shrink swelling. Sit down, James. My lord, if you would please remove his boot so I can apply the poultice . . ."

The earl, arching a black eyebrow at his cook, complied, saying, "What I do for you, James . . . You'd best be very grateful."

The smell of the thick yellow concoction was surprisingly sweet, like sugar mixed heavily with eggs and cream. James sat back, closed his eyes, and said, "When it's been on my ankle for an hour, Badger, may I please have a spoon?"

# ═══ 23 ═══

JAMES LIMPED ONLY a bit the following morning, going so far as to help Badger place the remains of the Herculean meal he'd brought to Candlethorpe in the wagon and assisting the Duchess to mount her mare, kissing her hand as he grinned up at her, waiting to hear Marcus growl, as he did, saying he'd thump James into the mud once he had fully recovered.

He and Jessie waved at them until they disappeared from view around the fat beech tree at the end of the long drive. James rubbed his hands together. He was filled with energy, impatient to accomplish something, anything, and ready to make up for two lost days. He was surprised to find himself eyeing Jessie at the breakfast table like a wolf who hadn't eaten for the entire winter.

She was chattering away, seemingly unaware of his ever-spiraling lust. He couldn't wait much longer. He hurt with it. This was the something he wanted to accomplish more than anything in the world.

"... don't you think we should have a pair of peacocks, then, James? I would like a Fred sort of peacock who's always pinning his sweetheart to the house or to a tree so he can steal a peck."

"Jessie, you may have fourteen peacocks if you wish. Just be quiet, finish your breakfast, and take care of me."

"What do you want me to do?" She looked wicked, those

red streamers of hers dangling down as she cocked her head to the side.

"You'll see. Are you done yet?"

She tossed down her napkin, smiling at him. "Yes, all done."

"Come along, then."

She raced him to the master bedchamber, knowing he was trying his damndest to pull that injured foot faster, but of course she beat him. She stood in the middle of the vast room, watching him as he came in, slammed the door, and turned the key in the lock. "There," he said, and turned to face her, his expression grim.

She fluttered her hands in front of her as if to ward him off. "Oh goodness, James. It's morning! It's not even raining and thus a bit dark. The sun is shining. You're not thinking carnal thoughts, are you? Your poor ankle, isn't it paining you something fierce?"

"Yes, you witch," he said, cupping her face between his hands. "So what?"

She stared up at him, grinning like a woman who knew exactly what she was doing and knowing she was doing it well. He kissed her once and released her. "Jessie, you're a tease. Glenda doesn't even come in a close second compared to you. You're wicked and you're driving me over the edge. Now, you know very well that all I've thought about since Clothilde kicked me is stripping off that gown of yours, knowing you're naked beneath, and kissing you until you yell and thump your heels on the mattress. Ah, that got you, didn't it? You're not quite as wicked as you thought just yet, are you? You've had no pleasure from me for two days now, and I'm determined that this morning you'll moan until you're nearly demented. No more teasing. Take off your clothes."

Her heart was slamming against her ribs. She loved him. She didn't care if he didn't love her yet. He was watching her, and she felt the warmth and that strange urgency building deep inside her, low in her belly. That there could be something so pleasurable for human beings, it boggled the mind of a female who'd never before imagined such a thing. She'd always believed men to be wicked because they were deficient in honor. She was feeling more wicked than a man with three mistresses at the moment.

He wanted her. All the rest be damned. It was morning and he wanted her naked.

So be it. She shied away from him. Let him think she was embarrassed, that she was shy. Her fingers were shaking as she took off her clothes, and it had nothing to do with shyness. She stood in front of him until he pulled her against him and began to kiss her and caress her and finally to take her to bed. His hands were all over her. He caressed her breasts, molded his hands to her waist, tickled her navel with his tongue, parted her so gently with his fingers, and stared down at her—just stared for the longest time, and she nearly died with the excitement of it. She pushed up her hips. He laughed, leaned down quickly to kiss her lips, then set his mouth on her. She screamed.

And that was just the beginning. She couldn't stop the moans, the marks she was making on his body. She was lost in the feelings he was whipping up in her, and she loved it. The old Jessie and the new Jessie—she didn't know the difference. Who cared? Finally when she was breathing as if she'd run all the way to Chase Park and back, he came down over her and kissed her, his tongue deep in her mouth, and to her utter surprise, those strange feelings were swamping her again. Instinctively she lifted her hips for him. It was all he needed. He moved within her, but he wasn't frenzied this time. He was controlled, and it drove her insane. She shouted his name, squeezing him as hard as she could, and she heard him laugh and moan.

James took his release, at last, his head hanging down,

his breathing hard and raw. Finally, he managed to look up into her glazed eyes. "Damnation, Jessie, you're going to kill me before I'm thirty."

"Some promise," she said, then squirmed until he was on his back and she was pressed against him, her head on his shoulder, her open palm on his belly. "You know," she said, her breath warm against his flesh, "it was so beautiful, James. You made me feel like a star bursting in the heavens. You made me a woman, James. I'm fulfilled now, and ecstatically happy."

He pushed her down onto her back again and began winding a streamer around his finger. " 'A star bursting in the heavens'? Is that what you said?"

"Yes, all sorts of white lights and rampant sorts of deliciously wicked feelings. I wanted you so much, James, and you gave me everything."

"I made you feel like a woman? You're fulfilled now? 'Ecstatically happy' you said?"

"Oh, yes. You're a wonderful lover, James. You're more a man than any man I've ever known, not that I've ever known another man intimately, of course. I'm very lucky." She gave him a fat smile and giggled.

He smoothed back the hair from her forehead. He lightly touched his fingers to her breast. Her flesh was so very white. He looked down the long line of her, her waist, her flat belly, the stretch of her white legs. He thought only fleetingly of the old Jessie and smiled at himself. Then he closed his hands around her throat and squeezed. "You're a wretched tease, Jessie Wyndham. The fact of the matter is that I did make you scream and drum your heels and do all sorts of nice things to me with your hands and your mouth, but not enough. You're still a neophyte. You're just a beginner in this business. But you're learning. Now, you're pretending that it's nighttime and you're exhausted. Well, it's time to earn your keep. Now, let's go to the stable.

There's always more than enough work to do.''

While he was pulling on his black Hessians, he knew how he was going to make his smart-mouthed wife pay for her games.

"More salt, if you please, Mrs. Catsdoor. Yes, that's better. That should be about right.'' James laid down the big spoon. The ham soup was seasoned perfectly.

"But I don't understand, Master James, I—''

"I want to serve my wife, Mrs. Catsdoor. You and Harlow may have your own dinner now.''

On his way to the dining room, James added even more salt to the soup. "Ah, here you are, Jessie. Consider me your servant for the evening. Soup, my dear? Mrs. Catsdoor does it very well. Yes, a nice big bowl for you. And a glass of my best port. It's heavy, I know that, but it goes perfectly with the ham soup, Badger's recipe.''

He watched her while she spooned a bite into her mouth. "It's rather salty,'' she said, picking up her wineglass and sipping at the hearty port. "Does Badger really put that much salt into it?''

"Oh yes. He says it makes the ham nearly jump around in your mouth, all that flavor. More port, Jessie?''

Fifteen minutes later she'd forgotten that he'd eaten very little, and none of that delicious ham soup at all, but as he'd told her, "I don't do well with ham. It makes my belly ache,'' and she'd thought that was fortuitous since it would make all that much more for her. It was the best ham soup she'd ever had placed in front of her.

He sat back in his chair, his hands laced over his belly, watching her alternately take a bite of the ham soup, then drink that sin-red port. He sipped at his water and ate a chunk of warm bread.

"Did I ever tell you about the time I stole a kiss from

Margaret Tittlemore? Out in her father's barn with a calf butting against my leg?''

"Margaret Tittlemore? Goodness, James, she's married now and has four children! You stole a kiss?''

"We were both fourteen and believe me, Jessie, she had the prettiest mouth, all pink and pouting. Anyway, after I'd stolen that kiss, she slapped me—not very hard because she'd wanted that kiss, too—but I wasn't expecting that slap, and it was enough to knock me off balance. I fell over the calf, who mooed loudly enough to bring his mother. She poked me in the stomach, sending me over backward into the hay bin. Unfortunately one of the stable lads had forgotten to remove the rake, and I landed right on the tines. I had four glorious holes in my butt for two months.''

She laughed, drank more port, watched James pour more into her now-empty glass, and drank that. "What was Margaret doing while all this was going on?''

"The miserable girl was standing there holding her sides, laughing her head off. I quite like Margaret. She's produced good children.''

Jessie laughed and laughed. She drank some more port. He eyed her joyfully. He counted the glasses she'd already drunk. He didn't want her to be sick the next day. He strolled along the table, then pulled her chair away and placed a hand on each arm of the chair. He leaned over and put his mouth against hers. "How do you feel, Jessie?''

"Marvelous. Oh, James, your tongue across my lower lip tickles. Do it again.'' She giggled, and her warm breath washed through him like a wave that couldn't wait to crest. She heaved a deep sigh when he kissed her again, his tongue slipping between her lips this time.

When he was carrying her up the wide staircase, knowing that Mrs. Catsdoor was very likely watching his progress, he leaned down and kissed her ear. "How do you feel, Jessie?''

"I want to kiss you," she said, leaned up, grabbing his shoulders, and nearly knocked him backward.

"In just a moment, you can do whatever you want to do," he said, and began to run. His game was fast turning back on him.

When he had her naked, flat on her back on the wide bed, he stripped off his own clothes and came over her, shuddering at the softness of her, the heat, the feel of her hands as they stroked up and down his back.

"James," she said, arching upward. He kissed her, moving over her, pressing himself against her belly.

"Slow down," he said into her mouth, and licked her lip, then quickly nipped her earlobe. She loved it when he kissed her breasts, massaging them, rubbing his cheek against her soft flesh. She giggled, leaned up, and bit his neck.

He grinned at her, butted her head back with his chin, and began licking and nibbling on her throat. She laughed, squirmed, and pulled his ear. "I want you to see lights. I want you to yell that you're a woman, that you're fulfilled, that you've had a glimpse of heaven."

"All that?"

"Ah, Jessie, take this."

She gave him an owl-eyed stare, kissed him, her mouth open, her tongue busy on his, and whispered into his mouth, "I know I probably shouldn't be telling you how wonderful you are, but it's true. You're grand, James, just grand. I hurt, deep down in my belly, I hurt, but I don't want it to go away, the way I would a bellyache. Make it keep going, James. Make it like the other times. Ah, is that a white light I see?"

"Yell, Jessie."

When his fingers probed to find her this time, she did yell, shattering his eardrums.

Port was a wonderful brew. But he hadn't needed it. There was no more game in his mind, there was only giving and taking and knowing soul-deep pleasure.

He held on by a thread. He wouldn't enter her until he'd given her pleasure. He kissed her mouth, her breasts, all the while stroking her, caressing her, pushing her. When she cried out, tugging at his hair, pushing her hips upward, he knew he had to be the happiest man on earth. She was wild with pleasure, clutching him to her as if she wouldn't survive without him. He pushed her and pushed her more, giving her all he could, and when he eased inside her, she moaned softly and whispered, "You were made for me, James. Just for me."

He agreed. He didn't have long to contemplate what she'd said. He was gone in moments, jerking over her, moaning as if he'd been shot, sweating like a stoat. When it was over, he collapsed on top of her.

"James?"

He was nearly dead. He didn't want to talk. He didn't want to think. He wanted to try to get through the next few moments still breathing. He'd been a wild man and she'd loved it. Both of them had gone mad. Everything had worked beyond the port, beyond his wildest dreams.

Utterly mad, and it had been beyond anything he'd ever felt in his life. He'd given her immense pleasure. He'd made her lose complete touch with the world. He was a happy man.

"James." How could she even talk? How could she even think of a single word to say? He was nearly beyond what wits God had given him, and here she was saying his name as if it were the easiest thing in the world. He supposed it was his responsibility to make some sort of response. He managed to grunt.

She giggled. "I feel marvelous. What's wrong with you? I've overpleasured you, haven't I? Ah, James, did you see white lights? Do you feel fulfilled as a man? Will you revere me for as long as you live?"

He groaned, tried to push his arms up to get his weight off her, then collapsed again. "I'll think of something. Just give me a while."

She wrapped her arms around him and said, "I'm tipsy. Not as tipsy as on our wedding day, but tipsy enough to know that when stallions cover mares, they surely can't enjoy it as much as I do. Having you inside my body, ah, well, perhaps if I had another glass of port—perhaps two—I would be able to express myself more properly."

"You're not being at all proper. Your mother would scold you. Glenda would smack your face. As for my mother, God alone knows what she would do."

"He speaks," she said, and laughed as she kissed his ear. "He speaks a lot. Your heart's slowing, James."

"I'll live. It was close, but I'm fairly sure now that I'll make it."

He finally managed to push himself up onto his elbows. He looked down at a face he'd known for six years, once a young girl's face, but no longer. She was a woman and his wife.

"The look on your face when you came to your release—it pleased me mightily, Jessie. You still look so bewildered, so anxious that whatever is happening is really going to happen again and again. It did. It always will with us. Did you enjoy yourself?"

"You didn't lie there like a dead dog, James. You surely enjoyed yourself as much as I did. You sweated more and you made more noises."

He kissed her. "Perhaps just a little. Am I an excellent lover?"

"The best. Am I your best lover?"

She regretted the words the instant they'd escaped unbidden from her mouth. Fool, she was nothing but a fool and now he would have to lie or he'd tell the truth, which would probably be worse. She thought of Connie Maxwell, of the countless other women he'd known, including his first wife, Alicia. Why hadn't she just kept her mouth shut?

He looked thoughtful. He moved over her, as if settling in. He was still inside her. The hair on his chest tickled her breasts. "That's difficult," he said finally, leaning down to nibble her earlobe. "You still don't know much yet, but your enthusiasm was deafening. My eardrums are still vibrating. I liked hearing you shriek."

"I don't remember shrieking precisely."

"You aren't a good liar, Jessie. Give it up. I love the feel of you. Every day, every night, perhaps after afternoon tea, perhaps just before lunch, and then there's—"

That was an excellent beginning, she thought. "You got me tipsy on purpose, didn't you?"

"You're sobering up too quickly. Yes, I wanted you to melt for me, Jessie, and you did. The fact that I melted right along with you, well, that means that we're very good with each other. I like to hear you giggle and laugh. Lovemaking should be fun. I always want you to enjoy yourself."

"You put salt in the ham soup."

"Yes."

"Am I going to want to die tomorrow?"

"No, you didn't drink that much. I was careful about your intake this time."

"You're still inside me."

He quivered, hardening again, coming deeper. She shifted and lifted her hips, bringing him even deeper.

"Jessie, you want me again?"

"I think so, James. Tomorrow, you know, I'm going to make you very sorry that you tricked me."

"If I'm to be punished on the morrow, then give me tonight," he said, dipped his head down, and kissed her.

He awoke to a shriek. He rose right up in the bed, shaking his head. Another shriek. It was Jessie, having another nightmare. "Jessie," he said, and lightly shook her shoulders. It was dawn and he could see her face. She screamed again.

"Jessie, wake up."

Her eyes remained closed. Her head moved back and forth on the pillow. Then she said quite clearly, "No, go away from me. No, stop it, Mr. Tom! Oh God, no, don't do that."

By all that was holy, it wasn't Jessie's voice. Well, it was her voice, but it was her voice of long ago, when she'd been very young, when she'd been just a girl who was obviously frightened out of her wits. What was going on here? It was the way her voice had sounded that first time she'd dreamed about this Mr. Tom in James's hearing.

"Jessie!"

He shook her until she opened her eyes. She looked up at him, but it wasn't him she was seeing, not in that instant. She tried to lurch away from him.

"No, Jessie, it's all right now. You just had a nightmare. It's all right. I'm here. I'm James."

"Of course you're James. Do you think I'm stupid?"

That was his Jessie, thank God.

"You had the dream again. No, wake up, Jessie. We've got to talk about this. Who was this Mr. Tom? You sounded like a little girl, like he was hurting you. Was he trying to rape you, Jessie?"

"Oh, James," she whispered, and the next moment she was asleep. He stared down at her, lightly smoothed her eyebrows with his fingertips, and kissed her slack mouth.

"Tomorrow," he said, "tomorrow I want to know all about this bastard."

But the following morning, Bertram kicked Esmerelda, who bit him on his neck, and together they kicked out their stalls. James was out of bed running to the stables, leaving Jessie to struggle into her clothes.

\*    \*    \*

Jessie couldn't believe her ears. "Who is here, Mrs. Cats-door?"

"It's Baron Hughes, Mrs. James. There's a young lady with him." This was said in a warning tone that didn't leave Jessie in any doubt she wasn't going to like this.

"I suppose we have no choice. Do show them in, Mrs. Catsdoor. Is Master James about?"

"I'll send Harlow to fetch him. I'll bring tea and some of Mr. Badger's lemon cakes he left me."

Baron Hughes stood in the drawing-room doorway, looking at her as if he'd like to shoot her where she stood. He gave her a travesty of a bow, saying, "Good day to you, Mrs. Wyndham. I would like you to meet my niece, Laura Frothingill, my younger brother's daughter."

Laura Frothingill was staring at her, weighing her, at least that's what it made Jessie think, and finding her wanting.

"You're a Colonial," she said.

"Yes, just like James."

"James is the product of excellent English blood, not some sort of mongrel of unknown antecedents," the baron said.

"Are you certain you wish to be in the same room with a mongrel, sir?"

"Don't you try to make sport of me, missie!"

"All right. Won't you come in and tell me why you've taken your valuable time to come to Candlethorpe."

"I wanted Laura to see what supplanted my Alicia."

The baron looked for the world like her father's thoroughbred Gallen, who got blood in his eyes whenever another racehorse got within six feet of him.

So she was a what, not a who. So be it.

She smiled and held out her hand to Laura Frothingill, who stared at her hand, which was admittedly tanned, as if she were diseased.

She withdrew her hand and said mildly, "You're very lovely, Miss Frothingill."

"If only James had met her, she would now be his wife."

"I doubt that," Jessie said in that same mild voice, "not if he saw the look on her face right now."

"What do you mean the look on my face? I am beautiful!"

"Not now, you're not. You look like a vicious mare I once saw who kicked in a fence, broke her own leg, and had to be put down."

"Be quiet, you damned trollop!"

"It just occurred to me," Jessie said in that same mild, easy voice, "that this is my house. You are both incredibly rude. I would like both of you to leave."

"Not until James meets dear Laura."

"Ah, I see it all now. You want to make him feel sorry that he married me?"

"He will feel sorry, damn you! Then he just might take care of you."

"Well, let's say you're right, sir. What will he do about it? Divorce me? Perhaps even strangle me?"

The baron literally gnashed his teeth. Laura Frothingill suddenly looked very uncomfortable. "Uncle Lyndon," she said, tugging on his sleeve, "let us leave now. She's right. There's nothing to be done."

"Dammit, you can't have him, you miserable slut! I won't let you have him, do you hear me? I'll kill you myself!"

He leaped at her, his hands outstretched. Laura screamed. Jessie jerked away, but she wasn't fast enough. In her own drawing room, she thought, as his hands came around her throat, she was being strangled in her own drawing room. But Jessie wasn't helpless. He was old, but damn he was strong. Laura continued screaming.

Jessie went limp. The terrible pressure around her throat

lessened just a bit. She brought up her hands and slammed them against his ears. He shrieked, pressing his palms against his ears. He stumbled backward, but not before he swung his right fist at Jessie, catching the side of her head and throwing her against the fireplace. Her head struck the edge of the mantelpiece.

James heard three horrible screams, each one louder than the one before. His blood curdled. Then he heard Mrs. Catsdoor yell from the drawing room doorway, "Be quiet, you silly girl! What have you done to my baby mistress?"

*What baby mistress? Oh God, Jessie!*

# $\equiv 24 \equiv$

JAMES BURST INTO the drawing room to see Mrs. Catsdoor slap a young lady he'd never seen before. Then she turned on the baron. What the hell was his father-in-law doing here? Who was that young lady who was shrieking her head off?

"You, sir," Mrs. Catsdoor was yelling, shaking her fist in front of his face, "you're responsible for this. I never should have admitted either of you to the house. You're wicked, sir, just plain wicked. It's not my mistress's fault that your daughter died, not her fault at all, and yet you blame her and try to hurt her. Oh, dear Jesus, just look at her. Have you killed my little mistress?"

The baron's voice shook with rage and the pain in his ears. "The damned bitch! She struck my head, a crude trick I should have expected since she's not a lady. Why, I'll—"

James saw Jessie lying huddled by the fireplace. He was on his knees beside her in an instant, feeling the growing lump at the back of her head. He laid two fingers flat against the pulse in her neck. Strong and steady, thank the good Lord. He quickly felt her arms, her legs. Nothing broken.

He closed his eyes a moment, gaining control, trying to come to grips with this show of hatred from his former father-in-law, with his unconscious wife lying by the fireplace. He rose slowly. Mrs. Catsdoor, bless her loyal heart,

was standing toe-to-toe to Baron Hughes; all that was between them was the exquisite silver tea tray the baron had
given to his daughter for a wedding present, one of many,
including Candlethorpe itself.

"Be quiet, whoever you are," James said to the young
lady, who'd just emitted another shriek and was pressing
her palm against the cheek where Mrs. Catsdoor had slapped
her. His voice was low and mean, and it instantly got her
attention. She shut her mouth and stared at him, looking
white and scared.

"She tried to kill Uncle Lyndon."

"She didn't succeed, did she? That's right, just keep your
mouth shut. Whoever you are, sit down and don't move."
James walked to the baron. "Mrs. Catsdoor, thank you for
dealing very nicely with these people. Have Harlow ride
immediately to York to fetch Dr. Raven. Mrs. Wyndham
has struck her head. Her heartbeat is steady, thank God, and
it doesn't appear that she's broken any bones. But there's a
lump burgeoning on her head."

"James, I didn't intend for her to be hurt," Baron Hughes
said, taking a short step back at the utter fury he saw in his
former son-in-law's eyes. Never had he seen James angry
before. It shocked him, this anger on the part of his son-in-
law, and all over this trollop of a girl who wasn't anybody,
less than anybody, a bloody American, for God's sake.

"Of course you meant to hurt her," James said, pleased
he sounded so calm, so in control of himself. "Listen to me,
Lyndon, I know you grieve still for Alicia. I do as well. I
know you miss Alicia. I miss her as well. Her death was
tragic, but there was nothing we could do to prevent it. She's
dead, Lyndon, and there's still nothing either of us can do
about it. It's been well over three years, sir, and I have
remarried the woman of my choice, not yours."

"I heard the rumors, James. You had to marry her because she seduced you. She counts for nothing. She's a trol-

lop. I brought Laura for you. Just look at her, James. She's a beauty. She's my brother's daughter. Her name is Laura Frothingill. She has a dowry to boot. She's lovely—just look at her a little bit. She's the poor girl that old harridan slapped, the one you told to be quiet. I've been saving her for you. Just look at her, James. She's a lady. Look at her—please just give a small peek at her. Her hair's a fine light brown, a neat figure she's got. She would grace your home, bring you heirs, provide you with wit and companionship—at least I've been told by her mama that her wit sparkles on occasion. Her shrieking may be perhaps a bit shrill, but a lady does that sometimes.

"But this other one lying there, she doesn't deserve you. Look at her again if you can, James, after looking at beautiful Laura. Just look at all that red hair. It's cheap and vulgar, that red hair, too curly, not soft and long like dear Laura's. And she was swimming naked in the pond. No, no, not Laura, this one here. Only a trollop would have done that, only a trollop would have known to slap her palms against my ears to get me off her."

James felt deeply saddened. "I suppose there's nothing for it." He sighed deeply, stepped forward, and sent his fist into the baron's jaw. Baron Hughes collapsed without another sound. Laura began screaming again, then stopped instantly when she saw Mrs. Catsdoor come running into the drawing room, her right hand raised.

Laura whimpered quietly, saying, "Did you kill him, James, for hurting your wife?"

"Don't be a fool, Laura. You don't mind my calling you Laura, do you? 'Miss Frothingill' seems a bit too ceremonious under these insane circumstances, wouldn't you say?"

"Call me Laura, please. You would have anyway had you married me—at least, most men call their wives by their first names. I'm sorry for being a ninny. It was just such a shock, all this violence. I didn't know any of this was going to happen, I swear it. My uncle asked me to come visit Candlethorpe with him, and I agreed. Alicia hadn't liked it here, but I was curious to see where you had lived and to meet you, that's all. I didn't know he planned to kill your wife.''

''It's all right. I suspect I won't see you again, Laura.'' He nodded to her, then said, ''Thank you, Mrs. Catsdoor for all your assistance. Now, I'm going to carry Jessie upstairs and put her to bed.''

''I'll sweep these two out once the noble baron here recovers himself. You, missie, see to your precious uncle. It will give you something to do rather than shrieking the ceiling down.''

What had Laura Frothingill meant, James wondered as he carried Jessie up the wide staircase, when she'd said that Alicia hadn't liked it here? She'd always seemed happy at Candlethorpe, until she'd told him that she was carrying his child, so short a time after they'd married, too short a time . . . He didn't want to think about it.

Jessie was a dead weight in his arms, her head hanging limply over his arm, her hair trailing down another foot. It had been at least ten minutes since she'd struck her head. Why didn't she wake up?

James continued to wipe a cool, damp square of linen over her face. It had been nearly twenty-five minutes now, and still she remained unconscious. Something was very wrong. He remembered a jockey in a race at York some two years ago who'd been kicked in the head. His heartbeat had been slow and steady, just like Jessie's, and everyone had been relieved. Only he'd never awakened. James's belly cramped, he was so scared.

Finally, he rose from her bed and stretched, walking over to the windows. There was no sign of Dr. Raven. It would take at least another hour. Darkening clouds were building up to the east. It would rain before long. He turned back to see Jessie move her left hand. She made it into a fist.

"Jessie?" He thought he'd burst from relief. "Jessie?" he said again, leaning over her.

Her eyes remained closed. Her head moved back and forth on the pillow. Then she said clearly, "My head hurts. None of this is amusing. That man is dreadful."

"Well, yes, he is." He leaned over her and yelled in her face, "Jessie!"

He shook her until she opened her eyes. She looked up at him, but he looked vague to her, hovering strangely above her, all his edges blurred, his blond hair circling his head like an angel's, all soft, beams of light gleaming through the strands. Had she died? Was she in heaven? Surely his eyes were as green as the small pond with all the moss growing around it just near the stable at her father's stud. Everyone knew that angels had blue eyes, but this angel had green eyes that mesmerized the one looking into them, making that person incredibly happy, at peace. Yes, this angel's eyes were green, as soft-looking as his hair, the deep green of a limitless stretch of trees in deep summer, as well as that pond. She blinked, trying to see him more clearly. "James? Is that you? No, it isn't you, is it? I died and you're an angel. That's why you're floating above me. You're such a beautiful angel, but I don't want to die and leave James even for you. My head hurts dreadfully."

"If your head hurts, then you aren't dead," said a prosaic voice that surely couldn't have belonged to an angel. "Doesn't that make sense?"

"Yes." She tried to raise her hand to her head, but couldn't manage it. Two tears seeped from her eyes and rolled down her cheeks. "You don't talk like an angel, but still you're here, all beautiful and vague with your blond hair and green eyes, and I don't know what to think."

"Then I have an advantage. No, don't move, Jessie. I

know it hurts, sweetheart. Just try to lie still. Can you see more clearly now?''

''It's getting better. You're not an angel, but you called me 'sweetheart.' I never heard that an angel was allowed to become so intimate. 'Sweetheart.' I like that. No one's ever called me 'sweetheart' before.''

He laid the damp cloth over her forehead, even as his belly cramped. No one had ever called her 'sweetheart'? Surely that didn't make sense. She was a sweetheart, kind and innocent and loving . . . ''No, I'm not an angel. If you doubt me, just ask my mother. Right now, you definitely are a sweetheart. I daresay if you remain as you are, you will be a sweetheart as long as you live. Does that help?''

''Yes,'' she whispered, and closed her eyes again.

James knew enough not to let her doze off. ''Jessie, come, sweetheart, wake up. I don't want you to muck up your brains. Wake up.''

He spooned tea between her lips to keep her awake. After half a cup, she became violently ill. He held her head while she vomited.

''Rinse out your mouth. That's right. Better?''

She managed to nod, but the pain was stark and raw now, like a hammer bludgeoning at the base of her skull.

''Did I hurt that horrid baron?''

''You did indeed. He still hadn't learned his lesson, so I had to tap his jaw. I laid him out flat on the beautiful Axminster carpet, this one a wedding gift from the Hawksburys. I hope Mrs. Catsdoor had Sigmund see them both off our property.''

''He's a very unhappy man.''

''That may be the case. However, it gives him no right to try to murder you.''

''He was strangling me. I used a trick Oslow taught me years ago. I went limp, then slapped my palms really hard against his ears.''

"You hurt him. I thought he would weep. That was well done of you, Jessie. I'm sorry I didn't come sooner." He'd tell her later that the baron had called her vulgar because she'd managed to save herself.

"Does he have a wife?"

"Yes, he does, but she wasn't very close to her daughter. I saw her last spring in Tutleigh, buying some ribbon at the milliner shop. She appeared glad to see me. I always thought she was a nice woman. I'm certain she knew nothing of this exploit of his." He was chattering nonsense but he knew he had to keep her attention, keep her awake. "I think the ribbon she finally selected was green, nearly the color of my eyes, she said when she first saw it."

"You do have beautiful eyes, James. The Duchess told me how all the important Wyndhams had blue eyes except for you. She did allow that your green eyes added diversion and interest."

"I've always longed to be a diversion. If you'll allow me, I'll try to divert you for the rest of our lives."

That sounded suspiciously permanent, and Jessie wouldn't think about what he'd said just now since her brains were a bit scrambled. "When Mrs. Catsdoor showed them in, I knew I wasn't in for a pleasant social call. I'm sorry, James."

"What? Oh, come, Jessie, you didn't do anything wrong. Now, do you think you can stay awake? Not quite sure yet. All right, I'll tell you a story, one that Oslow told me."

"I've probably already heard it."

"Then you'll hear it again. Keep your eyes fastened on my angel's face. I'll even try to twinkle my green eyes for you. Watch me hover. Now, it seems that the first thoroughbred to leave England for America was Bulle Rock. Did you know that?"

"Do you think I'm ignorant? Of course I know that."

"Ah ha, but do you know who Bulle Rock's sire was?"

"Oh dear, my head hurts awfully bad, James, so bad it's blocked out all my learning."

He kissed the tip of her nose. "I know your head hurts, but you're using that as an excuse. You can't fool me. Bulle Rock's sire was none other than the Darley Arabian, foaled in 1700, one of the three founders."

"I don't believe you. You're making that up."

"No. You see how quickly I fooled you? No, don't shut your eyes, Jessie. Let me think. Ah, did you know that Charles the First—before he lost his head—gave Newmarket its first Gold Cup in 1634? Jessie, dammit, wake up."

"Gold cups are nice. I have more than you do, James. At least, my papa does."

"Not many more, and I don't think they're all gold. In fact, none of them are—at least none of mine are."

"Mother made him melt the one gold one down a few years ago when our fortunes took a downswing."

"Oh," James said. "Who melted it down for him?"

Unfortunately her learning failed her again. She said instead, "Maybe that's why Nelda married Bramen Carlysle. She was afraid of being poor again, and he's very rich."

When Dr. Raven arrived, Jessie was counting the fingers that James held up.

"She's seeing clearly now," James said. "She vomited, but her stomach's better. Her brain still goes adrift a bit, but not badly now."

"Excellent," George Raven said, motioned for James to move, and took his place. "Hello, Jessie," he said as he pushed up her eyelids. Then he gently probed around the back of her head. "Good-size bump. Harlow told me you struck your head against the mantelpiece?"

She nodded.

He closed his eyes as his fingers lightly traced over the swelling. "This will take a while to go down, Jessie."

"I'm glad you call me Jessie. Everyone does, even Anthony. Even the horses would if they could speak human."

Dr. Raven said as he continued lightly touching his fingers to the bump. "Speaking of the little fellow, Anthony just wrote his first ditty. His mother is crowing about it. It's quite clever, really, all about his father giving a speech in the House of Lords and everyone falling asleep."

"I assume Marcus didn't find it as clever as the Duchess did?" James asked.

"It was difficult to say," Dr. Raven said. "He'd tucked Anthony under his arm and told him he was taking him to the lake to drown him. Now, Jessie, here's what you're going to do for the next three days."

"I don't like this, James."

"I know. Drink it."

She downed the brownish liquid, made from one of Mr. Badger's prized recipes, Mrs. Catsdoor had said, and fell back against the pillows, wheezing. "Oh goodness, that would make any sinner reform. It's far more vile than that hangover drink you made me swallow."

"Mr. Badger did say he gave it to his lordship whenever he was downpin," Mrs. Catsdoor told her. "He said it made his lordship as malleable as a sheep for at least an hour. Mr. Badger did allow, however, that seeing his lordship as malleable as a sheep worried everyone, even the scullery maid in the pantry. Now, you're to have some nice light soup, Mrs. James."

Jessie ate the soup, yawned widely, and went to sleep at 8:00 that evening. At 8:45, James, who was reading in bed beside her, suddenly stiffened at the touch of her fingers on his belly. He stared at her. Her eyes were closed. She looked to be deeply asleep. Still, those fingers of hers moved, downward now, through the hair at his groin, down until she was lightly touching him with her fingertips. James let out a whoosh of air, realized he'd been holding his breath, and leaned back against the pillow. She was touching him, now she was stroking him, closing her hand around him, and he thought he was going to expire with the pleasure of it. She was doing this in her sleep? While she was injured? Well, she had been knocked on the head, that was it, she didn't know what she was doing, she couldn't begin to imagine what she was—He moaned as her fingers tightened on him, moving now, touching, caressing. He couldn't bear it. "Jessie, you've got to stop this. I won't be able to hang on much longer. Oh God, that's wonderful. Don't ever stop."

"All right, I won't."

He nearly jumped out of his skin. As it was, the sheer shock of her voice pulled him back from the frantic urgency that was pushing him hard toward release. "Jessie, you damned tease."

"Yes, perhaps. I've wanted to do that for a long time, James. Do you like it?"

"You're ill. God, I love it. You must rest. You shouldn't be driving me mad like this. Don't stop, Jessie, don't stop." He moaned.

"No, I won't stop. I like the way you feel, James. My head just hurts a little bit, not enough to make me lie here any longer wanting to touch you. You don't mind, do you?"

"You're ill. I love it. Jessie, I'll lose everything if you don't stop now. I don't want you to, but on the other hand if you do then I'll just be devastated for a very few minutes until I'm inside you and then it will be wonderful again and I won't have to stop."

"All right, James."

He pulled her on top of him, jerked her nightgown over her head, and said, "Bring me inside you, Jessie. That's right, slowly, slowly."

It was nearly nine o'clock, his wife had struck her head not all that many hours before, and here she was riding him—slowly, to be sure—but she was moving on him, and she looked to be enjoying herself. He stroked her breasts, let his hands tighten about her waist, then lower until he found her and he stroked her until she was breathing hard, pulling him deep inside her, teasing him, and he said very clearly, "Jessie, it's time for you to climax now, all right?"

"Now?"

"Yes, now."

"Yes," she said. "All right." She looked amazed as she flung her head back, all that wild red hair of hers streaming over her shoulders and down her back, and surely throwing her head like that had to hurt her just a bit but all he could see was her pleasure, shimmering over her, making her cry out, making her ride him hard and harder yet and just as she was easing, he took his own release.

She was lying over him, her warm breath against his neck, and he was still inside her.

"You were ill," he managed when he could finally put two words together.

"Yes, but I'm much better now."

"I'd say you were the best. That was incredible, Jessie."

"Yes," she said, licked his neck, and snuggled back down. In a moment, she was asleep and he was still inside her.

He lay there a long time, his hands rubbing her back, stroking her, kneading her buttocks.

The old Jessie, the new Jessie, it didn't matter. She was his Jessie.

He didn't know when he fell asleep, but it seemed as if it were only three seconds later when he was jerked awake by a loud scream.

Dear God, had Laura gotten back into the house?

It was Jessie, thrashing around, her arms and legs flailing, screaming, then screaming again, sobs wheezing out between the screams, deep ugly sounds that scared the devil out of him.

She'd slipped off him. He grabbed her shoulders and shook her until she stilled. "Jessie," he said, kissed her, then shook her once again.

She opened her eyes, stared up at him, and screamed again.

"No, no, it's just me, James. It's all right."

"James," she said. Oh God, he thought, she spoke in that child's high singsong voice. He felt the hair stir on the back of his neck. That child's voice said, "I don't know a James. Who are you? Why are you here?"

"I'm taking care of you. You had a bad fall and hit your head."

"Oh, are you a doctor?"

"Perhaps that is what I am now." Didn't she know him? Had the child come into her and planned to stay?

"Dr. James. That sounds strange to me."

"Can you tell me what you were dreaming?" He tried to speak calmly, his voice as soothing as a father's to his child when the child is afraid and confused.

Suddenly, Jessie jerked away from him. She struck his chest and scratched his cheek before he pinned her arms to her sides. There was terror in her eyes, wild terror she couldn't seem to escape. "No, no," she said it again and yet again. "Let me go! Don't do that, it's horrible, stop, stop." It was that pathetic child's voice and it terrified him, hearing it come from a woman's mouth.

His eyes had become used to the darkness. He saw shadows now, saw more clearly the terror in her eyes. He said slowly, "Something happened to you, Jessie. Something to do with this Mr. Tom?"

She was straining away from him, looking at him as if she was waiting for him to hurt her, that, or kill her. He released her hands. She crossed her arms over her head to protect herself, lurched to the very edge of the bed, her legs drawing close to her chest, huddling down, trying to hide.

"It's all right," he said quietly, in that same soothing voice he didn't even know he had, knowing he was dealing with the child, not the woman. "You will be fine. Go to sleep now. I'll watch over you. I won't leave you. Sleep."

She fell asleep sobbing, her fist stuffed in her mouth. He was afraid to touch her. He was afraid to awaken her. He wondered if he did awaken her whether she would be herself or that terrified child again.

He waited until she was sleeping deeply, then drew her against him, nestling her into the curve of his body. She had no more nightmares that night, at least ones that drew her back to childhood and to terror. It occurred to him that she'd had this damned dream each time they'd made love. No, not the first two times when she hadn't enjoyed herself, but every time thereafter. They'd made love and then she'd had this horrible dream. Triggered by pleasure? He didn't like that one bit.

When Jessie awoke the following morning, a dark morning with rain slashing against the windowpanes, the wind slashing the oak branches against the side of the house, she opened her eyes and saw James sitting beside her not looking at all like an angel. He looked like a very worried man. But Jessie's thoughts were elsewhere. For once her nightmares had pierced through to memory. She sat straight up in bed, turned to her husband, and said, "James, Mr. Tom was a very bad man. But it's not only about him. It's about Blackbeard. It's all about the pirate Blackbeard."

# ≡ 25 ≡

THE EARL OF Chase said to his valet, who was regarding a sleeping Charles with a beneficent eye, "Spears, what do you make of all this Blackbeard nonsense? George Raven had precious little to offer about any of it, not that he knew much, but the fellow has no imagination at all, just rambled on and on about that wicked fellow Blackbeard, and how it all had come back to Jessie after ten years."

Spears cleared his throat and said in his deep voice, "The pirate Blackbeard, as he devised himself, was really named Edward Teach. He would appear to be in the forefront of this situation, evidently. If you know what I mean."

"I don't, but that's never stopped you before. Proceed, Spears."

"Yes, my lord. I spoke more closely with Dr. Raven. It would seem that Jessie hasn't had a vision. It seems she's remembered horrific details from her past—details that as a young girl she'd refused to remember. She hasn't revealed the details to anyone but James. Evidently while still a girl she fell ill right after this horrific experience, then awoke, remembering nothing of it. Mr. Badger agrees with me. He believes that a child will simply forget in order to survive. Miss Maggie disagrees. She believes Jessie's childhood fever acted like a blow to the head, causing her to forget. This new blow on the head, Miss Maggie believes, brought the memory back to life."

"What does Sampson think?" the Duchess asked, laying down the small exquisitely stitched shirt that, her husband had told her, would be ruined by Charles's drool within an hour of dressing him in it.

"Mr. Sampson, when applied to for his opinion, said that he believed none of it mattered, that what was important was that Miss Jessie tell us more about this Blackbeard fellow and why he's so damned important and what he has to do with this horrific incident from her childhood. Mr. Sampson, as you know, my lord, usually disregards any outward trappings and cuts directly to the chase."

The Duchess didn't so much as turn a hair when Esmee, the cat, jumped onto her lap, curled up in the middle of her sewing, and began to wash herself.

She calmly patted Esmee, who began to purr so loudly that Charles jerked awake, looked up at his papa then at Spears, and yelled.

"I believe the young master is ready for his midafternoon repast," Spears said.

"He's a bloody little stoat," Marcus said. "Duchess, I'll hold that blasted Esmee if you would like to see to him."

"There is no choice," the Duchess said as she rose. "The American Wyndhams will arrive shortly, Spears. Then all our questions will be answered." To her husband, she added, "My dear, I fear that Esmee does not intend to lie quietly while you pat her."

Marcus, the cat now on his lap, was staring down at her while she kneaded his thighs.

"A cat and a wife," he remarked to the room at large, as he rubbed Esmee's chin, "most of the time I can't tell her scratches apart from the damned cat's."

"And you, my dear," the Duchess said calmly to her husband as she leaned down to pick up her yelling son, "many times aren't able to perceive when you are very close to the edge."

Marcus burst out laughing, dislodging Esmee, who stood up on his legs, dug deeply, then bounded off. "I'll get you yet, Duchess," he said. "All I ask is that you lose that god-awful serene facade just once a week. Only one episode a week will satisfy me."

"The Duchess, my lord," Spears said, standing very straight and very stiff, eyeing his seated master, who was grinning like a glutton in a room filled with sweetmeats, "will now give suckle to your son. Then—"

"'Suckle,' Spears? Good God, that sounds biblical."

"I doubt, Marcus," the Duchess said as she swung Charles into her arms, "that you would appreciate a biblical reference were it to float into the space before your nose."

"Spears," Marcus said, "you're looking so puffed up with ire you look ready to explode. When will you ever realize that the Duchess has no need at all of your protection? Go away. Leave me in peace with this blasted cat."

The Duchess, laughing as she cuddled her son to her chest, left the drawing room, Spears, still high in his dignity, at her heels.

Badger handed a delicate Sèvres dish to Jessie. She looked at it, and her mouth began to water. "Your scones, Badger, with clotted cream. Oh dear, this is wonderful. If my head even considered hurting me, it would surely stop now."

"The scones are known for their restorative effect," Badger said, gave Jessie a close look, nodded, then turned to serve everyone else. The Duchess dispensed tea. James looked over at Maggie, gowned this afternoon in a soft peach affair, really quite demure for Maggie, that made her look as delicious as Badger's clotted cream. Sampson stood behind her, his left hand laying lightly on her shoulder. Every once in a while, Maggie patted her husband's hand.

"Actually," Jessie said, giving a demure look to her husband, "James is more effective as a cure than a scone could ever be. Forgive me, Badger, but it's true."

James choked. Sampson thumped him on the back.

"We won't wish to hear more of this," Spears said, but he wasn't frowning.

Jessie looked like an exotic flower next to Maggie today—surely a reversal—her red hair unconfined, because braiding it had given her a headache. It was full and wild around her face, a face that was still on the pale side, and that had worried him, but she'd begged and begged to ride with him to Chase Park, before she became as inert as one of her goose-feather pillows, she'd told him.

"Now that everyone is fortified for the upcoming disclosures," Marcus said as he ate the last bite of his scone, "it's time we know more about this Blackbeard fellow, Jessie. You didn't tell poor George a thing. The Duchess bullied him mercilessly, but still he wasn't at all forthcoming."

"His lordship is quite right," Spears said in his ducal manner, as distinguished as one of the royals, probably more so. "Dr. Raven is a fine physician, but he has no imagination."

The earl grunted.

Spears gently cleared his throat. "He doesn't inquire properly into matters. Now, Jessie, tell us everything."

Jessie looked around at all the people who had taken her in and been kind to her and guided her and held her close and had actually liked her and wanted her to be happy. It was just too much. She couldn't help it, she burst into tears.

"Jessie!"

James, utterly appalled, scared to his toes actually that she was unable to face this childhood terror—whatever it was—was on his feet in an instant. He sat beside her, which was difficult since it was not all that large a chair, and pulled her against him. "Shush, sweetheart, it's all right. It's your head, nothing more, and all those dreadful memories. You don't have to say anything if you don't want to."

"Jessie," Badger said, "needs a brandy. Mr. Sampson, would you care to pour her a goodly dose? It will clear an open path to her belly and warm her."

James took the snifter of his lordship's finest brandy from Sampson's outstretched hand and nudged it against Jessie's cheek. "Come now, drink it down. If Badger says you need it to open up your belly, then you need it."

She took too big a drink, thought her stomach would burn to a cinder, coughed until her face was as red as her hair, and wheezed out, "Oh my goodness, Badger, that is dangerous. How do gentlemen drink such quantities of it and survive to drink even more?"

"Gentlemen," Spears said, eyeing the earl briefly, "have remarkable adaptive powers. It aids them to survive when their brains don't function properly. Take just another very small sip, Jessie."

She did, felt the warmth fill her, and sighed.

"Do you feel up to telling everyone about that long-ago summer now?"

She nodded, looking suddenly embarrassed. "I was just a little girl, not more than ten years old if I remember correctly. My family has a house on Ocracoke, an island on a skinny strand of land off the coast of North Carolina that's called the Outer Banks or the barrier islands since it protects the mainland coast from Atlantic storms. It's a beautiful place in the summer, quite sunny, with long wide beaches, the water still cool but you can swim if you're brave. There are wild horses roaming all up and down the Outer Banks that many people believe swam to shore from a sinking Spanish galleon sometime in the sixteenth century. People who live there have tamed some of them.

"In the summer of 1812, I was always spending my days at the beach, digging around for clams, swimming until my skin was puckered and my mother threatened to tie me to my bed. There was this man who was living in this shack right on the beach. Everyone called him Old Tom. I called him Mr. Tom. I don't know now if he was really all that old, but since I was very young he looked ancient enough to be practically dead.''

"That's all very well, Jessie"—Anthony's voice came from behind the pianoforte in the corner of the drawing room—"but what about Blackbeard?"

"Anthony," his mother said in her calm, serene voice, "you will go to your father and he will gently place his hand over your mouth. You won't interrupt Jessie again, all right?"

"Papa's hand is very big, Mama."

"He'll be careful not to cover your nose as well so you won't suffocate. You will be careful, won't you, Marcus?"

"I didn't drown him, did I, and there was much more provocation.''

Anthony went to stand beside his father and stared toward Jessie expectantly.

"Well, Anthony, it turned out that Old Tom was Blackbeard's great-grandson. Blackbeard was an evil man, Old Tom told me over and over again, for he was very proud of Blackbeard. Aye, Old Tom would say, he was the most infamous, cruel, and ruthless of all the pirates. He robbed and murdered and terrorized everyone in the Caribbean and all the towns and cities unfortunate enough to have been founded on rivers or on the ocean.''

"I wonder if this is true, Jessie," Spears said. "We offered the blighter a pardon?"

"Yes, apparently so; way back in 1718, Blackbeard signed a paper renouncing pirate-hood and moved to Ocracoke. There used to be a ruined castle there in the village called Blackbeard's Castle, so it's said. Now, though, there are just some rocks lying around. So, was there really a castle? I don't know. There's also Teach's Hole, a channel that lies very close to the village. For years, this was where Blackbeard brought his ships to careen.''

"Jessie, what does 'careen' mean?''

Maggie said, "Master Anthony, when you careen a ship, you pull it up on shore and lay it on its side so you can make repairs and clean it off and whatever else it needs.''

Sampson gave his wife a surprised look. "However did you know that, my dear?''

Her eyes twinkled as she said in a voice as demure as a nun's, "There was this sailor I met just before I saved Mr. Badger's life in Plymouth. He, uh, told me ever so many things about ships and such.''

"I suspected as much,'' Sampson said. "My wife,'' he announced to the group, "has unplumbed depths.''

"Yuck,'' Anthony said, watching Sampson lean down and kiss Maggie's hand. "Tell us more interesting things, Jessie.''

"All right. After he signed the paper, he lived in his castle for a while, drank up all his rum, tormented his men, but soon even that got to be old hat. He got so bored that he slipped back into his evil ways. There were very few people living on Ocracoke at that time, only a few pilots, and he tormented them as well.

"Finally, the British went after him and a Lt. Maynard caught up with him. It's said that he fought madly for over three hours. He was stabbed twenty times, one slash nearly cutting his throat. He was shot five times and still he fought, until he simply had no more blood in him. Pardon me, Anthony. They cut off his head and hung it from the bowsprit.''

Spears cleared his throat. "Mr. Daniel Defoe wrote that his body was thrown overboard and that 'the Headless Corpse swam around the sloop Three Times in Defiance before it sank into the sea.' ''

"Did he eat people, Jessie?''

"I don't think so, Anthony, but he did cut quite a few

gullets. There's one story you'll like. It seems that their ship, *Queen Anne's Revenge*, was becalmed, everyone was bored, there were no ships in sight to plunder and destroy, and Blackbeard, drunk on rum, shouted, 'Come, let us make a Hell of our own, and try how long we can bear it!' They sat on the stones used to ballast the ship. Pots of brimstone—sulfur—were brought down and then the hatches were closed. Blackbeard outlasted the other men. One of his men shouted to him that he looked as if he were coming right from the gallows, to which Blackbeard is said to have roared that the next time they would play at gallows and see who could swing longest on the string without being throttled.''

"How do you know these stories?" Badger asked.

She blinked, staring off at something none of them could see. "They were in Blackbeard's diary. I read the stories over and over to Old Tom. I just now remembered them."

"Tell us more stories, Jessie," Anthony said, having slipped away from his father and sidled over to her, leaning against her shoulder. "I'll tell you more stories later, Anthony. The most important story is about Blackbeard's treasure. Old Tom believed there was a treasure. He believed the clues to the treasure were in Blackbeard's diaries. Old Tom let me read only parts of the two Blackbeard diaries he had, the parts with the stories, nothing else. He also showed me the two diaries that his own father, Samuel Teach, had written, but he didn't trust me enough to let me read any of them. There was one other diary, very old it was, the paper so yellowed I was afraid to touch it. He said it was written by Blackbeard's great-grandma, and being it was written by a woman and long before Blackbeard was born and buried his treasure, it wasn't important. I managed to read about half of that one before that day when things happened. It was fascinating. But it doesn't have anything to do with the treasure, though it does involve another mystery.

I'll tell you about it later. Then, well, the other happened."
She raised her chin and said clearly, "He tried to rape me.
I managed to get away from him. When he brought me
down from behind, I had a rock clutched in my hand. He
jerked me upright, and I hit him as hard as I could on the
head. It killed him. I was terrified. I got all the diaries together, wrapped them in an oilskin cloth, and buried them.
As far as I know, they're still there. I remember dreaming
about him the first several years after it happened. Then the
dreams just stopped until James and I married and we—"

James said, "It appears that our marital intimacy brought
the dreams back to her. I don't like it. Pleasure to be followed by that god-awful memory."

"A treasure, Jessie?" Anthony breathed, his beautiful
Wyndham blue eyes dark with excitement. "Truly, a treasure?"

"Yes, a treasure." Jessie was aware that everyone in the
room was staring at her, all but Anthony, who really hadn't
paid any attention to anything else she'd said. She just nodded slowly. "There was a third diary Blackbeard wrote that
a man named Red Eye Crimson had gotten hold of. Old
Tom met him in Montego Bay, in Jamaica. Red Eye had
been looking for him. He told him that he had a third Blackbeard diary and if they put all three together, then they'd
know where Blackbeard had buried his treasure.

"Evidently, Old Tom didn't have any of the diaries with
him, so they agreed that Red Eye Crimson would come to
Ocracoke to put his diary together with Old Tom's two diaries. Old Tom really was convinced that if they put the
diaries together they'd find the treasure. That same night Old
Tom's friend Red Eye Crimson came to my father's house
in Ocracoke and tried to kidnap me because he must have
seen me leave Old Tom's shack near the beach. He must
have known I killed Old Tom. He must have realized as
well that I'd buried the diaries. He had to kidnap me so I'd

give them to him. My dog saved me, but I struck my head and knocked myself out. When I woke up three days later, my parents told me I'd had this awful fever and nearly died. I didn't remember any of this.''

''You don't think Maggie was right? One knock on the head made you forget and the other brought it back?'' Badger said.

''No, it was our lovemaking. I don't want this to continue. Soon Jessie won't want to come to bed with me.''

Anthony was tenacious. He was jumping around from foot to foot waiting for the adults to be quiet. ''I'm glad you killed that awful man, Jessie, but that's not important. What's important is Blackbeard's treasure. I wasn't born yet when Papa and Mama found the other treasure, the Wyndham Legacy.''

''It would be your first treasure hunt, Anthony. I believe it exists, probably buried near Teach's Hole. We just have to go back and dig up Blackbeard's diaries to find out where all the booty is buried. Even then, it's possible we won't have enough clues because we don't have the third diary. My papa told me that the man who tried to kidnap me— Red Eye Crimson—would be in jail until he was ninety. So I guess we'll just have to make due with Blackbeard's two diaries.''

Spears rose. ''I did a bit of reading about this Blackbeard fellow after Dr. Raven gave us the name. I discovered that in 1811 a Boston theater presented *The Nautical Spectacle, Blackbeard the Pirate*. It was all nonsense, of course. I couldn't discover many believable accounts of him, other than that the English believed he was a Scot and everyone else believed he was an Englishman. We all agree with Jessie. This fellow, Old Tom, he was a bounder and a wicked sinner, but he did have the diaries. Jessie saw them.

''Now we know exactly what to do. We have all discussed it and decided that since the Duchess has wanted to travel for a very long time now, this is the perfect opportunity. We will journey to this Ocracoke place and find Blackbeard's treasure.''

Maggie said, ''That's right. We haven't found a treasure in over seven years. It's time to stretch our brains and find another one. I believe I would like a ruby necklace this time. What do you think, Mr. Sampson?''

''You would look delicious, dearest.''

''I could prepare native recipes,'' Badger said. ''I understand, Jessie, that your cooks who live near water prepare what's called a conch chowder that is cooked with potatoes and carrots. A simple dish but one that could possibly tease the palate if prepared properly. I will prepare it when we reach Ocracoke.''

''Oh, Marcus,'' the Duchess said, sitting forward in her chair, Charles's shirt momentarily forgotten on her lap, ''another treasure hunt and Badger's conch chowder. Is that some sort of fish, Badger?''

''It is a spiral shell, Duchess, and the sea-mollusk meat inside is what one cuts up and cooks in a chowder.''

''I have several conch shells,'' Jessie said to Anthony. ''You can use them like a horn for calling.''

The Duchess said, ''We would travel to America. We would visit James's Marathon. We would meet Jessie's parents. Oh dear, we would see James's mother.''

''Sorry, Duchess, but she is unavoidable.''

''Rather like the plague,'' Marcus said. He rose and began to pace. He said finally to his wife, ''This isn't something that happens in the course of three days, Duchess. We would be gone for three months, at the very least. It could be dangerous. Ocean travel is always uncertain. What would we do with the boys?''

''We will ensure that the boys are always safe,'' Spears said. ''The boys must accompany us.''

Anthony whooped and ran around the drawing room shouting with glee.

"Master Anthony," Spears said very quietly, "adult ears are too sensitive to be thus abused."

Anthony quickly walked to where his father stood beside the fireplace and planted himself beside him, not moving just as his father wasn't moving either. Marcus began to pace. Anthony fell into place behind him, matching his steps as well as he could to his father's.

The Duchess said, "You saw Alec Carrick just last week, Marcus. We could travel to Baltimore on one of his ships." She added briefly to Jessie, "He's Baron Carrick. He married a shipbuilder's daughter from Baltimore just three years ago. Alec had a daughter by his first marriage, Hallie, and now he and Genny have a son, Dev James. Perhaps you knew the Paxtons?"

"Certainly. I remember hearing that Genny Paxton was trying to run her father's shipyard. Now that I think back, there was an Englishman in the picture as well."

"That was Alec. They spend more time in England than in America, but they visit at least twice a year. Genny is a very capable woman. Rather than writing vulgar ditties like my wife and abusing my adult ears, Genny knows how to build ships."

The Duchess just smiled sweetly at him. "A treasure hunt, Marcus."

"I haven't seen such a sweet smile since I gave you that very special birthday present last year. Do you remember?"

The Duchess never changed expressions, though perhaps her smile softened a bit. "I remember everything, Marcus. Don't ever doubt it."

The earl looked around at all the expectant faces. He looked down at his son's upturned face. He recognized the excitement in everyone's eyes. He felt it twitching and quivering inside him.

He said slowly, picking Anthony up in his arms, "Perhaps we should think about this for another year or so. What do you think, Anthony?"

"Papa! No, please, you wouldn't!"

He began laughing and squeezed his son tightly against his chest. "All right. If we leave next week, will that be soon enough for you?"

"That's what I prayed to hear," James said. "You'll all be in this with us. I want to find that treasure as much as you do, but more importantly, I want Jessie to go back to Ocracoke and try to demolish all memories of Mr. Tom. I want her to see that old shack on the beach, look at it good, and remember every detail so that she can forget it and we can get on with things. I wish Maggie were right, that Jessie's latest knock on the head brought the memories back, but it didn't, more's the pity. I should be able to protect her from more blows to the head, but dreams, nightmares, tattered memories that haunt her, that's beyond me. I want her dreams to be of me, not of that demon from the past. I want Jessie and I to be able to make—" He looked at Anthony. "Well, you know what I mean."

"Indeed we do," Marcus said. "That would be damnable. Don't you agree, Duchess?"

"Pleasure and then pain? Most damnable."

"Although," Marcus said, with that glint in his eyes, "some people are very fond of that concept and—"

"Don't continue, Marcus."

The earl looked at his son, who was all ears, and sighed. "One must be perfect for the little heathens."

# $\equiv$ 26 $\equiv$

Copenhagen was the Duke of Wellington's
charger at the Battle of Waterloo.

*Marathon Farm*

"I'M SORRY, JESSIE. If I'd known, I would have done something—what, I'm not sure, but something. Damnation, is she
some sort of witch? No, don't answer that."

"How could she be here?"

James had no time to answer. All of them were tired,
Charles was fussing and hiccuping through his tears, and
Anthony was whining that he was hungry. Spears took his
hand and said, "You will be as brave and stoic as your
mama and papa, Master Anthony. All of us are hungry. All
of us are tired. If you whine, we will all think you are a
little boy. We will think of you as no older than Master
Charles."

"I am not Charles, but I am a little boy."

Spears said to the Duchess, "Most of the time it works."

"Ah, Thomas, you've gotten here before my mother has

come out. Well, just barely. Hello, Mother. May I ask what you are doing here?''

Mrs. Wilhelmina Wyndham gave her son only a cursory glance. It was the Duchess she was staring at, the glint in her eye malevolent. ''You,'' she said. ''I haven't seen you for seven years, not nearly a long enough number of years. You brought your entire household to protect you? I must say, missie, you will need them. How dare you come to America? To Baltimore? To my poor son's house? And you brought this girl back with you. How I prayed she would disappear and never show her miserable ruined face again, but she's here. Ah, you've got two children. You don't deserve them. Poor James lost his wife and his child. Why did he bring all of you here? You don't belong here, and I insist that all of you leave at once.''

''Mother,'' James said very quietly, ''that is quite enough. We're all very tired. We've been aboard ship for six and a half weeks. It took more hours than expected to get to the Inner Basin. Why are you here?''

''I knew you were coming,'' Mrs. Wyndham said in a dramatic voice, flinging out her arms. ''I knew and thus I came because I knew you would need me, my son. And you obviously do need me. I will remove all these English blighters who don't belong here in America.''

''Mother,'' James said again, this time taking her arm in a strong grasp. ''I want you to leave now. I will come to see you tomorrow. Thomas, please see my mother to her carriage.''

''But, dearest—''

''I will call tomorrow, Mother.''

She gave the Duchess a last malevolent look, shot Marcus a coy look, and ignored Jessie. She followed Thomas from the house.

''Oh dear,'' the Duchess said. ''This was quite a welcome. She was right. Seven years between visits isn't nearly long enough.''

"It will improve now, I promise," James said. "Jessie, you're exhausted, you look a bit green around the edges, and I don't think there's a handy chamber pot downstairs.''

"It's all your fault, James.''

"I know," he said, patting her cheek. "Badger promises me that you'll get fat and waddle, but you're still so thin. You want a chamber pot now, don't you?''

"Please hurry," Jessie said, and took short, shallow breaths just as the Duchess had taught her.

"Hold on, Jessie. You've done very well today. All this nausea won't last that much longer. Here's Thomas with the chamber pot. Excellent.''

It didn't even seem odd to Jessie to vomit in front of everyone, she was so used to it. Being in close quarters on a barkentine for more than six weeks lessened one's privacy, and she'd been sicker than a person deserved that last week of the voyage. James wiped her face with a nice cold, wet cloth. Badger handed her a glass of water.

James helped her to her feet and hugged her tight. Then he laughed. "I'll never forget how you were certain you were dying, lying there on that coiled rope on deck, moaning and looking pathetic. You look nearly well again. Even your streamers are beginning to perk up once more. Ah, here's Thomas to help us all arrange ourselves.''

"Men should be shot," Jessie said.

Spears immediately stepped forward and extended his hand to the tall black man. "I am Mr. Spears. You are Mr. Thomas?''

"Well, Mr. Spears," Thomas said slowly, wondering if the earth had suddenly turned faulty, "I suppose I'm Mr. Thackery." Then he smiled—a wide, quite nice smile, showing lots of even white teeth. Maggie winked at him.

At ten o'clock that night, all the servants and the families had been fed and given beds. But there weren't enough bed-chambers. For the first time since he'd bought Marathon, James was truly aware at how derelict his house was. There were patches of mold on the wallpaper, dark corners with mouse holes in them, poorly furnished rooms, and all he could do was apologize, which he did in each room they entered. Finally, the Duchess had said, "Enough, James. Candlethorpe gave me little challenge. Between us, Jessie and I will make Marathon the most impressive house in the area."

He believed her until he glanced at his wife, who looked ready to drop where she stood. She was staring owl-eyed at him. "James, will I sleep with you in your bedchamber? The bed's big enough, isn't it?"

"There's no place else for you. Let's get you to bed. Yes, it will hold the two of us."

"I guess I might as well, since you've already done your worst to me."

She'd never before seen James's bedchamber, and she found it to be as dismal as the rest of the house. The wall-paper was old and peeling near the windows where the damp had gotten in and was painted a mangy brown color. There was only a big bed with a scarred maple headboard and an armoire just as ancient as the bed, its doors as scarred as the headboard. There was one stingy braided rug of varying shades of brown in the middle of the floor. But she was too tired to care. She stood passively while James unfastened the buttons on her gown. When she was standing in front of him only in her shift and stockings, he said, "Let me get you a nightgown." Then he paused, his eyes dilating. "No, perhaps you'd best learn to sleep naked with me again. You won't always be feeling like a green peach that someone's bitten into. Spears says not more than a couple of more weeks, hopefully." He didn't add that Caroline Nightingale, an excellent friend of the English Wyndhams, had been ill for nearly five months with her second child. No, Jessie didn't need to know that.

"I always wear a nightgown, James. I thought you enjoyed jerking them over my head and tossing them across the bedchamber."

"Very well, just for tonight. All right? In America, I seem to lose all these little modesty rules." He rifled through her clothes in the open valise on the floor, tossed her a clean nightgown, stripped himself, and climbed into bed. "Hurry, Jessie. I'm cold and I need you to warm me up."

Actually it was quite warm, being the beginning of September. Thank God it hadn't rained during their trip from the Pratt Street docks to Marathon. A long hot trip, but it hadn't rained.

"The children are sleeping with Marcus and the Duchess. Damnation, I just didn't remember how very old and ratty everything was."

"It's all right," Jessie said as she climbed into bed beside him. "Just wait until they see the stables and your workers' houses. Then they'll understand where you spent all your money."

"Are you really tired, Jessie?"

She was snuggled against his side, her palm over his heart. "No, not really tired." Actually she was so exhausted she wanted to close her eyes and never open them again during this current week. No sooner were the words out of her mouth, no sooner had he assimilated them and begun to turn to face her, already harder than he'd imagined possible in such a short time, than he felt her kissing his shoulder. "No," she whispered, licking his warm flesh, "I'm not tired at all."

"Our first time in America," he said some time later when he could speak again. He kissed her again and again until he knew she was falling asleep. "That was quite nice.

I wonder if Marcus heard you yelling. If he did, I'll hear about it tomorrow. Sleep well, Jessie.''

She slept well until three o'clock, then she awoke screaming, her arms flailing. This time, Jessie woke up first, sweating, her streamers sticking to her cheeks, heaving so hard she thought her heart would burst. "Oh, God, it was Mr. Tom again, James. Why won't it stop? I remember all about him now. Why won't he just bloody stop?''

"Oh dear, I think I'm going to be sick.''

It was as black as the bottom of a witch's cauldron in the bedchamber, the downstairs clock just striking three o'clock. James rolled off the side of the bed, hit the floor running, and got the chamber pot to her in the nick of time. He held her, then gave her water to drink and wiped her face.

"I don't know why you're still dreaming about it, Jessie,'' he said at last when he held her in his arms again. "Just try to relax. Breathe slowly, that's good. Go to sleep. That's right, just go to sleep.''

Damnation, every time he gave her pleasure, this wretched dream came to her. Even now that she'd remembered the truth behind it, she still had troubled sleep. He wanted to leave for Ocracoke tomorrow, but he knew they couldn't. Everyone was exhausted. The last thing anyone wanted to do was climb aboard another ship. He stroked her face with his fingers. He wound a streamer around his thumb, then lightly ran his fingertips over her face, her ears, stroking her curly hair back from her forehead. "It will be all right, Jessie. It's got to be.''

"James, I think I'll go to the kitchen. Surely there must be something to take away this wretched nausea.''

"No, you don't know the house yet. I'll go.''

James went downstairs and out the back entrance. He walked across the bricked walkway to the kitchen. He knew

Badger had already settled in. Surely he'd prepared something. He never forgot anything.

He was surprised to see candlelight showing from beneath the kitchen door. Could Old Bess be preparing something at this hour? He opened it slowly, listening.

"Does everyone agree that this is the course to follow?"

It was Spears speaking, naturally. What course?

"The old besom will turn on Jessie as soon as she realizes her dear James married her," Sampson said. "Of course, then she won't be able to fire all her cannon at the poor Duchess."

"It sounds likely," Badger said. "Would you like more tea, Maggie?"

"Thank you, Mr. Badger. You've put some soothing herb in it, haven't you?"

"I have, Maggie. It will make you sleep. It will make all of us sleep. The good Lord knows we'll need it to deal with all the myriad problems that seem to abound here." He yawned discreetly behind his hand.

"Just fancy," Maggie said as she sipped her tea, "we're in the Colonies."

"Yes," Spears said, "and it's three o'clock in the morning and all of us were prowling around and are now in the kitchen trying to address all the damnable problems."

"What have you all decided?" James asked, coming into the large room.

"James," Spears said comfortably, rising from his chair at the head of the large table, "you should be with Jessie."

"I was, but she's ill and I've come here to find her something to settle her stomach."

"I made some more unyeasted bread," Badger said, and rose to cut it and wrap it in a napkin.

"What have you all decided?" James asked again, eyeing each of them in turn.

Spears, looking as elegant as ever in a brocade dressing

gown of dark blue velvet, said, "Do sit down, James. We discovered that none of us could sleep, except for Mr. Sampson, who is fortunate enough to sleep standing in a corner if he must. We decided to come out here and have a bit of tea and conversation. It's good that we did. We've come to a decision about Your Mother."

"Do you plan to strangle her and drop her into the Patapsco River? What about the poor fish?"

"That's a satisfying thought," Maggie said. "Too bad about the fish." She looked glorious in a peach confection that would look more natural worn by a rich man's mistress. Her red hair was loose. She looked delicious and knew she looked delicious. "How can it be that you're so nice, James, and she's such a terror?"

"It's a mystery," James said, seated himself, and accepted a cup of tea from Badger.

"I will speak for Mr. Sampson. Your mother, James, will make Jessie's life miserable," Maggie said. "We will protect her. Whenever your mother visits, all of us will take turns being with her so that the old bi—, er, the old lady doesn't whack her off at the knees."

James looked around the table at the three servants who weren't really servants and knew they cared as much about Jessie now as they did about the Duchess, Marcus, and him. He was profoundly grateful. He said, "The house is not what any of you are used to. I'm sorry that your accommodations are so inferior, but I ran out of money once I had dwellings for my servants built and the stables and paddocks redone."

"Where did the servants live before if not in houses?" Badger asked.

"They were slaves," James said. "They're all black and they were slaves. They were nothing but property. They were abused. Husbands and wives were separated. Children were taken from their parents. I hate slavery. As soon as I

bought the property, I freed all of them and began paying
them wages. They lived in huts that the filthiest rodents
avoided. I had to build them decent housing. I had to.''

"Quite right," Spears said. "Don't you agree, Maggie?"

"I think James is a man with a conscience. Just fancy,
and he's half American and not all English."

"Yes, fancy that," Badger said.

"I'll let you decide which is my best half," James said,
laughed, and drank down his tea. He took the wrapped napkin from Badger, bid them all good night, then said over
his shoulder, "There's not just my mother. There's also Jessie's mother. They never perform a duet. They always come
at you from opposite directions. You'll be pleased to know
that my mother also bullies Jessie's mother. They were girls
together, evidently." He smiled at their collective consternation and took himself back to his wife, who was huddled
in the middle of his bed, breathing through her nose.

"Jessie told me," Spears said after James had left, "that
her father was bound to provide a dowry for her. That
should be ample to bring the house up to snuff."

"We have two mothers to worry about?" Maggie said,
then sighed deeply, leaning her elbows on the kitchen table.

"It's all right, Maggie," Spears said, "we'll figure everything out."

"We always do," Badger said. "Tomorrow I must find
a recipe for conch chowder."

The dreariness of James's red-brick Georgian house was
very apparent the following morning when everyone was
seated in the dining room with its old table and twelve chairs
whose cushions had once been a vivid blue and were now
a tattered blue-gray. The walls needed paint and new wallpaper, and the carpet on the floor was clean but so old it
was splitting apart.

James was embarrassed, mumbling as he seated his wife

at the foot of the table, "I bought the property from Boomer Bankes. He'd been a widower for many years. He paid no attention to the house. I'm very sorry, Jessie, Duchess."

"I daresay we'll all survive," the Duchess said as she settled Charles in the middle of a blanket in the corner of the room, a sugar tit from Old Bess in his mouth. The moment she laid eyes on him, Old Bess adored Charles, cooing over him, telling him he was the sweetest little bite she'd ever seen and that his mama was the prettiest little sweetie she'd ever seen as well, not as pretty as the new mistress, but very fine nonetheless. "Loyalty," the Duchess had remarked to her husband, "is an excellent thing."

"The room's a nice size," Jessie said. "The windows are large, the prospect pleasing."

"Just fancy," Thomas said from the doorway, "the house is filled again. We're all so pleased that you're the mistress now, Miss Jessie."

"Thank you, Thomas. Oh dear, may I have a piece of that bread, please, Badger?"

"Of course, Jessie," Badger said. "Mr. Thackery, would you please give the bread to Mrs. James?"

After breakfast, James took Marcus off to inspect the stables. Thankfully, Anthony, filled with more energy than the rest of them combined, went with them. During breakfast he'd exclaimed that he couldn't wait to leave to find Blackbeard's treasure. The Duchess had said in her calm way, "That's fine, Anthony. You can go with your father to search us out a ship."

"Another ship, Mama?"

"Certainly. We can't very well go overland. We'll get to be on board a ship again, just fancy that."

Anthony hadn't said another word. All of them wanted a bit of a rest, but not a long one. That treasure was there waiting for them, they all knew it.

Jessie, her stomach settled down, went with the Duchess

into the parlor, as she'd told the Duchess it was called here
in the Colonies.

"Now, Jessie, before you and I begin to make plans, I
imagine that you will want to visit your parents and your
sisters."

*Not really,* Jessie thought, flinching from the idea of
Glenda staring at James's crotch. Surely she wouldn't do
that now that he was married, would she?

"I have missed my father."

"Thomas suggested that you write a note to your parents
and tell them that you and James will be visiting them for
luncheon. Do you feel well enough to do that?"

"It comes and goes," Jessie said. "I feel marvelous right
now, but in five minutes, I could be tossing up Badger's
wonderful bread and Old Bess's strawberry jam I ate for
breakfast."

The Duchess eyed her closely. "Your clothes are hanging
on you, too. You want to be the mistress of Marathon, Jessie, the independent, married relative, when you see them.
You don't ever want them to think of you as their daughter
again, thus someone they can bully and order around. Let's
speak to Maggie. Among the three of us, we can dress you
up properly."

"Unfortunately it won't matter," Jessie said, staring
down at her shoes. "My mother and James's mother grew
up together."

"Oh dear."

"At least my mother will be pleasant to you, Duchess."

It was two o'clock that afternoon when James and Jessie
rode in his old carriage to the Warfield Farm. All the trees
and flowers were still in late-summer bloom. The air was
rich with warmth and the scent of the land. "It's good to
be home," James said as he lightly flicked Bellini's reins.

"James, is Glenda going to stare at your crotch again?"

He started, jerking on Bellini's reins, and laughed when the horse snorted. "I hope not, but with Glenda I've learned over the years never to try to outguess her. If she does, well, just ignore it. Are you certain you're ready for this, sweetheart?"

Sweetheart. It sounded wonderful coming from James Wyndham to her, Jessie Warfield, the girl he'd considered an obnoxious brat for six years. Maybe he still did.

"Are you going to keep visiting Connie Maxwell?"

He didn't look at her, rather just kept looking through Bellini's ears. "I will see her, naturally, to tell her of my marriage."

"Oh."

"What does that mean? You think I'd still make love to her? Well, say something. Damn you, Jessie, we're married. I happen to believe in marriage vows. I won't betray you. You will never betray me either, because I won't allow it."

"All right," she said, feeling tears well in her eyes. She didn't understand herself. One minute she wanted to laugh, the next she was sobbing like a broken woman. It was unnerving. Maggie had just patted her hand and told her it was the babe making her behave in such an unpredictable manner. But Maggie didn't have any children. How did she know?

"Good. Now, here we are. Are you ready for this?"

She'd poked her chin a good three inches in the air. He lightly punched her chin, grinning. "You look beautiful. I like your gown. Is it one of the Duchess's?"

"Yes. Maggie took a few tucks here and there. She also washed my hair. It doesn't look too bad, does it, James?"

He hated that ridiculous doubt in her voice. "The streamers are even saluting." She didn't look bad for a woman who was clutching Badger's bread in one hand. He watched her take a bite then push the rest of it down into her pocket. He tossed Bellini's reins to one of the stable lads, leaned over to kiss his wife's mouth, and said quietly, "You are my wife. You are now independent of your family. Do you understand? Once we get all this family business over with, once we get furnishings ordered for the house, once everyone is ready to face a ship again, then we'll go to Ocracoke and get Mr. Tom out of your mind and out of our lives."

"Yes. The Duchess said the same thing, both about Mr. Tom and about my parents. She told me not to forget I was now a married lady and free of them or she'd write a ditty about me I wouldn't like."

"Good for her. Let's go." He lifted her down from the carriage, brought her close to him, and said, "Oslow grinned like a fool when I told him we were married. Your father will do the same."

Portia Warfield pushed past Polly, the black girl in her floppy mop cap who answered the door. "Well," she said, eyeing her daughter. In truth she could think of nothing more to say because her wayward daughter didn't look at all as she had when she left Baltimore nearly four months before. She looked elegant. It was disconcerting. It was infuriating.

"I know all about this illicit marriage of yours, Jessie Warfield. James, your mother visited me this morning and told me of this outrage. However, the reason for her outrage is quite different from mine. You don't look right, Jessie. You don't look how you're supposed to look, the way you've looked since you were a child. It doesn't suit you, all this silly finery, your hair all done up like a loose female's. You will change everything immediately. You will become yourself again. I order you to do as I say."

"I can't, Mama," Jessie said, squeezing closer to James.

"May we come in, ma'am? Jessie would like to sit down. The voyage was long, and she's still tired."

"You might as well. Poor Glenda is prostrate, has been for weeks and weeks. Now today she discovers that you stole away the man she was going to marry, Jessie. She is a shadow of her former self. She is miserable, the poor pet. She barely ate her breakfast.''

''I thought Mrs. Wyndham came here to tell you of our marriage,'' Jessie said, confused. ''Surely she didn't come before breakfast?''

''Don't be smart, miss. Your poor sister didn't sleep well last night. She probably had a premonition of what treachery was to come. She didn't have her breakfast, indeed her lunch as well, until after noon, and that is when James's mother came. You might as well sit down. I will have your poor father fetched from the stables.''

''Is something wrong with Papa?'' Jessie asked, thoroughly alarmed.

''Don't be a fool.'' Mrs. Warfield swept from the parlor.

James turned to Jessie and grinned. ''She puts on as fine a performance as does my precious mother. Don't heed her, Jessie.''

Jessie ran her tongue over her lips. ''I'll try,'' she said. ''But she just keeps battering at you. It's hard to get away from it.''

''Here, eat a bit of Badger's bread.''

She did and was still chewing slowly when her father strode into the room, shouting with pleasure when he saw the two of them. ''Ah, my boy, you married my little girl. A fine day it is for me. Jessie, goodness, girl, whatever have you done to yourself? You look like a princess, that's it, a princess, with that yellow gown and your hair all shiny and stylish. Just look at those cute little curls.

''And here's your mother again. Well, we can't have everything perfect, can we? My dear, can you have some tea fetched? Perhaps some cakes as well?'' He waited until his wife had left the parlor, then hugged his daughter and shook hands with his new son-in-law. He held both their hands as he said, ''You've pleased me more than I can say.

I don't know if either of you realizes it yet, but you really are well suited for each other.''

"I surely hope so, Papa, since James has gotten me pregnant.''

"What? You're with child? Now? But you've only been married a matter of short months, just a summertime of months, not more than three months and you're already pregnant? Oh goodness, I'm going to be a grandfather?''

"Papa, I'm going to be ill.''

It was nearly an hour later when Jessie was once again seated next to her husband in her mother's parlor, her hair brushed, her gown straightened. She was still too pale even after she'd pinched her cheeks, but her stomach had settled. James had fed her weak tea and Badger's bread until she was lying all relaxed on her old bed.

"When is my grandson going to be born?'' her father asked immediately, rubbing his hands together, looking more excited, his wife thought, as she stared at him, than he had when she'd been pregnant with their first. Damn him. Silly old man. So pleased he was when he knew that James should have married sweet Glenda, not her hoyden sister.

"Next April we think,'' James said.

Her mother stared at her with new eyes. Jessie, pregnant. It boggled the mind. For a very long time she'd been without anything to say. Now, she found her tongue, remembered her grievances, and said, "I doubt it will be a grandson, Oliver. If she's this ill, it's probably a girl. Another one in the family. It seems to be all the Warfields can breed.''

James said easily as he took Jessie's limp hand, "I would be delighted to have half a dozen girls, ma'am, all of them with splendid red hair and Jessie's beautiful green eyes.''

"She never before had splendid hair,'' Mrs. Warfield said. "It's her grandmother's hair. Jessie was cursed with it just as her grandmother was also cursed, but at least her grandmother kept it hidden beneath all sorts of frightful caps and bonnets so no one would gape at her.''

At that moment, Glenda tottered into the room. She looked as pale as Jessie, her eyes red from weeping, her gown wrinkled. James rose and smiled at her. Her eyes fell immediately to his crotch.

## 27

JAMES'S SMILE DIDN'T slip, something he considered quite an accomplishment. "Hello, Glenda. You're looking lovely as usual. I'm now your brother-in-law. And you are my new sister."

Glenda looked from James to Jessie, groaned, and said through tight lips, her voice quavering with pain, "I'm betrayed. I'm ground into the dirt. It's all your fault, Jessie, and yours too, James, for not paying heed to the one woman—me—who would have given you grace, beauty, and wit. Now look at what you've got and she will just breed more of what she is."

"What do you mean, Glenda, that I'll breed just more of what I am? Surely that doesn't make sense."

"You stole James from me, you miserable traitor! You were ugly, a pathetic girl who looked like a boy, and I never worried about you for an instant except to laugh at you because you looked and acted so stupidly. But just look at you. You've changed. You've become different, and it isn't right. I hate you, Jessie. You will breed just more of what you were, not what you've become. You'll change back, James will see that and hate you as much as I do."

No one had a thing to say to that. Glenda tottered out of the room. She stopped just outside the doorway, whirled around, her face mottled, and shouted in raw fury, "I'll kill you for this, Jessie! You ruined yourself and forced James to marry you. You even seduced him. Well, it won't last. You'll see. You'll bore him by the end of next week, if not by the end of today. You interest a man? It doesn't matter that you look different. You'll never interest any man. Ha! You don't know how to. Ha, again."

Oliver Warfield cleared his throat. "My dear," he said to his wife, "I ask that you speak to our daughter. Her behavior is tedious, if the truth be told. James never gave her a moment's encouragement."

"He didn't give any encouragement to Jessie, either, but she's pregnant."

"That's different," Oliver said comfortably as he rose. "Come, Jessie, let's go to the stable. The horses have missed you. You too, James."

"Oh yes, Papa, I'd like that very much. James?"

While Jessie greeted all the stable lads and patted all the horses and gave them carrots and sugar, Oliver Warfield pulled James into his office. He sat down behind his battered desk, pulled a bottle of port from one of the drawers, and poured two glasses. "Here you are, son. Ah, that sounds nice. Here's to your marriage to my best daughter."

"I'll drink to that," James said, and clicked his glass to his father-in-law's. The two men drank slowly without speaking.

Oliver leaned back in the rickety old chair that was the most comfortable one he'd ever sat in, and said, "Remember when Jessie ate an entire watermelon to keep you from having a piece?"

"Good Lord, that must have been at least five years ago. I don't think she'd even look at a watermelon now. There must be a point somewhere in this, Oliver."

"Only that you will make her content, James. Why won't she eat watermelon now? I have no idea, James."

James smiled into his port at the suddenly stern father's voice. "I will try. There are a lot of changes coming. Do you know that the English Wyndhams, their two sons, and their four servants traveled here with me?''

Oliver Warfield looked horrified. "They're all staying at Marathon? They're all in that house?''

"Unfortunately so. The Duchess—she's the Countess of Chase, you know—she assures me that I'm not to worry, that all of them understand perfectly and indeed applaud how I spent my money.''

"I thought you did too much, but that's neither here nor there. Those slaves now live better than many citizens.''

James felt the familiar curl of anger in his gut, but he held his tongue. He sipped more of his port and waited.

"Speaking of money, James, we need to speak about Jessie's dowry.''

James shifted in his chair. In his new role as husband to Jessie Warfield, he was frankly uncomfortable with Oliver, the man whose horses he'd tried to beat for years at the races, talking about giving money to him.

"You want more port?''

"I think I'd better have some,'' James said, and held out his glass.

An hour later James and Jessie finally left the Warfield Farm to return to Marathon. Jessie was talking like her old self, as chirpy as a magpie and excited about her father's horses. "Rialto will take on Tinpin with no trouble in the race on Saturday. Oh goodness, whom am I to cheer for? This is a problem I hadn't considered.''

James cleared his throat. "You're feeling well?''

"Marvelous. What will I do, James? And there's Friar Tuck and Miss Louise. I trained her myself. She's nearly three now and ready to race. She—''

"Jessie, when your father dies, you and I will own the Warfield Farm.''

She stared at him. "He's giving us everything? But he didn't tell me that.''

"No, not everything. He told me he's been very lucky the past few years. I suppose I didn't want to know how he recouped his fortunes. There is a dowry for Glenda, a sizable one, he said, since he's not all that certain she can catch a husband without one."

"But Glenda's very pretty. She's not at all like me, she—"

"Are you fishing for a compliment, Jessie?"

She gave him a long, thoughtful look. "I know what I am, James."

"Good. I want my wife to know that what she is first, is mine."

Jessie wasn't sure that she knew that at all, but she preferred James's line of thinking. "What about the house? What about Mother?"

"She is to live in the house until she dies. Then the house belongs to us as well. Which is a problem. Our properties don't join, so we can't just pull down fences and combine them."

"We'll figure out something," Jessie said. "Don't worry, James."

He knew that look in her eye—all sparkling energy and intelligence—and was pleased. Now if only their babe would stop sending her to her knees in front of the chamber pot.

She said now as she frowned down at her gloved hands, "Will we have money to work on Marathon?"

"Yes. A lot."

She gave him a fat smile. "Good," she said, and tucked her arm through his. "Papa asked me what I wanted, and I told him that the Duchess and I were going to fix up the inside of the house and we needed money to do it right. Odd that he didn't tell me about giving us the farm as well."

"That's properly a man's subject of discussion, Jessie. Your father was right not to mention that to you before he'd discussed it with me. I'm surprised that he even asked you about the money.''

''He told me that I'd earned all of it, since I'd been his best jockey for the past six years. I told him he was right. He kissed me then and hugged me. I love my father very much, James. I don't ever want him to die. At least for a very long time.''

''How can you be so nice and your mother so tedious?''

She laughed and laughed.

There was no particular pandemonium at Marathon when they returned, which was a relief. There was, however, James's mother, resplendent in purple silk, and she was seated in the parlor with the earl. *The Duchess must have escaped,* Jessie thought as she squared her shoulders and walked into the parlor beside James.

''My son,'' Wilhelmina Wyndham said, encouraging him to walk across the room to kiss her outstretched hand before she'd held it out for long enough to get a cramp.

''Mother.'' He kissed her veined hand. ''I'm surprised you're here. I was coming to see you. Don't you remember? I told you I would visit you today.''

''I couldn't wait. It's been too long since I've seen you. I told Ursula that she could wait, that I would come to dine with you this evening. She and Gifford can see you tomorrow.''

*Wonderful, just wonderful,* Jessie thought, wondering if she would make it through an evening with her mother-in-law without having to leave the room to retch.

When the Duchess came into the parlor, looking like the regal countess she was, slender and elegant and beautifully gowned in a pale yellow jonquil day dress, Wilhelmina Wyndham swelled with indignation. ''You're still here? I had prayed you would decamp. I don't mind that your lovely husband is here, for his only fault is that he had no choice but to marry you. He is an excellent man still despite the fact that you and he took everything that should have belonged to me. But you here as well? I won't have it. I wish you would die in your sleep.''

Jessie gasped. ''What did you say, ma'am?''

''Oh, I just said that I wished the Duchess won't ever sigh or weep. Life is so uncertain, you know.''

''Exactly so, ma'am,'' the Duchess said, and gave her quite a beautiful, serene smile. ''Badger wished me to tell you he prayed the food he prepared would give you bile.''

''How dare he! He said what?''

''Why, ma'am, Badger said it was his pleasure to serve you food that would make you smile.''

''You haven't changed,'' Wilhelmina said, lips tight, her powerful bosom heaving beneath the deep purple silk. ''You shouldn't ape your betters, young lady. It doesn't matter that you're a countess. You don't deserve to be. You're a fortune-hunting adventuress. Everyone knows it, even your poor husband, but he still married you seven years ago.''

''Exactly what I was thinking,'' Marcus said. ''Well put, ma'am. However, since I am married to the wench, since I can't very well boot her into a well, I suppose I must defend her to the best of my meager ability. Thus, ma'am, I would be pleased were you to drop yourself off a cliff.''

''Oh no, surely, no! What did you say, my lord?''

''Me? Oh, I just said I would be pleased if you were to drop yourself off a cliff.''

Mrs. Wyndham stared at him in consternation. There was complete silence in the parlor, with everyone staring at Marcus, who looked as bland as Old Bess's tapioca pudding. ''You didn't pretend,'' she said finally. ''That's not how it's done. You must pretend and find suitably matching words to cloak your meaning in banality.''

''How inept of me,'' Marcus said, and twitched a small piece of lint off his sleeve.

''Yes,'' Wilhelmina Wyndham said, leaning toward the

earl, "you could have said, for example, that you would be pleased if I were to take a good whiff of this excellent tea."

Marcus frowned. "No, that's not quite right yet, ma'am. Ah, I will have to think about it. When I decide, I will tell you and you can give me a critique."

"I would be delighted to," Wilhelmina Wyndham said, and patted the earl's arm. "Such a lovely material this is," she said, her voice all coy and flirting. "Such a lovely color, that deep blue."

The Duchess rolled her eyes. Could her wretch of a husband get away with any sin?

James, much enjoying himself, remained silent—at least he had planned to until his dear mother turned her guns on Jessie. She said now, "I am at a loss to determine why your beautiful husband doesn't leave you. You're not fit to live."

"What, ma'am?" Jessie felt her eyes begin to cross. The earl laughed deeply. "Well done, ma'am. Finish it."

"Certainly, my dear boy. Why, Jessie, I only told the Duchess that she had such wit to give."

James finally cleared his throat, drawing all attention. "Mother, let me give your thoughts another direction, perhaps a more pleasant one. You are going to be a grandmother come next April."

Jessie felt the force of her mother-in-law's shock, then her fury radiating now toward her. "So," Wilhelmina Wyndham said, pointing her finger at Jessie, "you did seduce my poor son. When he got to England you told him and he had to marry you. I wouldn't have minded if he had wed Glenda because she's an ignorant twit and I can control her quite well, both her and her ridiculously inept mother, who was my best friend when we were girls. How Portia birthed an oddity like you I will never know. It must be her husband's fault. Oliver has always been too sporting by half. Poor Portia writhes with the knowledge that you took poor

Glenda's husband, but she doesn't have the skill to do anything about it save moan and whine.''

"What would you do, ma'am?" Marcus asked, giving her a look that would vanquish any woman's defenses.

"Why, I would see that she's made so miserable that she traveled to Italy and lived the rest of her miserable life in a fishing village.''

"But, ma'am," Jessie said, rising now, wringing her hands, wondering if she would vomit on her mother-in-law's shoes, "I don't speak any Italian.''

"That, miss, is none of my fault. Speak to your mother. She gave you no suitable education. My James speaks fluent French. He even reads their outlandish literature.''

Before murder could be committed or laughter break through, James rose and held out his hand. "Mother, I believe you should be on your way now. You will come to us for dinner another evening. Bid your farewells to Marcus.''

"You continue to improve," Wilhelmina Wyndham said to the earl. "You may kiss my hand.''

The earl complied.

"As for you," she said to the Duchess, "I shan't forget you.''

"Thank you, ma'am.''

"Ah, Thomas, please have my mother's carriage fetched. Thank you. I will escort you, Mother.''

"It's your fault," Wilhelmina Wyndham said to both the Duchess and Jessie, and swept from the room on her son's arm. Jessie didn't imagine she'd ever totter, like Glenda. She heard her say to James in the small entranceway, "The earl is such a lovely man. It was *she*—that girl whose name is ridiculous! Duchess—of all things—it was she who kept the earl from giving us our due. Bring him with you to visit me, dear James. Leave both females here. They're better off here. Trust me.''

The Duchess, who was studying the fabric on the settee,

said, "You know, Jessie, I think we should visit Baltimore tomorrow and see what furnishings are available. But to be fair about it, I suppose we should consult James."

"Yes," Jessie said, looking thoughtful. "Knowing James, he'll have an opinion about everything." Jessie sighed. "I can't believe how you treated her, Marcus, yet she lapped it up."

"I'm irresistible," Marcus said.

His wife looked at him, a smile playing about her mouth. "I'm sorry, Jessie, but Wilhelmina is a harridan and the most vicious woman I've ever met. I appreciate how you, Marcus, protect me from the worst she dishes out. As for James, I noticed he kept his verbal distance until she set her sights on you, Jessie."

"He does well," Marcus said. "What else can he do? Toss her out of the window? Drop her off a cliff?" He laughed, rose, and stretched lazily. "I'm off to exercise one of James's horses." He kissed his wife and patted Jessie's cheek. "Relatives are the very devil," he said, and strolled out of the parlor.

"His mother," the Duchess said, "dotes on him as well. She adores him. She's always talking about his innocence, his purity. She's also decided that we suit each other, which is a vast relief. She spoils the boys shamelessly."

Jessie sighed deeply. "Can you see Mrs. Wyndham spoiling any offspring of mine shamelessly?"

"Well, perhaps not."

"What are we to do, Duchess? After all, she is his mother."

"Poor James."

## 28

JAMES WAS SO surprised, he stumbled over the three-legged
stool that stood in front of the winged chair and nearly went
crashing to the floor.

He flailed his arms to regain his balance, then stood there
rubbing his shin, cursing the stool, and staring at his wife,
who sat cross-legged in the middle of their bed, brushing
her hair over her shoulder, sending a cascade of red curls
nearly to her belly.

She was stark naked.

Not that he could see much of anything. Her thick hair
cloaked her white flesh as well as a shawl might. When she
raised her arm he could see through the hair to a lovely
expanse of white flesh just over her left breast.

James began to shake. Those glimpses of white skin, vis-
ible only now and again, would madden a man, any man,
particularly a man who was a husband of only three months
who hadn't touched his wife in two days for fear of inciting
another nightmare involving that blasted Mr. Tom. James
wanted to jump on her right then, at that very instant. "My
God," he said, taking one step forward.

"Hello, James," Jessie said with a fat smile. "A lovely
warm night, isn't it?"

"Yes, and for that I'm grateful." He took another step
toward the bed.

She pulled a thick mass of hair away from her body,

lifting it to studiously brush the curling ends over her fingers. As she brushed, she said, "James, will you make love to me if I promise you that I won't dream about Mr. Tom?"

"Well," he said slowly, "I'm not sure I can risk giving you any pleasure. I think it's connected — the pleasure and your nightmares. Although you didn't have any bad dreams the first two times we made love. But no, I can't take the chance. And how can you promise me you'll not have that hideous nightmare again?"

Jessie didn't answer. James took another step, then another. He couldn't take his eyes off her. "Can I brush your hair?"

"If you like," she said, and handed him the brush, handle first, as if she were handing him a foil. "I have a strong will, James. I won't dream about him. I also demand my share of pleasure."

He sat down beside her. Her white thigh was pressed against his. She was still seated cross-legged. He could slide his hands up her thighs and cup them over her. There was nothing to prevent him from doing that, from touching her intimately. She tilted her head toward him. He stared at all that shiny hair and said, "I think I want you to wear a bun right now."

She laughed, turning about to face him, her fingers on his face. "I've been sitting here for a good fifteen minutes brushing my hair. My hands are tired from wielding the bloody thing. You truly want it in a bun, James?"

"Yes. I want it away from you. I didn't realize you had so much hair. It covers far too much of your body. Put it high up on the back of your head."

"If you'll hand me the pins from atop the dressing table, I'll do it."

He was so close to her white flesh, so close to that mouth of hers and her belly and her thighs that he didn't want to move, but he did. He retrieved the wooden pins and handed them to her. He didn't seat himself again, but rather stood beside the bed and pulled off his clothes in record time. He even hopped on one foot to get off his boots.

When he looked again at his wife, her arms were above her head, her hands holding up all that hair, and she was utterly and completely white and naked. He thought he'd spill his seed at the sight of her.

"Your breasts are bigger," he said, and took a step toward the bed.

"Yes, they are, aren't they?" she said proudly. "Did you know that you're always big when you take your clothes off with intent, James? Just look at you. If I didn't know already that you did indeed fit, I would be howling with fear and running from this bedchamber."

James couldn't help himself anymore. He nearly leaped on Jessie but managed to hold himself back, taking another step toward the bed. He could see the soft flesh between her thighs, open to him. "You don't mind that I'm all hairy and different from you?"

She grinned and began twisting her hair around her left hand. "I look like goat milk, yard upon yard of goat milk with breasts that weren't anything at all before you got me with child. But you, James, yours is a complex landscape, all valleys and ridges and beautiful clumps of hair here and there, and your legs are thick and strong. I can see your muscles when you move. I don't have any hard muscles in my stomach as you do. I very much like to touch your body, particularly your belly, well, and other places."

"Manly places," he said.

"Yes," she said, "manly ones."

He closed his eyes as her breasts rose and fell as she twisted and retwisted her hair. She liked to touch him? He shuddered. He touched his fingers to his belly. He supposed she was right about the muscles, though he'd never thought about it. She liked—very much—to touch him there particularly? She could have all their lives to touch him there, to touch him wherever she wanted to.

"Your nipples are darker. They were a soft light pink before. Now they're richer, fuller. I want to take you into my mouth, Jessie."

"Oh. I didn't think you'd noticed so closely."

She was excited; she had to be at least as excited as he was. How long did it take to put hair in a bun? Not as long as she was taking, he realized, as his legs were now pressed against the side of the bed. "Jessie, you're teasing me. How long have you been planning this?"

"Since my stomach settled before dinner. Since I realized you were depriving me just because of Mr. Tom. Badger patted me on the head, he was so pleased I didn't retch up his delicious stewed mutton kidneys."

"Don't put your hair in a bun, Jessie. Just drop it down your back, that's it. Give me the brush. Thank you. Now, lie down on your back. I want to look at you."

He knew he'd taken control from her, but he couldn't help it. He wanted her so badly he knew he'd burst with it if he didn't get inside her quickly. Ah, the pleasure he would give her. He thought about Mr. Tom, then dismissed the phantom from his mind. She was his wife and she wanted him. He wouldn't deny her. Soon now, very soon, they'd leave for Ocracoke. He found he was thinking more of ridding her of a ghost than of Blackbeard's bloody treasure. For he was sure that was what he would do if he got to the bottom of the mystery plaguing her.

He stretched out his hand and gently laid it over her belly. He began to massage her. Her belly was still flat, but her flesh was soft and he continued to caress her, splaying his fingers out to touch her pelvic bones. He sat beside her, leaned down, and kissed a patch of white flesh framed by his fingers. He moved his hands a bit lower until the heels of his hands rested on her curling red hair. He kissed her, then caressed her with his tongue. He wondered how long he could do this without dying. "You are the most beautiful female person in the world," he said, breathing his warm breath over her flesh. Even as he was close to touching her, she found herself arching upward.

He laughed softly and took her in his mouth.

"James!"

"Hmmm," he said, but didn't raise his head. She tasted so sweet, so much like Jessie and that gardenia soap she used. Lust was battering him down, but he knew he had to hold on. But what if he came into her now, just this one time? No, he had to hold on, he had to do things properly. He didn't understand how he could want her more now than he had three months ago.

Her back arched up, he felt her fingers digging into his hair, into his shoulders, and she was whispering in a low, hoarse voice, "Please, James, oh please, please . . ."

He pushed her then, teasing her with his tongue, then caressing her deeply. When he eased his middle finger into her, she screamed. That high wail made him moan.

When he felt her pleasure explode through her, he wanted to shout with the joy of it. He pushed her, reveling in her pleasure, and knowing that soon, very soon, he would be inside her and it would be she who would be giving to him, she who would be reveling in his passion. At least he prayed a woman reveled in a man's passion. Jessie certainly always seemed to.

When finally she quieted, he lifted his head, smiled at her, and said, "Now, Jessie."

Then he was between her legs, holding her up. He wanted to shove into her immediately, all of him, but he took his time, and with every small bit he pushed into her he felt immense pressure that was surely pain, but he didn't want it to end, not ever. He was his full length inside her, at last.

At last. He came on top of her, balancing himself on his elbows.

"Jessie, how does that feel to you?"

She opened her eyes. "It feels rather nice, James. Of course you always feel nice. As if you're a part of me. Actually, if that's true, then I want you to be a part of me forever."

She lifted her hips, her legs going around his back, and he was lost. To his utter surprise, when he thrust hard into her, he felt her quiver beneath him, felt those quivers around his sex, pulling him deeper, squeezing him, and he reached between their bodies, while he still had the wit to do anything, and touched her. She cried out, a sharp cry, sounding as surprised as he felt. He kept up the pressure, giving her pleasure again, and as she peaked, he took his own release.

"Oh dear," Jessie said, kissed his shoulder, and pulled him down flat on top of her. "Oh dear."

He kissed her ear.

"That was embarrassing, James. I experienced pleasure two times. Surely that isn't all that common."

"All right, I'll never do it again."

She bit his nose. "It wasn't that embarrassing." She frowned, closed her arms over his back, and pulled him as close as she could get him. He was very heavy, she was having trouble drawing a full breath, but she didn't care.

"Do all women reward themselves as much as I just did?"

"No."

"Ah, so I'm special."

He shrugged and licked her earlobe. "A man has to do things right," he said, and nibbled her earlobe again. "Some men don't care, others just don't know what to do, and since women rarely know what's good for them, nothing at all happens. Can you imagine spending the rest of your nights with me with no pleasure at all?"

"No. Can we do this every night now?" She kissed his shoulder even as she squeezed his back. "I know you've held back from me for the past two nights because of the nightmares, but please don't anymore, James. If you do then I'll insist that we leave immediately for Ocracoke, and I really don't think anyone is quite ready just yet. Soon, though—very soon. And Blackbeard's treasure. Just imagine. Jewels, a ton of jewels and they'll be all ours. We'll be so rich we'll buy Maryland." She giggled and he grinned down at her.

"I like the sound of that. More giggles every day now, all right?"

"All right. James, what will we do about our mothers?"

"Ignore them."

"Does your mother always say awful things and then use similar sounding words to try to make them sound as though she said something different?"

"Just to certain people. When we were all at Chase Park, way back when the Duchess and Marcus were first married, she used to dish up the Duchess with every sentence she uttered. Then one day the Duchess actually did the same thing back to her. It was quite well done." He sighed, then stiffened like a hunting dog sighting a pheasant. Jessie's hands were stroking his back. She was caressing his buttocks. He felt himself filling her again. Her fingers went between his thighs and he thought he'd croak that instant.

"Do you know what you're doing?"

"I hope so, James, I surely do. Oh goodness, you're gaining in proportion again."

"A necessity, Jessie, a necessity."

"There's another mystery."

James, so exhausted he didn't know if he could even draw enough breath into his lungs, just stared down at her. He wanted to collapse, but he managed to keep himself up on his elbows. He'd nearly crushed her before, but she hadn't complained. But now there was a light of excitement in her eyes; unfortunately it had replaced that sated, vague look that had filled her eyes just five minutes before. Women, he thought, shaking his head to keep himself awake, were extraordinarily different from men. She should be whispering love words to him, rubbing her sweating body against his, then falling asleep even as he got hard inside her.

But she was wide awake. It was as if having all that woman's pleasure gave her new energy. He himself wanted to sleep for a week.

"What mystery?" He didn't give a good damn. Nor could he keep himself up for another moment. He pulled out of her and collapsed next to her, drawing her against his side. "What mystery?" he said again, trying to remember a time when he'd felt this content, this pleased with the world and his place in it. And the reason he felt this way was because of Jessie Warfield. The former brat. Amazing.

"Oh, I'm sorry, I forgot what I'd been thinking about. My thoughts drifted to thinking about how that felt, James, you sliding out of me and the way that made me all quivery inside."

"Be quiet, Jessie. I'm on the very edge of death. What mystery?"

"You've heard of the lost colony on Roanoke Island, haven't you?"

"Certainly. Sir Walter Raleigh owned the ships and was a major backer of the expedition. He shipped colonists to the Outer Banks, off the coast of North Carolina, to Roanoke Island. It was sometime late in the sixteenth century."

"Yes, in 1587. There were more than one hundred colonists from England, including women and children. In fact, the first child born on American soil was Virginia Dare, the granddaughter of John White, the leader of the colony. When it was time for Sir Walter to leave Roanoke Island, the colonists asked that John White return to England and make certain that they weren't forgotten and to see to replenishing their supplies. However, Spain attacked England in 1588 and thus no relief ships ever went to Roanoke Island. White wasn't able to return until 1590. When White and his men landed, there was no one there. Not a single soul. There was no sign of them, not even a trace. There hadn't been a massacre because there would have been bones, debris, wreckage, but there was nothing. The colonists had simply vanished. So what became of the colonists of Roanoke Island? It's been a mystery ever since. Many men have tried to solve it and have come up with outlandish theories.''

''Is this leading somewhere, Jessie?''

''Yes. I'm a woman and I've solved it.''

''*What?*''

''Well, I really haven't quite solved it just yet and by the time I do solve it, I won't have had to study it as all those poor men have in the past three hundred years. I just have to finish reading Valentine's diary—that's her first name, I suppose, but I'm not really sure. She only ever refers to herself by that single name. Of course we have to find all the diaries first.''

''Who the devil is Valentine? Where did she get that ridiculous name?''

''She was one of the colonists. She is also Blackbeard's great-grandmother. Yes, you heard me right. Evidently she was the one who passed on the habit of recording events in diaries. She was Blackbeard's great-grandmother, so therefore she must have survived and thus it's likely that all the other colonists survived as well. When we find the diaries on Ocracoke, I'll read the rest of her diary and know what happened to the colonists. I'd forgotten about her just as I'd forgotten Blackbeard.

''Her diary won't help us find Blackbeard's treasure. She

died long before he was ever born. But I imagine she can set to rest the mystery of Roanoke Island once and for all. Isn't that exciting, James?''

"I don't believe this. You've had too much sex, Jessie. You're not thinking with your brain, not if you're dredging up this ancient relative of Blackbeard's. You just want me to caress you again and come inside you and make you scream and moan.''

"Well, perhaps you're right about that.'' The hussy closed her hand around him and he nearly leaped off the bed.

"Stop that or you'll regret it.''

"Just how will you manage that, James?'' She leaned up and kissed his chest.

"I'm so tired I can't make you regret anything right this minute, Jessie, but there's always tomorrow. Actually, there's always two hours from now. I just need a bit of rest, only a small number of minutes. Blackbeard's great-grandmother, you say? This is surely too much. She was a member of the lost colony of Roanoke? You've lost your grip on things, Jessie my girl. You've been off a horse for too long. You've been wearing stockings and lovely gowns for too long. Those streamers have cooked your brain.''
There was no answer.

He nearly laughed aloud. Jessie was sound asleep, her fingers still curled around him.

There was no nightmare of Mr. Tom that night. James didn't mention it the next day, and neither did Jessie. Maybe the nightmares were gone for good. Maybe. But James didn't want to take the chance. No, he wanted to go to Ocracoke and he wanted Jessie to see where it had all happened. Then he wanted to find that bloody treasure, like everyone else in his house.

# ═══ 29 ═══

"WE'VE DISCUSSED THIS thoroughly and come to a decision."

Neither Marcus nor James looked the least bit surprised at Spears's announcement.

It was Jessie who said, "What is this decision you've come to?"

"Mr. Badger, would you do the telling, if you please?"

Badger handed everyone another of his delicious damson tarts while Sampson poured the port. He cleared his throat and said as he seated himself at the dining-room table, "It's all about this Valentine woman and the lost colony of Roanoke Island. You've added more spice to the stew, Jessie, and we all find this lost-colony business stimulating. Perhaps the stimulation could have come a bit later, but one must continually adapt, and we have."

"Fancy," Maggie said as she took a delicate bite of her tart, "a young woman who lived so long ago writing to us across the centuries. And here she is that evil pirate's great-grandmother."

"That certainly proves the lost colonists survived," Marcus said. "If this Valentine gave birth and her offspring survived, then others could have survived as well."

The Duchess's thoughts were more focused on the chair in the parlor she'd pronounced would belong to James—a huge, comfortable winged chair, as ugly as the devil in a tattered old brocade of pale brown. But her ears pricked at this talk of Ocracoke and a lost colony. "What about Valentine, Badger?"

"Jessie told us that she'd forgotten about Valentine's diary just as she'd forgotten all about Blackbeard's journals. This Old Tom was the one who told her his grandfather had gotten his evil hands on all the diaries. The only reason he'd kept Valentine's diary was because he thought it an oddity, and she was family, after all."

"That's right," Jessie said. "Old Tom let me read aloud to him part of Valentine's diary. I know a lot about how the colony lived. I'm certain that what happened to them will be toward the end of the diary. I fancy I could become very famous were I to publish her diary and present my conclusions."

"We are considering that, Jessie," Spears said. "It is another stimulating prospect. However, first things first. What we want to do now is journey to the Outer Banks to Ocracoke Island and dig up all the diaries. Then we'll locate that treasure. You can progress with your scholarship, then we will assist you to present it to the world. I fancy all of us are nearly ready to board another ship. It isn't all that long a distance, after all."

Maggie cheered.

Sampson lightly patted her lovely hand.

Badger said, "I have four more damson tarts. Who would like them?"

"Yes, let's go immediately," the Duchess said, leaning forward to take one. "Well," she added with a small frown, "perhaps not tomorrow, but soon. First Jessie and I must order all the furnishings we need for the house. When we return, everything should be about ready. Oh dear, there are the roses to be seen to. I've already asked Thomas to look into finding you a gardener, James. I can't bear to see the roses so bedraggled and I fear I don't have enough time to work on them myself.''

"Don't worry, Duchess," Jessie said. "Now that James and I have my dowry, we can hire three gardeners. I will make certain that when you come again to America the gardens will be what you're used to.''

"James," Marcus said, eyeing the last of Badger's damson tarts, "are we even necessary? Do you get the feeling that we might as well take ourselves back to England? That the ladies can see to these matters all by themselves?''

"James is very necessary to my happiness," Jessie said, and smiled at James, who seemed startled by her words. Then he gave her a wicked grin.

"My dear Jessie, that's not exactly what I meant, but perhaps that is a consideration.''

"What can I do, Marcus?" James said, snagging the tart before the earl could. "My wife will surely pine away without me if she and the Duchess go off adventuring.''

"We'd never leave you to yourselves. It would be too dangerous," the Duchess said, leaning forward, her soft white elbows resting on the white tablecloth.

"Do your ordering, Duchess," James said, "then we'll leave. But first, tomorrow night, we're going to a ball in Jessie's and my honor at the Blanchards', where it all started with Jessie falling out of a tree on top of me, after, of course, she'd shot Mortimer Hackey in the foot.''

"Oh dear," Jessie said. "Do you think that dreadful man will be there?''

"If he is," James said, stretching his legs out and crossing his feet at the ankles, that last damson tart chewed and swallowed, "and if he gives me any threatening looks at all, you, my dear wife, can pound him into the Blanchard rosebushes.''

Surprisingly, Jessie didn't laugh with all the others. She nodded solemnly. "Don't worry about Hackey. Surely he's feared me ever since I shot him in the foot.''

James rolled his eyes.

Spears said, ''Quite right, Jessie.''

Marcus said, ''I don't suppose, Badger, that you hid just one more damson tart? James has proved himself an unworthy host. He popped that last one into his mouth before I had a chance to snag it for myself.''

Badger, giving Marcus the same fond look he frequently bestowed on Anthony, lifted the corner of a napkin to reveal one last tart.

The Blanchards, immensely fond of James but not his mother, and equally fond of Oliver Warfield but not his wife or his daughter Glenda, were perfectly willing to accept Jessie once Mrs. Blanchard saw that she wasn't wearing trousers and smelling of the stables. Indeed, the Blanchards were so relieved to see something of a vision come into their house that Mr. Blanchard ordered more bottles of champagne to be brought up from the wine cellar.

He rubbed his beefy hands together. ''Ah, James, she's a fine girl, just look at that beautiful hair. Never noticed she even had hair before. And her, well, her other womanly parts look womanly, which is a vast relief, let me tell you.''

James took it all in good humor, just smiling and nodding.

Mrs. Blanchard wanted to exclaim her delight and her relief, but she was too in awe of the Duchess, this glorious English countess who surely could be a queen—filled with grace and charm and so achingly beautiful she knew all the gentlemen would fall over their feet to get near her. Not to mention that husband of hers—an earl!—and he was actually James's cousin. They'd known about the English Wyndhams, of course, but actually to have them here in their own house in Baltimore—it was more than Mrs. Blanchard could stand, nearly. Her hands were over her bosom as she listened with rapt attention to the Duchess's ever-so-refined voice, with all those clipped syllables and concise royal vowels. Mrs. Blanchard was filled to overflowing with sublime content, knowing that every matron in Baltimore and its environs would know of her brilliant accomplishment in hosting such fine guests. They'd worship at her feet. Which was of course the real reason they were giving the party for James and his new bride.

Mrs. Blanchard prayed that Wilhelmina Wyndham would be late. Indeed, she sent one brief, heartfelt prayer that Wilhelmina just might sprain her ankle as she stepped into her carriage. Maybe even break it.

*No such luck*, she thought, hearing Wilhelmina's ringing voice all the way from the front steps. It appeared she'd arrived at the same time as the Warfields. Surely Glenda wouldn't be with them. Surely.

James wasn't at all surprised to see Glenda standing stiffly beside her mama, wearing a gown that surely showed off too much cleavage. She looked very pretty, if the truth be told, not the kind of pretty that attracted him, for he'd discovered that Jessie's looks appealed to him now. He drew a deep breath, tucked Jessie's cold hand in the crook of his arm, and said, "Good evening, Oliver, Mrs. Warfield, Glenda."

That was the most optimistic line that came out of his mouth for the next five minutes.

"We are here because your father insisted we come."

"Actually," Oliver said under his breath, but not enough under it for everyone present to hear, "I wanted to come alone. I knew I'd have a better time if I came alone."

"You can come with me, Papa, and have some champagne punch." Jessie took her father's arm, and the two of them bolted toward the punch bowl. James grinned after her, then watched the Duchess reduce his mother-in-law and sister-in-law to stuttering supplicants. Glenda even curtsied. The Duchess gave her a gentle nod of approval.

It was excellently done. As for Marcus, he took care of James's mother when she swept into the Blanchard house, passing Mrs. Blanchard with a mere nod, heading straight toward the Duchess.

Marcus said to her without pause, "Charm is a very useful tool, if one has sufficient intelligence to realize it. Don't you agree, ma'am?"

Wilhelmina pulled up short, twitching her skirt away from the Duchess, who was standing six feet away from her, and smiled flirtatiously up at the earl. "My dear papa told me that I was endowed with more charm than anyone he knew."

That, Marcus thought, staring at that still-handsome face that had some of the look of James in it, was a possibility that hadn't occurred to him. It probably hadn't occurred to any member of her acquaintance. "I trust to see it oozing out of you tonight, ma'am. If it is not oozing out of you I will question my ability ever to converse with you again."

Wilhelmina felt put upon. She also believed the earl, whose threat was distressing. She'd wanted to preen in front of all her neighbors because she was actually a relative of this illustrious couple, but at the same time she'd wanted to dash the damned Duchess into the floor. It wasn't to be. Also, all her neighbors believed themselves more fortunate than God to have that damned adventuress and the earl in their midst. She drew a deep breath. She resolved not to insult the Duchess tonight. She wouldn't insult her son's new wife either, though that would be difficult as well. She didn't want to lose the charming earl and his charming conversation.

"We will waltz, my lord?" Wilhelmina asked, patting the fat little sausage curls in front of her ear.

"Certainly," Marcus said smoothly. "But first, a gentleman must dance with his wife."

"You're a smooth-tongued devil," the Duchess whispered to her husband as he whirled her around in his arms to the lively music played in strict three-quarter time by a small group of men at the far corner of the room.

"I will be disappointed in myself if she slips her harness tonight and allows her tongue to run riot," he said, kissed his wife's lovely ear, and whirled her around in wide, full circles. "I will have failed in my, er, mild threat. Pray that she doesn't, Duchess. My image of myself as a great diplomat would suffer." The Duchess choked as she laughed up at her husband. Neither of them was aware that all the guests were standing around in a huge circle staring at them.

"Well," Mrs. Blanchard said complacently, "they are nearly royalty. Of course one would expect them to dance to perfection. Doesn't the countess even laugh perfectly? Ah, and they are so beautiful, both of them. She in that dark blue silk and he in those splendid black evening clothes. I do wonder what is wrong with Wilhelmina. She has the amazing good fortune to be connected to them. She looks as if she's swallowed a prune pit."

"She always looks as though she's swallowed something," Mr. Blanchard said. "As for the earl, he's a damned good man, despite his being English. I suppose a fellow can't help his antecedents."

Mrs. Blanchard looked at Mr. Blanchard as though he'd lost his mental faculties. She was more grateful than she could say that for whatever reason Wilhelmina Wyndham hadn't held a ball for the English royalty and her new daughter-in-law. So that privilege was now hers. She turned to greet Compton Fielding and his mother, Eliza.

"Ah," Fielding said once he'd greeted and been greeted by the Blanchards, "I see that James and Jessie are here. I'm delighted they've married. It's quite a surprise, but a good thing."

"I was very surprised as well," Eliza Fielding said. "I believed James looked upon her as a little sister. Jessie is a delight. I remember I tried to talk her into taking violin lessons from me when she was young, but she was always horse mad. How lovely she's become.''

James and Jessie danced sedately. James didn't want to take the chance she'd turn green and end up in the Blanchards' garden vomiting up her dinner. Nor did he want to see the infamous tree that spat Jessie out of its lower branches and onto him.

It was midway through the evening when James finally got to speak to his sister, Ursula, Giff, and Alice Belmonde. He hugged his sister, thwacked his brother-in-law on his broad shoulders, and said to Alice, ''You're looking well. How do you feel?''

Alice gave him a brave sweet smile. She was pleased he'd married Jessie and told him so. ''Just look at her, James,'' she said, pointing to Jessie, who was talking to Compton Fielding. ''She's beautiful, so very different than the way she used to be. It's surprising that none of us realized what was beneath those old hats she used to wear. Or perhaps it all happened by magic when you put that wedding ring on her finger.''

''Jessie's still the same, Alice, just the outward package is a bit different. She's splendid, you know.''

Alice was surprised to hear James Wyndham speak of any woman, even his wife, with such pride. Jessie had been transformed, turned into a beauty. Alice hoped Jessie's inner self was still the same.

''I say, James,'' Giff said, ''I approve your choice of brides. I hope she can still ride a horse after the way she's changed.''

Ursula said, ''Is it true that Jessie's pregnant? Mother was going on and on about it, her lips all tight and pursed.''

''Yes. You can give me even more congratulations.''

''So you did ruin her,'' Alice said.

''No, Alice, Jessie isn't all that pregnant, only about two

months along, we think. I need to call Dr. Hoolahan over to Marathon to examine her.''

"Oh, here's Nelda," Alice said. "Excuse me, James, Ursula. Nelda and I are having tea tomorrow." Alice waved as she walked away. James looked down at his sister. "Would you care to dance, Ursula?"

When they were on the dance floor, James kept their movements sedate. He said, "I know you wonder why I married Jessie. As always, you're willing to bide your time. You have more patience than Job, Urs. You never let Mother rile you. I sincerely hope Giff appreciates you fully."

"Giff is a smart man, James. Of course he appreciates me." His sister gave him an impish smile. "Now tell me why you married Jessie Warfield, your nemesis on the race-track."

He said, "To be blunt, I married her because I wanted to. It's as simple as that. She's a marvelous girl. We share many interests, as you know."

"I'm not upset that I'll never know the whole truth, James. Mother is fairly chomping at the bit. I do hope she doesn't begin to attack Jessie once that beautiful Duchess has returned to England with her equally beautiful husband."

"If she does, then I shall have to call you to help me shut her mouth."

Ursula laughed, a deep, full-bodied laugh that sounded just like her husband's. "I will wish us both luck," she said, and stood on her tiptoes to kiss her brother's cheek.

"Ah," James said after he'd returned her to Giff. "Compton. Come on, let's have a brandy and talk about *Le Cid*. It's a marvelous play. You're the scholar here, tell me how accurate it is."

They spoke in French, James insisting. "If I don't speak French occasionally, my mouth muscles refuse to work properly,'' he said, and laughed. They spoke of the French playwright's plays for some time, enjoying themselves thoroughly. James said after a pause, ''Oh, Compton, do you know if our esteemed magistrate, Mr. Dickens, has managed to uncover anything about Allen Belmonde's death?''

Compton shook his head. ''No, he just dithers around, then goes home to bed his new bride. I've never before seen a man so smitten. Well, perhaps you fill the bill as well, James. I've watched you look at Jessie tonight. Your bride looks lovely.''

''I fill the besotted bill?'' James asked in some surprise. ''I'm very fond of Jessie, and the good Lord knows I savor all the other joys a man is offered in marriage.''

''You would be a wily diplomat,'' Compton said, and laughed. ''Did Jessie enjoy the latest diary I gave her?''

''Well, yes she did, actually. It's quite a coincidence about diaries, actually. You'll never believe what she remembered.'' James paused, frowning at himself, then continued easily, ''Well, never mind that. Tell me about your latest violin recital, Compton. I was sorry to miss it.''

James listened politely. Spying Jessie across the room, he smiled at her. She was having an animated discussion with Marcus, but seeing James, she smiled back.

Once Compton had finished describing his recital, James inquired again about Allen Belmonde. ''Gordon has no ideas at all? No one he can suspect?''

''No, not really.''

''Mortimer Hackey hasn't bothered Alice, has he, Compton?''

''Not that I know of. I do know that Giff has been keeping an eye on him. He's dealing with all Allen's banking affairs, you know.''

''Good,'' James said, wondering what Mortimer was up to. In James's experience, men like Mortimer Hackey didn't give up easily. He said as much to his brother-in-law a few moments later when he caught him alone. "I appreciate it, Giff. I can't help it. I just feel protective of Alice." He shook his head at himself. "So Gordon hasn't said a thing to you either?"

"Nothing directly pertaining to Allen's death, but he did say that one of his dock rats, as he calls them, told him that it was Belmonde who was behind that incident with Jessie — when someone tried to run her down. Apparently Belmonde hired a ruffian to do it. I can't understand why, but there it is."

James stared at Giff in utter disbelief. This was the first he'd heard of the incident. "What did you say? Jessie *what*? Someone almost ran her down? She's never said a word of it to me, curse her hide." He turned around to stare at his wife, and this time he wasn't smiling. She blinked at him in surprise.

"Yes, that's right. I assumed you knew. Gordon heard that Allen might have hired a man to do it. Gordon asked me if I could think of any reason why Allen would want Jessie dead — he didn't come to me until after both of you had left for England. I told him I couldn't think of anything other than that she always used to beat him racing. Then she saved Sweet Susie from those thieves. He seemed pleased enough with her then as I remember, at least until she threatened to butcher him after he threatened you."

"This is nonsense and I'm going to kill her," James said, plowed his fingers through his hair, and turned abruptly on his heel. "I will speak to you later, Giff."

Why the hell hadn't she ever said anything about it to him? Why hadn't anyone else said anything to him? He stopped a foot from his wife, who greeted him with a wide smile and a soft look in those green eyes of hers that some- how looked greener between her gown and her shining hair.

"Jessie."

"Hello, James. Do you want to waltz with me again? I would like that. You're so graceful and—"

"Be quiet. I don't want to dance with you. I want to strangle you. Come with me to the garden."

"Oh dear, is Mortimer Hackey here? I didn't bring my pistol, James. I'm sorry. I forgot. Are you certain you want to go to the garden?"

He ground his teeth, took her hand in his, and pulled her across to the long bank of French doors that gave onto a balcony with steps down into the garden. "We'll stay up here. I don't know what you'd do if you got near that tree again."

"I'd probably climb it again so I could fall on you. Now that I know what I could have done that first time, I'd like to try it again. Why are you frowning? What on earth is the matter with you?"

He took her shoulders in his hands and shook her, but not too hard because he didn't want her to turn green and heave up her dinner. "Why the hell didn't you tell me?"

"Tell you about what? What are you talking about, James? I saw you speaking with Alice and Compton and Giff and ever so many other people. What do you mean?"

"Giff told me that Gordon Dickens, the magistrate—"

"I know very well who Gordon is. Other than pompous and an idiot, he's got a father who managed to get him appointed as magistrate, truly a jest and—"

"It turns out that old Gordon heard from an informant that Allen had hired a man to run you down. Run you down how? When did someone try to run you down?"

"Oh, that." She had the gall to shrug. "If the truth be told, I'd forgotten it. I'm not so sure now that that man wanted to kill me. Maybe he was drunk. Maybe he wanted to mow Compton down. Now you say that Allen was behind it? That's surely odd and difficult to believe."

"What happened, Jessie?"

"It was last winter, James—well, late March actually. I was walking down Pratt Street, not paying much attention because I'd just seen Connie Maxwell and I knew she was your lover, well, never mind that. I went into Compton Fielding's bookstore and bought a book. He walked me out to the sidewalk. Then, with no warning, this man driving an empty wagon, two horses pulling it, came right at me. He very nearly got me, too. If it hadn't been for Compton Fielding, I fear I might have met my maker."

"What did Compton do?"

"He grabbed me by the seat of my pants and yanked me through the door of his bookshop. The man drove the wagon within a whisker of the bookshop entrance. Fielding didn't think it could have been an accident. The man whipped up the horses and was out of sight in seconds. Actually, what I remember most vividly is being furious because he was mistreating those horses. Neither Compton nor I recognized the driver or the horses. Actually Mr. Fielding couldn't recognize any horse—he thinks they all look alike—but I could, and I didn't. A good dozen people witnessed everything, but none of them remembered anything helpful."

"Why the hell didn't Compton tell me?"

"Why would he, James? Why would he ever think you were even interested?"

"He bloody well should have realized I'd be interested. He should have told me, damn his eyes. Did you recognize anything about the man?"

"No. My father sent a servant to fetch Gordon, and he came out to the farm. He treated me as if I were a moron. I imagine he would have thought I was making up the whole incident if it hadn't been for Mr. Fielding and all those other people. He told my father it was probably some man I'd beaten in a horse race. He then added that the provocation was great, for what man would tolerate being beaten by a girl?"

"Jessie, tell me about that damned man who was driving the wagon."

"He was wearing a handkerchief over half his face. His eyes were dark, I do remember that, and he had very black bushy eyebrows. He was wearing an old black hat pulled down to those eyebrows. Work clothes. Nothing else, really."

"You told this to Gordon?"

She nodded. "Allen Belmonde wanted to kill me? That's impossible. There's no reason. Besides, I'm not certain that the man was trying to kill me. Maybe he was after Compton. James, would you like to go walking in the garden?"

"What? Oh no, Jessie. I've got to speak to Compton."

She gave him a forlorn look. "You don't want to dance with me?"

"No. Dance with Giff or Marcus. Have you been the object of any other attacks, or was that the only time?"

She shook her head. "No, nothing."

James rested his elbows on the stone railing that lined the balcony. "That makes sense, doesn't it? If Allen was behind it, any attempts on your life would have stopped with his death. Think, Jessie. Why would Allen Belmonde want you dead?"

She just kept shaking her head. "I was good friends with Alice. Perhaps he didn't approve of that, but that isn't enough to push a man to murder, is it?"

"Belmonde was always a bloody ass."

"That's true. As to his wanting to murder me because I'd beaten him horse racing, I've beaten him for the past five years. There was nothing new in that."

"Damnation, you must have done something to make him want you dead. It just doesn't make sense."

"Perhaps Gordon's informant was wrong. That seems the most likely conclusion."

"Possibly. Come along inside now. I want to speak with

Compton again. You can dance with any number of men who now find you quite toothsome, what with your bosom showing all white as new snow and those streamers of yours tempting a man to wind them around and around his finger until he's pulled you right up to him and there's your mouth, all soft and inviting.''

"Are you interested, James?'' She had the nerve to bat her eyelashes at him. He leaned down and kissed her mouth, then lightly rubbed his thumbs over her eyebrows, smoothing them down. "Isn't it odd that some of the ladies are giving you venomous looks?''

"I used to get pitying looks. I like venomous looks better. The Duchess is exquisite. Why don't they give her venomous looks?''

"Because she's English. She's a countess. Everyone looks upon her as near-royalty. She's exotic. You're Jessie and you're supposed to be a mess. Since you're not, you've tilted everyone on his axis. Nobody likes to see change in another, particularly this kind of change.'' He lightly rubbed his knuckles over the tops of her breasts. His eyes dilated.

"I suppose you're right,'' she said with a sigh, and tugged on one of her streamers. "My mother told me that my streamers made me look like a hussy.''

"Your mother should follow Glenda's line of vision when she sights a man, if she wants to talk about a hussy. Now, let's go back inside before my right hand starts wriggling down the front of your gown.''

# ===≡ 30 ≡===

THE DAY BEFORE they sailed for the Outer Banks, Jessie's morning sickness abruptly stopped. "It's gone," she said blankly, looking toward the chamber pot she'd grown quite intimate with during the past weeks. "I feel wonderful."

"Thank God," James said. "You're so skinny, I could lift you over my head with one hand. I want some meat on your bones."

"I believe you will be granted your wish," she said, laughed, and threw her arms around his back. "I'm so excited," she said. "We're going to find that treasure."

James wasn't so sure about that. Her memories of the four diaries were the memories of a child. Would she even remember now where her childhood self had buried them? Who was to say that someone hadn't come across them in the intervening years? There had been several small hurricanes that had struck the Outer Banks, and innumerable storms. Naturally the beach had been flooded, probably the entire stretch of land from the sea to the sound. It was possible the sea had cut a new inlet through that area of beach, pulling the diaries and everything else out to sea.

The chances of finding the diaries were not very good. But no one would say that aloud.

That evening, with the entire group assembled, Jessie took the opportunity to tell them about Ocracoke. "I must be clear with all of you. You're from England where everything is finished and neat and one knows exactly where to go to buy anything at all or procure something. But on the Outer Banks, there's really nothing at all. The Outer Banks are barrier islands, protecting the mainland of North Carolina from the sea. Think of them as a sort of chain necklace. It's savage, barren, and the village of Ocracoke barely compares to a small English village. There are about three hundred and fifty people living in the village now, most of them pilots and fishermen.''

''What do you mean, 'pilots'?'' Anthony asked, looking ever so much like his father with his blue eyes and black-as-midnight hair.

''Ocracoke Island is at the end of this long chain of islands. You come around the south end and into Ocracoke Inlet. That's when ships hire local pilots. To sail across Pamlico Sound to the mainland is tricky. The currents and tides are nearly always contrary, and sandbars pop up where you least expect them. The one thing you can count on is change. Only the local pilots know where the new currents and shifts of sand are. To try it without them is foolhardy.

''Don't picture Hyde Park. It's more uncivilized than not. Since the barrier islands are constantly bombarded by the sea, the people who live their lives there are sturdy, strong, and incredibly resilient. I just wanted to warn you. It will be difficult. There won't be anyone there waiting to help us. We will be able to hire perhaps a couple of men and maybe a woman to help in the house, but please understand this isn't like going to Brighton to see the Regent's Pavilion. The village bustles with life. There's a Methodist church and there are several general shops that carry everything from thimbles to scrub boards, but nothing like you are used to. Everyone eats fish and the local fare is delicious — Anthony, you'll love croaker, a silver fish that, fried in butter, makes you sing hallelujahs.''

"Don't forget mullet, Jessie," Badger said. "I already have several recipes for mullet."

"And pigfish," Spears added. "A very infelicitous name, but we must try it."

"My very favorite is red drum," Jessie said, licking her lips. "Let me get back to Ocracoke. Although you will miss many of the trappings of civilization, the sea is beautiful, the air sparkling clear, the sun will still be warm, and you can tell how the world was a thousand years ago. Even better, it isn't storm season yet."

Spears said, clearing his throat, "We've discussed this, Jessie, and we understand what it will be like. I have even spoken, as has Maggie, to this Compton Fielding about Ocracoke and its environs. He provided us with several treatises to study, which we did. We understand we will be voyaging to a place as distant from what we've already known as it would be to travel to the moon. We've all decided that a bit of the primitive in life adds flavor. We won't fall apart not to find a charming bakery on Howard Street, an actual street in the village, Mr. Fielding told us."

Badger added, "Thus, we're bringing with us all the foodstuffs we'll need for at least two weeks, particularly vegetables and fruit. His lordship can hunt the local small deer I've been told are abundant. Also, Olivia will come along to take care of Master Charles. Bess will come to assist me and see to the housekeeping. As James knows, Gypsom is coming along to see to the horses we hope to rent there and anything else that needs doing. You've nothing to worry about. We will contrive."

Sampson said, "We have even discussed how to make a campfire—just in case the house we're going to has become uninhabitable. We have rain gear. We are prepared."

The Duchess cleared her throat and spoke in her serene, calm voice: "Maggie, Jessie, and I have even had very simple gowns made and purchased bonnets to protect ourselves from the seaside sun. We have stout boots. Anthony and his father will look like pictures of those strange men all garbed in buckskin with squirrel hats on their heads. I believe everyone has managed to see to everything.''

Jessie looked at her husband. ''What have you done, James?''

''I've called upon your father to keep an eye on Marathon while we're gone. Oslow isn't pleased with me since he is always the one in charge during my absence, but your father begged me, so what could I do?''

''Actually,'' Jessie said, clearing her throat, ''Ocracoke isn't all that uncivilized. There are roads—well, all right, perhaps more like rutted paths—and many houses, mostly clapboard and small, but people love it there. I hope all of you will like it as much as I did.''

They sailed aboard a small Baltimore clipper from the Paxton yard, all smooth decks, set low in the water, and faster than any vessel Jessie had ever been on before in her life. Capt. Markly blessed the still-calm water every morning, splaying his hands over the sea, and prayed for a continuance every night before he went to bed. He encouraged everyone to do the same. It was a ritual. Anthony was delighted with it. He practiced splaying his fingers just like Capt. Markly. His father remarked that the prayer must lose some of its efficacy because of the dirt beneath the supplicant's fingernails.

It was a bright, sunny morning when he pointed out Teach's Hole—where that infamous Blackbeard had careened his ship and spent several months on Ocracoke following his pardon from the Crown until he'd gotten so bored he'd begun to plunder ships again—and Springer's Point just beyond it. ''And there,'' he said, pointing to a spot just higher than Springer's Point, ''is where they will build a lighthouse next year. So many ships and men are lost each year when a freak storm blows up. Anthony, did you pray this morning?''

''I even washed beneath my fingernails,'' Anthony said proudly.

The warm weather continued. The air was rich with sea smells, the squawking of sea gulls and the half dozen cormorants that trailed off the bow all the way to Ocracoke. Capt. Markly brooded on the sheer number of cormorants, wondering aloud if it portented a bad storm, in which case he decided an additional afternoon prayer was in order. He worried until he discovered that Anthony was feeding them all the leftover bread from breakfast each morning. The six crew members snickered behind their hands, having heard the captain utter one afternoon prayer for the beneficence of cormorants.

They sailed between Ocracoke Island and Portsmouth Island and into Ocracoke Inlet three days after leaving Baltimore. Jessie told everyone that she'd seen maps showing a channel between Ocracoke Island and Hatteras Island, but there wasn't one now because of a hurricane that had struck sometime in the seventeen hundreds.

The small village of Ocracoke was impressive to all the English passengers, who, if the truth be told, had expected nothing but broken-down tents and dilapidated wooden buildings weathered gray and molded by storms from the sea. Spears said to Jessie, ''You led us a bit astray, Jessie. This is a thriving village. Just look at all those small fishing vessels. Look at all those well-mended nets.''

There were three wooden docks, all well built and sturdy. Buildings weren't clustered together, rather they were stuck in their own little spots, weaving themselves in between live oaks and cedars, some of them reaching nearly to the shore of the inlet. Captain Markly told them that the inlet was deep, thus they could sail nearly to shore. It had been a fine retreat for the pirates, he said, and laughed. ''No more of those blackguards around," he assured the ladies. "Prayer and the English navy put them to rout."

"Aye," Anthony said, "it was Lieutenant Maynard who killed Blackbeard. He shot him and speared him dozens and dozens of times."

"That is very nearly the truth," Spears said, beaming down at his boy, a look, Marcus thought, that he earned far less than Anthony did these days.

"What a pity that there's no more excitement," Maggie said, and gave the captain a smile that curled the toes inside his boots. He wondered about staying here in Ocracoke with his passengers for the next several weeks rather than sailing on to Puerto Rico with a load of tobacco leaves. Duty occasionally depressed a man.

"Perhaps it is a bit unfinished, as Jessie told us," Badger said, "but Mr. Spears is quite right. Just look at all the bustle. It's alive here, not desolate."

"There are several small stores," Jessie said, pointing just down the dirt road. "A Mr. Gaskill owned the one my parents always used when I was a little girl."

Mr. Gaskill still owned the small store that carried everything from thimbles to scrub boards, just as Jessie had told them, and even more, including buckets of oats for horses to new netting for the fishermen. "Why," the grizzled old man said, beaming at Jessie, "ain't ye Jessie Warfield? Aye, that's who ye be. Sech a cute little girl ye was back then. Yer father all right?"

Other Ocracokers came into the store, and Jessie was soon surrounded by the Burruses, the Jacksons, the Fulchers, and the Styrons. All exclaimed at how grown-up she was. The locals eyed the English contingent, saying little directly to them.

Mr. Gaskill's son, Timmy, hired out himself and his wagon to transport them and their goods to Oliver Warfield's house, which lay on the ocean side of Ocracoke.

Theodore Burrus, a young man near Jessie's age, nearly swallowed his tongue when he saw the Duchess and Maggie. He merely waved to Jessie, who had already garbed herself in practical trousers, boots, and a flannel shirt and leather vest. Jessie believed, though, that it was Spears who got the most unabashed stares. He looked like a royal personage leading his minions. His deportment was impeccable as were his black wool trousers and coat. His cravat was stark white. He looked magnificent.

One Ocracoker started to bow, then recovered himself in time and spat on the ground beside him.

"I'd rather have a horse," Marcus said, eyeing the back of the wagon where all of them would pile in, like a collection of bundles.

"We will figure it out," Spears said as his master climbed into the back of the wagon and took Charles from Sampson.

"It's only a mile to my papa's house," Jessie said, as James whipped up the sweet-tempered gray mare, who was nearly groaning at pulling the weighty wagon. "On the ocean side. He wanted to be a bit separated from the rest of the villagers. It was his retreat from the world, he would say." As they drove outside Ocracoke Village, the dirt road narrowed considerably. There'd been a recent rainstorm, for there were deep ruts filled with water.

"Now I feel as if I've been transported to another world," the Duchess said, breathing in the salty air, looking up at the sea gulls, the terns, and the oystercatchers. "What is that, Jessie?"

"What? Oh, that's a white ibis. See his red legs and red face? He won't let us come much closer. There's a swamp just beyond that mess of sea oats."

"I'd never imagined such a place as this," Maggie said, and pulled the bonnet lower on her forehead. "A lady could ruin her complexion very quickly here with all this bright sunlight and the salt spray."

James pulled the horses to a halt in front of a weathered gray clapboard house, which looked the way most of them had pictured all the houses in Ocracoke would look. There was a sign over the gate that could barely be read. "It looks so derelict," Jessie said, looking at the buckling gray boards, the weeds that grew nearly to her waist. There were several broken windows. A stunted live oak grew in the front yard. "A Mr. and Mrs. Potter are the caretakers. Why is the grass so high? Why are there loose boards lying around?" Jessie said. "After I recovered from the fever, Papa never wanted to come back, but the Potters should have taken care of things. Papa has sent them money over the years for repairs and upkeep."

"It appears," Marcus said, shading his eyes from the bright overhead noon sun, "that the Potters have taken themselves off to other parts, your father's money in their pockets."

"But why didn't anyone say anything about it to me?" Jessie said, nearly in tears.

"Enough dawdling," Spears said, lightly stepping over loose boards that had fallen from a low-lying water tank. "We will consider the air invigorating, the house a challenge. We are prepared."

Charles was crying but Anthony was running around, wanting to see everything at the same time. Spears finally called him to order, and to his father's disgust, Anthony obeyed immediately.

The inside of the house made Jessie's tears flow over. "It was so lived-in before. Now, just look at it. Everything is falling apart and it smells like mildew and other things I don't really want to try to identify. Why didn't any of them tell me what had happened? Surely they knew that the Potters had left. They had to have known. Why didn't they tell me?"

"No matter," Spears said, patting her arm. "Bess is

ready to work, as we all are. Don't worry. We will make inquiries tomorrow. There will be a sensible answer. Now, Jessie, you must rest.''

But Jessie couldn't rest. All of them rolled up their sleeves, scrubbed, and dusted, all in all exhausting themselves so that by that evening Badger's dinner of fresh baked croaker, brought over to them by Mrs. Gaskill, to which Badger added small onions and a sweet wine, potatoes boiled in butter and parsley, fresh peas from Mrs. Gaskill's garden, and a mince pie lifted everyone's spirits. Everyone ate in the dining room, the Potters having left the long dining table, probably, Sampson said, because it was too heavy for them to carry. There weren't enough chairs, but it didn't matter. There weren't enough beds either, of course, but Maggie and Bess had remembered to bring a trunkful of blankets and sheets. Since there were only four bedrooms, all of them very small, it was a tight squeeze, but everyone managed, Badger's excellent cooking keeping their testiness low.

That night after James had made love to her, Jessie dreamed again of that day when Mr. Tom had tried to rape her. It was vague this time, the terror blurred as if it were far away from her. Still, James held her close and rubbed her back until her breathing slowed. ''Tomorrow,'' she said finally. ''Tomorrow morning we will go to the beach and dig up all Mr. Tom's diaries. Then we'll know.''

''Then the bloody nightmares will stop,'' James said.

# ≡ 31 ≡

**The last of Blackbeard's fourteen wives was a "most charming young creature of twelve."**

THE MORNING WAS sunny and warm. They dressed and ate quickly. Everyone wanted to get to the beach to dig up those diaries.

Jessie was wearing her trousers—a bit more snug in the waist than they'd seemed yesterday, so it seemed to her— old boots, weathered shirt, and the rattiest hat James had ever seen, and he'd seen her wear some pretty ratty hats during the past six years.

They arrived in the wagon at the beach, not more than a half mile from the Warfield house. Anthony was whooping and yelling until his father put his head under his arm and began to rub the top of his head. "Be quiet, you young heathen. Your mother will become cold to both of us if you don't calm down. Now, before you ask, yes, when we arrive at the beach you may go wading. Be sure to roll up your trousers and put your shoes and socks at a safe distance from the surf. Don't go deeper than your knees."

"Yes, Master Anthony," Spears said in his calm, deep voice. "You will restrain your wild spirits until it is appropriate to unrestrain them. If you go beyond your knees, I will be excessively displeased. I will even hint to your papa that—"

"I swear I won't go any deeper, Spears. I swear it."

"He's as convincing as you are, my lord," Spears said to the earl.

"Anthony isn't going near the water until we find Jessie's diaries," the Duchess said, rubbing her son's head herself a couple of times.

"Here!" Jessie suddenly yelled. "Right here. Stop the wagon, Sampson."

Old Tom's dilapidated hut was no longer standing. There was still a porch of sorts, but the small wooden building had collapsed in on itself. Sea grass was poking tall from between every crevice in the rotting wood. It was obvious that storms had brought it down.

"This is where Old Tom lived?" Spears asked blankly.

"You were expecting perhaps Chase Park?" James said, and poked Spears on his arm, which made the valet turn slowly and look at James as if he'd never seen him before. It had been a poke between friends, not master and servant. James just grinned and nodded.

"I'm surprised so much of it is left," Jessie said, kicking boards around with her foot. "But it doesn't matter."

"No, it doesn't," James said. "I'm relieved it's here at all. Excuse us for a moment. We want to look at what's left of that shack."

They walked hand in hand to the crumbled structure. Only one wall was still partially standing. Sand and rotted wood filled the small area. It was empty of pain, or fear; all horror had disappeared long ago. It was as peaceful as the beautiful blue sky overhead.

"There's really nothing at all left," Jessie said, looking around. "Well, there's a crab trying to escape us."

"You want to find those diaries now, Jessie?"

"Oh, yes. There's nothing for us here, James, nothing at all."

"Excellent."

All of them stood there, staring out over the water, then to the north and south. Long, waving arms of sea grass that held the sand were alternately dense and meager. Sand dunes undulated for as far as one could see. The waves sounded rhythmic and smooth. The sun was fiercely bright overhead, making the water sparkle with starlike lights. Sea gulls swooped down around them, hopeful for scraps, squawking loudly when they didn't get any, then plunging into the water for food. There was a briskness to the air, but it wasn't cold by any means.

"I wouldn't want to be dropped into that water, despite the bright sun," Maggie said, clasping her arms around her body.

"Where, Jessie?" James asked, wanting suddenly to pull off his boots and feel the warm sand between his toes.

"Let me think," she said, and left them to walk toward the water, a good thirty feet from Old Tom's cabin. "I remember that I wrapped the diaries very carefully in the oil-cloth and buried the bundle beneath a small live oak. It's been ten years, so the tree will have grown considerably. If I look directly at the front of Mr. Tom's cabin and turn my head just about an hour to my right, then—There it is! That's the live oak. Goodness, look at how oddly shaped it is. But it's still here, thank God."

Jessie was running to the tree, Anthony tearing behind her, whooping louder than the black skimmers overhead, his ocean wading temporarily forgotten.

It was too easy, James thought. It was just too easy. The tree looked very strange indeed, nearly bowed onto its landward side by the harsh sea winds, its trunk twisted and coiled and turned around on itself. There were lumps and dents and hollows. It was possibly the ugliest tree James had ever seen.

"Bring the spade, Sampson," James called, and made his way after Jessie, who was already on her hands and knees, digging into the sand with her hands, Anthony beside her, flinging small handfuls of sand over his shoulder. A blue crab scurried away from the flying grains. Terns and sanderlings began to wheel downward, coming closer, scenting food. Sea gulls were bolder, some running nearly to Jessie's digging hands, then scurrying back when Anthony yelled in excitement, his fingers striking a root of the tree.

"Papa!"

"Be careful, Anthony," Jessie said, pulling his hands away. "We don't want to kill the tree. Just dig gently around the roots. That's right."

But they didn't find anything. Fifteen minutes later, all were standing in a circle around that stunted live oak, which stood alone now, like a castle surrounded by a moat.

Jessie was shaking her head. "I couldn't have dug any deeper than this. Where is it?"

James closed his arm around her shoulders and pulled her against him. "It's been ten years, Jessie. You've told me many times how the landscape can shift drastically in just one day. Ten years is a very long time, and there have been violent storms."

"This is depressing," Maggie said, standing there with her brilliant red hair glistening in the sunlight, her skirts billowing in the salty wind. "Jessie, one of your streamers is stuck beneath your collar. That's right, just pull it out and let it blow free. Much better."

Anthony sighed deeply. "I'd hoped we'd find a treasure, Jessie. Do you have any idea where Blackbeard could have hidden it even without the diaries?"

"No, I'm sorry, Anthony, but I haven't a clue."

"My first treasure and I won't find it," he said, shook his head, dropped to the sand, and began taking off his shoes and socks.

It was Sampson who said, "I say, Jessie, this tree looks like it should preside in a witch's forest. It's gnarly and all twisted about, and just look at that odd bulge. I didn't know trees could bulge out like that. It looks like an old man with a goiter.''

She frowned, stepped forward, and ran her hands over the fat bulge in the tree. ''I've heard stories,'' she began, and now her eyes began to sparkle, ''about how the water swept up by storms could nearly rip trees up by their roots. Just suppose something was buried at the base of those roots. Why then, the bundle might just get swept up into the tree and be stuck there. Then it just might continue to be pushed upward as the tree grew.''

''You mean,'' James said, ''that this unlikely lump here is really the oilskin bundle? It grew up into the tree itself?''

''Why not?'' Jessie said. ''Oh dear, we must sacrifice the tree. It is excessively ugly.''

''I'll get an ax,'' Anthony yelled, running back to the wagon, Spears on his heels.

A white ibis, its red legs and red face as vivid as a sunset, stood some twenty feet away and watched as they chopped down the tree.

''Oh dear,'' Jessie said. ''I feel guilty about this.''

The tree broke into two parts. Anthony, looking like an urchin, squealed, ''Look, Papa, it's hollow!''

James grinned down at her. ''It's your diaries, your treasure. See if your theory is right, Jessie.''

Gingerly, Jessie slipped her hand up into the tree. She felt scaly bumps, sharp jabs, spongy stuff she'd rather not think about, and then she felt cloth. Oilcloth. She could only stare up at James. ''I don't really believe it,'' she said finally. ''I'm tugging, but it's not coming loose.''

James managed to pull the rotting bundle from the tree. He held it like a precious gift in his palms. The oilcloth fell away. Inside were five books, not in the best of shape, but not utterly destroyed either.

''Oh goodness,'' Anthony said.

"Jessie," James said. "These are Blackbeard's diaries?"

"Yes. These two he wrote himself. These two Blackbeard's grandson, Samuel Teach, wrote. He was Mr. Tom's father. And this one that looks so old it will crumble in your hands, Valentine wrote."

"But that doesn't make sense, Jessie," the Duchess said, swiping a thick tress of hair from her face. "If the grandson had his grandfather's diary, then why wouldn't he have dug up the treasure? And what about Blackbeard's son? Why didn't he get the treasure?"

"Probably," Marcus said, "because the son and grandson weren't smart enough to catch Blackbeard's clues."

Badger said, "I'll wager that the son and grandson both probably got themselves hanged before they could search for the treasure. They both sound like wastrels."

Jessie said, "Don't forget Red Eye Crimson and Mr. Tom, Blackbeard's great-grandson."

It was difficult but Anthony managed to remain somewhat still while James drove the wagon back to the Warfield house. They all trooped into the small parlor while Jessie sat down on the threadbare carpet, the oilskin bundled up in front of her on the floor. Badger brought in tea Old Bess had prepared.

"All right," Marcus said. "Why didn't Blackbeard's son or his grandson, for that matter, dig up the treasure? Oh God, there wasn't a treasure, that's the only thing that makes sense." He stopped. Jessie was shaking her head madly.

"I remember now that Mr. Tom said something about Blackbeard's son not getting the treasure because he was caught by the British just after he'd found his father's diaries in his mother's attic. He only had time to pass them along to his son, Samuel Teach, Old Tom's father. So Badger was right. Why Samuel Teach didn't get the treasure, I don't know. Surely we'll find out when we read his diaries."

"Red Eye Crimson," James said. "What happened to

him, Jessie? Didn't you tell me he went to jail?''

''I was told that he wouldn't get out of jail for ninety years. I was mighty relieved.''

''Just perhaps,'' James said thoughtfully, taking her hand in his, his thumb smoothing over her skin, ''he did. Just perhaps this Red Eye is the one who killed Allen Belmonde when he found out Allen was trying to kill you. Just perhaps he's your savior and your devil. Just perhaps he's been after you, only you were lucky and he never got you alone. Then you went to England, and when you came back to Baltimore you were surrounded by a crowd.''

Jessie shuddered. ''I don't like to remember that night Red Eye came, James. He was so angry, so enraged. He wanted to kill me but he knew he couldn't at that point, not until I'd taken him to where I'd buried the diaries. I was very, very lucky.''

''If James is right,'' Marcus said, ''it means that Red Eye Crimson could still be lurking about. It's possible that he's here on Ocracoke, that he followed us, guessing what we were after.''

''We will keep a sharp eye out,'' James said. ''Did anyone bring a gun?''

Spears said simply, ''Naturally. I never travel outside my own environs without proper protection. If you will remember, my lord, I had a gun in Paris when we were encouraging you to marry the Duchess. Ah, that was a time.'' Spears cleared his throat and, to Jessie's astonishment, looked mildly embarrassed. ''I will fetch it shortly. But it's not enough. We will arm ourselves. May we procure firearms in the village, Jessie?''

She nodded numbly, somehow fancying that the world had taken a faulty turn. Red Eye Crimson killed Allen Belmonde because he knew that Allen was trying to kill her? It sounded beyond farfetched. Besides, why did Allen want to kill her? She said finally, ''Mr. Styron has a fine collection. If he won't sell us guns, he would surely lend them to us.''

"Well then," James said. "That takes care of the threat from Red Eye Crimson."

"Yes," Jessie said, drawing a deep breath. "Let's look at the diaries now. It's time, don't you think? Is everyone ready?"

# ≡ 32 ≡

"OH DEAR," JESSIE said, her turn again with the diary. "This is the last entry. It's very short and no mention at all of those English bastards or running low on rum or of where Blackbeard hid his treasure.

"It appears he married fourteen women and he calls the last a 'most charming young creature of twelve. Her name is Valentine, jest like my great-grandma. I took her on because of it. We'll see if she's too young to give me a babe. I like the little buggers. Makes a man feel immortal even when he's in hell playin' with the divil.' " Jessie looked up, stunned. "Valentine isn't a very common name. This is interesting. I told James about another Valentine who lived in Sir Walter Raleigh's colony on Roanoke Island. That was the colony that disappeared, simply vanished, sometime between 1587 and 1590. No one knows what happened to it. But we'll find out." Jessie held up Valentine's diary. "This will tell us what happened not only to Valentine but also what happened to the rest of the colony." She laid the diary on her lap. "You know what I think? I think Blackbeard's last wife, this second Valentine, was indeed Old Tom's great-grandmother. It makes sense, doesn't it?"

"It's almost as if it came full circle," Marcus said. "All these 'greats' and these 'grands,' " Badger said. "It makes a person's brain boil. All right, Jessie. This first Valentine who was on Roanoke Island was Blackbeard's great-grandmother. The second Valentine was Old Tom's great-grandmother, and Blackbeard was Old Tom's great-grandfather.''

"That's it.''

"All well and good,'' Marcus said, "but like Maggie, I want to know where the bloody treasure is. Blackbeard makes no mention at all of it, the damned bounder.''

"Maybe we'll find out more about what happened to Blackbeard's bride—poor twelve-year-old Valentine—when we read Blackbeard's grandson's diary,'' Spears said. He leaned down and patted Jessie's shoulder. "Don't give up hope yet, Jessie.''

It was Anthony who stood legs akimbo, his arms crossed over his chest. "We have three sets of diaries. We've only read Blackbeard's diaries. I think we should read the grandson's diaries. Perhaps his grandmother, Valentine, Blackbeard's wife, was still alive and she told him something. We're not going to give up until we've read every word in every one of those diaries.''

"Yes, you're right, Anthony,'' James said, but he didn't sound at all convinced.

"This pirate was a right smart villain,'' Badger said slowly, shaking his grizzled head. "I believe to renew my mental workings I will prepare a luncheon of baked sheepshead—he's a handsome fish marked with six vertical black stripes on his side; I counted them. Gypsom caught him early this morning off the pilings at the dock. Weighs a good twelve pounds, he does. Yes, I'll bake our sheepshead and we'll have some of those tasty little green peas that Bess bought from Mrs. Fulcher. The sweet lady insisted that Bess drink a bit of her cider. Bess came back smiling like a loon.''

Badger took himself off to the dilapidated Warfield kitchen, so ancient and battered Jessie wondered how he could continue to produce such magical meals.

*     *     *

After dinner that evening, everyone adjourned again to the
parlor, Bess and Gypsom included. "Why not?" Marcus
had said. "They're a part of this just as we are."

James said, "This evening we're going to read the two
diaries written by Blackbeard's grandson, Samuel Teach.
Maggie, you and Anthony begin. We'll put the original Valentine's diary aside and keep it for later."

Anthony, Sampson, and Maggie were a team. Suddenly,
in the utter silence of that evening, Anthony shouted. Maggie cuffed him and laughed. "Go ahead, Anthony, read
aloud what we found."

"Just listen, Papa," Anthony said, gently lifting the book
from Maggie's hands. "Old Tom's grandpa, Samuel Teach,
writes, 'I think my grandma, Miz Valentine, is daft, poor
old dear. Today she went on and on about a gold necklace
that her dear husband Edward gave her—Edward Teach was
Blackbeard the pirate.'" Anthony continued in his precise
schoolboy's voice, "Samuel goes on to say that he's writing
down exactly what she told him because who knew what
could come of it.

" '. . . He went out into the night, a stormy night with
waves pounding against those black rocks near the inlet, rain
whipping through the twisted trees, leaving me with three
of his men in that small stone castle of his that was so cold
and wet even under the hottest sun that I occasionally nearly
gained the nerve to say something to him. Of course I never
did. Ah, that night. Aye, I told him to send one of his men
out if he wanted something, but he just told me to warm
him some rum, not too hot, but just the way he liked it.
When he returned he looked fearsome, his black beard all
tangled and wet, steam rising from his wet clothes when he
got near the fire, his full-cuffed black leather boots squishing
from all the rain and covered with rank black mud. I gave
him the rum. He drank it all down and grinned at me. He

then pulled a huge rope of gold from beneath his shirt. He laughed in that terrifying way of his and wound it once, twice, thrice, around my neck. It weighed nearly as much as I did. This was good, I thought, so I gave him more rum for I'm not a stupid girl. He drank it down in one gulp, belched, said he'd soon breathe fire now, and pulled out another necklace from his shirt. This one was all colored stones—white so clear it looked like ice, red stones, deep and mysterious, and blue stones that a summer sky would envy. There were even some green stones and these weren't as shiny as the others. He told me as he patted my face with his big callused dirty hand that both necklaces he just happened to find in a neat little chest what was afloat near a sinking vessel.

" ' . . . I nodded, all serious, not believing him for a minute. He was as evil as that Jolly Roger flag they flew on the *Revenge*. I'm not a stupid girl. I'd always known he had a treasure trove and now I had the proof of it. It was here on Ocracoke. He'd been gone from the castle only forty-five minutes. I was lucky that I happened to notice that. His boots were covered with mud. I want that treasure. I deserve it. My pa sold me to the bastard. Aye, I deserve the treasure.

" ' . . . I turned thirteen years old that night. But then, not a month later, that ruthless devil got himself shot and stabbed more times than any normal man and that English lieutenant cut off his head, tied it to the bowsprit, and sailed off with it. He left me pregnant with your pa. Your pa was a rotter even when he was a little mite. I swore I'd never tell him about the necklaces. He left me, coming back only years later to bring you to me, Samuel. I sold those necklaces a bit at a time and lived well and your pa asked me again and again how I managed to have such a nice house and servants. I told him I was a whore. He believed that easily enough, the rotter. Samuel, there is a treasure. You're not stupid. I want to be rich before I die. Find that treasure, Samuel.' "

Maggie said, "Samuel writes that she's daft even though he's seen some incredible stones. He believes in the necklaces, but he doesn't think they're from Blackbeard's treasure trove. He says his grandmother is old and has brain rot. But he wants the rest of those stones. When she dies he'll find them. He can't leave her until she dies because, he says, he owes her because she took him in and treated him well and they had two servants and he had a tutor."

"Because of the stones from those necklaces," the Duchess said quietly.

"What a charming lot," James said.

"Samuel is Old Tom's father," Jessie said. "Old Tom was charming too, James." She shuddered, the memory of that day sharp and clear in that single moment in her mind. James pulled her close and kissed her ear.

Anthony looked up, his dark blue eyes sparkling. He looked ready to jump to the ceiling. "We know there's a treasure now. We know it."

"Blackbeard's wife," Jessie said slowly. "Twelve-year-old Valentine. He gave her two necklaces from his treasure. It's hidden forty-five minutes from his castle, probably less if he had to take time to dig it up."

"Where's this bloody castle?" Sampson asked even as he helped Badger pour out the tea for everyone. There were even lemon cakes.

"It's been gone a long time," Jessie said. "When I was a little girl we used to explore the ruins, just piles of rocks even then. Many say there never was a castle. Who knows? If there was, the Ocracokers have used everything over the decades. But I know where it's said to have been. But what does that matter? Forty-five minutes? Which direction?"

James said, after he'd chewed and swallowed a delicious lemon cake, closed his eyes, and cleared his throat, "It was raining that night. His boots were muddy. We'll try out every direction from the center of where the castle used to be.''

''Yes,'' Marcus said. ''Forty-five minutes would in most cases have you swimming in the water. This is possible, it's just possible that we can discover something.''

''I think we should continue reading,'' Maggie said, eyeing the last lemon cake but mournfully shaking her head. ''If we don't find anything else, then we'll try this castle trek.''

''The villagers will think we're daft,'' James said, and grinned at his wife. ''Can't you just see us all fanning out from the middle of this pile of stones?''

The old house was quiet. No more creaking boards because everyone was in bed, asleep, it was hoped—at least James hoped so because he didn't doubt for a minute that any sound he or Jessie made would carry to every corner of every room. She was lying on her back, her lawn nightgown covering every inch of her except her toes. Peach satin ribbons were tied just beneath her chin. He couldn't wait to pull those ribbons loose.

She was saying quietly, ''Marcus is right. Most directions that would take someone forty-five minutes to walk would be in the ocean or in Pamlico Sound.''

He came up onto his elbow over her. ''It's a moonlit night.''

''What? Oh yes, James. I can even see the deviltry in your eyes.''

''That's not deviltry, that's lust.''

She raised her fingers to caress his cheek. ''I don't know why I haven't told you that I love you but I will now. I love you, James. I've loved you forever, at least since I was fourteen years old.''

He felt panic, utter panic. Love? Certainly he liked her,

he enjoyed her body. She made him laugh. He cared mightily about her. But love?

Her smile didn't budge, but he saw the sadness in her eyes in the soft shadows cast by the moonlight streaming in through the windows. "It doesn't matter," she said, but he knew that it did. "I have more love than I'll ever need. You will love our child, won't you, James? Despite the fact that it's my child, too?"

"Don't be a fool, Jessie. I care for you. A lot. You're my wife. It's just that—"

"I know. You won't forget that both of us love horses, will you? I don't know if I love children or not, but am I not bound to love our child?"

"There's no question about it. You'll be a wonderful mother."

"And you, James?"

"I'll be the best of fathers, I promise you. Now, Jessie, I'm almost positive that everyone in this bloody house is asleep. If you promise not to yell, I'll make love to you." He lightly touched her breasts. "Are you sore?"

"Yes, but you're always so gentle." She closed her eyes as his fingers slowly traced over her breasts beneath the lawn nightgown. She said, all drowsy and interested, "I don't think Marcus or the Duchess is asleep. You should have seen the looks he was giving her in the parlor."

"Marcus is out of luck. Don't you remember? Anthony is sleeping in their bedchamber." His palm splayed out over her belly. He felt the bulge. His child was inside her.

"No. Anthony is with Badger and Spears. I heard Marcus make a deal with Spears. Charles is with Maggie and Sampson."

James laughed aloud, then quickly stuffed the sheet corner in his mouth. When he caught his breath, he said, "With a wife like the Duchess, I doubt Marcus will ever let her alone for a day, let alone two days."

"I wish I were as beautiful as she is, but I'm not, James. I'm sorry. I'm just me."

"Are you fishing for compliments, Jessie? If so, you don't do it well. You sound pathetic. Now, be quiet." He leaned down and kissed the tip of her nose. Her eyes were open and, as he lowered his head to hers, they crossed. He was laughing again, and this time he didn't stop. They played, tickling each other, giving kisses that landed in very odd places, enjoying themselves thoroughly until Jessie's hand suddenly closed over him and he forgot laughter, forgot everything—Blackbeard's treasure included, his own name included—except her warm hand caressing him.

When he came into her, deep and hard, she sighed, arching up against him, and whispered, "You are magnificent, James."

He was gone.

At least five minutes had passed before he managed to say, "Jessie, you nearly killed me."

"If you're sweet to me," she whispered as she kissed his sweating shoulder, "I'll try to kill you again."

He moaned, his energy returning at a great rate. He said to her later, "You said you've loved me since you were fourteen years old. Jessie, you've always fought with me, been in constant competition with me, insulted me, even hit me every time you could when we were racing. Surely that isn't love."

"It was my mating call, I suppose," she said, bit his shoulder, and giggled. "I didn't know what else to do. You thought I was an obnoxious brat, you used to give me those tolerant looks of yours, those looks that said clearly that you wished you could swat me, and I couldn't bear it. I had to make you react and so I did everything I could to push you over the edge."

"You pushed me over the edge more times than I can even remember." He began to laugh. "The best time though was when you fell through the ceiling of your father's stable and landed in the hay trough, mashed cucumbers all over your face, and that was just three months before I married you.''

''I hadn't intended to fall,'' she said, punched her fist into his belly, then lowered her head and kissed his belly where she'd struck him.

''You'd best think about this, Jessie.'' He groaned. She whispered against his hard flesh, ''Oh, I always know what I'm doing when I'm loving you, James.'' Her hands were soft, her mouth warm.

''I'm not going to make it this time, Jessie.''

She made very certain that he didn't.

There was no nightmare that night, to which James replied the following morning, ''I just knew that if you actually saw that place with an adult's eyes, then the terror would fade into nothing at all. And I was right.'' He gave her a fatuous grin, kissed her nose, and left her, whistling one of the Duchess's ditties.

''Well,'' she said to the empty bedchamber, ''he was right about that.''

$$\equiv 33 \equiv$$

He was a bold man that first eat any oyster.
—JONATHAN SWIFT

FROM THE LOOK on the Duchess's face the next morning over breakfast, Jessie realized it had probably been an excellent night for the English Wyndhams as well.

By the end of the morning, however, everyone was in a profound depression. They'd read Samuel Teach's two diaries yet again, thoroughly.

"Nothing," Marcus said. "Damnation, nothing more, except that he bored me nearly to madness."

"Curse him," Jessie said. "He said nothing more about the treasure. Didn't he even try to find it?"

"Evidently not," the Duchess said, sighed, and patted Charles's back. He obligingly burped, and she told him what a fine fellow he was.

"That leaves the castle, then," James said. "More than a long shot. An impossibility, if the truth be told."

Even Anthony was downcast.

"Let's forget about all this for the moment. Let's go to the ocean," Badger said, and off they went.

It was a lovely day, a bit on the cool side, but it didn't stop Anthony from running like a wild animal to the water's edge, shrieking when a wave caught him, splashing up to his knees. The Duchess was sitting beneath a lone live oak that provided some shade from the radiant sun overhead. Badger had brought lemonade and some delicious seed cakes that no one knew how he'd prepared, given the fact that he'd had no time and surely he'd slept throughout the night, hadn't he?

The men had rolled up their trouser legs and were playing just as freely as Anthony, enjoying themselves as they threw rocks to each other, running and leaping, sometimes falling.

"This isn't fair," Jessie said, drawing her knees up and wrapping her arms around them. "That's just what I did when I was little. Now I'm afraid to even skip because I might hurt the babe."

"Men," Maggie said, "always remain little."

"Yes, but they're having fun, Maggie. Wouldn't you like to be yelling and running around, chasing waves, finding crabs, pushing each other down in the sand, things like that?"

Maggie shuddered, not deigning to answer as she smoothed down a streamer that was flying around wildly with the stiff ocean breeze. The Duchess laughed. "It's no use, Jessie," she said. "I would like to perhaps walk along the water's edge. It's so incredibly lovely, so different from where we live in England." She lifted baby Charles, who'd just yawned from his nap, and cooed up to him, telling him what a big boy he was, how his baby yawns were even clever. Then she put him on a blanket and watched him crawl off into the sand. "Oh dear," she said, and scrambled after him. "I should have known the moment he woke up I would get all the exercise in the world."

"My dear Sampson has an idea," Maggie said suddenly, then tried to wave her words away with her hands.

"What's the matter, Maggie?" Jessie asked. "What idea does Sampson have?"

"He told me not to say anything, that he wanted to think

about it some more. But I think he's terribly smart. He thinks the key to the treasure is somehow tied to the original Valentine's diary, the one we haven't even looked at yet.''

"But how could that be?" the Duchess said as she managed to retrieve Charles again from the sand. "The original Valentine was Blackbeard's great-grandmother."

"She could have given Blackbeard the idea of where to bury his plunder," Maggie said simply. "That's what Sampson thinks — not realizing, of course, that there would be a treasure sometime in the misty future, but naming an excellent place to dig a hole, if you know what I mean. You did say, didn't you, Jessie, that the original Valentine was part of that Roanoke colony and that the colonists moved about with the local Indians? Maybe those Indians were here. Who knows?"

"Yes," Jessie said slowly, staring at Charles, who'd managed to dig up a blue crab, which was scurrying wildly away. "And she could have been in this area. Yes, it's very possible." Jessie jumped to her feet. She stared down at Maggie and the Duchess, but she wasn't really seeing them. "Yes, it's more than possible." She broke into a dead run down the beach to where the men were flinging clumps of sand at one another, laughing, and singing one of the Duchess's ditties at the top of their lungs.

She yelled, "Sampson's brilliant! Come along, all of you, we've work to do and treasure to find!"

Since it was Sampson's idea, he was the one given the signal honor of deciphering the very faded and spidery sixteenth-century writing penned by the original Valentine. He read silently for a very long time before he looked up, smiled, and read aloud,

" 'We've been with the Croatoan Indians for nearly a month now. Without them, we would have not survived. There was no food and so many were ill. They helped us pack everything and brought us back to their village. They have tended our sick with local herbs and concoctions they have known for hundreds of years.

" ' . . . Manatoa is my friend. Today he took me with him to fish in this small inlet that lies at the end of the chain of islands. After he caught nearly more fish than his small boat could hold, he rowed through this narrow channel that had thick poplars on both sides of it. There was also a high point of land that stuck up above the trees. Then the channel flowed into a much larger inlet. He said we were now looking toward the mainland, no longer the ocean. He said the narrow channel hadn't been there twenty years ago. He said everything changed here all the time.' "

"Do you think that's Teach's Hole?" the Duchess asked as she pulled Charles's fist out of his mouth.

"Very probably," Jessie said. "I was told that it was very different a long time ago. Today there are very few poplars left there and that point is gone."

" ' . . . Manatoa told me that a sand dune could disappear overnight. He said storms could carve a channel through an entire island or silt up an already-open channel. He said whole stands of trees could be gone after a storm, their roots ripped up and the trees pulled out to sea. He said he never hid anything beneath the ground. It would never last. He told me not to forget that.

" ' . . . Manatoa showed me one of the many marshes today and told me never to wade in it or stick my hand in the filthy water, even at high tide. He said there were snakes just below the surface and they would bite me and I would die. He told me about this one evil marsh. One day a villager came shouting into their midst that the marsh was empty. This had never happened before. All the other marshes would be empty or nearly so at low tide, but not this one. Everyone believed there was some sort of underground spring that fed it, but no one really knew. Manatoa told me that they went to marvel at it. There were snakes wriggling around in the black mud and crabs and slimy layers of sea growth that smelled awful. Everyone believed it either a miracle or a portent of doom. No one knew. One of Manatoa's friends waded into that black mud and discovered piles of huge rocks at the bottom sticking up through the mud. They were all round. He was terrified. I was the only one he told. He was afraid to tell any of the others. They might cast him out for being so foolish, for what if this had been an evil happening? He, by his action, could have cursed all of them. Manatoa told me those rocks were hard and big and wouldn't move regardless of any storm. He said those rocks had been at the bottom of that marsh for a very long time. If they hadn't disappeared by now then they probably never would. He said those rocks were the only things he would trust to survive on these islands.' "

"What kind of rock?" James asked.

Jessie said, "The stones remaining from Blackbeard's castle are limestone, quarried from the mainland near Charleston. I remember overhearing Mr. Gaskill talking to Mr. Burrus about it. As for the rocks in this marsh, I don't know. Round? How odd."

"Not odd at all," Marcus said, brushing off his sleeve, grinning like a pirate who'd lost his patch. He then jumped to his feet and spread his arms grandly. "Ballast stones, Jessie. They're ballast stones."

"Just like those stones Blackbeard and some of his men sat on while sulfur burned down in the hold," Badger said. "Good God."

"Valentine did give her great-grandson, Blackbeard, the solution for burying his plunder without danger of losing it in the shifting sands," Sampson said. "Lordie, this is just splendid."

"And it was your idea, my dear," Maggie told him fondly. She took his hand and kissed each knuckle. "You're magnificent.'' Anthony looked disgusted. Charles rubbed his knuckles over his new tooth.

"Jessie," James said, "just where is this marsh?"

It was twilight. The three scouts stood by the marsh staring down at it. There were only three of them, for they didn't want to draw attention to themselves. The last thing any of them wanted was for the Ocracokers to demand to know what they were doing. The scouts, James, Jessie, and Badger, stood at the edge of the marsh, which lay nearly a half mile from the village on the inland water side of the island. It was brimming with filthy black water that made Jessie shudder just to look at it.

"It looks evil," she said.

"It stinks, that's for sure," Badger said, nodding. He dropped to his haunches and stared at the motionless surface. Suddenly there was a ripple, then a cottonmouth poked its head up, and Badger fell back on his rear end, gasping.

"However did Blackbeard get the two necklaces for Valentine if the water was this high?" Jessie asked. "Surely he didn't stick his hands down there?"

"No," James said slowly as he took Badger's hand and pulled him up. "He would have used something—a long pole, perhaps, with a scoop on the end of it. Something like that."

Badger said, "It seems that Mr. Sampson's correct in his deductions. He thinks the treasure must be inside something metal, so the nasty marsh water wouldn't get to it. He thinks this metal casket is tied securely with chain to the ballast rocks."

"Yes," James said. "That's what Jessie and I think, too. We need to come back at low tide. In the meantime we need to make a pole sturdy enough and long enough to get the job done. Once the pole touches the metal casket, it's got to be strong enough to bring it up without breaking the pole."

"It's a start," Jessie said, hugging James to her side as they walked back into the Warfield house, which now didn't look quite so decrepit. "It's exciting."

"Nearly as exciting as you filled with my child," he said. He looked at the scythed lawn, the front door that stood open, looking inviting, not threatening, and said, "I think your father just might like to come back here to visit. It's a beautiful place, different from any place I've ever seen."

"Riding horses on the beach is fun, too," she said. "Perhaps now, with you, it would be more than fun."

"I would hope so. We must do it before you're too fat to sit behind me with your arms around my waist. I don't want you falling off the back of the horse."

She laughed, poked his arm, and they went into the house to the nearly overwhelming scent of Badger's oysters, simmering in wine, rosemary, and onions. "I hope he knows what he's doing," James said. "Oysters! They're slimy ugly things. What man in his right mind would drop one in his mouth?"

But they all did. If Jessie and Spears didn't care for them, Marcus and James waxed eloquent on the way they slid down the throat. The Duchess threw an oyster at her husband, who peeled it off his chest, wiped it with a napkin, and handed it ceremoniously to James. Oysters, the majority of the party decided, weren't at all a bad thing—as long, Spears announced, as Mr. Badger was there to prepare them.

The next morning Jessie arose full of energy. She met Badger, who was cursing under his breath, coming from the kitchen.

"Whatever is wrong?"

"I broke my special wooden spoon. I'm going to Mr. Gaskill's store to see if he has something I could use."

"I'll do it. I know you want to build the pole with the other men."

Badger nodded, clearly distracted, and took himself to the small overgrown garden in back of the house where all the men were gathered, their hands filled with tools, their heads filled with ideas, each different from the others'. She heard Marcus shout, "Dammit, Spears, you've got lumps in your brain! The prongs won't give us enough strength. The pole will break."

She called out, "Why don't two of you go to the marsh, stick the pole in, and see how long it needs to be before you find the ballast stones? I guess you just might want to make two poles, to give you more leverage."

She heard ferocious muttering. She shook her head even as she was grinning, as unrepentant as a child who'd stolen a forbidden sweetmeat.

"Men," Maggie said fondly, shaking her head as she came up behind Jessie. "That was a reasonable suggestion but since none of their exalted highnesses had thought of it, well, there must be something wrong with it."

"They'll go," Jessie said. "Won't they?"

"It's an even chance," Maggie said. "Your streamers are a bit on the edge, Jessie. Hold still. You must remember to straighten yourself up after James fondles you. He's exuberant, isn't he? That's nice."

Ten minutes later, Jessie picked up her parasol, for the morning sun would be fierce overhead soon enough, and headed for the village, but a mile away. She was humming, knowing that soon, one way or another, they'd know if old Blackbeard did indeed bury some treasure in that marsh. She hoped so, she surely did.

She was singing one of the Duchess's ditties about the troubles in his majesty's navy, what with all the beans and scurvy the poor sailors had to endure. It was sung everywhere, Marcus had told her, and the Foreign Office hated it. They'd been forced to find lemons, and that cost too much money. He'd grinned then and said his wife was a rabble-rouser and wasn't it fun.

She was utterly surprised when Compton Fielding, the bookstore owner from Baltimore, suddenly stepped into her path.

"Mr. Fielding! What a surprise! Whatever are you doing here in Ocracoke?"

He smiled at her and offered her his arm. "I am enjoying a well-earned week of pleasure," he said. "Shall I escort you to the village, Jessie? I was just on my way to see you and James. And here you are, right in front of me."

She took his arm, smiling up at him.

"You're very happy with James," he said, as thoughtful as a man with two bills to pay and enough money for only one of them. "I'm surprised. The two of you were always fighting. It amused me. Actually," he continued, looking up at a royal tern who was flying just overhead, "for a while I was convinced that you were one of those curious females celebrated by Sappho, the Greek poetess."

"Who was Sappho? She must not have written a diary, or else you would have given it to me. I don't believe I've ever heard of her."

"No, you wouldn't have. You're a Colonial, you're a female, you're horse mad, and there's no need for you to know that so many hundreds of years ago women celebrated their love for one another. She lived in the sixth century before Christ on an island named Lesbos. There were only women on the island, it is said. Fragments of her poetry remain today. It is passionate stuff, not poetry that a normal woman would pen. Stop looking so stupid, Jessie. We're not speaking of just spiritual love, as a daughter could have for a mother, or a sister for another sister, but carnal love, two women caressing each other, kissing each other, their bodies straining against each other."

Jessie knew she'd turned pale. She knew Mr. Fielding was trying to shock her but she couldn't think why. "I don't understand you," she said slowly. "Why are you saying these things?"

"Because, my dear Jessie, I have you now, and I don't intend to let you go until I've got my share of Blackbeard's treasure. Not all of it, surely not. I'm certain I couldn't manage all of it, but a goodly amount, enough for me to travel to Europe and live like royalty for the rest of my life."

She stopped then and stared up at him. She'd always liked Mr. Fielding, had spent hours in his bookstore, even more hours when she learned that James was there a lot of the time and she would have done anything to see him. And Mr. Fielding had always been kind to her, never talking down to her, offering her books to read—particularly diaries, yes, she remembered that clearly now. "You can't kidnap me, Mr. Fielding. This is Ocracoke. There's no place here to hide me. Besides, why? What is all this nonsense about Blackbeard's treasure?" Even as she said Blackbeard's name, she jerked free of his hold and turned on her heel. She picked up her skirts and ran back toward Warfield house.

# === 34 ===

JESSIE WAS IN fine physical condition, but her petticoats and skirts got tangled around her legs, making her trip and stumble. She cursed herself for letting Maggie talk her out of wearing her breeches. He caught her soon enough. He leaped at her from behind, throwing her forward onto her knees. She was breathing hard, the pain in her knees deep and raw. She was afraid now, very afraid, and it was her own fault. Why hadn't she realized she was going off alone? Why hadn't she *thought*? No one had realized it. Everyone was so excited about the treasure that no one had thought, not Badger, not she.

"What do you want?"

He jerked her to her feet and turned her to face him. He slapped her hard, first on her left cheek, then on her right. "You won't try to escape me again, Jessie, or I'll just kill you. I don't really need you. All I have to do is send a note to James and tell him I've got you and that I want my share of the treasure. He won't know until it's all over that you're well dead. Obey me, Jessie, or I'll strangle you right here, right now. I've absolutely nothing to lose now, you see."

She nodded slowly, her mind racing frantically, trying to figure all this out, trying to understand, to . . .

"Come with me. You'll like my little refuge. I've been there for two days now. Thank God the winter storms haven't set in yet. I found out all about the Outer Banks before I sailed here. I didn't want to end up drowned when my ship ran aground on one of these forever-shifting shoals.''

''Storms can hit at any time.''

''Yes, but they won't. I just feel it in my bones. At last my luck has changed.''

She walked beside him. Soon they left the rutted path to the village, veering toward the ocean. He said matter-of-factly, ''Yes, for the longest time I thought you were a lover of women. Many men have known passion for other men, but not all that many women that I've ever heard of. I watched you, and I was fairly certain, what with you always aping a man, wearing breeches, those ridiculous old hats, your hair ratty and in a braid. Yes, I thought, she's a student of Sappho.

''That's the reason, Jessie, that Allen Belmonde wanted you dead.''

Jessie, who had never imagined that two women would want to kiss each other as she did James, just stared at him, shaking her head. ''Allen Belmonde? What are you saying? This doesn't make a bit of sense.''

He swatted away a big fly, saying, ''He told me before I killed him—naturally I had to encourage him just a bit—that he'd tried to kill you because he was sure Alice was going to divorce him so she could live with you, be your lover. He wasn't particularly repelled by the notion. What he was, my dear, was desperate. He couldn't lose her money and he would if she left him. Her father, no fool, had protected her in that. Allen had to lower himself many times just to get enough money to pay his gambling debts. Thus, he tried to kill you. If you'll remember, I pulled you away from that wagon. I saved your life. That was happenstance, and I am grateful I was there that day. I already knew I needed you, you see, and thus when I discovered it was Allen Belmonde who wanted you dead, I had to eliminate that threat. I needed you alive. I killed him. I saved you. You should be thanking me.''

''Thank you, Mr. Fielding.'' She still felt utterly bewildered. ''I don't understand.''

''Oddly enough, Allen was right. His wife would have divorced him, but not for you. It wasn't you Alice loved. It was your sister. The two of them should suit each other quite nicely when old Bramen croaks.''

''Nelda? She's a student of this Sappho woman?''

''Oh yes, indeed she is. I imagine she and Alice will move to New York, away from the scandal their union would cause here in Baltimore. But that's not really important. Naturally Bramen will leave Nelda well provided for in his will. They will do well together. I just wanted you to know that you owe me, Jessie. You owe me part of that treasure because I protected you, because I saved you.''

''You wanted me alive, but why? How could you possibly know about Blackbeard? I didn't realize I had forgotten all about Old Tom and his diaries until just months ago.''

''Turn here, my dear. Yes, that's right, into this oak thicket. It's dense and protected in here, the sun doesn't beat through the thick leaves. Ah, but these trees are ugly, aren't they? So twisted and bent and gnarly, like old women shuffling down a road.''

''I've always thought of them as old men.''

''Turn in here, Jessie.''

She did as he said, still not understanding, but knowing he was enjoying telling her all about what he'd done. He was proud. She sensed the excitement in him, scarcely leashed. She'd walked away from the house, whistling, all happy, enthusiastic, and now look at her. In the hands of a murderer. What to do?

''Sit down, Jessie. Do you like my little refuge? See how I've woven branches together so they form a roof of sorts? It hasn't rained yet, so I can't be certain it will protect us.

But it's comfortable. The nights aren't too cold. Yes, sit down, and I will tell you the rest of it. There's plenty of time. I won't send a message to James until later today. I want him to know you're gone, to be worried, finally, to be frantic.''

He lightly touched his fingertips to her cheek. She jerked away, her eyes going wide.

''No, I won't rape you. Actually, to see you now, after your transformation, makes me wonder how I could have been so blind. My mother always told me that I was possessed of great discernment. But with you, I was blind. And you've a child in your belly, James's child. Who would have thought the two of you would have married? Who would have thought James would even want to bed you? Well, that's that and not really important now.

''You probably remember Red Eye Crimson.''

She stared at him. ''How do you know about Red Eye? Oh God, we all thought he was the one to protect me from. I remember him so well now, that night when he tried to kidnap me from Papa's house, how my pug saved me, how my papa told me he would be in jail until he was ninety years old.''

''Oliver was wrong. Red Eye Crimson came blundering into my shop one fine day last December. He wanted diaries, he said, Blackbeard's diaries. Did I have any?

''Of course I didn't have any. I'd never heard about that evil man even being able to write, much less keep diaries. But I was fascinated to know why this pathetic creature wanted to know about Blackbeard. I got him drunk. He told me finally how he and Tom Teach—you call him Mr. Tom—were partners, how he was supposed to have met Tom here on Ocracoke and together they would put the diaries together and then they'd have the treasure. He had Blackbeard's final diary, but it did him no good without the others. He was convinced that Blackbeard was a cagey villain and that he'd scattered clues throughout his diaries. Thus he didn't intend to kill Tom until he had his hands on the treasure. He was nearly in tears. He said he finally arrived only to find that you'd murdered Tom—he'd watched you sneak away from the shack on the beach. Evidently he didn't see you bury the diaries. You did bury them, didn't you, Jessie?''

''Yes. We found them two days ago.''

''Yes, I know. I've been watching and waiting for my chance. You were very lucky that the diaries had been pushed up into that tree, very lucky indeed. But back to Red Eye. He followed you home, then tried to take you that night. You escaped him and then you forgot everything in that illness that followed. A child has amazing powers for protecting itself. It was all so horrifying for you that you simply forgot it. As for poor Red Eye, he did indeed go to jail. He escaped and came back to Baltimore, to get you. I decided to make him my partner. I hid him in my house on Powell Street. I sent my dear mother off to visit her sister in Philadelphia. All went well until Allen Belmonde wanted you dead. I, of course, had realized that you had no memory of Old Tom or Blackbeard or the diaries. I simply told Red Eye that we'd have to wait. I told him it would do him no good to kidnap you because you didn't remember anything. I told him I would try to stimulate your memory. That's why I gave you all those diaries to read, Jessie, all from that period of time. You recall now how I also tried to question you closely, even touching on your childhood here in Ocracoke.''

It was all so clear now, Mr. Fielding giving her various diaries during the couple of months before she fled to England, most of them at least two hundred years old, reading to her, encouraging her. He'd wanted her to remember. She said, ''Yes, you always wanted me to look at your diaries. I never suspected. Why would I? I sometimes had horrible nightmares about that long-ago night, but they were vague and usually gone in the morning. I remembered everything when I was in England. I hit my head, and when I woke up I remembered.''

''I know. That beautiful Maggie Sampson told me all about it. It was her mission to help me remember any more details about the man who nearly ran you down in that wagon. A charming creature, your Maggie. It was difficult to act calm around you and James. I was so excited. I knew things would begin to happen now. I'd already killed Red Eye—I found I just couldn't control him, the blundering fool insisted that it was a mistake, that he shouldn't have listened to me, that he should have kidnapped you and he would have beaten you into remembering. So yet again, I saved you, Jessie. Yes, I killed him, saw no reason not to since I'd read Blackbeard's final diary. Blackbeard wrote that the answers were in his great-grandma's diary. He wrote, if I recall correctly, 'Deep in a pit, my treasure lies hidden, safe for all time.' You can't imagine how long I thought about that, but I had no answer. I needed Blackbeard's great-grandma's diary, not Blackbeard's other two diaries. Old Tom must have been a fool. Here you figured it out without Blackbeard's lame little clue, didn't you?''

She nodded. There was no point in lying, not now. It would gain her nothing. ''There was no need for that clue. His great-grandmother's name was Valentine. It's true. Everything was clear in Valentine's diary. Are you going to kill me, Mr. Fielding?''

''I don't want to. Don't make me.''

''I won't. Go to James, tell him what you've told me, and he'll give you a share. I know he will. Tell him how you saved me twice. He'll be grateful. I'm sure he'll share the treasure with you.''

''You are now, Jessie? I've heard everyone saying that even though you're a regular beauty now, James doesn't love you. He had to marry you because he seduced you.''

She swallowed. ''That's possible, but James is an honorable man. He'd give you some treasure to get me back.''

''We'll see. I wish to think more about it. Speaking to you of all the details helps me think things out. Do you wish to know about anything else, Jessie?''

''How do you know Nelda is a student of this Sappho person who lived in ancient Greece? How do you know that she and Alice Belmonde love each other in that way?''

''I saw them,'' he said simply. ''I had come to pay my condolences to dear Alice — I felt nothing but pity for the girl, being married to Allen, who was a bloody rotter. It was late, and I saw that people were there with her already. I waited and waited. Finally there was only one carriage left. I couldn't understand why the last visitor didn't leave. Then I thought that perhaps Alice was a sly baggage and had a lover. I stole up to the window and looked in. I saw Alice and your sister embracing. They weren't comforting each other, Jessie, they were passionate. It surprised me and I'll admit it, it made my own passions boil. Isn't that odd? I've imagined two women together now many times. Well, no matter, that's how I knew.''

Jessie knew then, deep down, that he couldn't afford to let her live. He'd murdered two men. He wouldn't have told her if he'd intended to let her leave alive. What about James? Oh God, she had to protect James, for surely Mr. Fielding would have no compunction about killing him, or killing any of them, for that matter. And she had to protect her unborn child. Her hands went to her belly and lightly pressed.

''Do you need to relieve yourself? I know that pregnancy makes a woman need the convenience more often. I overheard two ladies speaking of it. I must go with you, Jessie. I can't take the chance of letting you out of my sight. I won't watch, I promise.''

She did have to relieve herself. She forced herself to get it done, knowing he was but three feet behind her. He didn't look—at least she didn't think he did. When she was done, he led her back to the small bower he'd fashioned.

The silence between them stretched out endlessly. She was afraid, more afraid than she'd ever been in her life. It was a slow fear, not one of great urgency, which made it all the more frightening because it numbed her, it helped her hide herself from what she knew had to be the truth. Time stretched out, every minute longer than it should be, surely. But eventually there would be no more time, and then he would kill her. He would kill her baby. What to do? She said, "You're a scholar. I know what happened to the lost colonists of Roanoke Island."

His pale gray eyes glistened, he moistened his lips, then he seemed to catch himself. He laughed. "God, that's been a mystery for two hundred years. No one knows the answer, though many men have speculated about it." He laughed. "There's no way at all you could know anything about that."

"Oh, yes I do. You see, Blackbeard's great-grand-mother—Valentine—wasn't just anybody. She was one of the colonists on Roanoke Island. She recorded everything in her diary, and I've read that diary."

"A colonist of Roanoke Island spawned Blackbeard's ancestors? My God, that's amazing. Her name was Valentine? Strange name for a girl born in England."

"I know what happened to her, what happened to the colonists. You would like to know—I can see it in your eyes."

He laughed again. "Oh, Jessie, you're such a smart girl. Of course I'd like to know. But listen to me. Once I'm rich, then I doubt I'll give a good damn about any more of that nonsense, and that's what it is, nonsense. It's a way for poor men who are very smart to justify themselves to the world, to justify themselves to themselves, really, to convince themselves that it gives them some sort of worth. It's pathetic, really, but soon I won't be one of those men. I'll be rich.'' He sighed deeply, sat back against the gnarled trunk of a live-oak tree, and clasped his hands over his waist.

Jessie said, ''The colonists were starving, and there was rampant disease. They weren't going to survive.''

She saw the fascination in his eyes as they narrowed on her face. She didn't say anything more.

He said, ''In the packet just beside you is some food. I'm hungry. You must be as well. Soon James will wonder where you are. Soon he will go to the village to ask about you. Then he will know you're gone. Make me some food, Jessie.''

''All right,'' she said as she wrapped her fingers around the handle of a dull knife.

''Don't even consider trying to stab me. I'll punch you in your round little belly, and we'll see what happens to you and that get of yours.''

She couldn't bring herself to eat anything, even the cold slices of pinfish, fried and well spiced, placed between slices of dark oat bread. She'd prayed he'd be willing to compromise with her if she told him about Roanoke Island. She'd certainly whetted his interest. She'd just have to think of something else. She was surprised when he said some time later, ''I know what happened to the colonists. Most educated men do. It was duly noted by many that there's a group of Indians who live in the far west of Virginia. They're known to have blue eyes and fair skin.''

''You're dead wrong,'' she said.

''Well, yes, I suppose I am, particularly if this Valentine truly was Blackbeard's great-grandmother as she does appear to have been. He came from England. Well, it's a puzzle then.''

He looked hungry now, and she knew it wasn't for food.

She just shook her head. She would tell him no more. Compton Fielding said finally, "Very well. We will amuse ourselves. I will ask you questions about the colonists and you will answer."

"No, I won't, not unless you promise me you'll not hurt James or my babe."

He raised his hand, making a fist in her face, his smile never faltering.

# ≡ 35 ≡

SHE JERKED AWAY, rolling onto her side, her arms over her belly. He didn't hit her. He laughed.

"I'll find out soon enough all about Valentine and the lost colonists," he said. "Sit up, Jessie. I just wanted to make sure you believe I'm serious about all this. I'm pleased that you do. Also, you seem to care about the babe in your belly. I fancy that will make you all the more cooperative."

"What are you going to do now?" she asked as she righted herself, leaning back against the scruffy tree trunk, her arms over her chest. Her heart was pounding so hard, she was certain he must hear it.

"I already told you. We'll—" He broke off as a shout came from not twenty feet away.

"Miss Jessie! Where are you? Miss Jessie!"

"You make a sound, and I'll kill whoever that is."

She believed him. It was Gypsom. She held herself very still. But it wasn't to be.

Gypsom stumbled into the small clearing. He came to a dead halt, staring at Jessie, at Mr. Fielding, who was holding a very ugly pistol, pointed at him.

Gypsom said helplessly, "Miss Jessie, I saw ye walkin' with this man and ye must have dropped yer bonnet."

"Did you drop your bonnet on purpose, Jessie?"

"No," she said, and prayed she sounded as though she meant it. "It's all right, Gypsom."

"Actually it's not all right at all, Gypsom," Mr. Fielding said very pleasantly. "Miss Jessie came with me to this charming little den of mine. Why don't you sit down? You're one of James's stable lads. You're fine with horses, he told me. Yes, sit right there, Gypsom. Well, we're gaining quite a fistful of folk, aren't we? What do you think, Jessie? Should I kill him or send him back to James to get all this started right and proper?"

"Send him to James. Don't hurt him."

"I was going to write a note but perhaps it's better to send you, Gypsom. However, you know where she is. What will I do about that?"

"Why do you need to hide me at all? Just take me with you to the place where the treasure is. Gypsom can bring James. Then you can take what part of the treasure you want and leave us alone."

"You make it sound so very simple, my dear girl. Is it that simple? I wonder. Very well. Gypsom, listen carefully to me, for your mistress's life depends on your fine execution of my words."

Five minutes later Gypsom ducked beneath the live-oak branches and was lost from view.

"Now, my dear Jessie, why don't you take me to where the treasure is?"

"Compton Fielding? The bookstore owner? The scholarly man who plays the violin and speaks French as well as I do? That Compton Fielding?"

"Yes, sir, Mr. James. He decided to send me back to you, not to kill me. I was very glad about that."

"So," James said slowly, thankful for the moment that he and Gypsom were alone, as Gypsom had requested, "you and I are to take our poles and go to the marsh. He'll have Jessie there. We get the treasure out and he takes what he wants. Then he'll leave us alone."

"Aye, Mr. James. He said to tell you how much you owed him, what with him saving Miz Jessie's life two times. Mr. James?"

"Yes?"

"I think he likes you, but I don't trust him. There's something not quite right in his brain." Gypsom tapped the side of his head and rolled his eyes.

"Jessie was all right? You're certain?"

She'd been messed up something awful but Gypsom knew the master didn't need any more fretting so he said quickly, "She's jest fine, Mr. James. Jest fine."

"We'll leave now, Gypsom. Not a word to anyone."

Before he left the house, James slipped a small gun in his boot. Nothing else to do. Oddly enough, no one seemed to be around so he got out without questions. He didn't like keeping them in the dark, didn't like it one little bit, but he didn't see he had a choice. He wasn't about to take any chances with Jessie's life. And the babe's. James had known fear before, goodly doses of it, but nothing like this. If Compton Fielding wanted, James would give him all Blackbeard's bloody treasure. Who the hell cared? Only Jessie mattered to him. She had the spirit and the fearlessness of the best of his thoroughbreds, and that worried him even more. What if she tried to escape from Compton Fielding? He could even picture her attacking him. It made his blood run frigid in his veins.

That, he thought as he strode down the rutted path beside Gypsom, carrying one of the long poles, was a kicker. He frankly couldn't imagine life without her now. Life took odd twists and turns. He didn't mind that. What he hated was when life was out of his control, as it was now.

"Hello, James. I see Gypsom brought you. I've been watching you walk here. Fortunately there's a small rise just over there—at least until the next storm flattens it—and I would have seen if you'd brought any of the others with you. You didn't. You just might have saved your and Jessie's lives.''

James said, his eyes on Jessie, "Are you all right?"

"I'm fine, James.''

"Good. Now, Compton, you can have all of Blackbeard's treasure. I don't care. It's that simple. Understand, though, there might not be anything here. A lot can happen in two hundred years. It's possible that if the treasure was truly attached to the ballast stones, it broke off and sank. It's possible someone already found the treasure. It's possible it was never here in the first place.''

"We will find out shortly. You and Gypsom stick those poles of yours down into the muck. Be careful, James. I *will* kill her. I don't have anything to lose. Remember that.''

"I intend only to see if there's a treasure,'' James said. "If there is, take what you want and leave us alone.''

"I've always believed you to be a reasonable man. You're young, but you think things through. Jessie, here, is your opposite. Find that treasure for me, James, or I won't be happy.''

James took the long pole with the scoop on the end of it and eased it down into the dark, stinking muck. He quickly found the first ballast stone. "The stones are here,'' he said. He felt around the first stone, then eased the scoop down to the next stone and the next after that. There were so many of them, piled haphazardly. It was difficult to know if he touched every one of them. He was beginning to despair, for he knew that Compton Fielding was becoming impatient, believing James was somehow trying to fool him. "Just a moment,'' he called out. "I believe perhaps I've found something. Yes, it's a chain and it's wrapped around a ballast stone.'' Just as they'd all thought it would have to be. He'd prayed the chain would be stout, the links as strong as the devil, given the vicious tides, the storms that blew over the island and rearranged the landscape in a matter of hours.

"James? You've got it?"

"Yes," James said, so relieved he wanted to yell. "Come over here on this side, Gypsom. It's time for our two scoops to work together. If we find a metal chest at the end of this chain, it will be heavy. I hope the poles will be strong enough to bring it up."

The poles went deeper. It was getting close. James was beginning to wonder if that villain Blackbeard had just fastened chains to the ballast stones as a grand jest when his spade hit metal. Blackbeard's treasure trunk. "I've got it!"

It was slow, tedious work. They had to fit their scoops beneath the metal chest and slowly bring it up, and pray the poles were strong enough not to break in half under the weight of the chest and the filthy muck in the marsh. They couldn't take the risk of trying to pull the chain free of the ballast stone. If they lost their grip, the treasure could sink to the bottom of the world. Slowly, slowly, they worked it up. It was heavier than a horse that had once fallen on James during a four-mile heat. He'd been lucky, only three ribs cracked. If he failed at this, he wouldn't be as lucky. He'd be dead. Jessie and his babe would be dead. He didn't doubt that for a minute.

Suddenly, Gypsom slipped. The chest slid off James's scoop and fell down into the muck again. James cursed, then quickly turned. "Don't do anything, Compton. We'll just get it again. Wait, Gypsom, I feel something. Yes, the chain is wrapped at least three times around another of the stones. It's a good thing we've got more length of chain or else we'd never clear the surface of the muck."

"I know you didn't slip, James. It was Gypsom here. You afraid, boy?" Compton Fielding very carefully aimed the pistol and fired. Gypsom leaped backward as the bullet exploded the slimy ground at his feet and fell flailing into the marsh. He yelled as the black, filthy water closed over his head.

"Damn you, Compton!" James grabbed the man's arm and jerked him out of the marsh as quickly as possible. "I need him, you bloody fool!"

Gypsom stood there, his shoulders bowed, trembling from head to foot, covered with slime. "There's a hundert snakes in there, Mr. James," Gypsom was whispering, so afraid that he could scarce speak. "Snakes. I felt one of 'em slithering around my arm. Oh Gawd."

"That should teach you to be a bit more careful, Gypsom. Get back to work now before I become more impatient with you. Next time I just might force James to leave you in there."

"If you kill either of us," James said calmly, so enraged he wanted to close his fingers around Fielding's neck and choke the life out of him, "then who will pull up your bloody treasure?"

"I'll just tie Jessie up and be the second man. I'd just as soon not, but I don't want any more mistakes. Get to it now. I want what's due me."

All during their labor, he heard Compton speaking quietly to Jessie, terrifying her, telling her that her precious husband best not lose his treasure or he'd have a wife without a head. Yes, he'd blow her head off. It made James frantic. He looked over at Gypsom. He'd never seen such intense concentration on his face in all the years he'd known him. He smelled dreadful, black filth covering him, hardening into a mask as it dried on his face. But he was a fighter. The good Lord knew that before James had bought him and set him free, he'd learned to be a survivor. He wanted nothing to happen to Gypsom.

They couldn't lose the damned chest now. James had the three loops of chain free of the ballast stones. At last.

James said very quietly, "Does the chest have handles, Gypsom? Can you feel any?"

"I don't know, Mr. James. I'm afeared to search out a handle, I jest might drop my end of the chest. I can't do that, Mr. James. He'll send me back into that pit."

"That's what Blackbeard called it," Fielding said. " 'Deep in a pit,' that's what he wrote. It is a clue of sorts, but worthless out of this context. Now, James, how close to the surface is the chest?" He pulled Jessie forward as he spoke, bringing her to the very edge of the marsh now. The ground was soggy, the stench of rotted vegetation, of the gases in the marsh itself, were nearly overpowering. She was too scared to gag.

"We managed to unwind three loops of chain twisted around the ballast stone. It should give enough length to bring the chest to the top, but I can't be certain. Be patient. For God's sake, don't let Jessie fall in."

"No, I shan't lose her, James, don't worry. I'm surprised that you haven't demanded to know everything. I applaud your restraint. As I said before, you think. You know what's important at any given moment. Later, James, if all goes as I wish it to, you will know all you wish."

The chest broke the surface. There was a huge sucking sound as James and Gypsom managed to drag it over to the edge of the marsh onto the ground. James just stared at it for a long moment. He supposed he really hadn't believed it existed. "Thank God," he said at last. "We've got it."

"Excellent," Fielding said, so excited he could scarcely breathe now. Like James, he just stared for a long moment at that old metal chest, sludge and filth coating it. The lock was still intact. "My treasure. At last, all I've worked for."

"You didn't work a minute for this," Jessie said. "You don't deserve this." James wished he could stuff a sock in her mouth.

"It doesn't matter," he said quickly. "It's yours, Compton. Nearly yours if we can get it open."

James managed to grasp a filthy, rusted handle on the side of the chest and pull it along the slick, soggy grass. It was a good-sized chest.

"Oh no," Compton yelled, waving his gun wildly. "Damnation, just look. There're holes in it. It's metal. How can there be bloody holes in its sides?"

He jerked Jessie to her knees beside him as he fumbled with the locked clasp on the front of the chest. He couldn't manage it. He leaned back and fired into the lock, splintering it, sending its pieces flying into the marsh, making not a sound as they landed and sank.

He was chortling now, shoving back the metal lid. "My God, it's filthy, but there are jewels and so many coins—thank God they didn't fall out of those damned holes. Jewels don't rust or rot. Yes, there are jewels." He dropped his pistol and plunged his hands and arms into the chest.

And then he screamed.

He was on his knees in front of the chest, leaning over the opening. His arm was still thrust into the filthy pieces of jewelry and coin. Out of the depths of the chest rose a cottonmouth snake, surely the ugliest snake ever created, its body nearly as thick as a man's neck, its mouth a dead, puffy white—a white that looked like rancid maggot-covered meat. The snake's mouth gaped open. A rope of pearls hung out of its open mouth, falling on either side, like a bridle in a horse's mouth, the reins trailing. The snake stared at Compton Fielding. Then it lunged up his arm in the flash of an instant, its fangs going deep into his shirt. Another cottonmouth emerged, this one opening its mouth to show a necklace of emeralds, the snake's venom having cleaned off the gems enough to see the deep green of the stones. It wrapped itself around Compton's arm, so gently and slowly it seemed to move, and very smoothly, it opened its mouth, spat out the emeralds, and sank its fangs deep in the back of his hand.

"Compton, get your arms out of that damned chest! Damn you, move!"

Compton Fielding shrieked and shrieked but he didn't move. He seemed incapable of doing anything but scream. Another cottonmouth, this one slithering through one of the holes in the side of the chest, shimmied up Compton's chest, gently easing beneath his arm and viciously biting his armpit once, twice, three times before it slithered off him and sank back down into the chest.

Compton Fielding shrieked again. Still he didn't move. Couldn't move? James didn't know. He yelled at him, but it did no good. James jerked Jessie away when one of the cottonmouths turned in their direction, its open mouth yawning even wider. He pulled them both farther away from that cursed chest. James realized blankly that only seconds had passed, and yet it seemed like a bloody lifetime.

"Move, dammit, Compton! Get away from the chest!"

Compton Fielding turned his head very slightly so he could see James. He said in a soft tired voice, "I can't. Just look at them, James. They ate through the chest because they wanted the treasure. Just look at the one with those pearls looped through his mouth. He didn't even spit them out when he bit me. Oh God, just look at them, so many of them." Two more cottonmouths came up from the depths of the treasure chest. They had no jewelry or coins in their mouths. They moved slowly, as if they weren't really interested. They took their time, biting Compton Fielding's arms, his neck, then slithered back down into the chest and out the holes in the side onto the slippery grass. They slid back into the marsh.

James had been frantically looking for Fielding's pistol, then remembered he'd stuck his own into his boot. Cursing himself, he pulled the pistol from his boot and fired. One of the cottonmouths was still wrapped around Fielding's arm. He flowed off, sinking back down into the chest. James fired again, using his second bullet, knowing it did no good, but feeling angry and helpless. Why the devil didn't Fielding move?

The snakes were eating him alive. He hadn't so much as whispered for several minutes now, not even shuddering when yet another cottonmouth bit him. Just there on his knees in front of that damned chest, his hands and arms still plunged into its depths, letting the snakes devour him.

"Gypsom, take Jessie away from here. There might be more snakes. Get her to safety."

"I'll take her," Badger said, and he lifted Jessie into his arms.

"Yes, James, all of us are here," Marcus said. "Surely you must have suspected when you saw no one when you and Gypsom left the house with those two poles. Now, this fellow here is nearly dead. Who the devil is he?"

"We haven't seen a villain in many a year," the Duchess said, but she didn't step forward. "I hate snakes. God, these are hideous. Be careful, all of you."

"What should we do with this man?" Spears said. "I hate snakes as well, Duchess."

"I'm glad Maggie isn't here," Sampson said. "She wouldn't be happy were she here seeing those hideous snakes."

"Step back, James," Marcus said. "Let me see if I can't get rid of the rest of those snakes." He fired both shots in his pistol, then nodded to Spears, who then fired his two shots.

James waited. He saw no more movement, no more undulating swells beneath that pile of jewels and coins. He managed to pull Compton Fielding free of the chest. His face was the color of those damned snakes' mouths, a sickening, bloated white.

"Compton?"

"Yes, James," he said, his voice a hoarse whisper. "I can't see you, but I can hear you a bit. Where is Jessie?"

"I'm here."

"Please tell me what happened to those Roanoke colonists."

"They went with the Croatoan Indians when they had no more food. I imagine once they filled their bellies, they began to behave like the masters even though the Indians had saved them. The Indians, in retaliation, sold them to the Spanish. Valentine was taken to Spain. Later she traveled to England and married a merchant from Bristol. As to what became of the other colonists, I suppose most of them remained in Spain."

"Thank you," he said. "James, perhaps you won't tell my mama that I killed Allen Belmonde. She always liked him, even though I knew he was a scoundrel."

"I won't tell her," James said.

"Thank you," Fielding said, jerked once, then lay still.

A cottonmouth slithered up the bank and moved with incredible speed through the soggy grass, the pearl necklace still held in its mouth, its ends trailing behind him, perfect black circles becoming streaked with white as they were pulled through the grass.

"He's dead," James said. "All because of that damnable treasure."

"What shall we do with the treasure?" Jessie asked, eyeing the chest with revulsion. Even as she spoke, another cottonmouth poked its head through the surface, coins sliding off its thick head.

Sampson raised his pistol and fired. The cottonmouth fell back into the chest.

"It's horrible, James, just horrible," Jessie said, unable to look away from the chest. "These jewels and coins, all of it stolen from the people Blackbeard killed to fill this chest. I can't bear it.''

''I agree,'' James said, looking first at Spears, then Badger, then Sampson, and finally at Marcus and the Duchess. Slowly, each of them nodded.

''Let the filth and snakes have it again,'' the Duchess said. ''Let it sink to China.''

James and Gypsom both put their booted feet against the chest, kicking it hard. It fell back into the marsh, sinking slowly until it was nearly gone from view beneath the black surface. They watched a snake rise from the chest and out of the water, then sink down again as the chest disappeared.

Fat, lazy bubbles rose to the surface, popping, flattening. No one said a word, just watched until the black water again became still.

Gypsom said, ''I itch. Gawd, I thought I wanted to be rich, but not that way, Mr. James. Niver that way.''

Suddenly the Duchess leaned down and picked something up from the sodden marshy grass. ''Look at this,'' she said, and without thinking, cleaned it off on her skirt. It was a necklace, an elaborate chain of gold. In its center was a ruby, as deep a red as a winter sunset on the Outer Banks. The Duchess rubbed the ruby against her palm, then held it up. ''Look,'' she said. ''It's a swan.''

She handed it to James. He turned it over and over in his hand. The huge ruby was very warm against his flesh. ''There is printing on the chain,'' he said, bringing it up close so he could make it out.

''What does it say?'' Jessie said.

''It says 'Valentine Swann 1718 Edward Teach.' ''

They just stared at each other.

Which horse to cheer for? They all look the same to me.

—ANONYMOUS

"Go, Jigg! You can do it, boy, go!" Jessie was straining forward to see her beloved six-year-old quarter horse spurt through the pack to take the early lead.

"Not well done of you, Jessie," her mother-in-law said in a voice loud enough to be heard through all the cheering. "You're a Wyndham, not a Warfield. That's your father's horse."

"Oh dear, it's such a fast race, isn't it? Only a quarter mile. Go, Console. Go, boy! Yes, Console, you can do it!"

Her father frowned at her and shook her arm. "You were shouting for Jigg. Now you're shouting for a Wyndham horse. Where are your loyalties, Jessie?"

"Oh dear. Both of you, run! Run! Move, Jigg! That's it, Console, you can do it!"

James was riding Console and losing. The other jockeys weighed less then a sandbag, James would say and curse, saying he'd have to shoot them to win. But he tried, flattening himself against Console's back, hugging his neck.

Jessie couldn't help herself. She yelled at the top of her lungs, "James, you can do it! Give Console a good kick with your boot heels! He loves it!"

Console got two sharp kicks. He burst forward, like a ball out of a cannon, surprising the crowd of at least two hundred people, who, for the most part, had bet against him. James was just too big to win a fast race like this. His friends always rubbed their hands together when he was riding, knowing they could safely bet against him.

He won this time. It was those two kicks that did it. Jessie was certain of that. Console flung himself across the finish line a good length in front of Jigg, from the Warfield stable. Sweating, grinning like a sinner in a roomful of Puritans, James kicked himself free of Console, handed his reins to Oslow, and strode like the conquering hero to his wife, who was standing there, as white as a sheet, staring up at him.

"What the devil is wrong with you? I heard you, Jessie, and I did give Console that little nudge. It worked, didn't it?" He kissed her hard, hugged her until she gasped, then turned without losing a beat to her father: "Well, Oliver, I fancy after Marathon wins the next three races today, you'll be coming to our house, a big bottle of champagne under your right arm, bowing and scraping to me, the winner. You can bow and scrape to Jessie, too. She's the winner's wife."

Jessie tugged on his sleeve.

James turned toward Console, who was blowing hard, looking pleased with himself. "Just look at him. What a heart Console has. Jessie was right—he did need the boot heels. He nearly left me behind, he spurted forward so quickly." He was rubbing his hands together, still elated from his unexpected win, still grinning from ear to ear, words bubbling up in his mind to describe the brilliance of his horse, how Oliver should just give up and offer James a standing offer of champagne. Jessie tugged on his sleeve again. He turned, smiling. "What is it, love? You want to give the conquering hero a kiss?"

She said very clearly, enunciating each word slowly, "James, I think our baby is coming."

James stared at her blankly. "No, Jessie, that can't be right. The babe isn't due for another week, at least. Don't you remember? You told me that coming to the race today would be good for you, you needed to be out in the fresh air, you needed to exercise your lungs shouting for our horses to win. No, surely you're wrong about this. I didn't hear you shouting for your father's horse, did I? No, you wouldn't do that."

"She did," James's mother informed him. "However, I speedily brought her to her senses."

Suddenly Jessie gasped, her arms hugging her big belly.

"Oh my God!" shouted Oliver Warfield. "James, do something. She can't have my first grandchild here at the racecourse. Damn you! What did you do to my little girl?"

James knew exactly what to do, but he wasn't permitted to do a thing. As soon as he laid Jessie down on their bed back at Marathon, Dr. Hoolahan—who'd been waiting—shoved him out of the way. "You're not a doctor—you're a husband. Go away, James. This isn't the place for you."

But Jessie whispered, her lips already dry and cracking from the cries she couldn't seem to hold inside her, "James, don't leave me. You promised me that you wouldn't let anything happen to me."

James gave Dr. Hoolahan a look and sat himself down beside his wife. "It won't take long, Jessie. Just hold onto my hand when the pains come. It will be over soon, I swear it to you. Yes, I know it."

"How the hell do you know how long it will take, James?" Dr. Hoolahan asked, looking up. "You're not a bloody doctor. All right, so you might help mares when they're foaling, but that's nothing like this. I'm the doctor here. This is Jessie's first child. It will certainly take more than the next twenty minutes. It will probably take hours, maybe even days. Why, I knew one first child who required a full four days to be born.''

Jessie moaned at that.

"Don't say that, damn you," James said, turning. "You're scaring the hell out of her and me. Just get on with what you have to do. Don't listen to him, Jessie. Listen to me. I'm your husband, and I know what I'm talking about. Dancy is good for stitching up cuts, but he doesn't know all that much. He's just bragging about that baby that took the four days. No, you're coming along very nicely. It will be over soon.''

"Hurrmph," Dancy Hoolahan said.

"I hate this," Jessie said, closing her eyes as she felt Dr. Hoolahan's hands move between her legs and to her belly. Then a pain struck, and she wouldn't have cared if the entire population of Baltimore had trooped into her bedchamber and commented on her bent, sprawled legs. The pain was ghastly, unimaginable. It was ripping her apart, she knew it. Four days? No, that couldn't be possible. No human could bear this pain for four days. "I'm not going to survive this, James," she said, panting between gritted teeth. "My mama didn't tell me it would be this horrible. It's worse than horrible. I wish it were you, James, not me. Why the devil can't it be you?''

Dr. Hoolahan snorted as he stood up between her legs. "James couldn't bear it, Jessie. He'd be a pitiful mess after just one bout of contractions. Women are much better at it. Think about the beauty of the experience, how God ordained that you, woman, would be the vessel to carry all generations, think of how blessed you are, think—''

She screamed, nearly lurching off the bed.

"Shut your damned trap, Dancy," James said, nearly yelling. "No, not you, Jessie. You shout as much as you want to. You're doing very well. How close are her pains, Dancy?''

"Coming more closely together, obviously. I'm doing other things, James. I haven't timed them. If you're so bloody interested, time them yourself."

"You're nearly there, love," James said, "nearly there. That's right, push as hard as you want."

To Dr. Hoolahan's absolute astonishment, and a bit of chagrin as well, Jessie birthed a boy exactly twenty minutes later.

"I don't believe this," Dr. Hoolahan said, holding the bawling infant by his heels and giving him a good smack on his tiny buttocks. The yell made both James and Jessie smile. "This wasn't supposed to happen. This must be some sort of record, Jessie. I will write to the medical journals and report this. Of course, they'll believe I'm lying just to enlarge my reputation. Jessie, would you mind coming with me if they do disbelieve me and testify that I did indeed birth your child in a mere twenty minutes?"

"I don't think so, Dancy," Jessie said, staring toward the naked baby he held in his arms, seemingly unaware of him. "If you don't mind, that is."

"I suppose not," Dr. Hoolahan said, looking down at the baby, who promptly yelled.

"He sounds just like you, James," Jessie said.

"I was thinking that was your voice I just heard, Jessie."

"Actually," Dr. Hoolahan said as he cleaned the baby and wrapped him in a soft towel, "I was thinking he sounded just like James's mother."

Both new parents groaned.

An hour later, Jessie was cleaned up, dressed in a fresh white nightgown, her hair brushed and braided. The baby was asleep in the cradle next to the bed. She watched James stare down at their tiny precious son, then lean down and lightly kiss his forehead. He then turned to her, smiling widely. "You did it. In twenty minutes flat. For a while there I thought Dancy was going to cry, then when I reminded him that he'd just been present at a new record, he did brighten up a bit. He asked me when you were feeling a bit stronger to give his request some more thought. I fear he's serious. He would delight in presenting you to his colleagues.'' James laughed as he shook his head. ''I told him to go get drunk on his success.'' He bent over and kissed her mouth. She was still too pale for his liking. He sat beside her, took her hand between his, and said, ''I did mean to say this sooner, Jessie: I love you.''

''I'm sore,'' she said, not looking at him.

''Yes, but you'll mend. You didn't tear, and that's good. I'm so proud of you. And I do love you. Very much. I've felt love for you for a good long time now, ever since Gypsom told me that Compton Fielding had taken you. I realized then that I loved you, that I couldn't bear it if I ever lost you.''

''You're saying that because I just gave you a son. Every man wants a son no matter what he says to the contrary. It's brought forth all sorts of grateful feelings in you.''

''Where did you get that bit of errant wisdom?''

She had the grace to flush. She still wouldn't look at him. ''From your mama.''

He smacked his forehead. ''I love you. I love our son. I would have loved our daughter equally. When the hell did you ever believe anything my mother said?''

She looked thoughtful even as her hand stroked up his arm to his neck, to his cheek, where at last her fingers caressed him.

''That was the first and last time. I swear it.''

''See that it is.''


''He looks exactly like his father,'' Mrs. Wilhelmina Wyndham announced to the parlor at large, as she looked down at her week-old grandson. ''A chin as beautiful as Apollo's.''

"I think he looks like my little Jessie," said Portia Warfield. "Just look at those green eyes and that sweet little dimple. Jessie had a dimple just exactly like that one, but she lost it when she was no more than five."

"You don't lose a dimple, Portia," Wilhelmina said, her disgust evident. "She never had a dimple. It's my James who has the dimple. About her eyes. Eyes always change color, but not with this darling child. He will have green eyes, just like James, whose green eyes are a richer and deeper green than Jessie's are. Yes, they will be James's eyes."

James looked from his mother to his mother-in-law and said, "I think he looks more like Bellini, my three-year-old, when he was just foaled." He laughed and laughed when the two grandmothers turned on him, outrage stiffening every bone that wasn't already stiff from age in their bodies. "After all, he was all wobbly, wet, nearly bald, but he had the cutest mouth, opening all the time, showing a tongue surely the size of a hand. Just like Bellini when he was foaled."

"James, that's ridiculous," said his mama. "You will cease such comparisons."

"Yes, James, this is my grandson. He is surely beautiful. He is surely perfect."

"Just wait until he begins wailing. You will run from the room covering your ears." Jessie grinned at the people in her parlor as she walked into the room. "In fact," she said thoughtfully, "I think he should begin to realize he's starving any minute now."

Everyone stared at the white bundle in James's arms.

In one minute to the second, Taylor James Warfield Wyndham let out a yell that set the crystal trembling on the mantelpiece.

YORK, ENGLAND
DECEMBER 1825

### *York Races—the Day Jessie Wyndham Beat Everyone*

It took Jessie only a minute to realize that all the jockeys around her were protecting her from the few jockeys from other stables. At first she wanted to yell at them, curse them with every foul word she'd learned from her earliest years in the stables. Then she began laughing. *Well,* she thought, *let them keep up.* She kicked Dorsett in his sleek sides and shot forward. The wind pulled at her hair, she felt the air burning her face, she felt a thousand pounds of horse pounding beneath her. She loved it. Lord, she'd missed racing. She quickly outstripped her jockey honor guard. Then she saw one of them out of the corner of her eye. She'd known that any self-respecting jockey wouldn't allow her to walk away with the race. But she beat him handily, laughing when Dorsett flashed across the finish line, blowing hard, head high. The other horses pulled into a circle around her, and the jockeys threw up their hats and cheered wildly. James walked toward her, looking furious.

Oh dear, was he blind? There'd been no danger, except perhaps from one of her protectors accidently running into Dorsett's rear end, which hadn't been at all likely. She wouldn't have let that happen. She was by far too good a jockey.

"Madam, what the devil do you think you're doing?" He clasped her around her waist and lifted her down. "Just look at you, your streamers are tangled and blown apart. That bloody hat—you look like a beggar. I don't know what I'm going to do with you, damn you."

"How about giving the winner a cheer, James."

He stared down at her, pulled a streamer from around her neck, and stepped back. "May God grant me patience," he said, then grabbed Marcus's hat off his head and threw it into the air, yelling, "May our son be as excellent a rider as his mother!"

"Hear, hear," the Duchess said. "Well done, James."

"I'll kill her when we're alone," he said. "You outran your protectors. You left them to swallow your dust. You didn't give a good damn about your own safety. You"—he stared down at her, his heart in his eyes—"you, Jessie Wyndham, were magnificent." He then took his son, Taylor, from Spears. "What do you think?" he asked his son as he nuzzled his throat. "Do you think I should throttle your mama?"

Three-year-old Taylor said in a voice loud and clear, "My mama told me she was the best jockey in all the world. My grandpa said it was the truth. She said you were good, Papa, but you're too big a man. She told me she hoped I didn't grow as big as you."

James groaned, pulled Jessie against him, and said, "I don't stand a chance."

She turned a glowing face to him. "Isn't life wonderful, James?"

"It's the best," he said, and leaned down and kissed her. They heard cheering all around them. Taylor let out a yell that nearly felled his father.

"Dr. Hoolahan was right, James," Jessie said. "Those are your mother's lungs. They just get stronger by the year."

# ═══ Epilogue ═══

MARCUS WYNDHAM, THE Earl of Chase, not only became a father to four children (all by the Duchess), but also became active in the House of Lords in the Melbourne government. In 1837, he was appointed an advisor to the new queen of England, Victoria. It is said she would have married him if she could have because he was so "wickedly fair of person and so wickedly wicked of tongue." This was her last witty remark.

The Duchess, the Countess of Chase, became the most famous ditty writer of her time, although Queen Victoria is said to have complained that "some of the ditties hovered on the precipice of *The Vulgar*," to which a journalist replied in an impertinent column, "Then tootle them not, your majesty, and leave them to your salty dogs." In the English navy today, her famous *Sailors' Song* is still one of the favorite drinking tunes.

In 1837, Anthony Godwyn Ruthven Wyndham, Viscount Radcliffe and eldest son of Marcus and the Duchess, married Cecilia Derwent Nightingale, eldest daughter of North and Caroline Nightingale, whose wild antics fascinated Anthony and terrified her parents. He called her his devilkin. Queen Victoria was persuaded by the Earl of Chase to be godmother to his grandson, Marcus James Bentford Wyndham, born in 1838. It is said that many busy fingers counted months until the birth of their child, which, fortunately, arrived only one week early.

Charles, second son of Marcus and the Duchess, married a Russian duchess—whose mother was English—and moved to St. Petersburg only to return with his wife to England after but one Russian winter. Charles later became the British ambassador to Russia, though he turned down the post twice before finally accepting it. He said that "even my dear wife's fiery kisses can't keep me warm enough in that bloody climate." His wife, Marianna Shelley Petrovinka Wyndham, sang her mother-in-law's ditties far and wide in a rich soprano voice and wrote two gothic novels in the 1860s.

North and Caroline Nightingale, Viscount and Viscountess Chilton, helped revitalize the tin-mining industry in northern Cornwall with the aid of Rafael and Victoria Carstairs. They brought five children into Cornwall, all of them hell raisers, their eldest daughter, Cecilia, leading the way, their father said many times in near-despair. Their two younger blue-eyed daughters married twin-brother robber barons from New York and moved there in 1846. North and Caroline's sons, Edmund and Alexander, both became vicars, strangely enough, after having sowed enough wild oats for a calvary battalion, their father said, shaking his head whenever he viewed his sons exhorting their flocks from behind their pulpits.

North walked on the moors with his hounds once a year just to remind himself how very sweet life was and how very warm it made him feel to hear his wife's rich laughter upon his return. Owen Ffalkes married Miss Mary Patricia. His adopted son, Owen, became a famous violinist and composer and moved to Prague. His first sonata was dedicated to his mother, Alice, who had died birthing him. Mr. Ffalkes remained at Honeymead Manor until his fond wife happened to find him dead in a ditch, supposedly of too much drink, in the late fall of 1832. No one questioned her closely.

Caroline never ran out of laughter. Her two godly sons tried to populate Cornwall double-handedly, she was heard to say when her fourteenth grandchild was born, healthy and loud, another prospective hell raiser, North added, rubbing his hands together, seeing revenge in the future.

James and Jessie Wyndham, the American Wyndhams, lived a Proserpine arrangement—six months at Candlethorpe in Yorkshire and six months at Marathon in Baltimore. They brought three children into the world. Taylor, the eldest, was as horse-mad as his parents. In 1844, he married Marielle Elizabeth Wyndham, his first cousin, born sixteen months after he was, saying just after their wedding that "I've known her since I was one and a half years old. I might as well stay with her to see how she turns out." Both of them turned out very well. Marielle became more American than English, though she continually mixed her idioms.

James and Jessie spoke rarely of Blackbeard's treasure, but they did occasionally visit the Warfield house on Ocracoke in the summer. They rode horses bareback on the beach, Jessie's streamers tangling wildly in the wind. Jessie published a treatise on the lost colony of Roanoke, but it wasn't well received. She was promptly accused of having falsified Valentine's diary, being a woman and thus unskilled in proper forgery methods. Wilhelmina Wyndham bullied her grandchildren until the day she passed on to her just reward, which all her relatives prayed was truly just. As for Alice Belmonde and Nelda, widow of Bramen Carlysle, Compton Fielding was right. Upon her husband's death in 1824, Nelda and Alice moved to New York and became famous literary hostesses. Jessie passed down the Valentine swan necklace to her eldest daughter. It is still in the Wyndham family despite outlandish offers made by collectors.

\*    \*    \*

Spears and Badger remained with Marcus and the Duchess, becoming godparents many times to all the Wyndham offspring, both English and American. They spent at least a month every year in Baltimore with the American Wyndhams, Spears informing Marcus that ''Mr. Badger and I know our duty. Indeed, we do enjoy ourselves in assisting James and Jessie to improve upon their child-rearing practices.'' Marcus, never one to complain, nonetheless forewent writing any major speeches for the House of Lords until Spears had returned to provide him nominal assistance. It is said that Badger once cooked for President Andrew Jackson.

Sampson and Maggie also remained part of the Wyndham household. Maggie gave birth to Damon Arthur Lancelot Sampson in 1825. Damon became one of the most famous actors on the London stage in the entire nineteenth century, excelling in his roles of Othello, Hamlet, and Shylock. He was extraordinarily handsome, charming, and witty, but he never married. He always gave thanks to his beautiful mother who, he was fond of saying, ''sacrificed her own acting career to the rigors of motherhood.'' No one ever challenged this.

Wyndhams and Nightingales are everywhere. Perhaps one is a neighbor.

Turn the page for an exciting excerpt from
*ROSEHAVEN*
by Catherine Coulter


In 1277, Severin of Langthorne returns to his family's
estate from the Holy Land, only to find the lands devastated.
As the new Earl of Oxborough, his station in life seems
enviable, but he is saddled with a wife who detests him, a
staff that distrusts him, a mysterious property called Rosehaven, and a clever pet marten that seems determined to
bring him together with his reluctant bride.

Now available in paperback from Jove Books.

*Oxborough Castle, home of Fawke of Trent,
Earl of Oxborough*

HER FATHER DIDN'T like her, but he would never do this to her, never.

Even as she swore over and over to herself that it couldn't be true, she couldn't stop staring at the man. The air seemed to stir in seamless folds about him as he stood utterly still and silent. But not yet, not until he had judged all the occupants of the great hall of Oxborough Castle. Only then would he act.

His face was dark, his expression calm and untroubled. Sharp sunlight poured in through the open doors of the great hall framing him there as he stood motionless. She stared at him from the shadows of the winding stone stairs. She didn't want to look at him, didn't want to accept that he was here at Oxborough. But he was here and he didn't look like he had any intention at all of leaving.

His eyes were as blue as the sea beneath the bright morning sun yet they seemed somehow old and filled with knowledge and experience a man his age shouldn't possess, and distant, as if part of himself was locked away. She could feel the strength of him from where she stood, feel the determination in him, the utter control, the deliberate arrogance. He looked to her like the devil's dearest friend.

His finely made gray cloak moved and swelled about him even though there was no wind. The black whip coiled about his wrist, seeming to whisper in that thick contained air. But he made no movement. He was still and calm, waiting, watching.

He wasn't wearing armor, the whip around his wrist and the huge sword that was sheathed to his wide leather belt were his only weapons. He was dressed entirely in gray, even his boots were a soft supple gray leather. His tunic was pewter gray, a rich wool, his undertunic a lighter gray, fitting him closely. His cross garters were gray leather strips, binding his leggings close.

No, her father couldn't mean this. Surely this wasn't the man her father had brought to Oxborough to marry her. Hastings wasn't afraid. She was terrified. Marry this man? He would be her husband, her lord? No, surely this couldn't be the man, more like he was an emissary from Hades or a messenger from the mystical shades of Avalon.

Her father wanted to make this man of his line? Leave him all his possessions and land? Bestow upon him his titles since all her father had produced was her, a single female, of little account in the long scheme of things. Except for this marriage. Except to bind her to a man who scared her to her very toes.

This was the man her father's longtime friend, Graelam de Moreton, wanted her to marry? Lord Graelam was her friend too. She remembered him throwing her squealing into the air when she was naught but seven years old. Graelam was as good as family, and he wanted this unearthly creature to be her husband too? Indeed it had been Graelam, now striding into the castle great hall, who said this man was a warrior to be trusted, to be held in respect and awe, and who held honor more dear than his own soul. Hastings didn't know what it meant. Of course she shouldn't have heard his views, but she'd been eavesdropping two months before, bent low in the shadows behind her father's chair. Now her father no longer sat in his chair. He no longer ate his dinner in the great hall, in his finely carved chair, served by his page and squire, both vying to give him the tastiest cut of beef. Now he sipped broth in his bed, praying it would stay calm in his belly.

The man's cloak seemed to move again and she thought she'd scream. All the Oxborough people in the great hall were huddled together, staring at the man, wondering what would happen if he became their master. Was he violent and cruel? Would he raise his hand when it amused him to do so? Would he brandish that whip as her father had done when he had found that her mother had bedded the falconer? Hastings hated whips.

The man's cloak rippled yet again. There was an unearthly shriek. She stuffed her fist into her mouth and sucked herself farther back into the shadows.

The man slipped his gloved hand beneath his cloak and pulled out a thickly furred animal with a bushy tail. There was a low hiss of fear from all the Oxborough people in the great hall. Was it a devil's familiar? No, no, not that, not a cat.

It was a marten. Sleek, thick furred, deep brown in color save for the snow white beneath his chin and on his belly. She had a beautiful sable cloak made from this animal's fur. She'd wager this animal would never have to worry about being a covering for someone's back. Not held so securely by this man. What was this warrior doing with a marten?

The man brought the marten to his face, looked it directly into its eyes, nodded, then very gently slipped it once again beneath his cloak inside his tunic.

She smiled, she couldn't help it. The man couldn't be all that terrifying if he carried a pet marten next to his heart.

Graelam de Moreton stepped up behind him and slapped the man on his back—as if he were just a man, nothing more than a simple man. The man turned and smiled. That smile transformed him. In that moment when he smiled, he looked human and very real, but then he wasn't smiling, and he was as he had been, a stranger, a dark stranger, with a marten in his tunic.

The two of them were of a size, both taller than the oak sapling she'd planted three summers past, big men, too big, taking too much space, crowding everyone around them. She'd never feared Graelam, though. She knew from stories her father had told her since she'd been small that he was a warrior that other soldiers backed away from if they could, that her father had once seen Graelam sever a man in half with one swing of his sword and kill another three men with the same grace and power. She had never before considered that a man could be graceful while he butchered other men.

"Graelam," the man said, his voice as deep and rough as a ship pulling at its moorings in a storm. "It has been too long since I have tapped my fist into your ugly face and watched you sprawl to the ground. All goes well with you?"

"Aye, too well. I don't deserve what I have, the luck God has bestowed upon me, but I give thanks daily for my life. I caution you never to call my face ugly in front of my wife. She has a fondness for it. She may be small but she is ferocious in her defense of me."

The man said, "She is a special lady, unlike any other. You know why I am here."

"Naturally," Graelam de Moreton said. "I regret that Fawke of Trent is very ill and cannot be in the great hall to welcome you. Hastings should be here to greet you but I do not see her. We will sup then I will take you to him."

"I wish to see him now. I wish to have this over with as quickly as possible."

"Very well." Graelam nodded to her father's steward, Torric, so thin Hastings had once told him that she feared he would blow away whenever there was a sharp wind off the sea. Graelam then motioned for the man to proceed him up the winding stone stairs that led to the upper chambers. "Then," he said to the man's gray-cloaked back, "you will want to meet his daughter."

"I suppose that I must."

When they were out of sight, Hastings drew a deep breath. Her future would be sealed at her father's bedside. Her future and the future of Oxborough. Perhaps the man would refuse. She walked into the great hall. She called out to the thirty some people, "This man is here to see Lord Fawke. We will prepare to dine."

*But who is he?* she heard over and over.

People were whispering behind their hands, as if he could hear them and would come back to punish them. Their faces were bright with curiosity and a tinge of fear. This was the sort of man who would wage a siege and show no mercy.

She said aloud, "He is Severin of Langthorne, Baron Louges. He, Lord Graelam, and their men will dine here. MacDear, please return to the kitchen and keep basting the pork with the mint sauce. Alice, see that the bread remains warm and crisp. Allen, fetch the sweet wine Lord Graelam prefers." She shut up. They were all staring at her, all filled with questions. She raised her hands, splaying her fingers in front of her. "I believe," she said finally, "that Lord Severin is here to wed with me."

She didn't listen to the babble. She was frankly surprised that everyone, all the way to the scullery maids in the kitchen, hadn't known who he was or why he was here. A well-kept secret. She knew he had just returned from France to find his older brother murdered, his estate beggared, his peasants starving, nothing there but devastated fields destroyed by marauding outlaws.

Aye, he was here to wed her, the Heiress of Oxborough. She'd heard this when her father had asked Graelam what he knew of the man, what he thought of him and his honor and his strength. And Graelam had praised him, told him how King Edward had requested Severin ride at his right hand when they had been in the Holy Land during those final battles with the Saracens. He had stood beside Edward on the ramparts at Acre.

He was called Severin, she'd heard Graelam say, then he would add as he rubbed his calloused hands together, "Aye, Severin, the Gray Warrior."

"Severin is here, Fawke."

Fawke of Trent, Earl of Oxborough, wished he could see the young man more clearly, but the film that had grown over his eyes was thicker than it had been just this morning, blurring everything, even his daughter's face, which was good since she looked so much like her mother, and it pained him to his guts to look at her. Too much pain, and now death was coming to him. He hated it yet he accepted it. At moments like now, he welcomed it, but first he had to see this through.

"Severin," he said, knowing he sounded weak, and despising himself for it.

The young man gripped his wrist, his hold firm and strong, but it didn't hurt Fawke. It felt warm and powerful, a link to both his past and the future, a future of many generations and his blood would continue to flow through those warriors who would come after him.

"You will wed my daughter?"

"Aye, I will wed her," Severin said. "I thank you for selecting me."

Graelam said, "I have told you she is comely, Severin.

She will please you just as you will please her.''

Fawke of Trent sensed the young man freeze into stone when he said in that damnably weak voice of his, ''All I ask is that you take my name. I have no son. I do not want my line to die out. You will own all my lands, all my possessions, collect all my rents, become sovereign to all my men. You will protect three towns, own most of the land in the towns, accept fealty from three additional keeps. I have nearly as much coin as King Edward, but I have told him I am barely rich for I don't wish him to tax me out of any of my armor. Aye, you will wed my daughter.''

''I cannot take your name, Fawke of Trent.''

Graelam said, ''Severin, you need not efface your own name. It is long known and you will continue to wear it proudly. Nay, what is to be done is that you simply add the family name of Trent to yours and the earl's title to your current one. You will then become Severin of Trent-Langthorne, Baron Louges, Earl of Oxborough. King Edward agrees and has given his blessing to this union.''

It would serve, Fawke thought, wishing again that he could see the young man clearly. His voice was deep and strong. Graelam had assured him that he was of healthy stock. He said, ''My daughter will be a good breeder. She is built like her mother. She is young enough, just eighteen. You must have sons, Severin, many sons. They will save both our lines and continue into the future.''

Oddly, Severin thought of Marjorie. He remembered clearly the glory of her silvery hair, her vivid blue eyes that glistened when she laughed and darkened to a near black when she reached her release. Then her image dimmed. He had not thought of her in a very long time. She had long since been married off to another man. She was buried in a past that he would no longer allow to haunt him.

He said to Fawke, ''Graelam has told me her name is

Hastings. Surely a strange name for either a male or a female.''

Fawke tried to smile, but the muscles in his face wouldn't move upward. He felt the deep weakness drawing on him, pulling his toward bottomless sleep, but he managed to say low, ''All first-born daughters in my line since the long ago battle have been named Hastings in honor of our Norman victory and our ancestor, Damon of Trent, who was given these lands by William in reward for his loyalty and valor, and, of course, the hundred men he added to William's force.''

His eyelids closed. He looked waxen. He looked already dead. He said, voice blurred with pain and weariness, ''Come to me when you are ready. Wait not too long.''

''Two hours.''

Graelam motioned for Severin to follow him from the chamber. He nodded to a woman who went in and sat beside Fawke of Trent, to watch over him whilst he slept.

''Aye, if we can find Hastings, it will be done in two hours,'' Graelam said. ''She is usually working in her herb garden. Aye, it must be tonight. I am afraid that Fawke won't survive until the morrow.''

''As you will. Trist is hungry. I would feed him before giving my name to this girl Hastings.'' Severin reached his hand into his cloak and pulled out the marten. He raised the animal to his cheek and rubbed his flesh against the soft fur. ''No, don't try to eat my glove, Trist. I will give you pork.'' He raised his eyes to Graelam's face. ''No other of his species eats much other than rats and mice and chicken, but when I was captured near Rouen last year and thrown into Louis of Mellifont's dungeon, he had more rats on his dinner plate than a village of martens could eat. He didn't have to hunt them down. All he had to do was wait until one came close, kill it and eat. After I escaped, he wouldn't hunt another rat. I believed he would starve until he decided that he would eat eggs and pork. It is strange, but he survives and grows fat.''

Graelam said, ''He poked his head out a few moments ago. It seemed to me he didn't like being in Fawke of Trent's bedchamber. He quickly withdrew again.''

''He remembers the smell of sickness and death from the dungeon. Not many of us survived.''

''Aye, well now he will eat all the pork he wishes.'' Graelam paused a moment on the winding stone stairs. ''Severin, I have known Fawke and Hastings for nearly ten years. Hastings was a clever little girl and she has grown up well. She knows herbs and over the years she has become a healer. She is bright and gentle. She is not like her mother. As the heiress of Oxborough, she will fulfill her role suitably. I will have your word that you will treat her well.''

Severin said in an emotionless cold voice, ''It is enough that I will wed her. I will protect her from the scavengers who are already on their way here, just waiting for the old man to die so they can come and steal her. That is all I promise, that, and to breed sons off her.''

''If she were not here to be wed, then you would have to become another man's vassal. You would still be Baron Louges but you would watch your lands turn hard and cold with no men to work them.''

''They are already hard and cold. There is naught left there.''

''You will have the money to make things right. You will have Hastings as your wife. She will oversee the management of Oxborough when you are visiting your other estates.''

''My mother wasn't able to oversee anything. When I arrived at Langthorne, she was huddled in filth, starving, afraid to come into the sunlight. I doubt she even recognized me. She is a woman with a woman's mind and now that mind is mired in demons. She is quite mad, Graelam. She could not hold Langthorne together. She could not do anything save whine and huddle in her own excrement. Why would I expect anything different from this Hastings? From any woman? What do you mean she isn't like her mother?''

''Her mother was faithless. Fawke found she had bedded the falconer. He had her beaten to death. Hastings isn't like her mother.'' He thought of the girl Severin had wanted to wed, this Marjorie. He had spoken of her long ago, with a dimmed longing. Did he think little of her also?

''We will see.''

Severin was a hard man but he was fair, at least he was fair to other men. Graelam knew there was nothing more he could do. He missed his wife and sons. He wanted to leave as soon as these two were married. He rather hoped Hastings would approve her father's choice, though that didn't particularly matter.